NO PERFECT PLACES

Also by Steven Salvatore

Can't Take That Away
And They Lived . . .

NO PERFECT PLACES

STEVEN SALVATORE

BLOOMSBURY

NEW YORK   LONDON   OXFORD   NEW DELHI   SYDNEY

BLOOMSBURY YA
Bloomsbury Publishing Inc., part of Bloomsbury Publishing Plc
1385 Broadway, New York, NY 10018

BLOOMSBURY and the Diana logo are trademarks of Bloomsbury Publishing Plc

First published in the United States of America in May 2023 by Bloomsbury YA

Text copyright © 2023 by Steven Salvatore
Map by Steven Salvatore and Jeanette Levy

Bloomsbury books may be purchased for business or promotional use.
For information on bulk purchases please contact Macmillan Corporate and
Premium Sales Department at specialmarkets@macmillan.com

Library of Congress Cataloging-in-Publication Data
Names: Salvatore, Steven, author.
Title: No perfect places / by Steven Salvatore.
Description: New York : Bloomsbury, [2023]
Summary: After their father dies unexpectedly in prison, twins Alex and
Olly's relationship becomes fractured as they cope with their loss very differently,
and to make matters worse, Olly is hiding the truth that Tyler, who recently arrived
at their lakeside town for the summer, is actually their half brother.
Identifiers: LCCN 2022047373 (print) | LCCN 2022047374 (e-book)
ISBN 978-1-5476-1107-2 (hardcover) • ISBN 978-1-5476-1108-9 (e-book)
Subjects: CYAC: Twins—Fiction. | Siblings—Fiction. | Grief—Fiction. |
Family problems—Fiction. | Secrets—Fiction.
Classification: LCC PZ7.1.S2543 No 2023 (print) | LCC PZ7.1.S2543 (e-book) |
DDC [Fic]—dc23
LC record available at https://lccn.loc.gov/2022047373

Book design by Jeanette Levy
Typeset by Westchester Publishing Services
Printed and bound in the U.S.A.
2 4 6 8 10 9 7 5 3 1

To find out more about our authors and books visit
www.bloomsbury.com and sign up for our newsletters.

For all the time lost,
the great escapes we couldn't make,
and the hope of one day finding perfect places

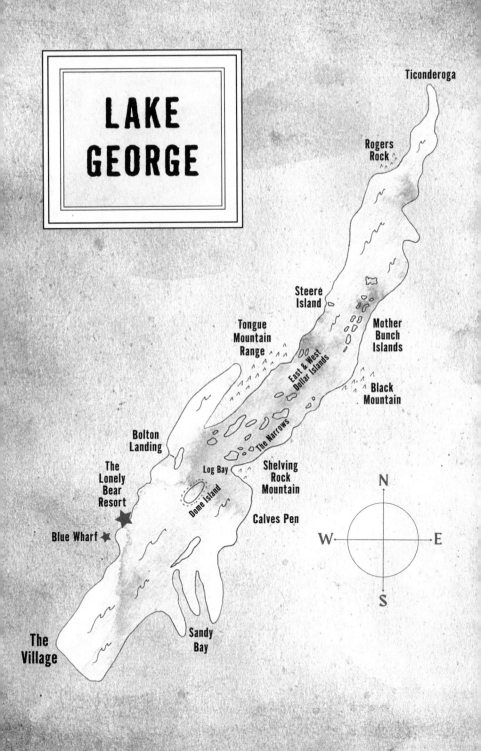

NO PERFECT PLACES

THE SUMMER BEFORE

OLLY BRUCKE

You don't have to be arrested and sentenced to prison to serve time.

Trust me, I know.

Junior year is over—if it were a person, the body would still be warm—and I should be spending time on the lake, but I'm trapped in this shitty car, where Alex forbids me from putting down the windows because of her hair, with an endless loop of Lorde–Olivia Rodrigo–Billie Eilish. She won't let me listen to the *Star Wars* film scores, even though she's passed out in the passenger seat, face smooshed against the window, most likely leaving a trail of drool.

I can think of a zillion different ways I'd rather spend my time, hard-earned gas money, and the beginning of summer break, like surprising my boyfriend, Khalid, with a cheesy romantic date. Or working to save for a hot-air balloon ride for his birthday. Especially since I blew through my savings on making my latest film, *Barefoot*, which thankfully is off my plate and submitted to the Saratoga Film Festival, two months early! I shot it documentary-style between last summer and this spring, going around Lake George to uncover the "truth" behind the reported sightings of Bigfoot.

I interviewed wildlife and conservation experts, and the first half was like a straight-up Discovery Channel show. But then! In my search for Bigfoot, I uncovered an entire world of magical creatures hidden in plain sight! I got to hone my mad CGI skills, and by the end, it became a commentary on how we've disturbed our environment so much the magic of the land has all but vanished.

Now I'm creatively tapped out, broke, and on my way to prison.

Alex and I are missing out on two days of work at the Lonely Bear Resort right at the start of the sole money-making season on Lake George, New York, to make the nearly nine-hour drive to see Dad, who is currently serving time in a minimum-security federal prison in Nowheresville, Ohio.

So, really, anything would be better than this.

I'm only here for answers. Not like Alex, who actually misses Dad.

A text from Mom dings through the car speakers: **Are you almost there okay text when you are there safe love you bye end text**

She loves voice texting but thinks it's like leaving a voice mail. Bless her.

Mom couldn't come. Actually more like *wouldn't* come. In the mornings, Mom works at a busy breakfast spot in the village, in the afternoons she fills in as a temp answering phones at a small real estate agency, and at night she bartends. Sometimes she'll clean houses on the weekends and cut hair for her former clients, making house calls when her schedule permits. She claims all of her bosses wouldn't let her off work because it's tourist season, but I know she didn't try to take off. I can't blame her. If she didn't work, we would be homeless. I wish Alex would cut her some slack, though.

Alex is stirring; it's like her body knows we're close.

I fire off a quick text back to Mom before Alex wakes up and yells at me for texting and driving: **Ten minutes away. This drive is TORTURE. Love you.**

"Olly, get off your phone! I'm too cute to die," Alex mutters, her voice froggy.

Olivia Rodrigo screeches through the chorus of "Brutal" in the most perfectly timed sequence, like the universe cued it up for me to say, "Gosh, it's brutal *in* here."

"Are we there yet?" she asks.

"Says the girl who slept seven out of the eight hours when she promised to keep me company." We left at three a.m. to get here during visiting hours, and we'll leave tomorrow after visiting is over. I'm already looking forward to a twenty-piece nugget, fries, and apple pie from McDonald's before passing out in a lumpy-ass motel bed.

Picking up her head, she turns and grins, her eyes hazy with sleep. "You love me."

"Do I?"

She ignores me, stretches, and grabs her bag with her hairbrush and eye makeup, then sets to work transforming from my hot mess twin into the carefully curated, ultra-blonde Instagram version of Alex Brucke, albeit toned down for prison.

Driving past barbed wire fences and armed security guards locks my bones in place and sets my jaw on edge. I shift into park when we reach the lot, then sit back, sucking in a breath that hurts my lungs.

"Thanks for coming with me," she whispers, putting her products away and turning to me. "When you didn't want to."

I pull her close, and she rests her head on my shoulder. "You're my person," I say.

But she has no idea what I'm about to do, and my stomach gurgles in discomfort.

"He'll be so happy to see you, Ol. He misses you," Alex says, her hazel eyes wide and watery. "Think about what Dad is going through." She's never ready to see Dad in his ill-fitting khaki jumpsuit.

This is where Alex and I differ: I don't have sympathy for Dad. If she knew about Tyler Dell, she wouldn't either.

Last night before bed, I read the letter I received in the mail a month earlier so it'd be fresh in my mind when I confront Dad:

May 25

For Oliver and Alexandra Brucke:

I'm not sure this is your address, so if a random person opens this letter instead, surprise! Please enjoy the plot twist.

Excuse the bad joke. Truth is, I've rewritten this letter a bazillion times. Nothing feels right, but there isn't a "right" way to say this, so here goes:

I'm your brother, biologically speaking.

Sounds ridiculous and impossible, but we share a father. In case you don't believe me, I'm including the results of the paternity test my mom had issued at birth, and a photograph of the only time we ever met. I was five and you both were three, I think. You probably don't remember that day, and I was only five, but I do. We played arcade games and I won a stuffed dragon off that one where you have to squirt water into a clown's mouth. I gave it to Oliver and Alex wouldn't stop crying because she wanted one too, but I couldn't win again. I tried, for what it's worth. I got her a plastic tiara by playing a ring toss game and Oliver stole it from her. I don't remember how the day ended but maybe if I would've begged our moms to stay longer everything would have been different. I don't know. Maybe not.

I don't want anything from you or our father, only to know you both.

My email is TyeDye1505@gmail.com, and my cell is 610-555-1505.

Tyler Dell

PATERNITY TEST

CASE #3843873	CHILD	ALLEGED FATHER
	(Tyler Dell)	(Cameron Tyler Brucke)

Probability of Paternity: 99.99996%

"I hate this part," she says, snapping me back to reality.
I take a deep breath.
Alex doesn't know about Tyler, and I'm done keeping Dad's secret.
"Me too." *More than you know, Sis.* I start humming Lorde's "Royals." It's her go-to pump-up song.

7

A laugh catches in her throat. "Hate you," she mutters, but she can't resist humming along with me, even if it is breathless, the words snagging on her teeth.

We stretch our tired legs and stare at the façade of the Federal Correctional Institution, Elkton, Ohio, which looks less like a prison and more like a shitty, abandoned elementary school. The ghost-like refractions of other kids inside waiting to see their loved ones haunt me. The mirrored windows are scuzzy and blurry, and Alex and I look like funhouse versions of ourselves as we make our way to the entrance. There's a short fence braided with barbed wire running along the tree-lined perimeter, which according to Dad doesn't do much to stop some of the inmates' family members or friends from sneaking close enough to the fence to bury dumb-phones in plastic sandwich bags. Despite it being summer, it looks seasonless here, lacking color and life.

The first time we visited, Dad sent us instructions via email on what to wear. He told me to make sure Alex wore a big hoodie and loose jeans, nothing to draw attention to her curves, and for me to dress as plainly as possible. Normally, she wouldn't be caught dead in anything not borderline couture, nor would she leave the house without a full face of makeup, but even she didn't argue with the need to blend in, not stand out, in the prison visitation room. We can't wear shorts, despite the summer heat.

Sweat snakes down my back. We carry nothing but our government-issued IDs and a clear Ziploc bag of dollar bills and quarters for the vending machines, so we can feed Dad something other than jars of stale peanut butter, ramen, and whatever cardboard food facsimile they serve daily.

She grabs my hand.

This never gets easier.

At least we have each other. That will never change.

I hold my breath and open the heavy door to the large waiting room filled with people of all ages, races, and backgrounds. Mostly families. Mothers with babies, mothers with toddlers, mothers with whiny ten-year-olds who'd rather play on their Nintendo Switches, mothers with kids our age who hold their hands.

Mom *should* be here with us.

"Made it under the clock," the guard says, cold-faced. If more than three hundred visitors come in one day, the guards start to turn people away; according to Dad's emails, most of the guards are assholes, so it's happened. He claims to try to stay on their good sides, but there is one in particular who likes to antagonize him. He never mentions the guard's name because they review all correspondence, and all phone calls are monitored. Dad doesn't think it wise to make enemies while he's here. He has enough of those outside the prison's walls.

Once we check in, we wait with the other visitors.

Iron bars separate the visitation and waiting rooms.

My foot taps restlessly.

Alex bites her manicured nails, a habit she picked up recently.

"You okay?" I ask.

All she does is shrug, fear etched across her face, her posture tensing. She moves as close as she can get to me, and I grab onto her in a side-hug.

The guards call for a line-up. Alex and I look at each other, and I recall our first visit where we weren't sure what to do and watched as families lined up at the locked prison gate. This time, we don't hesitate, and we're the first in line. It's almost like being next in line for the first row of a roller coaster, if the roller coaster had a known break in the tracks and ended in a fiery blaze.

"All right, listen up," one of the many guards shouts. He has a rough voice and a thick accent I can't quite place. "I'll only say this once. If you don't adhere to the rules, you will be ejected and will *not* get to visit with your loved one." He looks around, and nobody says a word, except for a small toddler who begs his mother to be picked up. He clears his throat. "So quiet down."

Alex and I stare straight ahead. We know the drill: pay attention and stay, or ignore his rules and leave.

He scratches his shiny bald head. "The guard at the gate will check your government ID against your signature and the list of approved visitors. If there are any discrepancies, you will be asked to step aside and/or leave the premises. Once inside, please proceed to the seating area and wait for the inmates to be searched. When the guards give the okay, your loved one will walk to you. Do not get up and go to them. They will come to you. You're allowed to hug, but anything longer than a guard deems appropriate, and your visitation could be terminated."

Alex's whole body shakes, no doubt remembering the last visit when, upon saying goodbye to Dad, she had to be pried off him by a guard whose force left a slight bruise on her upper arm.

Inmates start to file in. Alex grabs my hand again and digs what's left of her nails into my skin when we see him. He's gaunt. The skin on his face clings to his cheekbones, and his once-thick hair has thinned and grayed. He puffs out his chest, the way he used to when he would walk into rooms and wanted to feel powerful, but there's hardly enough meat left on his midsection to have any real effect. His eyes are sunken into dark fleshy mounds, but when he sees us, they light up and fill with tears.

Even *I* get choked up, unable to speak as he walks toward us after the guards pat down each of the inmates and give them all the go-ahead to approach their respective families. I don't want to cry. I won't. He doesn't deserve my tears. But I can't help wanting him to hug me, despite the anger driving me to confront him.

I let Alex hug him first. She needs him. She hugs him so tight he winces a little, but he doesn't even try to get her to loosen her grip. He wraps her up in his arms and squeezes his eyes shut. When he opens them, a tear rolls down his cheek.

"You dyed your hair. Looking good, pal." He moves to hug me, and his grip is still strong, despite how weak he appears. I hug him back, almost searching for the love I once held for him. When he pulls away, I'm deflated like a wrinkled helium balloon after hours in the hot sun.

Dad seems softer as he talks about how many books he's reading and the exercises he's doing to occupy his time, running around the busted, pothole-littered track even though it's too cold to stay outside for long, especially in the paper-thin uniforms and jackets they provide, and over the past few weeks, he's been feeling weaker. "A little lightheadedness. But I think it's the lack of good home cooking from my princess." He grabs Alex's hand and squeezes. Though it's not *just* lightheadedness—it's heartburn, nausea, and trouble sleeping because it feels like when he lies down, he's out of breath.

"*Demand* to see a doctor, Dad," I say.

He scoffs. "It's not that easy. I've put in a request at the infirmary.

It'll take a few weeks before it's processed and I get cleared to see a doctor. I'm keeping my head down in the meantime."

He tells us not to worry, but I'd be lying if I say I'm not a little concerned; a few years ago, right after all his legal shit started going down, he had a "minor" heart attack. I didn't understand how a heart attack could ever be "minor." The word "attack" sounds so aggressive and horrifying. But he notices the worry on both of our faces and pivots quickly, regaling us with stories of the friendships he's made with a few other guys. He's even teaching one guy to read.

That should make me feel proud. But it doesn't.

It's merely a survival tactic for him.

As Alex hangs on his every word, he goes off about Mom being too drunk to meet with his lawyers to "get him out"—as if it works like that—and how it hurts that she's not here now and hasn't "bothered" to come visit him.

Alex nods her head. "She complains too much. She's not the only one hurting."

"Mom has to pay the bills." I look straight at Dad. "You know. Rent. Food. The bills for your lawyers. All the debt you left us with." My teeth grind.

His gaze travels above my head. "I told her to file bankruptcy. The government won't stop coming after her, like they used me as a scapegoat. If she only filed—"

"Dad, please stop with this bullshit," I say. Alex kicks my feet to stop, but I hate when he rails on Mom, and I don't get how Alex doesn't see what he's doing.

"Watch your mouth." His lips purse like the end of a drawstring bag, white, drained of all blood. "I'm still your father."

He hasn't changed at all. He's still doubling down on the same stories: his wife, whom he cheated on, doesn't visit him because she's drunk and doesn't care; the government is after him; he did nothing wrong; he's the ultimate victim in a conspiracy scheme, details be damned.

"Can you both please stop?" Alex hisses, turning her body away from us.

"Sorry, kiddo," he says, placing a hand on her knee. He looks down at the floor and asks, "Did you bring any money? I could use a cup of coffee."

"Do they still have those powdered donuts you love?" Alex asks, eyes wide like she's five years old again.

I reach into my pocket and pull a handful of quarters and dollar bills from the Ziploc. "Go wild."

He clears his throat. "*I* can't, remember?" Right. Inmates are not allowed near the vending machines. It's only for visitors. We have to go to the machines and get him food. "I have to take a leak, anyway." He stands up, looking around for the nearest guard who, within seconds, moves toward Dad. We watch as Dad is escorted to the bathroom, patted down and searched thoroughly, a process that will repeat when he reemerges.

Alex and I pick out a packet of cinnamon sugar donuts, a bag of deli-style potato chips (for me), a Snickers bar (for Alex), and a large cup of coffee from the assortment of vending machines.

"They have Hot Pockets. Meatball," I say. "He loved it last time."

Alex's face scrunches and her whole body convulses, and she's probably thinking, *Give me a barely stocked kitchen with some spices and I'll whip up a feast.* Alex is our resident chef; she has a love for food like I have for film. "This shit is gross. It hurts my soul, Ol."

"It's either that or microwavable fish sticks."

Alex makes vomit noises and a nearby family hovering close to the single dirty microwave, waiting for their fish sticks to finish nuking, looks our way.

"What? You don't want to give Dad food poisoning?"

Her head whips toward me. "Not funny, Ol."

"It's a joke."

"Except, is it?" Alex furrows her brows as she peels back the Snickers wrapper.

I pop the Hot Pocket into the now-empty microwave. "He's lucky I'm here at all."

Her face softens. "I want to know why." She pauses, crinkling her forehead. Questions pull at the corners of her eyes.

I want desperately to tell her about Tyler. This is the first time I've ever voluntarily lied to my sister. Patting the outside of my pocket, I feel the letter addressed to Alex and me folded into eighths carrying news of our secret brother. It's a cinematic plot twist I couldn't make up if I tried. The day it arrived, I had gotten the mail after school—Alex was over at her friend Ashleigh's house—and it was sitting right at the top of the stack. Handwritten addresses on the envelope. The novelty of getting physical mail excited me, so I tore it open, hoping Alex would forgive me later for not waiting. I read it a hundred times, trying to make sense of it until Mom came home from work.

"What's wrong?" She plopped down on the couch, nursing a Big Gulp–sized glass of red wine. Her eyes were glassy, either from working a double shift or the sulfites in the wine. She set down the glass and straightened herself up, motioning for a hug I couldn't give her.

I sat down next to her and pulled out the letter and picture. "Who is Tyler Dell?"

Mom sucked in a breath and held it. She picked up the picture first. Her hand trembled, so the photo shook too. Alex and I were babies. Three, if I had to guess, based on the length of Alex's short, Shirley Temple curls. We were at some boardwalk by the beach, a Ferris wheel in the distance and people walking with cotton candy and funnel cakes behind us. Off to the side was a wooden Jersey Shore sign. Next to me was a boy, clearly older, a good foot taller than either Alex or me, with his arm around me, and I'm cheesin' big time as I hold my favorite stuffed dragon. He looked a little like me, but more like baby pictures I'd seen of Dad. Off to the side was half of Mom's body, intended to be outside the frame.

She gazed at the photo like a long-lost artifact, a family heirloom she was certain was lost for good. Her face softened, then hardened, then softened again.

Impatient, I dropped the letter into her lap.

She let the breath out slowly, a leaky balloon releasing air, until she had completely deflated. "I knew this would happen. Eventually. I told your father—"

"So it's true?" I asked and she nodded. "How long did you know about Tyler?"

"A complicated question," she said, taking another gulp of wine until there was nothing left. She reached for the bottle, but I snatched it from her, and she recoiled. "I don't know if you're old enough to handle—"

"Mom. Please. My father got arrested and went to prison before my fifteenth birthday. I can handle it. Uncomplicate it. *Please.*"

Her voice shook. "I was twenty when I married your father. I didn't know anything. I thought I was in love." She began to pick her cuticles. "So I ignored all the signs. He would come home late, always with an excuse. He had—" She continued, using air quotes rather liberally, "'Meetings' or 'things going on' at work. When I asked for details, he would get angry, accuse me of not trusting him, told me I was lucky because every other man cheats, but not him. I wanted to believe him." Her voice trailed off. "But I knew."

"How'd you *know*?"

"I caught him. With my former best friend. We'd been married for three years, and I'd gained a little weight. I was unhappy. And he never missed an opportunity to tell me I needed to lose weight. *She* was thin and beautiful. I caught them at his office when I brought him dinner because he was 'working' late. This was two years before you and your sister were born."

I did the math in my head. "Tyler's mom?"

She chuckled, but it was hollow and pained. "No. She was one of many." She had tears in her eyes as she continued, "I knew about a few of your father's girlfriends. But I thought once I was pregnant, he would stop. And for about three years, everything was good. Really good." She stood up and walked to the front closet. On the floor was a safe where Mom kept all our important documents, in case of a fire or a robbery or something. You know, birth certificates and social security cards and stuff. The dial lock clicked until it beeped and creaked open. She rummaged through her files, digging to the very bottom for an unmarked, sealed envelope. Inside, a typed four-page letter and pictures of a young boy in a Buzz Lightyear costume.

"Tyler's mother, Vivian," Mom confirmed. "You can read the

letter. She said she wasn't looking for anything from us. She wanted her son to know his siblings." Mom's voice was thick with mucus. At the end of the letter was a copy of the paternity test, in case Mom needed proof she was telling the truth, but it was evident from the picture of four-year-old Tyler, a clone of Dad.

"I was devastated," Mom said, wiping her nose. "But the more I thought about it, I realized you and your sister should know your brother. So without your father knowing, I contacted her and we spoke for months before deciding to meet."

I grabbed the photo of the three of us at the Jersey Shore boardwalk. "Explain."

"Tyler's mother had moved to Pennsylvania to be closer to her parents. I didn't want anyone here to see me. I always loved the shore growing up, so it seemed like a happy medium. Remember jumping waves together?" The puffy bags under her eyes and blotchy, tear-stained cheeks told me she was reliving it all over again.

I remembered waves, looming large overhead and threatening to crash down on me, to pull me under. Mom was there to hold me. "Why don't I remember *him*?"

"It was the only time we ever got together. Your father found out when Tyler's mother reached out to him." She cleared her throat. "He was adamant Tyler wasn't his son. There's no denying it, though. I took one look at the kid and knew. But he threatened me, said it was Tyler or him. If we ever saw them again, he'd get a restraining order against them and ruin Tyler's mother's life."

Bile filled my mouth. "So, you both let us grow up not knowing we had a brother?" Every bone in my body ached with rage, but I was anchored in place as her story whirled around my head.

"That wasn't what I intended. But I didn't want anything to ruin this boy's life either. I wanted to leave your father, but I wasn't strong enough." Mom grabbed for my hand, but I pulled it away.

I knew I shouldn't be mad at her. She was a victim too, but nothing made sense. Dad stacked his lies, one on top of another like a Jenga tower, until we were all buried under them.

"Please, Olly. I did what I thought was right. To protect you and your sister. And Tyler." She held the photograph close to her heart. "I knew this day would come." She looked up at me. "Don't tell your sister. Not yet."

"I can't keep this from Alex!" I yelled.

She grabbed me hand. "When the time is right. Alex can't handle this right now." Ever since Dad's arrest, Alex has been walking a shaky tightrope between functional and total meltdown. A little slack in that line could mean disaster.

Back in the prison visitation room, the microwave beeps. Dad's Hot Pocket oozes pasty sauce. Alex moves in to grab it with a wad of napkins like a makeshift oven mitt.

"Can I talk to Dad?" I ask, walking back toward him. "One on one."

She hands the Hot Pocket to him and excuses herself to use the bathroom.

Dad and I sit across from each other in a stare standoff reminiscent of Luke Skywalker and Darth Vader at the climax of *Return of the Jedi*. I'm trying my best to remain calm, but, like true opposing Skywalkers, we're inches away from a lightsaber duel.

"How's the lake? Warm yet?" Dad asks, his mouth full of cheese and sauce.

I *hate* small talk.

He doesn't give me a chance to respond before saying, "You don't answer my emails anymore."

"Why didn't you want Tyler to be a part of our lives?" I blurt.

He nearly chokes. I toss a napkin onto his lap. "Excuse me?"

"You heard me." All the blood rushes to my head. "Tyler Dell."

Fear shadows his face. "What did your mother—"

I cut him off. "Mom didn't say anything. He sent a letter to Alex and me."

His eyes dart around the room, searching for Alex.

"Don't worry, she doesn't know. Yet."

He exhales. Relief. "I did what I thought was best for *my* family."

I block his defense. "No, you did what was best for you." I rise to my feet.

"He's not my kid." He stands up too, holds out his hand for me to stop, to lower my voice. Some of the guards look our way, but I don't care. "His mother lied. He's—"

"There's a paternity test."

"It was faked."

I step back. "Why can't you own up to it?"

There's a moment where he stops and thinks, and I wish I knew what was going through his head.

The guards notice us standing and glare at us, hands on the guns in their holsters.

"I don't want anything to do with *him*." Dad eases back down sheepishly. "I'm not talking about this. And I forbid you to have *any* contact with him."

My mind splices alternate footage of a conversation in which he doesn't deny or deflect or demand anything of me he has no right to demand, but there's no audio and it quickly sputters out.

There's so much I don't know. There's so much *he* doesn't know.

His eyes are stony. "You're old enough now to man up and realize your sister should be left out of this." It's a Sith mind trick, to shame and subdue me.

Man up? Screw that heterosexist nonsense. It takes all of me not to scream, but if I do and this escalates, it'll end visitation, and I can't take that away from anyone else here.

"If *you* don't tell her," I threaten, but it's no warning, "I have to."

His fists clench and he puffs out his chest. "Don't open doors you can't close, kid."

This door wouldn't exist if it weren't for *his* actions. I've felt trapped in my own prison built by him and his lies, and I want out.

Alex emerges from the bathroom and notices me towering over Dad's skeletal frame. Before she can hear me, I say, "Enjoy prison, Dad. You belong here."

She quickly makes her way toward us. "Everything okay?"

The anger loosens in Dad's jaw as he grins up at her. "Everything's great, kiddo."

"I'm waiting in the car." I drop the bag of quarters in her hands and don't look back. I didn't get the explanation I came for, but at least I know what I have to do once we're far away from him and he can't manipulate either one of us. What I should have done the second I got the letter: tell Alex the truth.

ALEX BRUCKE

AirPods in, I click play on "Secrets from a Girl (Who's Seen it All)" by Lorde and sink into the heat of the kitchen at the Lonely Bear.

Though it's barely begun, it already feels like the longest summer on record; good thing I fucking *love* the heat.

There's something meditative about the small window between prep and the dinner rush, when the servers are out of the kitchen and Chef isn't bitching about his girlfriend or the menu and there's nothing but silence and the gentle hum of the gas lines running to the ovens. I did everything myself today because Chef is running late, which is perfectly fine with me—I love him, and he's taught me a lot, but sometimes I think he's too caught up in the idea of perfection, of a standard American fare menu he designed ten years ago and hasn't changed since. When I get to call the shots, I revel in that power and freedom. It makes me feel alive.

In this state, now, behind the line—the narrow space where all the cooking and prep is done—caught between the heat of the ovens and the breath before the rush, I'm zen as fuck.

"Alex, what the hell is this?" Chef erratically waves the special menu in front of my face. "Sheila showed me tonight's specials! Ruby red grapefruit scallop crudo? House-made sweet potato gnocchi in a truffle butter sauce with portobello mushrooms?" He goes off in Spanish and I pop my tongue, waiting for him to stop so I can stare him down.

"Are you done?" I ask with a smile.

"You didn't run this by me," he says. "I told you, every dish goes through me—"

I cut him off. "You told me I could create two specials this week."

"I did no such thing."

A typical hot-blooded man who has to piss everywhere to mark his territory, Chef needs to feel like he's in charge at all times. I've gotten good at managing his ego and getting what I want.

I fix the cute pink camo bandana covering my hair. "You said I could experiment before it gets too slammed. I gave you a rundown of the ingredients and I priced everything out the way you taught me, and you approved it last week at the bar." Granted, he was two tequila shots and three Coronas deep, but that was part of my strategy. "I made sure to add everything to the order sheet, plus Sheila approved it." I resist the urge to pull the "Sheila Addington owns the Lonely Bear Resort" card. Sheila is Mom's best friend, one of the only ones who didn't stop picking up the phone when Dad was arrested. Actually, Sheila called her, took her out for lunch and manicures and spa days and footed the bills. She offered Olly and me jobs—she knew I wanted to be a chef, and she knew Olly was a better boater than 95 percent of the adults on this lake. Olly takes hotel guests out for a day on the lake, or for short spins around the cove where guests can waterski or tube. Olly's had his boating license since he was fourteen, but Mom and Dad practically raised us on the water, teaching us how to drive our boat at ten. Sheila has been incredible, and I've really learned a lot about working in the kitchen here, thanks to her. And Chef.

Instead of using the Sheila card, I go with, "I've been prepping since I got back from, um." My voice gets lower, softer. "Ohio yesterday." I clear my throat and shake it off. "You have nothing to worry about."

For a few seconds, he doesn't say anything. His lips curl in distaste until he feels like he's officially postured enough to scare little old me into a state of submission. *Whatever you need to feel like a big man, Chef.*

"You remind me of my daughter." He says this all the time. Sometimes, I like the idea of pretending he's my dad. Not because of anything having to do with my actual father, but because Chef is physically here and maybe if I close my eyes and tap into Olly's imagination I can feel like Dad is next to me and not nearly five hundred miles away.

I give him a toothy grin. "Beautiful, strong, capable, take-no-shit—"

"Frustrating, stubborn, doesn't listen to directions," he finishes with a wink. Chef is a tall, broad-shouldered man in his late forties, jet-black hair dotted gray, full beard and moustache, and a shaved scar line in his eyebrow he says came from a hot cast-iron pan he was taking out of the oven when he slipped on some grime on the terracotta tile floor and slammed his face into it. I don't believe the story, I'm certain he shaves the line himself, but he likes to tell it to new back-of-house staff to instill fear in people: clean the floors, watch your step, move fast with agility and focus, not panic.

He folds his arms over his chest. "So show me this prep work before the rush."

As I take Chef through everything, demonstrating exactly how to put together a dish in the methodical way he taught me, I can't help but notice he seems somewhat impressed, which fills my chest with a warmth that makes the back of my neck prickle with sweat.

Once I'm certain I have his approval, I take off my gloves so I can head to the bar for a seltzer, and his eyes widen.

"Mija." He grabs my hand with force. "Explícame."

I stare him down. He's about to yell, but I don't give him the satisfaction. "What?"

"Your nails." His face is always so snarled.

"You shouldn't frown so much, you're getting lines in your forehead."

"Don't change the subject—"

"There's a place in Saratoga that does Botox—"

He cuts me off. "Why do you insist on having these long nails?" The frustration builds again, and he starts pacing back and forth behind the line and muttering in Spanish. "One day, they're gonna pop off in someone's lobster bisque."

"It's like a King Cake," I jest. "Instead of finding a little plastic baby, you find a flawless nail tip."

"Not funny," he says.

"Take a joke, Chef. You know, laughter. Does the body good. Plus, you already have me in this bandana that makes me look like a lunch lady in a hairnet!" I couldn't go visit Dad with stiletto nails, so I made an appointment for this morning, using money I'd been squirreling away for self-care purposes. I click my nails together like an evil sorceress.

"Dios mío!" Tossing his hands up, he looks to the ceiling.

"It takes money I don't have to look good."

He throws his hands up in the air again, shaking his head. "And nobody sees you back here! You are too much like my daughter!"

"You never know who you're gonna meet." I push open the swinging double doors leading from the kitchen into the service area of the Lonely Bear's restaurant, ripping off the red paisley bandana because I refuse to be seen in public wearing it, and fluffing my long curly blonde hair.

Olly and I have worked here for so many summers now, it feels like this place is my second home. Okay, well, technically this is only our third summer, but with Mom bringing us here so she could hang with Sheila, we basically grew up here.

Through the large floor-to-ceiling windows at the far end of the restaurant overlooking the lake, I can see most of the Lonely Bear Resort, teeming with life. Vacationers who save up for the year to come to the Adirondacks and spend a week on Lake George. The way the sunlight hits the water, scattering glitter across its gentle blue waves. The beach lining the shore to the docks where Olly is no doubt cleaning Sheila's boat for tours or selling a guest on a tour package with his immense love of this lake. Sometimes, I marvel at Olly's ability to still love this place so completely.

I can't think about what it was like to live here before Dad got arrested. Before the swirling red and blue lights. Before his trial. Before the constant barrage of local newspaper article head-lines. Before he had to surrender himself to a federal prison. Before my large group of close friends started dwindling into a couple confidantes who I'm still not sure I can trust. Before the whispers turned into something louder. Before, before, before.

This is why I thrive in the thick of the kitchen; there's not much room to think in the heat, when you have to perform, when you have a certain set of tasks and countless people are counting on you to get everything right—perfect—on the plate. Ingredients, measurements, timing, design: all things under my control.

Okay, well, technically *Chef's* control, but I'm the fucking boss.

"Alex!" A familiar voice calls out from the other side of the bar.

Ashleigh Rodriguez stands at the door on her tippy toes, trying to get my attention. She's gorg as always, a black-haired Gigi Hadid with a penchant for fashion. Next to her, Becca Arnold is on her phone, looking predictably over it. The three of us have been friends for as long as I can remember, which tends to happen when the number of students in your entire grade is in the double digits. We called ourselves "The Bad Bitches," a moniker Becca heard while she was smoking in the girls' bathroom during third period our freshman year. But ever since Dad's arrest, trial, and surrender, Becca doesn't talk to me. She fakes a smile and nods with one eye trained on me, the other looking around as if at any moment I could implode her entire social status. It gives me the ick, being around her. I've tried to explain this feeling to Ashleigh, but she doesn't see it. "Becca loves you. She's still here, isn't she?" Shitty argument, but who am I to question *any* friendship right now?

Still, I've got one eye trained on Becca, too.

I go behind the bar, grab a clean glass, and fill it with ice and seltzer, then snatch lemon, lime, and orange slices and squeeze the juices until the citrus properly infuses.

Big sip. Fuck yes. "What're you guys doing here?"

"Surprise, bitch!" Ashleigh says. "I would've texted you, but I knew you were working." Becca nods tersely, hitting her shoulder into Ashleigh. "We're with, um, Hunter. We came by boat. He had to pick something up from his aunt."

Hunter Addington is Sheila's nephew, and because his aunt owns the place, he thinks he can walk in and boss everyone around. Including me. He looks like one of those walking Abercrombie & Fitch ads, but he's about as deep as a glossy billboard. Captain of the varsity football team as a junior, ridiculously rich, entitled, everyone's contact for coke. Drugs are as prevalent as clean, fresh drinking water in Lake George, but nobody suspects beautiful, privileged Hunter Addington, with his tube socks all the way up his calves and bright-white smile and daddy's BMW. His presence is like a tightly knitted Ralph Lauren sweater loosely wrapped around the neck in the dead of summer: cute aesthetically but you can't trust his choices. Which is a shame because we used to be friends.

"You're here with *Hunter*?" I ask incredulously.

Ashleigh shrugs.

I hum and take another sip, and the bubbles tickle my throat.

Becca harrumphs, still staring at her phone. "This kid from Albany, Chris, texted. He has good stuff, apparently." She runs her fingers through dyed red hair. So *that's* why she's hanging out with Hunter. "Meet me outside, Ash." It's not a question, more like a command. Becca waves goodbye.

"Nice to talk to you too, Bec!" I shout, but she's out the door already, running toward the parking lot. "Since when does Becca get high like *that*?"

"Oh please, Lexi, don't act like you don't."

"Not Hunter-high," I say. "Weed is one thing." Without it I probably wouldn't have been able to sleep over the last year.

Something is off with Ashleigh, who half-listens and hugs her body like she's hiding herself away, her eyes darting around.

"You okay?"

Her eyes catch mine, and she can't look away. "Sorry, yeah, totally. I'm in a weird headspace."

"Becca rubbing off on you?" I'm joking, but I'm also not joking at all. Anxiety bubbles in my gut like soda. I've been nervous Ashleigh could emotionally abandon me the way Becca has.

"What?" Ashleigh asks, looking around nervously.

My brows furrow. "Ash?"

"There's a lot on my mind right now."

"What's going on?" I ask, but Hunter appears at my side before she can answer.

"Hey, beautiful." His heavy arm snakes around my shoulders and constricts me, distracting me from whatever Ashleigh was saying.

"What do you want, Hunter?" I ask.

He laughs and it's so fake it makes me want to laugh at him. "Saw you here and couldn't resist."

"Resist," I say. "When all else fails, never trust your gut."

He runs his free hand inside his tank top and up and down his abs, clearly in a move to show off. "Who could resist this?"

"Who *does* that?" I say out loud, giggling at him.

Ashleigh concaves further into herself.

Keeping one hand wrapped around me, he pulls me closer to him, while the other is feeling his washboard abs like a laundress in the 1800s, which makes me laugh harder.

"What?" He's so oblivious. But he does smell good. Like

sunscreen and sweat and really expensive cologne, the kind of bougie shit that really blends into the skin, not the gross knockoffs they sell at the pharmacy on the outskirts of town. "So when are we gonna hang?"

"Who's *we*?"

He shrugs and flashes his five-hundred-watt smile. "Us. We can chill at my place. I got the whole basement to myself, you know. Hot tub. Or go for a spin in the Formula. Maybe do a little nighttime skinny dipping."

A pained, "Romantic," slips through my gritted teeth.

"You know what they say?" he says, expecting me to fill in the blanks as if I know his personal tagline. Probably has to do with the size—or lack thereof—of his dick.

"Let me guess, *Just do it? Gotta catch 'em all? Melts in your mouth, not in your hands?*"

It takes him a second—or thirty—but when he starts to laugh, I weasel out from under his grip and sidle up next to Ashleigh.

"So you coming or what?" he asks.

I say this slowly, enunciating each word and syllable: "I. Am. Working. You know, work. Job. Bills. Money."

"Oh, yeah," he says, as if he doesn't know I work for his aunt. Everyone knows everything about everyone in this backward tourist-trap town. "I'm sure Aunt Sheila would let you off if she knew you were coming with me."

"The fuck she will!" Chef shouts from behind the bar. "Let's go, Brucke, we got our first order of gnocchi, and I need you behind the line."

Hunter furrows his brow. "Right, guy." He turns to Ashleigh. "Who *is* that?"

Normally, Chef would be all, "You know who the fuck I am!" but everyone lets Hunter's bullshit slide because of Sheila. And his parents' money.

"Text me later, Ash," I say, pulling her into a hug. She reluctantly hugs back.

Chef is still leering at Hunter as they walk out and toward the docks. "I don't like him." He shakes his head, and his lips curl into a sneer. "Don't get mixed up with him. You hear me?"

I nod, watching as Hunter puts his arm around Ashleigh. Is that why she was so squirmy? She's with Hunter? No, they wouldn't be together without me knowing, and he sure as hell wouldn't hit on me right in front of her if they were. Would he?

I whip out my phone and text her. **Are you into Hunter?**

I watch as she slides her phone out of her short jean shorts and quickly types something before putting it back. My phone dings immediately: **HELL NO!! Gross. I'm here for Becca!**

Relief washes over me.

"He's the guy you go to when you want to avoid your life, not the kind of guy who helps you grow. He's a weed, not a flower," Chef says, his voice softening. He coughs, clearing the sincerity from his throat as he wipes his hands on his white jacket.

Looking up at him, I ask, "Speaking from experience?"

"As a man, I admit we suck. Though some are better than others."

I knock into him. "Maybe more than some." I want him to hug me like I'm his daughter, but that would be weird. Nice, but weird.

"I know things," he says, adjusting the white bandana around his forehead.

"Do you have an actual order?" I ask, noticing the empty restaurant.

"A room service order came in, but I took care of it. Burger and fries."

"How exciting."

"You know how it is around here. It's a Burger and Fries Paradise. You're a Gnocchi and Crudo kind of girl." He gently places his hand on my shoulder, the way a teacher looking over your shoulder might. "When you're thinking about colleges for next year, keep that in mind. I didn't go to culinary school, and I'm lucky Sheila took a chance on me when she built the restaurant here. Everyone said she was out of her mind, and I agree." He chuckles. "Point is, you have talent. Raw, natural talent. You can go places." He looks out the window toward Hunter and Ashleigh. "Things are hard for you right now, and I want to make sure you're keeping up with your college applications."

Fucking hell, I was not prepared to cry today.

"Come here, mija," Chef says, tentatively pulling me close in a sideways hug.

Olly didn't come with me to see Dad yesterday. He stayed at the motel until checkout, and then drove around in Khalid's car until visiting hours were over. All Dad and I talked about was how angry Olly is, but Dad avoided me when I asked why Olly walked out on him the day before. Olly won't tell me either. When I got too fed up with all of it during the last hour of visitation, Dad changed the subject to college applications.

"You staying on top of everything? I emailed Ms. Rodriguez and she said she would do everything she could to help you and Olly out." His smile was so weak, but there was a resolve in his voice.

"Yeah, Ms. R is helping me line everything up for culinary school." Our school guidance counselor is also Ashleigh's mom, which makes talking with her both easy and weird because of how well I know her outside of school. "She really wants to highlight my community service work," I said, prattling on about the fundraiser I organized with Sheila for Planned Parenthood and volunteering with Olly at the LGBTQ+ community center in Saratoga last summer.

Dad's eyes sparkled with pride. "Great, kiddo!" He grabbed my hand. "You *need* to set yourself up for success. I won't always be around and the world won't always be kind, so when opportunities come, take them." He let go before he got in trouble from the guards. For a second, I imagined us sitting around our old dining room table in the beautiful house we used to live in on the lake, Dad and I immersed in one of our hours-long talks about life and school and other normal shit. "With any luck, I'll be out in time for graduation next year," he said, and my heart sank. "Might still be at a halfway house, but they'll at least give me leave for the day."

I held back tears. "Only for one day?"

He could hear the disappointment in my voice. He quickly grabbed my hand and held it, bringing it to his chest, right over his heart. I felt it beating fast.

"Will things ever go back to normal?" I asked him.

One of the guards started to shout, "Hey, hey, hands to yourselves!"

I recoiled as Dad said, "A new normal."

That stuck with me like a bad song on loop in my head, and talking to Chef now is really nice, but he's not my father, and the sincerity of it all makes me want to scream. I don't want this new normal.

Everything is so fucked up.

Before I hugged Dad goodbye, he said, "Thanks for doing what you can to help your mother. Working to help pay the bills isn't ideal for you or Oliver."

"At least I'm getting experience," I said, not wanting to dig into the hell of having to work off-the-books for the last two years so we could survive. The last thing I wanted was for Dad to feel worse than he already did. He was already serving his time to the government.

Then again, I am too.

Chef nervously lets me go. "You good, mija?"

I shrug, and it's heavy and pained. "Aren't I always?"

He shakes his head and sighs.

Together, we walk through the double doors and get to work.

Sizzling pans.

Butter and garlic and fresh truffle.

Flames and the sound of ceramic clacking on steel.

The heat lulls me into the best kind of trance, my body able to withstand the fire.

Plating my first gnocchi order as Chef looks on with pride, then the next one, and the next, I am the next Julia fucking Child or Pía León.

Chef takes a taste of a leftover plate for an order I made twice by accident when a dupe didn't end up on the finished ticket spindle. "Music, mija! A symphony of flavors! You truly have a gift." He savors another bite before shuffling me out of the way to grab a handful of fresh parsley.

"You think?" I ask.

"I *know*," he corrects me.

"Fuck yes!"

He raises an eyebrow as if he's about to scold me. Then cracks a smile. "If you were my daughter, I'd wash your mouth with soap. Now get me more fucking garlic from the back. We're out."

"Yes, sir!"

On my way to the walk-in, I catch Olly and Khal making out in the unused corner of the kitchen.

"Jesus, can y'all get a room? I'm sure Sheila has some vacancies."

Khal's face turns bright red, but he still sticks his tongue out.

I wave the image out of my head like a horrible smell. At least they're getting out and being more adventurous; Olly and Khalid are basically married, attached at the hip. All they do is watch old-ass movies at the drive-in and have sex. At least Olly has someone who isn't me. "How's the boat? I'm so jealous I'm not out there with you guys."

"You're in your element, Sis." With his hands, Olly mimes filming me. Then he pops up and gives me a high five.

The second our palms slap, we both stop. Dead.

"Oh god," Khal says. "Not this again."

At once, Olly and I both jump to attention, crouching low in a sumo wrestling pose. I stare into his face and he scowls, which almost breaks my composure, but instead, I scowl back. When he winks, we break into an epic Miss Mary Mack secret handshake extravaganza, something Olly and I started doing when we were six on the playground. It involves us doing the whole hand game routine, followed by jumping up and down and kicking our heels, doing the monster paw we stole from Lady Gaga's "Bad Romance" choreography, screaming random throwaway lines from *SpongeBob SquarePants* only we find funny, and ending with Olly posing like he's behind a camera, and me holding an imaginary fork and putting my hand to my stomach and saying, "Mmm, mmm, good," while rubbing it in circles, twice.

"You guys," Khal begins. "Are truly the most embarrassing. You all need help."

We collapse into each other.

"I hate you," I say to Olly.

Olly pulls me into a hug. "And I love you." He kisses my forehead.

"BRUCKE! WHERE THE FUCK IS MY GARLIC!" Chef screams.

"Shit, I gotta get back before Chef lights me on fire." I dash to the walk-in, yank open its heavy metal handle, and dart inside. The cold feels amazing, like a five-second full-body rejuvenation at the spa. I grab the garlic, along with more herbs and vegetables I saw we were running low on, and slip out.

"You wanna hang tonight?" Olly asks. "After work? We need to talk."

My stomach drops. "Everything okay?"

Olly looks to Khal. "Totally. Why wouldn't it be?"

I furrow my brows and stare him down. Sometimes it feels like I'm walking on eggshells with him, especially where Dad is concerned. After visitation, Olly wouldn't talk to or look at me for the whole car ride back home. If Olly is pissy, he projects it onto everyone around him like a film reel.

"Text me when you're done," Olly says. "I'll be down at the docks."

Which seems normal.

Except.

The last time he said "We need to talk" was the day he told me Dad was going to prison.

OLLY BRUCKE

"You really ready for this?" Khal leans against a dock post in my favorite rainbow tie-dye hoodie, looking all sorts of kissable under the lamplight. He finished covering the bow of the boat, so now he's watching me finish up the back.

"Is anyone ever ready for the 'Hey, Sis, we have a secret brother' talk?" My arms overextend to hard-to-reach snaps as I balance myself on the wakeboard tower.

It took me eleven days to get up the courage to send Tyler Dell an email after receiving his letter. I wasn't going to until I talked to Alex about it, but I kept reading and rereading the letter, and every time I put it down, I kept wondering what it would be like to know this stranger I share blood with. It tugs on my chest every single day. How can I want to know everything about a person I didn't know existed a month ago? Part of me wishes it could be an easy Insta-relationship, to slip into a brotherhood like a well-worn hoodie. So I couldn't resist sending him an email a few weeks ago:

FROM: DirectorOlly@gmail.com   June 10

TO: TyeDye1505@gmail.com

SUBJECT: Long-Lost Brother?

Hey Tyler,

I'm not sure if you've ever seen the movie *The Parent Trap*—either the far superior 1961 version with Hayley Mills, or the fun 1998 version starring a pre-cocaine Lindsay Lohan—but Alex and I used to watch both versions all the time with our mom and we'd have debates for hours about which version was better. Alex was #TeamLohan, and I was #TeamOriginal, though I made concessions for the Chessy character from the Lohan remake. Anyway, I used to love how these (very obvious) long-lost twin sisters randomly ended up at the same camp and figured out they were sisters after feuding with each other and I would think, "That wouldn't happen in real life because in real life, I would immediately know Alex and she would know me because we're one and the same." I used to think it was an outlandish premise for a movie because what kind of monsters would separate their kids and never tell them about the other? And then I got your letter and the picture of you with me and Alex and I guess that actually happens? Idk, I'm rambling. This movie clip says it all:

YOUTUBE LINK: The Parent Trap I Chessy Finds Out About Annie

I wish it were as simple as a movie scene. Something scripted, revised, edited, spliced together in a satisfying ending for both characters and audience. But real life is not *The Parent Trap*. Either version. Even with Tyler responding and us exchanging a few back-and-forth messages since I took the plunge.

As I snap the last buttons of the boat cover to the back swim platform, I propel myself off and onto the dock.

"You're hot when you do that." Khal moves close to me. "Like a Sea Captain America."

"You like sea men?" I ask, wrapping him up in my arms.

He scrunches his nose and waves me away. "Majnoon. Have you heard from Alex yet?" He rubs my back as we sway on the creaky wood boards.

"Nothing. Restaurant looks busy still." I look up at the stars. "Wanna hang here?"

Hand-in-hand, we move to the edge of the dock and dangle our feet off the edge. He's shorter than me, so his toes don't touch the water, but I'm submerged up to my ankles. I rest my head on his shoulder until he rustles, causing me to shift. I can't stop thinking about Tyler and Alex and Dad and Mom and how my entire life over the last few years has been flipped upside down and shaken and cut back together in a montage of memories I'm not sure are real or imagined, and until now, nothing was in my control.

Enter: Tyler Dell.

While nothing has felt truly grounded, at least knowing Tyler is something I can do on my terms. Build a new foundation.

Unless Alex feels otherwise. She used to be able to handle the truth, but she's become a lot like Dad lately, with a tendency to lash out or run. She insists Dad is an innocent bystander, a fall guy for someone else's mistakes or whatever story of the week Dad cooked up to convince her of his innocence. His stories never worked on me, not when I read all the online articles I could on his case. Alex purposely avoided anything posted online. I didn't want to run from it.

"Don't worry, babe." Khal's lips brush my forehead. His irises resemble tiger's-eye gemstones with golden flecks. "Alex is strong. And she'd want to know. Even if it hurts for a little."

If anyone knows Alex like I do, it's Khalid Zaid. Without him, I don't think Alex and I would have survived sophomore year, not after Dad was arrested. He was my best friend and, for a while, our only shared friend at school after everyone else wrote us off because of our criminal dad. Khal was a patient ear for Alex, and my distraction from the chaos. He was a gardener caring for us, watering our plants after a drought and pruning back our dead leaves. He never seemed bothered by Dad's story as it played out on the local news, and he never failed to stand up for us when the whispers in the hallways or cafeteria grew too loud.

For so long, it was the three of us, but over time, I fell hard; when I was around him I held my breath and when he looked away was when I could exhale. He would sit close to me on the couch as we binged old episodes of *Schitt's Creek* and *The Good Place* while eating homemade popcorn sprinkled with fresh olive oil and za'atar, my body aching for him to move closer—the two inches between us was a continent I couldn't cross.

One Saturday night when Alex was at culinary classes at the nearby community college at Mom's insistence, Khal and I decided to watch *Love, Simon*. I watched his face during the scene where Simon's mom told him she could feel him holding his breath for years, but now he could finally exhale, and Khal's eyes were wet, his entire face red from a breath he'd also been holding. I grabbed his hand, which was sweaty and limp, and held it until he finally let go and cried into my shoulder.

Nothing happened between us that night. But the tension, *whew*!

"Thank you," I say.

"For what?" he furrows his brows.

"Everything." I pause, then repeat to him what he said to me the night we watched *Love, Simon*, not knowing I would hold onto the phrase and ask him what it meant later: "Ana bahebak."

"Love you too, Ol." He kisses my forehead again. "Everything'll be fine once you tell her."

My phone buzzes. "Speak of the devil." A text from Alex: **Sorry Ol! Chef needs me to do inventory. Mom is gonna pick up me later. BECs at our spot tomorrow AM?**

I send back a quick: **Sounds good. Khal and I are heading home.**

She hearts the text. **Gross. Love ya!**

"You okay?" Khal asks, reading the screen.

"The universe is telling me something." I slip my phone back into my pocket.

"Come on, let's go." He hoists me up, and we walk to his car.

"Stay over tonight? My mom doesn't give a shit," I say. "She's working late and will be out early."

He shrugs. "My mom would die if she knew about the nature of our sleepovers."

I hook my arm into his. "Just cuddles tonight?" I'm not in the mood for sex.

He squeezes my ass. "Cuddles are everything."

He's everything.

On the car ride back to my small, dingy, empty apartment, I scroll through Tyler's emails on my phone.

FROM: TyeDye1505@gmail.com   June 11

TO: DirectorOlly@gmail.com

SUBJECT: Re: Long-Lost Brother?

Hey Oliver,

I may or may not have found both versions of *The Parent Trap* on Disney+ and binged them last night after my mom went to bed. Didn't want her to wonder why I'm watching old-ass movies about long-lost sisters. Stupid, I know, but she's a big worrier. When I told her I made the lacrosse team sophomore year, she basically had a meltdown because she thought I would get hurt on the field. My first game, she came with this massive first aid kit and cried every time I got to play. So distracting. I couldn't concentrate. I had to ask her not to come anymore. That didn't go over well, either. I didn't quit in the middle of the season because I never would have been able to live with myself, but I didn't try out the next year. I stuck with basketball. No contact, really, and Mom was used to watching me play. I'm better at it anyway so I guess it wasn't the end of the world, but sometimes I wonder, you know? I loved lacrosse. Anyway, while my mom told me about you and Alex, and she supports me contacting you both, I haven't told her I actually did yet. I don't want her to worry. I will soon.

Do you play basketball too? Always wondered if it came from my father.

To be real, I didn't expect to hear from you. I wasn't sure if the address I found was right and I'd been holding on to my letter for a while. I spent senior year in therapy trying to figure out how to cope with the father who never wanted me, but my therapist helped me realize what I really wanted is to know you two, so I took a shot.

You wanna know something ridiculous? I've been googling "secret siblings" and obviously *The Parent Trap* came up, and I watched about a billion different *20/20* YouTube clips about people who found out they have siblings they never knew about. There's even a TikToker who chronicles her finding out she has like fiftysomething siblings. I might've spent an entire night down that rabbit hole haha. But then I found this whole psychological breakdown of *Star Wars* (I don't know if you've ever seen it, I haven't. Space wizards are not my thing) on Reddit. Dude, some people are OBSESSED! 😱 Anyway, I watched a clip where Bad Helmet Dude told Luke he was his father (spoiler?) and kind of freaked out a bit because I was imagining Luke's reaction was you and Alex reading my letter:

YOUTUBE LINK: The Empire Strikes Back I Luke, I Am Your Father

I'll take the Chessy reaction, btw.

Tyler
P.S. I'm #TeamLohan. Sorry.

TO: DirectorOlly@gmail.com

SUBJECT: Re: EVIL SPACE WIZARDS!?

Oliver! Or should I call you Olly? Your email addy is "Director Olly," but not sure it's cool or not.

This is gonna be a short email because I have to get ready for senior prom tonight. Pick up my girlfriend's corsage and get a haircut. My buddies and I and our girls are spending the weekend at one of their houses in the Poconos. Have you ever been? I've heard it's similar to Lake George. Mountains and lakes and stuff. Maybe one day I'll get to see for myself.

You mentioned in your last email you haven't told Alex about me or the letter yet. Can I ask why?

Ty

P.S. I totally snort-laughed when I read your spiral about me calling *Star Wars* a bunch of space wizards!!! Your obsession has been noted. 😆

P.P.S. You had me rolling when you said, "Hand-eye coordination and sportsball has never been my thing." LMFAO. That's cool your boyfriend plays lax tho. Maybe one day we can all play a game.

TO: DirectorOlly@gmail.com

SUBJECT: Re: Happy Prom!

Sup Olly,

Prom was awesome, the weekend was okay. Lots of stupid drama with my friends, which I don't have any time for. But it was nice to get away. Graduation is in six days, which is wild. I can't believe in, like, two months I'm going to be a college freshman! 🎓 Sorry you and Alex couldn't afford to go to your junior prom, but man I was cracking up when I read your last email about you guys and your boyfriend having your own prom by dressing up in old costumes and camping on an island on the lake. That's so cool! I'd love to do that. The video you sent of you guys drunk around the campfire with Alex singing Doja Cat in a pink wig killed me 🤣 She seems mad cool. You done with final exams yet? Officially a senior!? Any fun summer plans?

I guess I understand why Alex doesn't know about me yet. I have a very strong instinct to protect my mom from all the shit in the world, and from what you said, she's pretty close to your dad. (*Our* dad? That's weird af. Biological father? Sorry, processing out loud. My therapist tells me it's okay to do if I feel safe. Taking a chance here.) Take your time telling her. I'll wait.

Ty

FROM: TyeDye1505@gmail.com   June 27

TO: DirectorOlly@gmail.com

SUBJECT: The Future?

Ol-master! (Trying something out. Feel free to tell me to fuck off.)

Wait, you work at a resort on the lake? And you do boat tours?! So
dope! I've been on my friend's pontoon boat on Lake Wallenpaupack.
Have you been? It's dirty af. I hear the lakes up in the Adirondacks
are all so clear and blue. That's what my mom tells me anyway.

It's doubly cool you work at a hotel because I'm a hotel
administration major. Or, I mean, I will be once I start at Cornell
in the fall. My gramps used to own a bed & breakfast down here
in PA, and I grew up working there, so being a hotelier is in my
blood, I guess. When he passed away a few years back, my
mom made the decision to sell it because she couldn't take it
on, and I was too young. But man, I'm still sad about it.

What about you? Do you know what you might want to study
after HS?

Good luck visiting your dad. I hope it goes well. (Don't) tell him
I said hi!

😬 Ty

I haven't written Tyler back since we got back from Ohio.
There's so much I want to tell him about my life: who I want to be,

who I hope Alex becomes, my relationship with Khalid, and my love of movies and filmmaking and how I want to go to film school in Los Angeles or New York to study with the greats. Call me Veruca Salt because I want it all when it comes to a relationship with Tyler, and I want it now! Is that so bad?

Khalid tells me to slow down, to stop recording when the film runs out, that life isn't a privileged rich girl who gets whatever she wants, whenever she wants it, and these emails are a reminder. Right now, Tyler exists as a tiny version of himself in a faded picture and a collection of words in emails, and I don't really know him.

Right now, it's an illusion. He's not flesh and blood, and we haven't met.

Being an amateur filmmaker, I've learned sometimes illusions are all we have. Something might look real, but that doesn't mean it is. The only difference is what our imaginations are willing to do with the supercut in front of us.

ALEX BRUCKE

"Sparkling Diamond" booms through my dreams like some sort of psychedelic acid trip, horns trumpet me awake out of a dead sleep. I had been dreaming about making angels on untouched snow, and I bolt upright like I'm about to be murdered.

And there's Olly, hanging onto my bedroom door like a boozy lounge singer, draped in a sparkly pink feather boa singing the old-ass song from *Moulin Rouge!*, a movie Mom used to watch on repeat when we were toddlers, so naturally Olly is obsessed. He used to make me dress up like a burlesque dancer, with a black lace placemat he fashioned into a corset, and always talked me into letting him do my makeup, which should tell you everything you need to know about my impaired decision making. But Olly was always the visionary. We would recreate scenes from the movie musical, and he would film them and have viewings with Mom and Dad and our friends. Back when "friends" existed.

We lost the footage, all on old handheld video cameras from the early 2000s, when the government seized our storage units after we got kicked out of our house.

"It is way too fucking early, Ol." I run my fingers through knotted hair and wince. This is what I get for passing out as soon as I get home after working a double. My curls smell like a deep fryer, and there's a fresh burn mark on my wrist from when I wasn't paying attention last night during the rush because Hunter took it upon himself to waltz into the kitchen to hit on me. I wasn't aware of my hands, and I accidentally tried to rest on a searing-hot pan full of chicken piccata. The bright red patch has already bubbled. Add it to the list of scars.

"It's never too early for burlesque!" he shouts quickly before returning to the lyrics to belt his heart out. I really admire that about Olly: no matter what's going on, no matter how serious he can be—and goddess, he can be so damn serious sometimes—he can still find the joy in a feather boa. He looks like Dad when he smiles, but that's really the only time I see Dad in Olly. Like Dad, he's a bit stocky with sky blue eyes and a balloon head inflated with ego. His natural hair is Dad's ashy blond, but he dyes it now to draw a contrast between him and Dad—lately, he's been going a dark chestnut brown, which totally washes him out, but I don't tell him. He doesn't have to dye his hair though, because he looks more like Mom, with full lips, a striking Mediterranean nose, and rosy cheeks. I look way more like Dad, all German, all temper.

Olly laughs as he sings and it's infectious; we haven't danced it out together in so long. My stomach winces because it's been days since Olly said he needed to talk to me, but Sheila and Chef needed me to work double shifts over the Fourth of July weekend. It's been nothing but work and sleep.

We're at my favorite part of the song, where she lists out Tiffany and Cartier and segues into Madonna's "Material Girl," which I could never resist.

I hop up onto the bed and sing along.

Holding out my hand, I pull him up with me, and we're both jumping up and down on the squeaky mattress, alternating between lyrics like we used to when we were kids and begged Mom to replay the movie so we could study this number.

"Lady Marmalade" blasts through Olly's portable speaker next, and we immediately slip into our previously assigned characters. I take the Mýa and Pink parts, and he gets the Christina and Lil' Kim sections. You would think since he used to make me dress up like Christina, I would also get to sing her part, but out of the two of us, Olly is the true diva. No matter how much I fought him, he always won. Stubborn bitch.

I still remember the choreography I made up. I took dance classes, so obviously I thought of myself as an expert who tried— and failed—to teach Olly how to dance. Olly tries to mimic my movements, but bless his gay soul, he's so uncoordinated.

When the song is done, we collapse into a fit of laughter, both of us sweating from dancing and belting. Both the upstairs and downstairs neighbors are banging on the ceiling and floor, respectively, shouting for us to "turn it down."

"What's gotten into you? Khal must've put out."

"Alex!"

"Prude. We share a wall, you know."

Olly works to hide his smirk. He tries hard to pick up the slack Dad left and fill the hole from Mom's constant absence, and it's rare to see him let loose. Olly hides a lot, buries it deep down for me. I'm grateful for Khal because he's the one perfect place to which Olly can escape.

"Don't be jealous of my man," he says.

"Hardly. Speaking of, guess who keeps asking me out?"

He eyes me curiously. "Who?"

"Hunter Addington."

"Gross," he says. "Again? Can't he take a hint? How long has he been trying?"

"Way too long. It's desperate now." I don't tell him about Hunter showing up to the Lonely Bear late last night, alone, and how he sat with me while I finished cleaning my station. I choose not to tell Olly how after work Hunter and I went down to the beach and sat for a while. We didn't say much of anything, but it was oddly nice. He didn't make a move at all, but at the end, he whispered, "I like you," and kissed me on the cheek. Strange. I didn't hate it.

"It's a shame something so slimy comes in such an aesthetically pleasing package." Olly used to have a crush on Hunter back in middle school. Then again, who didn't? "There's a rumor he's fucking Becca, you know."

Olly developed a keen ear for the rumor mill after Dad's arrest. I mean, I can't really blame him. Small town and all. He wanted to know everything everyone was saying about our family. I wanted to know nothing. Ignorance and bliss and shit.

"Doubtful," I say, thinking about how Hunter also put his arm around Ashleigh. He's a numbers guy: try with everyone, and eventually someone will bite. "I would know."

"Would you though?"

"Points. But even if Becca wouldn't tell me because the bitch acts like I don't exist, I think Ashleigh would tell me."

He shrugs. "I guess."

"You don't think so?"

"She's been acting weird," he says. "You know I love her, but—"

"Everyone's acting weird around us, Ol. It's the Brucke curse." I lean back against my headboard, the one I've had since I was six years old and Mom and Dad said I could redesign my room myself. I chose a white pillowy headboard, which fit so perfectly in my old bedroom with the cathedral ceilings. In here, in this dingy gross apartment, it barely fits in the space, with little room to walk around the bed.

"True." He's staring off into outer space, off on some distant moon in a star cruiser looking out on the horizon.

"What's up, Ol?"

He sighs, then starts and stops a good three times before saying, "Wanna go swimming?" His tone reminds me so much of Dad: the cadence and tone, a little goofy but with a serious edge.

Sounds perfect.

Khal drops us off beyond the property line of our former house, and we quickly skirt around the edges and traverse the beach, hopping up on the dock and settling into our spot. Our legs dangle into the cool lake as the sun beats down on us, neither of us ready to dive into the waters yet. I need the heat first.

Blue skies, boat engines humming, mild waves slapping against smooth rocks on the shoreline, all of it is like cool aloe on an everlasting sunburn. But temporarily, it provides some relief. I haven't been back here in nearly eighteen months. It hurts too much. Olly goes without me now, which hurts too.

"It's weird, isn't it?" I ask. "This dock. It's like—it hasn't changed."

My fingers run along the divots in the wood, carved by tight boat lines.

A car rumbles down the road, slowing at the entrance to the driveway.

I look to Olly, and we both turn, noticing the car and the figures inside, who are clearly squinting at us. I don't want to move. I don't think I should have to move. This is my land. I claimed it. I was here first. *We* were here first.

Jackie Henderson and her wife, Genny, emerge from their perfect suburban SUV. "Oh, thank god, it's you two!" Jackie shouts as she picks their son up and out of his car seat. "How are you both? Long time, no see, Alex!"

Olly and I wave. The perfect little family. Pangs of jealousy and anger and sadness attack me, all at once.

I fake a smile. "It's been a busy few months."

"I hope finals were good. You working at the Bear again?" Jackie must own stock in plaid flannel shirts because that's all she wears, even in July. Though, to give her credit, it's a cute short-sleeve button down, probably cotton. She owns a local brewery nestled in the Village, one of the only places in town open year-round. She sells brews with weird names like Mother Punch and Hairy Chest and, during Pride month, a specialty that always sells out: The Adirondyke.

"You know it!" I say. "Never ending."

It's hard to fake a smile seeing them here. In *our* house.

"Hi, Olly, Alex," Genny says, reusable grocery bags in hand.

"Hope you don't mind us," Olly says.

I roll my eyes. *Of course they don't mind, Ol; they're not demons.*

"You know you're always welcome here," Jackie says as if this wasn't our house first. Our property. Our dock and beach.

Guilt strikes me. Because they *are* nice. Too nice. They let us come here even though this house hasn't been ours for a while. Their kindness opens old wounds.

When they're not home, I can pretend this is still our house and Dad is home with us and not in prison. That everything is as simple as aloe on a sunburn.

"Do you want to come in for lemonade?" Genny, a kindergarten teacher who loves paint-splattered smock dresses, is a lot softer than her wife.

Under no circumstances do I want to step foot inside *their* house.

"Let them be alone, Gen," Jackie says. "You two have fun. We have to put the kid down for a nap. If you need anything, bathroom, cold drink, come up!"

"Will do!" Olly says, a lump in his voice. "Thank you." I love him for knowing he has to do the talking because if I open my mouth, chances are I'll start crying. He puts his head on my shoulders. "Always a jolt of reality."

Sometimes I think he's my only safe haven. The shelter from storms that always come. Then he ruins it by pretending to shove me off the dock and into the water.

An ear-piercing scream leaves my mouth. "The worst!"

His laugh fades into a low hum. "Whenever I see the Hendersons here, it's like turning the lights on after an incredible movie and realizing I was never part of the movie at all."

Oh, we're being serious now. Jesus, Ol, give me whiplash! "Like the silence after a Lorde song ends and nothing else plays because nothing else can ever follow *that* up." I love the way she can throw all her contradictions into her music and sing like she gives zero fucks and every fuck at once. "Do you think this will ever get easier?"

He squeezes my hand. "Which part?"

"Any of it. All of it." I wait for an answer that never comes.

He doesn't say anything.

I miss Dad. I want to say it out loud, but Olly's been so hard to read with anything Dad-related lately. I take out my phone and open my email app, refreshing it. I haven't heard from Dad in three days. It's weird. If I can't see him every day, at least I can hear what he's up to. Most of the emails are the same: prison sucks (no shit), the food is awful, he spends whatever money Mom sends him on jars of expired peanut butter and packets of ramen at the commissary (a gross injustice on many levels, especially if you eat them in close proximity), he's getting jacked and teaching other inmates how to read (which basically makes him Superman), and he misses me (same).

I pull up his last email and reread:

FROM: Inmate #98723473   July 2

TO: Lexigurl@gmail.com

SUBJECT: Miss you

Hey Kiddo,

Happy almost Fourth! How's the lake? I miss it so much. Thinking a lot about our summer days on the water, bringing hot dogs and burgers to an island and watching the sunset. Going out on the water late at night for fireworks. Wish I could be there with you.

Have you spoken to Oliver? I haven't heard back from him since he stormed out. Maybe we can plan a time when you're together and I can call you. I'd like to hear your voice, too. It makes the days in here pass more quickly.

There are some things I'd like to tell you. Things you should hear from me first. No matter what happens, always remember I love you, and want you and Olly to be good to each other.

Dad

Ominous as fuck, right? I mean, it's not like he never got sappy. His emails around the holidays are always raw. The ones at Christmastime and Thanksgiving were gut-wrenching memory dumps of happier times and how he would spend his Christmas playing chess with other inmates and eating boxed stuffing, wishing he were home with us. The Valentine's Day one waxed poetic about how much he wishes Mom would visit him. They soaked me in guilt, chilling me to the bone. But at least those emails were specific and focused. But this email is vague and came two days early. When I first read it, in the middle of working at the restaurant, it didn't register.

Now, it's growing like an invasive weed in my stomach.

I realize I never responded.

The weed in my belly sprouts thorns as I remember I ignored his last call because I was sleeping and too tired to pick up after working all night.

"Have you heard from Dad?" I ask Olly, putting my phone on the wooden planks.

He shakes his head. "No, but we need to talk."

My chest flutters.

He does this shit too much. Tries to sit me down for a conversation that will alter my entire fucking existence, and it's always been that way. "We need to talk" about my best friend saying shit behind my back in the fifth-grade lunchroom. "We need to talk" about my first "boyfriend" kissing Shannon Woleski at Barrett's eighth-grade birthday party. "We need to talk" about Dad getting arrested. "We need to talk" because Dad told him there's a good chance the jury at his trial is going to convict him, and he could be sentenced to up to eight years in prison. That last one nearly destroyed me. For months, all Dad said was that he was innocent and his lawyers were fighting to disprove the charges against him. Dad said we had no reason to worry, despite us having to move out of our beautiful home and into a dump before we settled into the shitty apartment building we're in now. I thought the worst was over. But Olly always forced me to face reality. I try hard not to resent him for it because he's my twin and I love him, but.

I don't want Olly to say anything. Sometimes it feels like Olly wants me to hate Dad the way Olly does. I can't. I *won't*.

Olly's phone rings as I steady myself on the dock. "I'm gonna hop in the water." I propel myself into the lake, the water engulfing my body, cleansing the memories and the bad tastes and all the negative shit away. Holding my breath, I slip beneath the surface and glide weightlessly, eyes open until my lungs hurts and I have to come up for air.

The water covers my ears, muffling the noise of boats zipping across the lake and Olly yelling to get my attention. If he wants to talk to me so bad, he can dive in.

He starts kick-splashing me with his feet.

I smirk and dip beneath the water, flipping over like a dolphin and propelling myself back toward the dock. I'm going full *Creature from the Black Lagoon*—I blame Olly for knowing that film reference. Once I'm close to the dock, I crouch down and spring up, grabbing Olly's legs, causing him to lose his balance and topple into the lake.

I'm laughing like hell when he emerges, but he's not.

I brace myself for him to scream and curse me out, but he doesn't.

Once he's done snotting water from his nose, I register his bloodshot eyes. He's been crying.

He lifts his hand, showing me his waterlogged iPhone. "Mom called." Olly's voice is dry, hollow. "Lex, it's Dad."

Suddenly, the entire world goes silent.

OLLY BRUCKE

I always thought getting cremated would start from a grand funeral pyre, a noble send-off for a warrior.

Or a fallen hero.

But there's no such thing.

It's a lot like baking a cake. You turn on the oven to eighteen-hundred degrees, slide the tray—a cardboard box holding a body—inside, and watch as the heat dries the body and the bones calcify. At the end, all we have is a pile of ash. The funeral director told us the process is a spiritual one that returns the body to its base elements: oxygen, carbon, nitrogen, hydrogen. Dad will be reunited with the earth. Or something.

Before the cremation, I got to see Dad's cold, dead body clad in the khaki jumpsuit three sizes too big for him, emphasizing the weight lost to prison. It took over two weeks to transfer the body from Ohio; we couldn't get into the medical examiner's office to see him, as his death became another number, a kink in a flawed system that needed to be sorted through, autopsied over and over again to exonerate the federal prison system. Verdict: heart attack. That's it.

One minute, a beating heart, the next, a pile of ash and earthly elements.

Maybe this is all we are: oxygen, carbon, nitrogen, hydrogen.

Now, next to his urn, the only thing running through my head is the ending of *Return of the Jedi*. Why does Luke burn Darth Vader's body in a funeral pyre? Technically, it's Anakin Skywalker, not Vader, who "died" the moment he decided to kill the Emperor and save Luke. Am I really supposed to believe decades of pure evil can be wiped clean with one act of good? And Luke, all contemplative as his dear old dad burns, is at peace with everything Vader did, as if all the genocide and attempted murders (plural!) of his own kids is somehow offset by one moment of not being a total dick?

I didn't buy it then, and I don't buy it now.

Google alerts ping on my phone like an alarm:

LAKE GEORGE TRIBUNE
CONVICTED LAKE GEORGE
BUSINESSMAN DEAD AT 50

Cameron Brucke, 50, the former CEO of ColdFire Technologies, who pled guilty to charges of tax evasion, embezzlement, and fraud, died of a heart attack in his prison cell at the Federal Correctional Institution, Elkton, Ohio, Friday morning.

Brucke, a once-prominent tech entrepreneur in the area, was arrested on charges two years ago after the FBI found Brucke had falsified bank documents to secure multi-million-dollar loans for his company, which Brucke then used for personal gains. The scandal rocked the region due to the nearly one hundred local residents who lost jobs in the shuttering of ColdFire.

According to a spokesperson for FCI Elkton, Brucke had been making "remarkable progress, and was well-liked by most inmates." A medical examiner noted an undetected heart condition like Brucke's could have flared at any time. There are currently no further internal investigations planned, and the official cause of death was heart failure. Brucke had served eighteen months of a forty-eight-month sentence.

Brucke is survived by his wife, Gabriella; son, Oliver; and daughter, Alexandra. Services are being held at Diamond Point Funeral Home.

Not even one day of peace.

Even with the Google reminder, it's like I'm at someone else's funeral, watching from a distance.

The first time I ever went to a wake was for the father of one of my mother's friends. Alex and I were ten and, according to Mom, "old enough to pay our respects." I remember walking into the funeral home, notes of mothballs and lemon antiseptic hiding beneath layers of potpourri, staring up at wall-to-wall people dressed in black, all of them tense, all of them speaking in whispers so as to not wake the dead. If someone laughed, all heads turned; Alex and I overheard so many *I'm sorry for your loss*es we started to laugh, nervously at first because it seemed so empty, but then a little bit louder until Dad gave us The Look and we shut up. The closer we got to the open casket, the more people were crying. Mom dug her nails into my shoulders to steady me, but I was okay. I wanted to cry but couldn't because I didn't know him. I thought it made me a horrible person, especially because Alex was bawling. She always felt everything a hundred times more than I ever did.

But this? It's like a scene in a movie where time is sped up all around me, but I haven't moved an inch.

Mom zips around the empty room, fixing flower arrangements and smoothing out the wrinkles of her skirt, fluffing the mothballed pillows on the couches "just so." I don't know why she cares so much. A grand total of eight people have shown up today, if you include Mom and me. We *have* to be here. Mom makes excuses for the lack of bodies. "It's the end of July, everyone is away on vacation or otherwise occupied." Right.

Looking around, feeling the emptiness, and watching Mom try to fill that void with her small frame and frantic obsessing over throw pillows is what breaks my heart.

She straightens out the guestbook and the accompanying pen on the table.

"Mom, it looks good." My hand tries to steady hers.

"Nobody came." Her hand shakes.

I list off the people who came—Sheila Addington; Sheila's brother, Ritchie, and his husband, Noah; Ashleigh; Ms. Rodriguez, our guidance counselor at school; Chef from work—but Mom ignores me.

The hardest part of all of this for Mom is how this appears. She's always been most concerned about how people perceive her: the projection of perfection in practiced smiles, perfectly curled brown hair, sleek *Breakfast at Tiffany's*–tight dresses, manicured fingers and toes. Even when Dad Death Star–ed our entire lives, she Kellyanne Conway–ed for the entire town, pretended like everything was fine and we were still the perfect nuclear family, even as our ashes smoldered around her.

"*Where* is your *sister*?"

I shrug.

The day we got the news, I thought Alex's screams would echo in my ears for the rest of my life—that's how blood-curdling and raw and guttural they were. Time stood still and I watched her crumble with the minutes until she was a pile of rubble. Though I stood in her wreckage, I was numb. At home I fell asleep next to her, and when I woke up in the morning, she was gone and I was alone.

Mom was so busy trying to get Dad's body brought back to Lake George and arranging the funeral she hasn't noticed Alex barely comes home to sleep, reeking of skunked beer and weed. Alex doesn't return my texts or calls, and when I try to keep her home, she glares at me and leaves anyway. At least she's still showing up for work, even though Chef has told her to take time off. But I've seen her through the windows of the restaurant: a robot when it's slammed, a zombie after the rush.

When Ashleigh was here earlier, she took me aside and asked how Alex was doing because Alex was ignoring her calls and texts too. Thankfully Mom didn't hear, since Alex has been lying to Mom about spending time at Ashleigh's house.

Thank goddess for Khal, who hasn't left my side since the morning Alex left. I instinctively look around for him, wishing he were within arm's reach right now.

"Where's Khal?" Mom asks, right on cue.

"He went to get us pizza."

Mom's lips purse. "You think that's appropriate, Oliver?"

"It's food, Mom. Nobody's here anyway. Who will know?" I say, and Mom winces, a side effect of the constant "breaking" headlines about Dad over the years. "What's the worst that'll happen? We wake up to another article? I can see it now: Cameron Brucke's Funeral a Pizza Party, Source Says." I can't help but laugh. Our entire lives for over three years have been governed by newspaper headlines and breaking news on the local stations and Google alerts.

"It's not funny." A hint of a smile grows on Mom's face.

"It's a little funny." It feels weird to laugh here, but Mom looks relieved, a bit more relaxed as the tension in her shoulders melts.

She pulls me into her. "Thank you for being you." She kisses the top of my head and returns to fussing over the guestbook. "Alex should be here. What do I do with her?"

I stand at the window looking out over the empty parking lot. The more I stare, the more certain I am Alex isn't coming.

I try calling her for the millionth time, but it rings once and goes straight to voice mail.

In the silence, my mind starts to drift to the last time I saw Dad. Part of me wonders if it *is* my fault he died. When I confronted him about Tyler, maybe I caused his heart unnecessary stress. But I quickly push that thought out of my head. Dad's had heart problems for years. It's not my fault the prison wouldn't expedite a doctor visit.

Right?

Enjoy prison, Dad. You belong here. Guilt wraps around my lungs and squeezes out every last ounce of air until the walls around me start to close in. My chest heaves, and the funeral home falls away until everything is hazy.

It wasn't my fault.

It wasn't my fault.

It wasn't my fault.

I steady myself against a coatrack, using its wooden skeleton for support, while I count backward from one hundred, a trick Khal taught me when this happened the first time a few days ago.

One hundred. Ninety-nine. Ninety-eight.

Why did I make Khal go out for a pizza?

Ninety-seven. Ninety-six. Ninety-fuck this shit.

Sweat pools at the small of my back and snakes down into my boxer briefs. I rip the suit jacket off and fumble with it, trying to hang it on the coatrack, but my fingers are rubber and it slips through and crumples to the floor.

"Oliver—" Mom reaches out, but I dodge her.

"I'm fine." I don't want her taking care of me.

Not today.

Not now.

I'm fine.

I stumble into the bathroom, turn on the faucets, and splash cold water on my hot cheeks repeatedly until I can feel the sting and my breathing returns to a normal state. Propping myself up against the blush-pink porcelain sink, I stare at my reflection in the mirror. Traces of Dad linger in my eyes, around my chin and the balls of my cheeks, his dirty-blond roots peeking through a shitty dark dye job.

The awful yellowing floral wallpaper from the 1950s certainly doesn't help.

I check the time. We still have two hours left before this hell is over.

A text from Khal pops up on my screen: **Be back soon. Everything ok?**

I slide open my phone to respond, but instead I find myself opening my email and rereading Tyler's last few messages.

FROM: TyeDye1505@gmail.com   July 7

TO: DirectorOlly@gmail.com

SUBJECT: I'm so sorry

Olly,

I don't know what to say. I heard the news. I'm so sorry.

I never knew him, but I know what it's like to lose a parent.

I'm here, if you need.

Tyler

FROM: TyeDye1505@gmail.com   July 8

TO: DirectorOlly@gmail.com

SUBJECT: Re: I'm so sorry

Olly,

I'm glad to hear you're doing as well as you can. There's no real way to grieve, so don't feel bad about not crying.

I don't talk about this ever, really, but I'll make an exception. My mom got married to a guy when I was seven. He never officially adopted me, but to me, he was my dad. A few years ago, a couple of months after my grandad passed away, my dad died in a car accident. I didn't cry until after the funeral, once everyone left and I was alone in my room and I thought I heard him walking down the hall and calling for me. I lost it.

I think the worst part is never knowing what could have been, you know? Where do you go from here once someone you thought should be here, isn't?

It doesn't get easier, but it does get better.

(Stupid question, but) how is Alex doing?

Sending you . . . idk, so much, man. I got you.

Ty

I got you. I'm stuck there, not quite sure what it means. I haven't responded to the email yet, and it's been weeks.

How can he "have me" if he doesn't know me?

I wish he could, though. Is that weird?

Pangs of guilt rack me. I can't abandon Tyler, not now, not after emailing each other back and forth and him pouring out his guts to me when he didn't need to.

I won't be my father. I tap the reply button, filling Tyler in on everything: how we found out about Dad's death, how Alex has reacted by going off the grid, how Mom is acting like a grieving Stepford Wife, and how, even though it's been weeks, I still haven't cried but I have developed some lovely panic attacks because of what I said to him the last time I saw him. In an act of desperation—for answers or help or to get it out of my system so I'm not the only one holding onto this—I tell him how Alex is numbing herself beyond recognition. The morning after we got the news, Alex disappeared. She comes home reeking of booze. I'm not sure what to do. I'm scared. Typing furiously, I end with: Thank you for offering to be here for me. I really appreciate it, even though I didn't know how to react when I read it. I don't know if I've said this yet, but I've been thinking it for a while: I'm really glad I have a brother. Love, Olly.

I hit send before I even realize what I said.

Love? My emotions are all over the place and I don't think I meant it, but I can't unsend an email.

Shit.

With any luck, he won't notice, or he'll chalk it up to grief.

The smell of pizza—and the allure of Khalid, who will no doubt talk me down from this ledge, too—lures me out of the bathroom.

The front door of the funeral home flies open.

Alex carefully moves inside like a frail porcelain doll in over-sized sunglasses and a tight black dress.

I nearly choke on my own vomit when a suited-up Hunter Addington trails behind her. What the hell is *he* doing here? And why did they come together?

Mom walks over to Alex and pulls her into a hug. But Alex doesn't lift her arms to hug her back. She perches her head on Mom's shoulders and glares straight ahead, no doubt staring at the urn at the other end of the room. Mom attempts to fix Alex's hair, brushing it out of her face and behind her ear, then moving to Alex's black dress, checking for wrinkles. Alex slips to the side and groans, so Mom moves on to Hunter.

He lays on the charm pretty thick with an "I'm so sorry for your loss, Mrs. Brucke." He nods at me but doesn't offer anything more. Dirtbag.

Mom is in the middle of asking Alex if she wants a lint brush—because of course Mom brought a lint brush to the funeral home—when Alex, ignoring Mom altogether, walks into the room with Dad's urn and sits in the back row of empty seats.

"Mom, go sit with Sheila and Richie? They're always good for a laugh," I say.

I walk up behind Alex and lean against her chair.

"You're late," I say, unable to help myself from stating the obvious.

Alex doesn't say anything.

"I'm glad you came." What an odd thing to say, but it's all I can think of in the moment. I put on my best concerned patron voice to hopefully get her to laugh. "I'm sorry for your loss."

She smirks. "Not funny."

"She speaks!"

"When she wants," she whispers.

"Why're you whispering? It's so loud in here from all the voices talking at once I can barely hear you!"

As quickly as it came, her smile disappears. "Has it been like this all day? Was it busier earlier?" She smells skunky, like weed.

I shake my head. "This is it. Ms. R and Ashleigh came earlier. They waited around to see you but had to go."

She wants to say something but grinds her teeth instead. She knows Ashleigh probably blew up her spot.

She slides over so I can sit next to her. I've missed her so much it makes me want to cry and laugh and punch a wall. All I've needed is to put my head on her shoulder. She takes her sunglasses off. Her cheeks are puffy, her eyes bloodshot, from tears or weed or both.

"I don't think I can do this, Ol." Her eyes fixate on the wall.

I grab ahold of her hand and squeeze. "You don't have to do anything."

"No, I mean, I can't be here." She loosens her grip and slides her fingers out from mine. She shakes her head, her chest rising and falling.

I move closer and say softly, "Talk to me, Lex."

Her head snaps toward me. "Talk to *you*? Why don't *you* talk to *me*? You've basically been acting like all of this is for some stranger. You haven't even cried. Once. And you want me to tell you how *I'm* feeling?" Her voice rattles, her hands shake. She's nothing but a thin layer of glass: one nick and she shatters into a million pieces. "The last time you saw Dad alive, you stormed out on him. You don't get to act all, like, superior now." She slides so far away from me, she might as well be in a galaxy far, far away.

"What's going on here, guy?" Hunter says, sauntering over.

"Guy? Are you kidding me?"

"Olly, please," Alex begs. "Don't."

"You okay, babe?" Hunter says, motioning for her to stand up and come to him. Like she's a dog.

Standing on command, she asks, "Can we get outta here?"

"Anything for you, babe." Hunter kisses her forehead.

I stand and move toward her. "Alex . . ."

"Sorry, Ol. Dad's not here." She covers her eyes with sunglasses and dissolves. "He won't know I'm not either."

ALEX BRUCKE

"Shotgun!" Hunter exhales smoke into my mouth. "What do you need, babe?"

I wrap myself up in one of his hoodies, stretching the bottom over my bare legs, pulling them close to my chest. My mind drifts to the funeral home and the anger I have for Olly, for how much he hated Dad and never made it right with him before he—no, I push every thought out of my head. I have to. "To forget."

"I got you." Hunter slides out of his bed and pulls up his boxers from a ball on the floor before crossing the room and rummaging through a drawer at his desk. Whatever he comes back with, I'll try. I don't care what it is.

"You're safe. Remember that." He instructs me to stick out my tongue and puts something on it. "Think about something happy, and this'll do the rest."

It's not long before my head is fuzzy, my body goes cold, and Hunter wraps me up in a blanket. Everything goes white, a blizzard swirling in my mind.

I drift into a memory from a year and a half earlier, right before

Dad's sentencing when everything changed and the ground beneath my feet started crumbling. Back at our old house with Olly, standing in the snow.

"Oh my goddess, Olly, it's fucking freezing. How'd I let you talk me into coming outside?" I missed the balmy heat of summer in the Adirondacks. My fingers were numb. Nearly blue. "If I lose a finger, I'll murder you. Especially since I got these done today." I flashed him my new stiletto nails.

"Love those, by the way." He whipped out an extra pair of gloves from his pocket and handed them over. "I found this for you." An old Princess Leia knitted hat with built-in earmuffs in the shape of her classic cinnamon bun hairstyle.

"I *cannot*. How!? Last time I wore this I was, like, five." I tried not to crack a smile, rolling my eyes instead. "I'd rather freeze than mess up my hair."

He shrugged and put it on his big-ass head, pulling it down hard so it stretched. "You're a few degrees away from Rose-on-the-door-after-*Titanic*-sank."

As much as I hated the cold, I always loved the snow. When everything was still.

Quiet.

The docks were covered in feet of snow, but we managed to tunnel our way to the end and carve out enough space for our asses to squeeze between the posts.

Olly stretched his foot beyond the edge of the dock so it touched the top layer of ice. His video camera was slung across his shoulder. His nose pink from the cold.

A line of snowmobiles raced by on the frozen, snow-covered

lake in the distance, fanned out in a V-formation, the leader a bright yellow machine.

"Remember when we took out Dad's snowmobile without him knowing?" I asked. We were twelve, and Dad was supposed to come home from work early so he could take us out on the lake after a night of nonstop snow. Mom was at work, and we waited for hours, watching the road for his truck. When it was clear he wasn't coming, Olly decided he could drive it himself. I warned him Dad would kill us if he found out. The snow was so deep atop the lake it was impossible to see the heaves in the ice. When the temperature drops, the ice contracts, allowing unfrozen water into cracks, eventually expanding and pushing up against the shore, creating unseen walls of ice beneath the freshly fallen snow.

"When I went sixty miles an hour over an ice heave I couldn't see and launched twenty feet in the air?" He buried his face in a gloved hand as I cackled. "You flew off the back and into a snowbank and I was convinced you'd died."

"I was in shock for a good five minutes. I almost died, Ol," I said with the straightest face I could muster, and he looked at me with stupid puppy dog eyes. I tapped my gloved, perfectly manicured nails together like an evil witch. He had freaked out when he couldn't find me, yelling my name like a crazed banshee, so loud nearby ice fishermen perked up to see what the fuss was all about. When he found me, I was laughing hysterically, tears frozen to the corners of my eyes. He had thought I was crying and started to do the same, then made the sign of the cross, but it looked more like voguing than a Hail Mary.

"You were *so* extra." I smiled and shoved him.

"The extra-est extra who ever extra-ed." He wrapped his arms around me and pulled me close for warmth.

Armed with a lump of fluffy snow, I smooshed it into his face the way Kermit the Frog would slam a whipped cream pie into Fozzie Bear's face on *The Muppet Show*, one of Dad's favorite shows.

He sat still for a moment, no doubt strategizing. The drums of war had been pounded. Shots fired. No white flags for the Bruckes.

I bolted upright and traversed the slippery, snowy dock toward the yard, ducking behind a tree in our old yard where we used to erect forts out of old blankets and fallen tree branches in the sweltering summer heat. This was where Olly shot his first movie, a sprawling epic about a mermaid (yours truly) who washed ashore and was jealous of the humans, so she decided to split her fin in two with a magical dagger (there was so much fake blood we were grounded for a week because Dad had to pay to have it removed so it wouldn't pollute the lake).

Olly dashed toward me, determined to tackle me.

Time for an epic Alex fake-out: I crouched down, screamed like a scared child, and then, once he got close enough, jumped up and took his bitch ass out.

Victory. He fell for it every time.

But he wrestled me down to the ground and shoved a snowball down the back of my jacket, which rocket-launched me into the air.

"You. Are. Going. Down!" I jumped up and down, wrenching my back to get it out, but it snaked slowly down my skin until it was nothing but a tiny clump of slush clinging to the fabric of my undershirt. I bent down to arm myself with the biggest snowball I could form. As I was about to rain hell down on his face, he started making a snow angel.

That was always the first thing we did as kids when it snowed: find a patch of untouched snow close to the house. To be the first ones there, to find something just for us, was beautiful.

I turned around and launched off the balls of my feet into the fluff.

The world became quiet. Cold. My limbs numbed. I felt nothing at all.

Feel nothing.

Olly's voice—no, Dad's—calls out to me, but it's too far away. I can't hear his words.

Everything fades away, even Hunter's basement.

Hunter's voice lulls me away. "You feeling anything yet?"

"Numb," I mumble.

"Good."

I stay frozen in snow, lost in the blizzard of my mind, of these memories. In the dead of summer, I stay dreaming of angels.

THE SUMMER AFTER
ONE YEAR LATER

OLLY BRUCKE

"Cut!" Ms. Rodriguez swats me away.

I try to dart out of range but I'm not quick enough, and her hand comes down hard on my video camera.

Rage bubbles in my gut.

It's not her fault, Olly.

I take a deep breath. I can't get mad at Ms. R. Not only is she my guidance counselor, but her family has a history with mine, and she's legitimately concerned. She didn't mean to hit my camera. It was *my* fault.

"You know, only I can yell 'cut,' Ms. R." I flash her a wide smile, but my eyes focus on the small collection of original *Star Wars* action figures on the shelf behind her desk, wedged in between photos of her family. Ms. R has good taste.

"Can you put the camera away so we can talk?" Her head dips to one side with concern or pity.

It was worth a shot to try and derail her, to make it out unscathed. "It's hard to put the camera away when the deadline for this year's Saratoga Film Festival looms on the horizon." I hold out my free hand toward her, using my thumb and pointer fingers to frame her face. "Inspiration can come at any moment." I didn't win any of the awards last year, but one of the jurors pulled me aside afterward and congratulated my loss by telling me the votes were tight between *Barefoot* and the winning film, but because I was seventeen at the time of *submission*, they thought me "too green" to win, whatever that means. I turned eighteen right after the festival last October, but that didn't make a difference. Elitist, ageist film snobs. I hate them and want to please them, all at once. I almost pulled the "dead dad" card, but.

But I'm fine, now. Totally unscathed. Consolation prize: a fire in my belly to win.

I've gotten really good at swallowing my anger. Or filming my way out of feeling much of anything.

"This is serious, Oliver. Please." She motions toward an empty chair. "Have a seat." Ms. Rodriguez looks harmless enough, with her assortment of pink sweaters and hair always tied back in loose ponytails with scrunchies from the nineties, but I've never been dumb enough to let her lack of fashion sense fool me. She's a suburban Jedi, known to mind trick quite a few students. She slides a manila folder with "Alexandra Brucke" written across a white label toward me.

I knew it. My finger flicks the off switch on the camera and I place it gently on her desk. "I am not my sister's keeper." I can't look her in the eyes. If I do, it's all over; she's way too good at reading faces. Especially mine. Maybe because I wear my emotions like cheap ChapStick: shiny, obvious. So I glance between the college pennants on the wall behind her: Penn State, Cornell, Pepperdine, Culinary Institute of America. All colleges Alex could have applied to if she cared about herself. I make the mistake of biting my lip too hard and drawing blood, which makes me wince.

Ms. Rodriguez seizes the opportunity to move in closer.

I've lost. She might as well be wearing a sand-colored cloak and waving her hand, because I've been Jedi mind-fucked.

"Oliver." Her voice is thick like molasses, the kind of syrupy concern literally everyone has expressed since Dad died. I almost believe it. Almost. "It's almost been a year since . . ." her voice trails off. "How are *you*?"

"I'm fine." I'm not the kind of person who would lie to a guidance counselor, especially Ms. Rodriguez. She can sniff out lies.

I have to give her something, but I spent all morning in the hot, sweaty gymnasium for graduation, staring at Alex's empty seat beside me, knowing she wouldn't—couldn't—show, but hoping beyond reason she would.

For the Bruckes, hope is a futile war nobody ever wins.

In between salutatorian and valedictorian speeches waxing poetic about "life beginning now" and "all the memories we made together" like some cheesy Disney+ *High School Musical: The Musical: The Nightmare* song, I stared at the industrial fans humming loud like mini factories and wondered what the point of all of this was. Nobody here, with the exception of Khal, cares. Not about me, or Alex, and to be real, the second I got my diploma and moved the ridiculous tassel right to left, I checked out. Ready to put Lake George High and the last four years behind me. Footage for the cutting room floor.

My first mistake, because Ms. R was waiting for me by the door. "I was hoping to catch your mom, but I see she left."

"She had to get to work," I said, doing my best to hide my

disappointment. While everyone was getting ready to go to their own family parties celebrating the end of an era, Ms. R was asking me back to her office.

Her shoulders stiffen as she sits back in her chair, defeated. "Oliver." The way she says my name *repeatedly* makes it clear she thinks I don't take my sister's frequent disappearances seriously. I grind my teeth so hard my jaw goes numb. "You've had a rough year, *years*—"

"I don't mean to sound disrespectful, Ms. R, but I'm fine. Really, I am. It's been eleven months. I can't keep telling people I'm fine and not have them believe me."

"Grief takes many forms."

"That's the thing," I interrupt, again. "I'm not grieving. Everyone thinks I have to be sad or something is wrong with me. I'm *not* sad. There's *nothing* wrong with me. As for Alex, you'll have to find her to ask her what's up with her." My fists clench talking about her. I flash her a toothy smile to prove I'm totally, completely, one hundred percent *fine*. "But I'm not—"

"Your sister's keeper, I heard you." The whites of Ms. Rodriquez's eyes have little red veins crawling out and away from the irises. She clasps her hands on her lap and lets out a little sigh. "I don't make it a habit of talking to other students like this, but you're practically family and I've tried to get through to your mom, but." She clears her throat and her eyebrows crinkle as she negotiates something with herself. "I don't think I have to tell you her attendance this past school year has been nonexistent. She never sent in college applications and didn't show for her final exams. We've sent notices home"— which I've never seen, so Alex must have intercepted—"and called and left messages for your mom—" The cable company shut off our internet and cable and cut our landline three months ago. Mom has one of those cheap dumbphones and she doesn't know how to check her voice mails herself. She continues, "About Alex not being eligible to graduate, but." She waits for me to respond, but I don't have a response for her. She takes a deep breath. "Her teachers were willing to help her out, given the enormous loss, but her last chance went out the window when she didn't bother showing up for finals. There *might* be something I can do to push her past that finish line, but she *has* to come see me. You really don't know where she's been?"

It takes all of me to hold back the rage building in my chest for the last year. I spent so much time covering for Alex, but I couldn't take her finals for her. The guilt thrums against my rib cage, making it hard to breathe.

In losing the father who abandoned us years ago, I've lost Alex too. She's a ghost, dissolving through the walls of our apartment as if she were never there at all. Mom has been holding herself together with cheap thread, and she's inches away from unraveling and becoming a ghost like Alex. And not the good Force Ghost kind, but the kind that decay inside walls and feed off the fear and loneliness and anger of the people left behind.

"I really wish I did, Ms. R." I check my phone. There's a text from Khalid asking where I am. I don't try to hide the frustration in my voice. I fire off a quick text to Alex: **Where are you? Ms. R wants to talk to you. She wants to help you graduate.**

READ 1:02 PM.

No response. Typical.

"Can I go now?" I ask. "I have to be at work soon."

Ms. R glances at the clock on the wall. "Ashleigh's graduation party is tonight. Will we see you two?"

She knows good and well Alex and Ashleigh don't speak anymore.

"I have to work."

She concedes. "Please, if you can, try to get Alex to come see me." She nods toward the door, so I grab my bag and camera, but she stops me as my fingers grace the handle on the door. "What's your new film about?"

I exhale until all the air has left my lungs. "I don't know yet. I've been so busy with work I haven't been able to come up with a real concept for follow-up."

She hmms. "I've seen you with that camera every day for the last year." She's right—I've been filming everything I can, hoping for inspiration.

"It helps to view the world through a lens, and not my own eyes."

"Makes it easy to lose perspective."

My torso turns toward her, keeping one hand on the knob. "I wanted to catch the vultures picking apart our family bones and whispering behind our backs on camera." I'm only half-kidding. I have no idea what story I want to tell; I need *it* to find *me*.

If I were anybody else, I can almost guarantee Ms. R would say something like, "Nobody is whispering behind your back," which is a lie; the whole town has been talking nonstop about Dad and his masterminding of the Great Lake George Scandal for the last four years. When I thought the voices had finally disappeared, his death ratcheted up the volume because now it became, "His poor children. Fatherless before graduation. How sad! And have you seen the Brucke girl?" Thanks, Pops.

Instead, she says, "What story do you *want* to tell?"

Catching a glimpse of my reflection in the glass of her degree, I say, "The story of the gay existential crisis known as 'bleaching my hair white.'"

"Your hair looks great, but you're deflecting," she says, putting her counseling degree to good use.

I glance at the folder with Alex's name on it, and then my gaze falls to the floor. "The truth."

"Which is?"

We're no longer talking about my illustrious filmmaking skills. "Everyone assumes I'm broken by my father's death. I'm not broken. I'm pissed." My hand releases the doorknob and I walk back to the empty chair across from her. My temples throb as the whole Tyler secret I've been keeping from Alex swirls around my head, and it's become heavier over the past year, especially as Tyler and I have become closer. But I can't tell Ms. R this. "I'm angry all the time. At my dad. Alex." My hands are shaking. This confession surprises even me, and it takes a second before I realize she did, in fact, Jedi mind trick me into talking. If I weren't slightly embarrassed, I'd be impressed.

Jedi Master Rodriguez: 1

Padowan Olly: 0

I try to swallow, but the anger feels too impossible to bury. "Even dead, he's finding a way to destroy us." My face is a hot Mustafar lava pit about to explode.

"I don't know what you're going through. I can't imagine, actually. So I'm not going to attempt to say I understand because you're smart enough to know it'd be a lie. But I do know what it's like to have a parent—and a spouse—who abdicated responsibilities. What that does to a person."

"Sometimes I think the anger is too much," I admit.

"Let me put it in terms I think you might understand." She takes a deep breath and her eyes study mine while she thinks up something prophetic, as she is known to do. "You're familiar with *Star Wars, Episode V: The Empire Strikes Back*, yes? For the longest time, I never understood why Darth Vader appears on Dagobah while Luke is training with Yoda."

"He didn't," I cut her off. "It was a vision, a manifestation of Luke's fears."

"Exactly. But *why* does Vader appear? Do you remember when Luke asks Yoda what's in the cave?" she asks, and I nod. "What does he say back to Luke?"

"Only what you take with you."

"And then what happens?" she asks.

"Luke goes into the dark cave, cue dramatic music, Vader emerges in slo-mo with all his asthma, and Luke lops his head off. But it wasn't Vader. It was *actually* Luke! Dun dun dun!" I've gone over this so many times for a film essay I abandoned last fall when I decided not to apply to any colleges. Ms. R and I have spent many after-school sessions talking through my decision, and she helped me sketch out a few road maps:

Plan A: The Saratoga Film Festival has a grant for young aspiring filmmakers (requirements for entry: high school degree plus an original film capturing your essence as a filmmaker), so while *Barefoot* doesn't qualify since it placed last year, I can emphasize my near-win as part of my submission letter, and I have to come up with a new film to submit by the August deadline.

Plan B: Apply for paid internships and entry-level production assistant jobs on film sets and at film studios either in New York (to be closer to Khal) or Los Angeles (though those will require housing, which, given our family's current financial status, seems farfetched).

Plan C: Use Plan A to help fund Plan B.

So far, zero responses from any internships or PA jobs, so cue: anxiety!

"Sure, but you've missed a few key details," Ms. R continues.

I suck my teeth. "Like what?"

"Before he goes into the cave, Yoda tells him not to take his weapons, but he does anyway. It stands to reason Luke saw Vader in the cave in the first place because he went in ready for a fight. He let his fear and anger guide him. Go back and rewatch that scene: Luke draws his lightsaber first." She leans back, allowing her keen *Star Wars* knowledge to thoroughly impress me.

"So, you're saying because he went in as the aggressor, the cave showed him as Vader? I don't get it."

"If you confront darkness with darkness, you're feeding into your fears."

"Should I confront my fears and make a documentary about my family?"

"I didn't say that. I don't think—" She rubs her temples, clearly annoyed. "Luke saw Vader in the cave because he was afraid he would become Vader."

I sit back in the chair and scrutinize her critique: the way Vader's mask explodes and Luke stares at his own face, the cutaway to Yoda subtly shaking his head, knowing Luke had failed the test.

But Luke *wasn't* Vader. That was the whole point, so I don't know what Ms. R is trying to say, unless—

She thinks *I'm* Luke Skywalker–as-Vader.

I sling my bag over my shoulder and palm my camera tightly. "I'm not my father."

"That's not what I was saying, Oliver," Ms. R yells, but I'm already out the door.

The second I'm outside, I pull out my phone and there's a new email notification.

FROM: TyeDye1505@gmail.com   June 25

TO: DirectorOlly@gmail.com

SUBJECT: CONGRATULATIONS!

Olly!

Dude! You're a high school graduate? How does it feel? I wish I could've come and cheered you on. I know you said not to because your mom would probably freak and you're not having a party or anything, but I still would've liked to come. Have you thought any more about meeting up? You said after finals was good. Thoughts?

Hope you're doing something fun today. Like, legit fun, not just watching old movies and writing a dissertation or some shit. Hanging with Khal at least? The selfie you sent of you guys in your caps and gowns this morning in front of the lake was really cool! Shame Alex wasn't there. Looks beautiful there. Can't wait to see it in person.

Proud of you, little sib!

Ty

P.S. You're still working at the Lonely Bear this summer, right?
Message me back whenever you can. I have something to tell
you. Actually, can we officially move to texting yet? Let me know if
you need my number again.

I live for new emails from Tyler. Each one makes me smile, and
I want more, but it's not long before the guilt arrests me because he's
become my deep, dark secret. I wish I could meet him, and he's tried,
but it seems like the ultimate betrayal to Alex. That's why I never
gave him my number. Keeping him in email feels safer, less real.

Tyler and I graduated to "big bro" and "little sib" in our closings
last fall, and it seemed oddly natural. He noticed my "he/him/they/
them" signature, and naturally went with "sib," which meant the
world to me.

Then he started hinting at wanting to meet up. I scroll back to
last October.

FROM: TyeDye1505@gmail.com   October 30
TO: DirectorOlly@gmail.com
SUBJECT: Midterm Hell

Sup little sib!

Sorry it took me so long to respond. Midterms were hellish. I met
with my advisor who is gonna help me lock down a summer

internship. I feel like I barely started here and we're already looking ahead like eight months!? There's a lot of pressure. Everyone at Cornell is so intense. Sometimes I wonder why the hell I chose to study Hotel Management at one of the toughest schools in the country. I've seen people have complete breakdowns in the library after studying for ten hours straight. The culture here is so weird, too, because those same people then go out and get wasted on Friday and Saturday nights at the frat houses and then are right back in the library on Sunday stressing about their exams on Monday. My only reprieve is basketball with the guys after classes. Oh! How'd the film festival go?? I wish I could've made it.

Ty

Sometimes, I read his emails to feel like I have a connection to Alex. Sounds ridiculous, but he asks what I'm doing creatively and says he's proud of me and I wish Alex cared like that. Instead, I'm stuck rationalizing her behavior to everyone. With Tyler, I talk about my day like I'm normal.

I keep sifting through, rereading, which has become a habit when I feel like I need to be tethered to a sibling.

FROM: TyeDye1505@gmail.com   November 3
TO: DirectorOlly@gmail.com
SUBJECT: Re: Link to watch BAREFOOT

LITTLE SIB! WHAaaaaAATTT!!! What what whoa! I watched your movie last night . . . I can't believe you made that! Holy shit. I'm floored! I loved the subtle commentary about deforestation and how man disturbs the ecosystem in pursuit of glory and fame and the material. The natural lighting and the gritty nature of it juxtaposed with the fantastical CGI. I get why you call it a docu-fantasy! (Sorry, I'm taking a film class as an elective so I'm in critic mode. Thought it'd be cool to see what it is you like about movies.) But seriously, it was brilliant, and CONGRATULATIONS on placing second!! That's HUGE!!! I hope you don't mind, but I showed it to my roommate and some of my buddies. You got fans at Cornell!

And you were right. Lake George seems beautiful. One day . . .

One day.

Sometimes I think Tyler is a fantasy I created in my head: a fake brother to deal with a villainous father and very real sister. I'll respond to his latest email later. But for now, Khal is waiting. I switch on the GoPro strapped to my helmet before taking off on my bike down Mountain Road toward 9N; I rarely ever go through the footage, but it's nice to have a camera at the ready in case something eventful happens; it's good for establishing shots or B-roll.

I pedal so hard the tendons in my knees burn and pop. My jaw is clenched so tightly beneath my helmet that my head pounds. I can focus on the pain in my knees or the throbbing of my temples so I don't actually have to focus on my *I-am-not-my-sister's-keeper* and *I-am-not-my-father* thoughts.

It's incredible how fast you can get somewhere when your mind is buzzing on autopilot. I bank a right into the Blue Wharf neighborhood and snake my way down toward my old house. Part of me is hoping Alex will be here, in our spot, waiting for me. But she hasn't been back since the day Dad died.

The houses here are so pristine, each one its own perfectly designed lake house suited to the families who reside within them: a robin's egg blue Cape Cod–esque ranch for the elderly couple married for forty years, who now spend their winters in Florida; a log cabin tucked high on a hill for the single father who liked to hunt with his kids, both of whom graduated a few years back and moved to the city; a pristine navy-blue colonial with white shutters and a white picket fence for the ex-friends of my parents who completely cut off their friendships with Mom at the first sign of Dad's scandal. Every lawn is impeccably manicured, and each house is designed to protect the inhabitants inside from the horrors existing beyond their peripheries.

I stop at our old home, a carriage house converted into two-story open concept, tucked neatly behind a line of trees away from the street. When we lived there, we looked like the perfect nuclear family: Mom, Dad, two kids, a fluffy dog—a freaking *CW* show. Except we weren't, not really.

The ghosts of who we all were haunt it now. I wish I had a proton pack or something, so I could at least fight them off, but alas, I'm no Ghostbuster. If only I could trap the ghost of my dead dad and blast the ghost Alex has become and maybe jostle her back to reality. If I could wave a wand and capture all my ghosts in a box, everything would be fine. Right?

Filmmaking is a way to blast the ghosts, to capture the messy and make sense of it all in some sort of magical supercut. I can digitally create ghosts and kill them with my editorial power. Real ghosts possess your heart and head and nibble at your nerves until you're nothing but a bundle of frayed emotions.

I make my way toward the private beach where Alex and I used to build sandcastles and fight over who got to be the queen of the kingdoms in our imaginations. Faded images of us dancing on top of hot sand, a delicate choreographed scene, the moves to which only we know, a montage playing for nostalgia but serving no practical purpose for our current divergent stories.

Khalid sits at the edge of the dock, waiting. His family threw him a surprise graduation dinner last night, which I helped organize alongside his bestie Lia, at the Lonely Bear. They knew every place would be booked solid today and tomorrow, and they like to be ahead of the curve. His mom told me last night, as we toasted to Khal's next journey studying psychology at NYU in the fall, that he asked if it was okay to spend the day with me today because he knew I'd be alone. Cue: endless tears.

My bike crumples on the grass. I slip off my socks and sneakers, plop next to him, and dangle my legs off the ledge so my toes graze the surface of the cold water.

He turns to kiss me and it's soft. His hand finds its way to my thigh. He smells like cinnamon oatmeal and sweat, and I bury my nose in the olive skin of his bare shoulder.

"What'd Ms. R want?"

"Alex. What else? I basically only exist at this point so my twin doesn't die."

He rolls his eyes. "That girl . . ."

"Will be the death of me." My fingers rub the peach fuzz on the back of his head. I take a deep breath and wonder how many more of these days we have left, with him in New York City and me most likely heading to Los Angeles. If I can get a job as a production assistant or something, anything, the most basic-bitch entry level of positions at a film studio.

I remember the first time we kissed at the homecoming dance the fall of junior year, after I found him pacing outside the back entrance to the gym.

"Where's your head at?" he asks as I stare out at Diamond Island in the middle of the lake. The sun's rays bounce off the small, glittering waves. Between the view and Khal's strong body holding me up, I can stay here forever.

"Remember when you kissed me for the first time?"

He laughs. "How could I forget? It was, uh, the winter dance?"

"I hate you." I nudge him in the side. Khal is great at so many things: anything involving even a modicum of athleticism, talking to and empathizing with anyone, getting me out of my comfort zone and pushing me to do something like make a movie. But one thing he's not: a good memory bank of dates.

"No, wait, homecoming, right?" His eyebrows arch as he looks for confirmation.

"You don't remember how much of a mess you were?" I ask.

"I don't know what you're talking about." He looks away, but I still see the smile plumping up his round cheeks. That night he was pacing and mumbling to himself under the yellow overhead lamplight, and when I finally got his attention, he blurted out, "I like you!" His shoulders relaxed and I said something super cringey I can't remember now, but it was probably like, "I've always liked you, stupid." I definitely remember saying, "Can I kiss you?" and before I knew it, we were hardcore making out. Sure, it was sweet and tender and timid at first, but only lasted a hot second before I pushed him up against the brick wall, our hands exploring each other's bodies over our ill-fitting suits. It was like we were both finally breathing. I was his oxygen and he mine.

"My head still hurts from how hard you pushed me against the wall," he says.

"Lies," I hiss.

"I like it rough." He nibbles on my bottom lip. When he pulls away, I inhale sharply, trying desperately to catch my breath. Khalid Zaid is a movie montage, a reel playing over and over in my head when I want to feel something. Some directors spend their entire lives trying to create the magic of someone like Khal on film, but I get to experience it in the flesh.

"You know what else I like?" he whispers, and the melody of his voice lulls me into a false sense of security. I hmm, and he says, "When I get you wet."

He doesn't give me time to register what he says before the hand he had wrapped around my back forces my body off the edge of the dock and into the lake.

The icy waters are a quick shock to the system, but it's refreshing, like my body is able to release all the built-up Dad-related toxins. The lake is the one place I can clear my mind, breathe, and just *be*.

Usually, I would let myself float, but I can't let Khal get away with such a treasonous act as he laughs his ass off from his warm, comfortable perch.

I break through the surface and scream in pain. "My knee! I busted it on a rock!"

Without hesitation, Khalid slips his phone out of his pocket so it doesn't get wet and jumps in after me. The second his body hits the water, I lose control and laugh.

"How many times are you gonna fall for that?" I struggle to get the words out as my arms pump harder to keep my body afloat after laughing weakened my resolve.

Khalid, not the strongest swimmer, doggy-paddles and stretches his neck to keep it above the surface. He's basically one solid muscle, so he can't even rely on the buoyancy of body fat to keep him afloat. He sputters out a wet, "Bitch."

The tips of my toes dig into the smooth, sandy bottom. "C'mon, babe, you know the water is pretty deep here," I say, but now's not the time to use logic against him, not when he himself doesn't have a prayer of standing—he's a good seven inches shorter than I am.

A short king. My short, brown, muscly king.

I reach out to hold him up, but he pushes me away.

"One day, I won't jump in after you." He reaches up for a strong-hold on the dock.

I pout and swim closer. My fingers tease his slick skin and the goose bumps bubbling to the surface beneath my touch. I gently kiss the water droplets on his forehead.

"You won't?" I ask, already knowing the answer.

"Shut up." He latches onto me like a koala on a bamboo stalk, wrapping his legs around my torso, and we bob in the waves.

I could stay like this, with him, forever.

I close my eyes and imagine Khal and I somewhere other than Lake George. I wish we could float away from everything. The breeze kicks up and as we float, I picture us sailing high above the mountains all around us. Khal always says he wouldn't mind getting into a hot-air balloon and flying away; wherever we land, that's where we'll live.

Toward the middle of August, Lake George has a two-week festival culminating in a four-day hot-air balloon extravaganza: hundreds of balloons in the sky all weekend. We can never afford to get into a balloon, but I've been saving over the last year for Khal. He doesn't know, and I don't tell him. It'll be our last surprise hurrah before he leaves for NYU and everything changes.

I don't want Khal to leave, or for this to end.

I have a lot to do before then: start and finish a new film project (maybe a documentary about my family?) for the Saratoga Film Festival, pack an entire lifetime into this last summer with Khal, and somehow convince Alex to get her life together (and tell her about Tyler) before she becomes another Lake George townie burnout.

It might be easier to learn how to fly.

ALEX BRUCKE

Pitch black.

A sliver of light peeks out from behind blackout shades.

It reeks. Weed and skunked beer and cologne and sex.

My phone buzzes from somewhere in the bed.

Can't find it, not after I spent the morning watching and rewatching Instagram and Snapchat stories from everyone in my class at graduation.

I smothered my phone in the comforter, but the damn graduation march song still hums along merrily in my head like a fucking TikTok sound. Everyone posing and throwing their shit in the air like they did something great. Families hugging and crying. "The end of an era." I can't escape it.

I unearth my phone and squint to read the message from Olly:
Where are you? Ms. R wants to talk to you. She wants to help you graduate.

Leave me alone, Olly.

I rub sleep out of the corners of my eyes and click the button on the side of my phone to check the time. One p.m.? Graduation has come and gone. There is no "helping me graduate." I know it,

Ms. Rodriguez knows it (she's either too naïve to admit it or she doesn't want to add another statistic to her file), so it's best Olly does too. I toss the phone on its screen side. Back to black.

Hunter's king bed is so warm, and the air outside the blankets is icy. I slide out from under the sheets and ask Hunter's HomePod to play my music on shuffle. Harry Styles's "As It Was" plays, and I remember blasting this with Ashleigh in her car all melancholily talking about how this song must be what it'll feel like when we're apart for college. A whole-ass year and an entire lifetime ago. So much for college. And friendship. Ashleigh can suck it now.

Hunter's football hoodie is three sizes too big, but it's perfect right now. Warm and fuzzy and makes me feel small enough to escape.

An email alert dings on my phone.

FROM: SheilaAddington@LonelyBear.com   June 25
TO: Lexigurl@gmail.com
SUBJECT: Welcome Back!

Hello Bear Employees!

Another summer is upon us, and we're so happy to have you back as employees (and for the first timers, we look forward to welcoming you to the team)! Tomorrow is the first—and most important—full staff meeting, so make sure to arrive on time, at 8 a.m.

Nope.
Nope, nope, nope.

I love Sheila, I do. And I'm grateful she's given me the flexibility to come and go depending on what I can handle, and sometimes working at the Lonely Bear is all I can handle, but everything has a time limit. We need the money, and the Lonely Bear's restaurant can't afford to lose any help during the summer months, but.

But.

My toes fidget and my lungs start to drink in air like I've been oxygen deprived.

I have to move.

Pacing Hunter's empty room—his perfect doctor mom and pilot dad allow him the entire basement in their hella massive mansion on the lake—I trick my brain into caring if he's enjoying his rich-ass celebration with his picture-perfect parents at the bougie-ass Sagamore, where they rented out the entire outdoor pavilion, a move for only the richest assholes in town. It's not like I don't care about Hunter. I do. How could I be with someone for almost a year if I didn't, right? He's been good to me, lets me crash here most nights so I don't have to go home, and holds me when I cry (even though it's in the middle of the night when he's dead-ass asleep because I *never* cry in front of him when he's awake, but still—it counts). He's been the perfect escape. A warm body to hold and a good blunt. Plus, when I did go to school, and he had his arm around me in the hallways, nobody bothered me. Nobody said a word. No false platitudes, no pity, and no whispers. Well, none I directly heard. He was my human shield; if he stood in front of me, nobody got to me. He liked being my entire world.

I feel bad I'm not at his graduation party. He wanted me to go, but nothing sounded worse than celebrating everyone else's graduation when I'm a perpetual senior. Oh goddess. Am I officially a—

—dropout?

Throat closes.

Temples pound.

If I don't seek out Ms. R, if I don't graduate, if they don't let me back in—they have to, right? I mean, Olly said there's still a chance, but what if I have to go back in the fall as a senior and do everything all over again? I could never face myself.

The fear of failing so spectacularly isn't a fear, it's reality. I couldn't sit in classes day in and day out and pretend my entire world wasn't turned upside down and lit on fire by a fucking blowtorch until it was nothing but a pile of—

Ash.

In an urn.

My chest tightens, and it's like a million horses are stampeding through my body.

I rush to the bathroom and steady myself on the sink.

There's a box of dark-brown hair dye I stole from Rite Aid months ago. Tearing it open, I follow the instructions, smothering every square inch of blonde. The smell of ammonia gives me a heady high. When I'm done, I change out my new septum piercing, and stumble out, wet hair and all.

I need air, or a hit.

Yanking open the bedside drawer, I hastily rummage through Hunter's shit: loose condoms, lighters, a bottle of lube, cash, a few dime bags of blow, mini Tito's bottles, old iPhone cases, the class ring Hunter had to have but never wears, a small felt pennant from Texas A&M, where he's heading for college to play football and probably learn how to become a Republican senator.

Found it. A small plastic Extra gum box Hunter uses to store his personal blunts. The good stuff. The quality weed laced with whatever designer drug du jour Hunter can get ahold of—a far cry from the regulated shit he sells to freshmen who've never been to a dispensary and don't realize he upsells and makes a killer profit.

He calls himself an entrepreneur. A burgeoning businessman. Dreams of working in finance or whatever his dad tells him to do.

I don't give a shit what he calls himself. As long as I don't have to feel anything.

The sliding glass doors leading out onto the lush green lawn from his bedroom-slash-apartment are jammed, and I have to use my shoulders to jigger them out. You would think with all their money they'd have working sliders, but I guess even the rich have problems.

I curl up on a lounge chair near the edge of the lake, tucked on the other side of a tall pine tree casting shadows over the water.

Looking at the lake, the water moving shore to shore and refilling from mountain springs, I remember swimming with Olly and sitting on Dad's lap as he drove our boat, learning to waterski with Mom spotting and screaming at me to hold on for dear life because she was afraid I would let go and spin out of control. The swirling cop lights and ice heaves and snow angels and water angels and one minute Dad is here and the next he's gone, and it doesn't make any sense because in some ways him leaving for prison felt like he'd died, but we could still go see him and hug him and email him and talk on the phone the way some people visit tombstones and mausoleums and plant flowers for their loved ones as if they could see.

Then he was really gone.

A tear escapes as I zone out, memorizing the shape of the waves as they fall at my feet over and over and over again. Like I'm trapped in a loop.

A never-ending summer.

It's last summer and the summer before that and every summer I have yet to see.

Now I wait for sleep, for snow to fall again and the world to become a blank slate.

Between the heat from the sun baking the hoodie on my body, and fog from the blunt, I start to mellow and sink into the haze.

Until I forget, again.

OLLY BRUCKE

"Oliver, Khalid. You're *late*." Sheila Addington stands in the foyer of the Lonely Bear Resort's main office staring at a clipboard. She doesn't bother looking up when we enter and the bell above the door jingles. Sheila looks like your typical suburban soccer mom: short safari khaki shorts, a red polo shirt with the Lonely Bear logo—a black bear wearing white sunglasses inside a purple inner tube atop a yellow Adirondack chair—embroidered onto the breast, and short, angular, honey-brown bob with blonde highlights and feathery bangs. When she finally looks up from under the brim of her visor, she glares at us. "Where's Alex?"

The million-dollar question.

"Running late." I haven't heard from her this morning. Or yesterday. Or the day before. She hasn't been home, which isn't out of the norm. But still.

Sheila's face softens as I plead with her silently. With a heavy sigh, she returns to her clipboard.

I can't take more guilt. I take out my phone and fire off rapid-fire texts to Alex: **Where are you?!? and Hello?? and Sheila is asking. It's not for me. You know how much she's done for us.**

I don't expect her to even look, but immediately I get **ugh stfu i'm coming.**

Khal peers over my shoulder and mutters, "Mashallah."

"There's a first for everything."

The main office isn't very big, but it's crowded with bodies and most have their backs turned to us. So many new people, and I always wonder how the new personalities will gel with the old. Behind Sheila, Chef offers a small wave, his eyes lighting up. He mouths, "Alex?" and when I shake my head, his shoulders slump.

Sheila clears her throat dramatically. "Okay, welcome to another great summer at the Lonely Bear!" She beams up from her post and her smile is infectious, injecting us all with energy. "Most of you know your way around here, but we have a few new faces I'll introduce once I go over staff rules and changes, and give out the summer assignments, though most of you will be working the same positions as last summer." Seventy-five percent of the staff leaves in the fall when Lake George becomes a virtual ghost town as the leaves on the mountains turn robust shades of orange and red and yellow. It's a skeleton crew of locals who stay on through the winter months. She goes over the rules for new staff, the usual lateness policies, time-off requests, coverage, sick days, and staff housing for those who come here to work for the summer, many of whom are from Russia. "If you haven't finished filling out the necessary paperwork, please see Ritchie behind the front desk."

Ritchie, a fabulous older gay with perfectly coifed hair and sun-ravaged skin, waves. He offers friendly winks to Khal and me, and

I can't wait to go over to him and get the dirt on all the new folk. Then he gives me a concerned look and cocks his head like he's trying to tell me something but he looks like he's seizing.

I throw up my hands and shake my head. I think he mouths, "Talk later." Great.

"Since we emphasize our *family* values here, how about we go around the room and introduce ourselves and our duties," Sheila says. "Oliver, why don't we start with you!"

Heads turn. All eyes on me like I'm back on stage after placing second in the Saratoga Film Festival and having to give a "thank you for not picking me" speech. *That* was a lesson in restraint.

"Oliver here. Y'all can call me Olly. He/him, or they/them, whatever energy you feel I give off on any given day, go for it." The back of my neck prickles with heat and I clear my throat. "I run the boat excursions. Been boating since I was a fetus. Tell your guests to book a ride or a tour with us." I point to Khal. "Khalid is my, um, first mate. We also fill in wherever Sheila needs help; that's what we do around here."

"Way to sugar her up," Khal whispers.

Sheila beams. "They've been here longer than anyone else, except me of course, and they've worked every job possible, from housekeeping to bussing tables to manning the front desk, so they know the ropes. Even when they're not paying attention. If you have any questions, I'm sure they'd be happy to answer."

"Dynamic duo!" Chef shouts as one of the groundskeepers shouts, "Get a room!"

Khal's cheeks turn a deep shade of red.

Chef grimaces, knowing he's caught us fooling around once or twice in an empty room or in the backup walk-in fridge because

Khal thought it was hot. He shakes his head as he walks out of the office and heads back to the kitchen. His tolerance for staff meetings is nonexistent.

"Settle down," Sheila orders. "Thanks, Oliver, Khal." She continues with the veteran staff before moving onto the noobs.

An unexpected yawn grabs hold of me, and nearly takes me out. Khal spent most of the night thanking me for throwing him a graduation party the night before, riding me until I was on the brink of destruction. And then he woke me up early this morning because he was in a rare mood to top. He never wakes up early, and never wants to top, so I have to take the opportunities when they come. Of course, now my thighs are burning and my back aches and I'd rather spend the day in bed because I'm zonked, but it was totally worth it. I lean against the door frame to rest my eyes like a grandpa.

Khal elbows me, and at first I'm certain it's a mistake, but then he legit shoves his pointy-ass arm into my stomach, jolting me to attention. "Can I see your phone?"

I roll my eyes and growl, slapping my phone into his hand.

Peripherally, I watch as he zips into my email app. Khal is always keeping his mind and hands busy, and I never ask him questions. He's always buzzing with brain activity he can't turn off, so at this point, I appease him. But I watch as he taps the TYLER DELL email folder and scrolls until landing on one particular email Tyler sent about a month ago with a few selfies of himself outside on Cornell's campus after finals. Tyler has the signature Brucke dirty-blond hair, the same color I bleach and dye to look less like a Brucke, Alex's nose that balls at the end, my cerulean eyes. Tyler looks like a male Alex—the only real differences between them are the shape of his eyes, which are more almond-like than hers, and the dimples in his cheeks, which Alex doesn't have. His scruffy blond stubble and ridiculous, unobtainable muscles are very Chris Hemsworth. If my soft mushy body stood next to his I'd never stop being self-conscious.

Khal taps on the first picture and sucks in a breath. He zooms in on Tyler's face. Then looks up. Back to the screen. Up again.

"The hell, Khal?"

Slowly, he turns to me and licks his soft lips. "I wasn't sure, but—" He points toward the window, to a silhouette washed out from the morning sun. Then the shadow moves out of the light, and my breath catches.

My chest sinks.

Earth literally stops rotating.

Because he's here.

Tyler.

I grab onto Khal's shirt, which tears a little. My tongue is limp, no words come out.

"What's he doing here?" I hiss.

"I thought you would know," Khal says.

I shake my head. How would I know? He didn't say anything about coming here.

Holyshitholyshitholyshit.

This can't be happening.

I have to get out of here. Because if I don't, I'm going to throw up. Or we're going to have a melodramatic confrontation that'll be secretly recorded and uploaded to TikTok, and I've already had enough of my private life documented by people other than me. Maybe Ms. R is on to something with this idea about making a film about my life, on my terms.

"I'm out," I say, tossing open the lobby door to the outside.

At that moment, a souped-up BMW with black-tinted windows rounds the corner at top speed into the resort, tires screeching as it treats the front entrance like a scene from *Grand Theft Auto*.

It comes to an abrupt stop mere inches from the main office door and the vibration from the speakers shakes the room and tickles my entire body. Alex flings open the passenger-side door and a cloud of stanky smoke pours out like she's some washed-up pop star emerging on stage to a billowing smoke machine.

Hunter Addington sits in the driver's seat.

Everyone inside, including Tyler, moves to get a better look.

Only a douche would have a "PSSYKLLR" vanity license plate. Hunter, despite having the IQ of bedrock and being the rumored source of most of the Adderall and coke flying around school, was also captain of the varsity football team and a legacy student at Texas A&M. And he's treated like royalty because he looks like a tired Abercrombie model. He even smells like one of the stores too.

When you're rich, you can afford to speed around town with a blunt hanging out of your mouth and nobody gives a shit.

Hunter rolls down the window and nods at me, his eyes bloodshot. I notice right away he's shirtless. He sees me staring and makes his sculpted pecs dance. "Like what you see?" he asks with a wink.

"Not even a little," I say.

He snorts as if what I said is impossible. "Hey, baby," he beckons, and my sister's head rolls toward him. "Come here."

Curly dark-brown hair billows behind her as she walks up to the window and bends down to kiss him. *What the*—she changed her hair!? That's deep end for Alex. The deep streaky color washes her out, even with her fake tan, and it's so dry.

He sucks smoke into his lungs, pulling so hard I cough on his behalf, and grabs the back of her head to shotgun it directly into Alex's mouth.

Not taking his eyes off me as his window rolls up, he accelerates so fast Alex stumbles backward. I look at her in natural light for the first time in weeks; her suntanned face is puffy, and her makeup is smeared. The way she moves it's like her body is Sally from *The Nightmare Before Christmas*, a tangled mess of limbs stitched together. Her face is blank. I can't read her. For our entire lives, up until Dad died, when one of us has been in pain or sad, the other could sense it, no matter how many miles apart we were. Now, she's barely a few feet away, but there might as well be an entire solar system between us.

She barrels right past me toward the office door and says, "Don't look so serious, Ol. It's not the end of the world," and glides inside without another thought, remnants of who she used to be hanging in the air behind her like ghosts.

As the door swings shut, Tyler stares at me through the glass.

ALEX BRUCKE

The smell of Hunter's tires lingers in the air alongside his pungent cologne. A trace of weed and something else dances on my lips as I push open the door to the lobby.

"Nothing to see here!" I shout. It's painfully obvious everyone watched Hunter slam in and out of the lot, even though I asked him not to show off; I wanted *one* day of not being the person everyone stares at. He likes being stared at; it gets him off. If he was concerned about my punctuality, he would have stopped smoking with his dumbass friends earlier to drive me here, not when it was convenient for him. Instead he said, "It's my aunt's place, chill. You'll be fine." He always says I have nothing to worry about, he'll do all the worrying for me, I'm dumb for worrying because he's all I need.

I'm used to people staring, but I haven't put myself in the position to be the center of attention in a long, long time, preferring to sail beneath everyone's radar, drop off it completely. Now, all eyes are on me, and my neck is hot. I smile like a puppet on strings. My lips tighten as all the new staffers freeze in place, like I'm a bomb about to explode.

So what if I am?

To diffuse, I offer an awkward curtsy because I'm a fucking lady.

Someone starts a slow clap. "Ladies and gentleladies, the legendary Alexandra Brucke!" Khal follows up his introduction with a loud "Woo!" and soon, everyone follows suit.

I mouth *thank you* to him. "I'm here all summer!" I shout at my new adoring subjects.

"If they're going to talk, might as well give them something to talk about." Khal scoops me up into a hug. Well. Not *scoop* because he's too short to scoop, but he gives the best hugs anyway, firm and full, like he actually cares.

Olly judges me from afar.

"You okay?" Khal whispers, and I shrug. His skin smells like fresh lake water and oatmeal.

"How pissed is Sheila?"

"She's coming over now so here's your chance to find out okay-loveyoubye!" He dips out quick.

"Nice to see you, Alex," she says, not even bothering to furrow her brows. I mean, I wouldn't blame her for a furrowed brow or two right about now. Everyone always seems so damn bothered by my presence—or lack thereof—except Sheila. She never flinches. She expresses her worry differently than everyone else, straight to the point. Which I appreciate. No hysterics like Mom or Olly or Ms. Rodriguez. Everyone is intimidated by her; between her Latvian heritage, statuesque height, and Boss Bitch energy, nobody messes with Sheila. It helps she has the best stank face ever. Goals.

"Are you ready to come back? This summer won't be easy. And I need you here, Alex. You know how the kitchen gets slammed once the season starts, and I can't have you calling out or not showing up. I have an inbox full of résumés from people who would kill for your spot in the kitchen."

I blink. It takes every molecule in my body to say, "I'm here." If I had any balls, I would tell her being here is painful, walking in this office felt like sucking out every drop of energy remaining in my body, and cooking is the absolute last thing I want to do. But Mom needs help with the bills, and I can't let Sheila down. Not after the opportunities she's given me to learn in a real kitchen, with Chef. But the spark for cooking?

If I've learned one thing over the last year, it's that you can't bring back what's dead. This is about survival. And dulling the constant aches.

She leans in close. "I am too."

Everything is still so fresh. Flashing lights, trials and headlines, snow angels, Ziploc bags of quarters and khaki jumpsuits, booze and pills and weed and a funeral I didn't attend. I never saw Dad again before he was reduced to ash.

I hate that he left me.

Everyone is still staring at me.

Anxiety bubbles in my belly.

I need to curl up with a blunt and disappear.

Push all the bad shit away.

Shove it into a suitcase.

Tie it up with chains and weights.

Toss it in the lake.

"Are you okay?" Sheila asks, but her voice is far away, an echo. My vision frays and I'm at our old house sitting on the dock with Olly, who has a map of the lake drawn with crayon with a giant red X on Dome Island where we expect to find buried treasure. My feet dangle in the water, waiting for Dad to get home from work early, like he promised, so he would take us out on the boat. Like a montage in one of Olly's movies, time passes by in years and he never shows up, no matter how long I wait.

Wake up, Alex!

Cold palms slap against my clammy skin. Sheila's voice again, far away, shouts, "Someone get me a glass of water!"

Olly's hands prop me up. I want to tell everyone to shut up, get away from me, but my mouth can't form words.

"Drink, drink." Sheila's voice is under water.

My rubbery fingers grab the cold glass and the cool liquid splashes down my throat and out the sides of my mouth. My breathing steadies.

Someone's hand grabs mine and squeezes tightly, urgently. Olly.

Mere seconds before the world around me comes into sharper focus. Beaded sweat drips down my back.

Olly's in my ear like a voice-over. "Lex, I'm right here." His fingers squeeze mine, and I turn my head and he comes into focus. "You're okay, you're okay. Think of snow angels." His voice settles in my head as I make snow angels in the white-out of my mind.

"Should we call 9-1-1?"

"No, please," Olly begs. "This happens sometimes. She'll be fine."

All I want to do is sleep. Someone puts a wet cloth on my face. Ritchie. Seeing his face is like waking up to the smell of freshly baked apple pie, and I can't help but smile.

"Welcome back, baby girl," he says. "Hey, Sheil, she's awake."

Olly's eyes are wet. His fake smile, full of concern, kills me. All I want to do is bury my face in him. "Khal is pulling up his car. Let's go home."

"I don't want to go home." I bite my lip.

"Mom is worried." He looks away from me.

"You called Mom?"

"*I* did," Sheila interjects as Khal reemerges by the front door of the main office; his car idles outside. "Olly wouldn't let me call an ambulance. You okay to stand?"

I nod and offer a weak smile to reassure her, though it does nothing for me.

Olly leans in to grab my arm and hoist me up. "I saved you the embarrassment of her showing up here. You can thank me later."

Olly thinks he knows what's best for me. I hate his self-righteousness.

"Breathe, Alex." Sheila's voice becomes a whisper. "I know you don't want to go home, but it might be good for you. If you need a place to stay, my home is yours."

Breathe. It takes all of me just to breathe.

"Do we have to go in?" I stare up at our run-down apartment building. The cracked bricks are a faded yellowish orange, and nearly every window has a moldy air conditioning unit dangling out of it, propped up with broken pieces of wood or cement dug out of the "garden"—it's not so much a garden as a trash receptacle with overgrown bushes and the occasional stretch of dandelions—wrapping around the building. It's a far cry from any of the houses surrounding Lake George. Our apartment building may be just one town over, but it's legit a different country.

"Get it over with. Mom leaves for work soon anyway, so it's not like she can rail into you for longer than . . ." Olly stops to check his phone. "Twenty minutes, tops."

"Enough time to kill myself."

Olly stops and whips his head to me. "Don't joke."

The anxiety flares up again and the bubbles get caught in my throat. "Lighten up, Ol." I look to Khal for reassurance, but he doesn't give me anything but a concerned look.

It *was* a joke.

Can your eyes roll so hard you strain the muscles or tendons holding them in place? Because if so, yeah. My eyeballs strain. Everyone is so sensitive these days. If I want to joke about death, I'll do whatever the fuck I want. "Joking."

He grinds his teeth. "If you're not gonna take what's happening with you seriously, why should I? There are other things I could be doing, you know."

"Damn, Ol. That's cold," Khal says.

I'd be angry if it weren't true. I'd slap him if I cared.

"Are you staying, Khal?" I ask, and he looks to Olly for the answer. When they first starting dating, Olly used to sneak Khal in after Mom went to bed, but it got too complicated when Mom started passing out drunk on the couch by the only exit, and Khal had to climb down the rickety fire escape that rusted so bad it eventually eroded and crashed to the ground, which thankfully happened long after Khal descended. The landlords never fixed it, and Khal had to basically Spider-Man his way down. Not exactly safe. Or smart. And Mom wasn't dumb either. She knew Khal was sleeping over, but she waited until the perfect moment to say something, swearing me to secrecy. One morning while I was eating breakfast, she asked me to pretend she was leaving for work and hid in the coat closet by the door. Once I slammed the door and yelled "she's gone!" Khal came out in his boxers and Mom jumped out and his face went fire-engine red. I'd never heard a boy scream the way Khal did. And Olly. He fell to the floor like a demon had been exorcised from his body. I recorded the whole thing on my phone for the day they get married. Mom really didn't care. It's not like Khal or Olly could get pregnant, and they were each other's firsts, and Khal is adamant about frequent STD and HIV tests. They only had to endure the "make sure you use condoms" talk once. Once! Mom tries to lecture me every damn week, if she happens to be home when I wander in.

"I should give you guys time," he says.

"I'm not staying long," I mumble.

Olly loosens his grip and his voice softens. "You could?"

"After all the beautiful shit you said about me? I'll pass." I don't know how to explain I can't be around Mom. Our tiny apartment is a coffin.

Dad's things are gone. There's nothing left of him.

Except Olly, who looks at me like we're six and still believe in twin magic.

"Stay, Khal." I don't want Olly to be alone when I leave.

The apartment door is unlocked and our floofball of a dog, Dracarys, nearly pisses himself when he sees me. He's the size of a fat squirrel but somehow manages to jump halfway up my body. I scoop him up and snuggle him close. He's the only one in this house who doesn't care how much of a fuckup I am.

The walls are so bare. No pictures of us anywhere, only cheap dollar-store décor Mom bought to make it look livelier, since all of our stuff was repossessed and sold off. The only real photographs on the wall are of Dracarys as a puppy; the other is a stock photograph of a family of model actors. Mom liked the frame and I guess intended to use it for a picture of Olly and me, but never got around to it. She hung it anyway because it made her feel happy to see their smiling faces.

Mom is at the table with a mug of piping hot tea, an unopened package of Stella d'Oro biscuits, and, behind it all, a glass of red wine. Because of course.

"My baby! Are you okay?" She rushes over to me, tries to catch me, but I'm slick and, unfortunately for her, in no mood for her hysterics. I quickly slide into one of the empty chairs and reach for a cookie. Without a word, she slides a paper plate beneath my hand to catch the crumbs. That's Mom, always caring more about the appearance of crumbs than the source of the mess.

My legs tap restlessly. My fingers twitch. I need a hit of something, anything, but my pockets are empty—my emergency blunt must've fallen out at the Lonely Bear.

Olly wraps his arms around Mom, and she latches onto him like a life raft in a storm. Olly has a bond with Mom I'll never have.

"What happened?" she asks, her eyes wet.

Words tumble out of my mouth like crumbs. "If you paid attention, you'd know."

"Alexandra." There's a tension in her jaw. She's been crying. But tears are useless. Tears won't bring Dad back. Tears won't erase the last few years. Tears won't suddenly make me better. And her lack of words right now speaks volumes.

"Well, I'm fine," I finally say. "Right, Olly?"

His eyes are loyal to me. "Yeah. She's fine."

Mom closes her eyes and reaches for her wine glass. So much for tea time.

When she opens them, it's like she's an entirely different person. "Hi, Khal! Would you like some tea?"

"Hi, Ms. Brucke," Khal says. "I'm good. Thank you."

"Khal, when're you gonna call me Mom?"

"You trying to marry Olly off?" I interrupt. "We're kids."

"Oh, are *we*? *We* certainly are." Mom: Expert Shade-Thrower. "Listen. We have to talk." She's sucked all the air out of my lungs. Dracarys squirms in my arms, but I'm not ready to let him go. He nibbles on my fingers as she continues. "Ms. Rodriguez called. I told you, you needed to go to her if you wanted to graduate, and I don't have time to babysit you. Not anymore." Of course she doesn't. I'm surprised she doesn't just want me gone for good. "What the hell is going on with you?"

I don't know how to answer her. It's like, I can identify the problem, but the solution doesn't exist, so I'm suspended in limbo. Like floating out on the middle of the lake at midnight, no boat or life raft, no lights, just still waters and no way to shore.

The creases in Mom's forehead have become more and more noticeable these last few years. Before Dad was arrested, her skin was flawless, smooth, and she barely looked a day over thirty. Time and stress have carved their marks on her face. The creases around her eyes and the frown lines around her mouth were chiseled by Dad. "I work three jobs. I'm so tired, Alex, but I do it for you and this is how you repay me? By getting high and flunking out of school and not even bothering to meet with the guidance counselor to see what your options are moving forward? I can't force you to fix your past, but you're destroying your future!"

I start to power down. "I don't know how to respond to any of this." My voice is robotic. Dracarys slips from my weakened grip and dashes into the next room.

"You don't think it was *hard* for me not to see you walk at graduation?" Mom asks, her bottom lip quivering. Her emotions are swinging wildly, as per usual.

"Let us help, Lex," Olly says.

"You spent years dreaming of going to culinary school," Mom says. "Remember all those days and nights we spent cooking together and reading Archies? What happened to *that* Alex?"

Cooking and Archie Comics, the only things we ever shared. Mom used to dream of owning a small restaurant, where one day I would take over when she got too tired to work. We'd change up the menu daily or weekly depending on what ingredients were the freshest and what was grown locally. We'd experiment in the kitchen together, merging Mom's old family recipes with my instinctual twists. Afterward, we'd read her old collection of vintage Archie Comics and bond over hate-watching *Riverdale*. Mom always loved Veronica Lodge, even modeling her style after Veronica: skintight clothes always accentuate her cleavage, brassy black hair, bright red lips, and jewelry to match. She never leaves the house looking less than stellar, even to go to the store for milk. Even without money, how she looks is the one thing she can control. That and her never-waning love of cooking. For so many years, I wanted her dream too. Now, where I used to find passion for cooking, I find myself wanting, like turning the knob on a gas stove and waiting for that *click, click, click* to light a fire, but nothing happens beyond a slow leak of methane and a wicked dizzy spell.

A part of me wishes I could curl up on the couch with Mom and ask her to read me a comic book. But she can't without pestering me, harping on me, saying I'm doing *something* wrong. When Dad went to prison, she always found something to nitpick. So I walled myself off from her for protection. After he was *gone*, gone, she only thought about how *she* was handling it. How it looked for her. She never once asked me how I was doing. Not. Once.

"Do you wanna end up like me?" Mom says. "No college education, married at twenty, kids by twenty-five, relying on a man to pay the bills and when he can't even do that, waiting tables and bartending and cleaning houses to put food on the table for two kids who don't care enough to go to college?"

"Nobody asked you to do all that." I almost feel bad. "It's not *all* about *you*."

"Lex," Olly starts, but Mom has already been detonated.

"You're right, Alex. Nobody asked me to have children. You think I don't wonder what my life would've been like if I went to college and avoided your father? If I didn't fall for his bullshit and abandon my dreams?" It's like watching a bomb explode in ultra slow motion. Little by little her body expands until fragments of her soul scatter around us. "But I chose to stay with a man I knew would wreck me. Because I had to. I had *you*."

"I'm out." I stand. The storm inside is getting harder to quell.

"You don't get to be done. I've given you space to process your father's death and I thought eventually you'd—"

"I'd what?" I snap. "Move on? Like he never existed."

"No, that's not wh—"

"I wish it'd been you," I snap.

Time stops.

I immediately wish I hadn't said it.

"Lex, not cool," Olly says.

Mom's face falls. Sweat pools on her brow, tears forming in the corners of her eyes. All the air has been sucked from Mom's lungs; I feel her struggling to breathe, and I want to be her oxygen mask, even though she was never mine.

"Mom, I—" I start to apologize, but she cuts me off.

"Leave, Alex." Her voice is cold.

"What?"

"You're going to leave anyway. I can't keep doing this. I can't keep worrying about you every night. Waiting up for you. Neither can Olly." She looks to him. "I know you've been taking care of her every night, when she does make it home. Making sure she doesn't choke on her own vomit." Then she turns to me, and her eyes are vacant. "Don't you see what you're doing to us?"

"To *you*?" It's always about everyone but *me*. Inside my younger self screams for help. She's trapped, desperate to break out, to be heard.

Mom's right. I can't be here.

With jellied legs, I grab an old backpack I left by the door weeks ago and race down the stairs, skipping steps and using the rickety banister to hold my weight up. I nearly trip as I launch toward the door, jerking it open and bolting toward the curb.

I send out two texts, one to Hunter, **come get me now please**, and one to Khal, **i'm sorry. Take care of olly plz.**

Digging through the backpack, I find a bowl, a lighter, and a dime bag of weed. I pack it clumsily, some bud falling to the ground, light it, and pull a hit so harsh it coats my lungs, and I exhale smoke through my nostrils like an angry dragon about to charge. I don't know how long I've been out here, but Olly comes up behind me and sits down on the curb, pulling his knees up to his chin.

"Lex, please don't go. I need you here." He hands me my favorite oversized flannel. He always knows what I need before I do. Or, at least, he *did*. It's a nice gesture, but it doesn't make up for the months of silence between us. When we were younger, if Olly so much as stubbed his toe, I felt a phantom pain in my own toes. But something shut off our connection like a light bulb and I don't know how to flip the switch.

"I can't deal with Mom. She doesn't get it." I try to wrap the flannel around my bare shoulders. There's a bite to the air that makes my body shiver.

"She's trying, Lex." *Tick, tick, tick.* He exhales so loudly it startles me. "You know, I dropped everything for you. I always drop everything for you."

"I never asked any of you to do anything for me." I don't know what else he wants from me. Does he *want* to make feel awful? Does he think I like the way things are?

Maybe. But I don't know how to fix it now, so why bother?

He moves closer and I let him. "You're mad at Mom, and me. I get it."

"Do you?" I ask. "Mom acts like she's so concerned, but she hasn't been there for us, not really. Ever since Dad was arrested, she's been MIA. Working all day and night." My words are garbled, blended up in tears and mucus. I can't get out the rest, how all I needed from her was a goddamn hug.

My lungs work overtime, but no matter how hard I try, I can't seem to take in enough air to steady myself.

He nods. "Mom's been dealing with all the shit Dad left us in. So have I, and there's so much you don't know." He takes a deep breath and holds it in, suspending us both in silence. His lips spasm. "There's something I *need* to tell you. About Dad. And—"

No. My head pounds. "Ol, I can't." I have no idea what he's about to say, but whatever it is, I do *not* want to hear it. "You and Dad were in a weird place, and I don't know why, but I can't handle hearing the reason. Please, Olly." I don't want to know why Olly has pulled back. I don't want a justification for Mom not being the woman I needed.

I don't want to hear anything that will destroy what's left of Dad.

Tears cascade down my cheeks. I'm willing my bones to fortify so I don't completely fall apart. "Dad was everything to me, so whatever you're about to say, don't." The muscles in my face ache from crying so much.

Hunter's BMW screeches around the corner at the end of the block and though it takes mere seconds, it feels like so much longer.

"It hurts how you never wanna hear me." Olly's soft words disintegrate in the air.

I want to tell him I love him, because I do and I'm hurting him, but I can't be who he thinks I am, so it feels cruel and empty.

All I say is, "Don't wait up."

After I get in, Hunter revs his engine and whizzes around the block.

From the rearview mirror, it looks like Olly is crying.

I wipe the tears off my cheek and say, "We partying tonight?"

Hunter speeds through a red light. "All summer, babe. It's the end of an era!"

But I'm barely listening. I pop in my AirPods and let "Homemade Dynamite" by Lorde drown out Hunter, his music, and every thought swirling around my head.

OLLY BRUCKE

Khal doesn't say anything on the drive back to the Lonely Bear, but he holds my hand, his thumb gently stroking mine. It's a good thing I'm not in the driver's seat because it would take every last bit of strength not to veer off course and head to Hunter's house. Khal knows too, because we've been through this a zillion times.

It always ends up in the same place. "Am I supposed to give up on her?"

Like always, Khal is silent, calm. Instead, he lifts my hand to his lips and kisses the soft pillow between my thumb and pointer finger.

This time, though, it's different. I *was* about to tell her about Tyler. I don't really have a choice now.

"*He's here.*" The words come out in one breath. Not like I could forget. The entire time Alex was melting down, all I could think about was how Tyler could, at any moment, send her over the edge. Which is why we're headed back to the resort now, to head him off at the pass, a football metaphor I learned after Tyler's post–Super Bowl email a few months back.

Khal's hand goes stiff. "Are you freaking out? I mean, holy shit, Ol! I've been dying to talk about this! Did you know? You didn't know, right?"

"You think I wouldn't have told you?"

"You *can* be forgetful—" Khal's eyes widen.

"The shade! Maybe I lose my keys and forget where I put my phone—" I start.

"All the time," he adds.

"But this? Come on. *Of course* I had no idea!" I pull up Tyler's last few emails and comb through them carefully. "Okay, wait. Look at this: he's always saying things like, 'I wish I could come' or 'One day I'll get to see the lake' and you know he's been hinting at us getting together, which I did want but—"

"Alex," he fills in the blank.

"Yeah," I say. "But look at this. His last email. Holy Spaceballs, it was there and I didn't realize it." I read his message to Khal: "'You're still working at the Lonely Bear this summer, right? Message me back whenever you can. I have something to tell you. Actually, can we officially move to texting yet? Let me know if you need my number again.'" I stare in shock. "It was *right* there."

"Clearly he wanted to tell you he was gonna show up at the Bear," Khal says.

"Who *does* that?"

Khal shakes his head. "I dunno, Ol. This is like a Netflix show or something."

"How do I do this?" I plead with him. "What do I do? I have a sister who hates me and is sliding into a big black hole, and a long-lost brother randomly showing up to a new employee welcome meeting at *my* job, in *my* town! And I didn't get a chance to tell Alex yet. I know I've had a whole year, but—" I don't have to finish. Khal knows the rest.

"Remember what I asked you after you said you emailed Tyler for the first time?"

I shake my head no, but I remember.

"I asked what you wanted from Tyler." Khal licks his lips. "You said you wanted to know him." He sighs. "You can only know someone so well over email, Ol. Eventually, this was going to happen. You could've told Alex a million times, but was she ready? Is she now?"

Alex herself said she doesn't want to know anything bad about Dad.

"You tried," he says, as if he knew I needed to hear that out loud.

"Maybe," I say, but I can't spend time thinking about what I didn't do. He's here now. "It's not that I want to, I *need* to know him." Ever since I found out about Tyler, I've been living with immense guilt that wrecks my body daily. I bite my nails, ripping skin from cuticles. My stomach is constantly in horrible sailor's knots. The guilt unsettles me. Guilt for what Dad did to him, and the feeling I could maybe make up for lost time. Guilt for not knowing my brother, even though, objectively, this wasn't my fault. Guilt for keeping it a secret from Alex because, as frustrated as I am with her, she's my best friend. I would do anything to keep her safe. And if she knew this, she could spiral so far out of control she might never come back. Hunter has the means. Keeping this from her might be the only way to keep her safe. I can't get her image out of my head. The way her whole body shook, so subtly yet violent, like a dormant volcano. The way she destroyed her beautiful hair. Her bloodshot eyes staring off into the distance and asking me not to tell her anything. She's so much like Dad, incapable of facing the hard stuff. But I'm not. And Tyler deserves the Olly he's been emailing with. "He's my brother. But am I doing the right thing?"

Khal shrugs. "I can't say."

Slices of lake appear between towering pines as we wind around the mountain.

"You're lucky." He flicks the turn signal lever before making a wide right turn into the Lonely Bear parking lot, in front of the main office.

"Lucky?" This catches me off guard, and I slide my hand out from his. "Really?"

Khal looks me right in the eyes, unfalteringly, and snatches my hand back to let me know he's about to say something I need to listen to. "Alex isn't ready, but that doesn't mean you should waste a chance with Tyler. Even if he did show up without telling you. It's been years since I've talked to my brother. He barely calls my parents, and they're getting old." He looks down and shifts uncomfortably in his seat.

Khal never talks about his brother. Khal calls himself an "oops baby." His parents were in their early fifties when his mom discovered she was pregnant. His brother was a little younger than we are now when Khal was born and he moved back to Lebanon. He got married and has kids now. They never visit, and Khal wishes he had a relationship with them outside of FaceTime. All he knows are the photographed memories his parents keep on the otherwise stark walls of their house, like a memorial to what is and could be. As Khal talks about him now, I realize they're basically strangers.

"So don't waste this chance. Talk to him about why he showed up out of nowhere. Maybe it could be good?"

I hate when he's right. "You're coming with me, right?"

"You think I'd miss this? After hearing you talk about this for months, I deserve my popcorn and front-row seat."

I reach for my video camera out of habit, but Khal places a hand on it and says, "Leave it." While it feels weird not to have my camera on and rolling, he's right. Not everything needs to be recorded on film. "*Yalla*," he commands, hopping out of the car.

Ritchie Addington walks out of the main office as we get out of the car. I'm drawn to him immediately. When he moved to town a few years back, he took me and Khal under his wing, and once a month, he and his husband invite us over for dinner. In a small town like Lake George, I can count the number of out, known, or suspected LGBTQ+ people on two hands (including me and Khal), so growing up, I never saw the life I wanted for myself in action. Until Ritchie. He's passionate and creative, and he has a room in his house dedicated to old Hollywood memorabilia. He has a replica of the spiky black headdress Cher wore to the 1986 Oscars on display next to a pair of Alexander McQueen heels worn by Lady Gaga he won at auction. But the most beautiful aspect of Ritchie is getting to see how much his husband loves him, and how much they both love their son. He's the father I never had but always wanted.

He waves us over excitedly. "How's Alex?"

"Rallied and back with Hunter," I say, giving him a hug. He wraps his big arms around the both of us at the same time like a momma bear.

He sighs loudly. "Record timing." He lowers his voice. "She'll realize my nephew is not good enough for her at some point. Mark my words. She's smart."

"She's hurting," Khal adds.

"Hurt people seek out other hurt people." Ritchie takes a step back and stretches out his arms. "That's the version no one wants to admit to." He's clearly spent the day behind the cramped front desk, and his back cracks like a snapping carrot. "You both going to play mini golf?"

"Mini golf?" Khal asks.

"The new staff are going into the Village tonight. I figured you were going."

"You going?" I ask.

"My old ass is going home." He glances toward the late afternoon sun and yawns. "Noah took the kid to Six Flags today, and they're on their way home now. He'll be good and tired, so Noah and I can have a nice, quiet night on the dock. Mini golf is the absolute last thing I want to do."

I smile at the thought of Ritchie and his husband, Noah, lounging under the stars while their son sleeps inside. Alex thinks I'm certifiable when I tell her Khal and I want that exact life, but after all the nights Alex and I were kept up by the sounds of Dad yelling and Mom crying into bottles of wine, and us putting on our favorite Disney films to drown out the noise, I knew what I didn't want.

"When are we doing our dinner again?" Khal asks.

Ritchie's eyes light up. "Soon! And don't forget, next weekend is our annual Fourth of July mocktail party/bonfire for the Lonely Bear staff."

"We'll be there," Khal says.

"There's a new guy. Tyler *Something*." *Be more obvious, Olly.* "Have you seen him?"

Ritchie eyes me curiously. "Nice kid. He's down at the docks with the others."

"Right," I say. "Thanks, Rich."

He locks eyes with me, but I duck him. "Have a good night, boys. Stay out of trouble, Oliver." He starts toward the main road on foot; his property is right next to the hotel, so he gets to walk to work every day.

Nothing else stands between me and meeting Tyler.

Except all the new Lonely Bear staff.

Ten of them are down at the docks, all in some combination of hoodies with shorts, talking and laughing and passing around a cooler full of beer bottles and colorful cans of spiked seltzer. I immediately spot Lia Francisco, Khal's best friend whom he helped get a job here for the summer so she can save up before she heads to Columbia, who is deep in conversation—with Tyler!

She has her hand on his arm smiling, no, *laughing*, and he's laughing too. Maybe even blushing. A pang of jealousy twists in my gut. I should know Tyler before anyone in my orbit.

Lia sees us and skips over to Khal and wraps her arms around him.

"You are everything right now!" Khal says, waving his hands in the air around her body. Her white lacy jumpsuit pops against her dark-brown skin, and her floppy white hat is a serve. I told her a trillion times not to dress this nicely when she's working, but she's not a fan of the frumpy resort T-shirt-and-shorts look. Can't blame her.

She bows like she's on the royal court. "I needed an excuse to wear this. It's too cute to sit in my closet all summer." Her smile is infectious. "I heard about Alex. I tried texting her, but she didn't answer."

I shrug, unsure how to answer. Thoughts of where she is, what she's doing, if she's okay, tug at my brain. "She's with Hunter."

"Ugh." Lia touches my arm gently. "I was texting Ashleigh before you got here. She said she heard Hunter's having a party tonight."

"I didn't know you and Ash were friends like that," I say.

"We bonded during spirit week. We were part of the same organizing committee," she says. Of course they both were behind spirit week. Ashleigh, the daughter of the best guidance counselor at our school, and Lia, the world's biggest overachiever.

"Also, didn't Ashleigh go completely off the grid? She doesn't hang with LG people ever, especially Hunter's crew," I add. "She's too busy spending time in Queensbury and Glens Falls."

"You're trying to get intel," Lia says. "Text Ashleigh yourself." She grabs my arm. "She heard about what happened to Alex in the office."

I sigh. "How?"

"Word travels fast here," she says. "Apparently Hunter is throwing a rager tonight. Everyone knows about it."

Not me. "Is Ashleigh going?" I want eyes on Alex, and it can't be me. I would never go to Hunter's house. Plus, I now have an unexpected Tyler-shaped situation on my hands.

"Text her," Lia says. "Alex is strong, Ol." Lia gives me a hug, and it's unexpected because as much as we like each other, our only connection has always been Khal. She squeezes so tight the tension in my muscles relax.

Over her shoulder, I spot Tyler staring at us, alone and awkward, and my body goes stiff again. He's no longer merely a collection of emails and hyperlinks, he's more flesh and blood than the paper and ink of his handwritten letter. I knew he was out there, a few clicks away, but with him a feet away from *my* lake, the convergence of worlds feels too surreal. He shoves his hands in his pockets and his shoulders tense as he sways his torso back and forth, offering me a slight nod.

I pull away from Lia.

Khal's eyes go wide.

"I'll catch up with you guys in a sec."

This is it. Here goes nothing.

ALEX BRUCKE

Dad always told me I was a beautiful cherry blossom tree, one that flowers in the spring for a short time and thrives afterward with green leaves. I used to think he was saying I wasn't pretty enough to last through the seasons, but he laughed and explained: "Cherry blossoms bloom once a year, and people wait all year to see their beauty. Anybody you choose needs to be able to wait for you to be ready, and even then they'll never be ready for how beautiful you are. But as long as they love and water you all year, that's what matters."

I wonder what Dad would say about Hunter Thaddeus Addington III, Son of Hunter Thaddeus Addington II, Third of his name, Keeper of White Male Privilege.

Hunter used to be a sweet guy. And sometimes, those moments shine through the hard veneer he's manufactured.

He walks over, a casually too-large baseball shirt draped over his muscled torso. "What happened today?" He places a hand on my back. When nobody else is around, he's different. Almost sweet.

I shake my head. I don't like talking to Hunter about my family.

"I don't feel like I belong anywhere," is what I settle for, an arrangement of carefully chosen words that cut my mouth like shards of broken glass.

Slowly, he rubs my back. "You belong here, with me."

"What happens when you're gone?" I ask, because the end is nigh. We haven't talked about what happens when he goes to Texas because he's all about "the here and now." But I'm stuck here, in Lake George, and when he's there, he's going to be surrounded by thousands of girls like me, but without all my bullshit.

I'm not even sure I would care, though, which I guess says everything. It's not like Hunter is the love of my life, and I figured out a long time ago I don't love him. I like him, and he takes care of me. Looks out for me. Gives me a place to stay when I can't go home. In less than two months, he'll be gone, and I'll be here alone.

Everyone leaves.

"Babe, don't worry." He offers me a blunt, and I pull. We fall back on his bed. His grip is hard on my arms so I cuddle into him as I get hazy.

I wish this were something real, lasting, but it's another hallucination, one I've visualized repeatedly: golden boy and fallen girl, prince and damsel in distress, a type of fairy tale where two misunderstood people find each other, and in each other, find a love neither ever had. When I'm high enough and we're alone, I can pretend like he's someone who rescued me from a life I didn't want.

The summer before sixth grade, when his family moved to town, our parents and his parents became fast friends through Sheila, his aunt. Hunter's father, Sheila, and Ritchie all grew up here, but his father had spent the majority of his adult life in Texas, building a small aviation empire while his mother was a surgical resident at

Baylor University Medical Center, which meant Hunter was often alone, raised by neighbors who had children his age. This was part of the reason the Addingtons moved back to New York, to be close to family, but Hunter's mother also got an offer to reform the entire surgical center in Albany's main hospital.

That summer, Hunter, Olly, and I played together every day. Hunter and Olly bonded quickly, but I could tell it was because Olly was enamored by him. It was hard not to be. He was fearless, climbing to the very peak of Calves Pen, the high cliffs on the other side of the lake, and jumping without hesitation. Where Olly was afraid to waterski, Hunter was jumping in and out of the wake, doing 360s and catching hella air. For two months, Olly felt like he was in on something no other boys at school would allow him to be part of.

After a couple of weeks of knowing each other, I started finding cute little notes in my bedroom from a secret admirer. One night, Mom and I barbecued—okay, really Mom cooked, but I watched her skillfully handle the grill like a pro, while I prepped the ice cream sundae bar. Hunter and I were eating our sundaes on the deck, watching the sun set as his mom came by to pick him up. Before he left, he leaned down and whispered in my ear, "I like you." That night, I found a note on my bed:

Be my girlfriend?

We spent the last month of August in blissful puppy love. We held hands, and one night, he asked if he could kiss me, and then he kissed my cheek. His lips were chapped and it was so quick, more like a bird peck, but I refused to wash my cheek. When he would pick wildflowers for me from the long stretch of woods in between our inlet neighborhoods, I would yell at him and tell him to leave them alone to grow and thrive on their own, but he told me I reminded him of a wildflower, something beautiful popping through a forest floor of dead leaves and twigs and moss. I would tell him I was a tree, like Dad told me, and he said he could pick flowers for me, but not chop down trees. I don't think he got it, but he was cute. He told me he always felt alone, but moving here and meeting Olly and me, but especially me, he wasn't anymore.

Then school started, and Hunter was the shiny new object, the good-looking stranger who captivated everyone, and between his good looks, family's wealth, and instant popularity, he stopped being the sweet boy who left me notes and started pretending Olly and I didn't exist. The worst was when a group of his new friends called Olly the F word, and Hunter stood by and let it happen. Right in front of me. I vowed to never speak to him again, not if I could help it.

The clout and adoration were highs he couldn't come down from, and once his new groupies realized Hunter was often alone in his mansion, it became the place to party. Lake George has a low year-round population, so our joint middle-high school made it possible for middle schoolers like Hunter, who saw massive growth spurts early, to fit in with high school sophomores, juniors, and seniors.

I don't know when Hunter started dealing, but he quickly learned the more access he had, the more people he could surround himself with. And everyone clamored for Hunter. Every girl had a crush on him, and every guy either wanted to be him or buy from him. He was voted Most Likely to Become a Successful Entrepreneur in our senior yearbook, which made me chuckle due to the irony because the more time I've spent with Hunter, the more I've come to understand how shallow and surface level everyone in his orbit is. They want him for what he gives them.

The night before I found out about Dad, he showed up to the Lonely Bear looking for his aunt Sheila. His eyes were red, and I figured he was high, but the closer he got, I could see he'd been crying.

Against my better judgement, I asked, "You okay?"

He shook his head.

"Wanna talk about it?"

He shook his head.

"Cool." I put my hands on my hips.

Before I twirled away from him, he blurted out, "My mom and dad and I had a massive fight."

"Parents fight," I said heartlessly. I had no time for his First World problems.

"No, I mean, they both fought with *me*." Hunter's beautiful Abercrombie face was twisted in pain. "My mom found out about the stuff I sell and told me she regretted having me."

I moved closer to him and took him into my arms. Though he was a full foot taller than me, it was like he had shrunk to child-size. "I'm sure she didn't mean it."

"No," he sobbed. "She did." He told me his mom said she begged his dad to let her abort Hunter. She never wanted children in the first place, but he convinced her to keep him. She called him a disappointment, and his father smacked him upside his head and he swung out of instinct and punched his father in the jaw. His father laid him out, and all he remembered was scrambling out the door and getting into his car and driving to the Bear to spend the night at his aunt's. He said he felt lightheaded, fuzzy. He probably had a concussion because he'd felt like he'd been tackled playing football.

I didn't know what to say, but I told him he was safe. And I spent the night sitting with him at the beach, not saying anything at all.

When he kissed my cheek and told me he "liked me," I remembered how I felt with him at eleven years old when he first moved to town. I saw the boy I used to know.

I still see that boy from time to time. He's sad and lonely and hates himself.

And sometimes, when we're alone, he hates me too. Grabs me hard. Yells. But he says he doesn't mean it, he's "messed up."

I'm messed up too.

Maybe two messed up people deserve each other.

Even as he holds me tight now, I worry about what happens when the door opens and his "friends" pour in and he becomes the Hunter Addington III they created and the little boy I once saw goes into hiding to protect himself.

A holler pierces through the silence, a siren call for Hunter, who had been waiting to reactivate, to be the center of attention, the life of the party, the man with the axe.

And I'm a tree that can't blossom.

OLLY BRUCKE

I'm in the passenger seat, not breathing, staring at Tyler in the back-seat through the rearview mirror as Khal drives us all into the Village.

"Olly, what do they say in *Star Wars*?" Khal asks. "You'll never find a more touristy hive of scum and trash like the Village."

Essentially two perpendicular streets, the Village is a series of the same kitschy souvenir shop over and over sprinkled with the occasional arcade, ice cream parlor, tattoo and hemp shop, and overpriced, underseasoned restaurant serving the worst frozen food, deep fried. During the summer, it perpetually smells like a mix of patchouli and fried dough. At night, the neon signs in every store window act as beacons for people with bad taste in fashion.

Tyler chuckles at Khal's joke. Lia is texting, so the bright light of her phone screen illuminates Tyler's face from below. At least he looks uncomfortable too.

"Since you're new, you have to get pastries from the LG Baking Company," Lia says. "I swear, the bread will destroy you. Oh, and—" Lia excitedly gives Tyler a talking tour of all of her favorite places, and it quickly evolves into a "We should go sometime" with a peppering of "I'll have to take you myself so you can get the true experience."

Meanwhile, my ass is clenched, my hands gripping the handle, unable to say anything at all and hoping we park soon.

Okay, let's rewind. Back at the Lonely Bear, right before we were about to have what could have been a tearful—good or bad, who's to say—brotherly reunion, Lia hooked her arm into Tyler's and pulled him toward Khal, and said, "Come on, new guy!"

And I couldn't exactly say no without looking like a complete asshole, or blowing up my secret, and Khal was probably too shocked—and, knowing him, slightly amused—by the ironic outcome of Lia's boldness to say anything, so here I am, staring at Tyler, unsure of what to say as Lia prattles on about goddess only knows what.

I keep catching Tyler staring at me in the rearview mirror and looking away.

"You guys are so quiet tonight!" Lia says, before pointing out the Pink Roof, an outdoor ice cream parlor where she tells Tyler about her favorite coconut milkshake, and I can't tell if I hate her for calling out my silence or if I love her for not dwelling on it.

I nod but say nothing. Lia can't know anything about Tyler. She has a propensity for gossip.

Khal pulls into the parking lot of Around the World/Around the U.S. Mini Golf, which is nestled right off the main drag in the Lake George Village. The course is across from the *Minnie Ha-Ha*, *Mohican*, and *Lac du Saint Sacrement* steamboats taking eager tourists on plodding cruises with tired tour guides to various points on the lake. Even though it's still relatively early in the season, families in various shades of matching Easter pastels are lined up for the sunset cruise.

"Looks cool," Tyler says.

Khal laughs. "Olly'll kill you."

"Oh yeah?" Tyler says, his voice lingering on the last syllable. "Why?"

Khal speaks for me. "You can't experience the majesty of the lake on those tin death traps. We'll take you out on Sheila's boat."

My mind whirs with all the things I want to show Tyler: the cliffs to jump off, the rope swing in Paradise Bay, the hidden coves, Shelving Rock Falls, hiking to the top of Black Mountain.

"Olly knows the lake better than anyone," Lia says. "We should all go out one day." My face heats; I want to be the one making plans with Tyler.

"I'm down, if that's cool with you," Tyler says, reaching forward and placing a hand on my shoulder.

I nod, but no words come out.

"He's shy," Khal says. "He'll warm up."

"Shy?" Lia scoffs. "*Olly?*"

"I'm shy too," Tyler says.

"Could've fooled me," Lia says to him. "I'm not here for the weird energy in this car. It's mini golf, not brain surgery. I'll be an incredible brain surgeon one day. I have steady hands." Say what I will about Lia, I love her self-confidence.

"I've noticed," Tyler says, turning toward her.

Of course Tyler would show up here out of the blue, no warning, and immediately pick up my boyfriend's best friend. Straight guys are the worst.

Khal and I exchange knowing glances, and he nods subtly, understanding.

"What a line," Khal's always plucking words straight from my brain. Though it sounds cute and playful coming from him.

The second we're out of the car, Khal wrenches Lia away from Tyler. "Girl, let's organize this mess. These newbs don't know where they're going." He points toward the rest of the Bear staff and, ever the leader, she immediately seizes the reins and herds the bodies like cattle toward the golf course. He turns to me and winks.

Tyler hangs back, resting against Khal's car.

We're alone.

Awk. Ward.

"This place looks cool." He scratches the top of his head. "Like an old photograph." He peers over the wooden fence at the grounds. Around the World Mini Golf is a gaudy town staple. There are two eighteen-hole courses: One takes players to various states across the United States, complete with zany sculptures of a giant Georgia peach, a half-naked Hawaiian surfer, or a fairly spot-on replica of the New York City subway, complete with the pungent smell of rot and sweat that develops naturally in a structure without proper ventilation. The other course takes players to different countries, where you have to hit the ball around the rim of a giant Mexican sombrero, or make it sail off a ramp and into the pouch of a life-sized kangaroo in Australia, or hit it straight across a rotating platform through a small red guillotine-like structure labeled "Iron Curtain."

I nod. Does he expect me to ignore the giant elephant in the parking lot? Like, if there were an actual elephant, it would be as long as Lake George—thirty-two miles—and pink with purple polka dots and shouting, "WE ARE SIBLINGS!!!!" at the top of its lungs while dancing to a Megan Thee Stallion song.

"This is weird, huh?" he asks.

"You think!" My lips are uncorked like a shaken champagne bottle. "What the hell, man! You show up unannounced?! No heads up? Nothing? What the hell!" My chest expands and contracts, and I think I shouted because passersby are watching.

"I tried to tell you—"

"Did you though?"

He sighs. "I wanted to. I thought." He sucks in a deep breath. "I didn't think you'd ever want to meet. You always avoided my questions. And I thought—maybe."

I open my mouth, but *maybe* hangs on the tip of my tongue.

Come to think of it, he always avoided being direct when I would ask him in my emails how his search for a summer internship was going. Vaguely worded, evading responses. A lot like Dad with an air of, "I got a couple of things in the works," something he said nonstop while the feds prosecuted our entire lives. I guess avoidance is genetic.

I cross my arms and hold my body tight.

He shoves his hands in his pockets and doesn't look at me. His gaze is fixated on something behind me. "It was dumb. I wanted to see if maybe I had a reason to be here, as if it would be, like, natural or something." He kicks some rocks in the lot. "I kind of drunk applied to the Lonely Bear one night and I didn't really remember doing it, but I remember being deep in my feels, you know? This girl I was seeing, it wasn't really working out and she kind of cheated on me even though we weren't really together, I don't know—" he's rambling, and the nervous energy radiates off him. "Then it kind of snowballed because I got an email from Sheila and I freaked out a bit because I remembered what I did and I wanted to tell you but honestly I was like, 'I'm not gonna get it' because Sheila said herself she's never done an internship thing with any college or university so she would have to talk with the program director and obviously I didn't want to look like an idiot so I connected them and it happened so fast and I tried to drop hints but you never bit and I got in my head and then it felt like it was too late. I was kind of hoping it'd be—"

"Like *The Parent Trap*?" I ask.

His eyes sparkle as he cracks a smile. "This is very *Parent Trap*, huh?"

"Credit for that."

"Your fault, little sib. You introduced it to me." I've seen the moniker "little sib" in his emails so many times it started to feel natural. But it's different hearing the words out loud. I feel like freezer-burned ice cream softening in the hot sun.

Plus, I can't argue with him. This is *my* fault. I emailed him thirteen months ago when I should've waited for Alex. "So what do we do now?"

"I can leave if you want," he offers. "Go back to PA."

"No!" I say quickly, surprising myself. "Um, I think. Uh, maybe let's sleep on it?"

He nods slowly, cautiously. He studies me, rocking back and forth on his heels.

"What? Do I have shit in my teeth?"

"Nah, nothing." He pauses. "This is cool."

"Is it?"

He shrugs.

I shrug back, a small hint of a smile on my lips.

"Should we like—" He takes his hand out to shake mine, and I hesitate. When I move in toward him, he makes the split-second decision to instead pull me in for a hug, so my hand spears him in the stomach. We both laugh nervously and he extends his hand but this time I go in for an awkward hug and our bodies sort of mash together the way a child tries to make two unmatched puzzle pieces fit. But as I wriggle my arm out from between us and wrap it tentatively around him, I instinctively pull him closer to me, and he squeezes me back, tightly, if only for a second.

Stepping back, he clears his throat. "Cool. Which course are we doing?"

"Around the World. Always. Around the USA is fine, but it's too easy. There are insane obstacles in Around the World. It's a work of evil genius," I say, resisting the urge to make some sort of passive-aggressive comment about how he'd probably rather play with Lia, but Khal's in the back of my head telling me to not be Petty Boots.

He nods his head. "I like works of evil genius."

I smile. "Same." We start walking.

One of his eyebrows arches. "Favorite evil genius? Go!"

"All mine are directors: Peele. DuVernay. Zhao. Spielberg. Lee. Lucas. Hitchcock. Nolan."

"I don't know any of those people."

I stop almost immediately. "Jordan Peele? *Get Out*?"

"Uh, I thought you said we could sleep on it?"

"No, I mean the movie *Get Out*! It's brilliant. The social commentary. The deconstruction of casual racism!"

"Oh," Tyler says. "Sounds intense."

"Literal horror," I say. "Ava DuVernay, Spike Lee!" Drowning in more nos. "You kinda know *Star Wars*–ish, which is George Lucas, and Christopher Nolan did *The Dark Knight* trilogy, *Inception*, *Interstellar*?" He nods like he might know what I'm talking about. "Steven Spielberg did *Jurassic Park*, *E.T.*, *Indiana Jones*, *Jaws*, *The Color Purple*? No? Nothing?" I reach into my Wikipedia of film trivia. "Oh, *Ready Player One*?"

"I know that one! That was killer!" Tyler shouts, proud of himself. "*Jurassic World*, those too."

"No, *Park*, not *World*." My head throbs. "This is unacceptable. We have to fix this."

My brain engine revs, thinking of all the ways I can let him into my world. And hopefully he'll figure out how to do the same. I can see us now, staying up late, watching movie after movie, talking about every moment of our lives up to the point we met, filling each other in on existing gaps to make up for lost time. I have a tendency to get ahead of myself when there are fifteen missing years that can't be reclaimed, but I'm picturing him and Alex sitting next to me at the Academy Awards in ten years as I wait to be called to the stage to accept my first Oscar for directing, and in my speech I'm thanking both of them for being the best brother-sister team I could ever ask for and they're applauding and crying and by the next morning, the whole scene has been turned into viral memes.

"I love sports movies. My favorite is *Creed*," Tyler says.

Okay, I can work with that. I'm clearly not a film snob by any means—I hate it when people look down on blockbusters or franchises. Let people like what they like! And a movie like *Creed* gives me a way in to Tyler. "I don't like The Sports, but I love Ryan Coogler, who directed *Black Panther*."

Boom. His eyes light up. Now we're down a rabbit hole of our favorite Marvel movies.

"*Guardians of the Galaxy*, hands down," he says as the girl behind the counter hands him a bright-blue golf club and a beat-up orange ball.

"If you like *Guardians*, you have to appreciate *Star Wars*. Green, please." I point to the green club and one of the matching Ninja Turtle–green balls.

Tyler shrugs. "Meh. The ones my roommates were watching were so old looking. Cheesy, man." He bounces the ball on the concrete and I use his distraction to study his face, imprinting seventeen years of missed basketball games—his, not mine, clearly—and movie-watching experiences. He sort of looks like Captain America: all-American blond-haired kid with a chip on his shoulder. Maybe if I stare long enough, a memory will surface from that one day we spent together fifteen years ago. His golf ball flings sideways and onto the practice green. He furrows his brows before laughing the way a young child might.

"*Cheesy?* Much work to do with you, I have," I say in my best Yoda, which makes him tighten his lips in a I'm-about-to-laugh-at-you way.

"We'll get there," he says. It's oddly comforting. "Favorite Marvel movie? Go!"

"Oof, that's hard. *Black Panther* was incredible, from a storytelling and world-building perspective. *Doctor Strange in the Multiverse of Madness* was a beautiful exercise in the chaos of grieving with the Scarlet Witch's storyline. I also loved the whole allegory in *Captain Marvel* where Carol's autonomy and power was controlled by a man who wanted her to be less than she was because it threatened him."

I can tell by the look on his face he's never thought about this stuff. "As a male-presenting person with nonbinary energy, I relate a lot to female characters who struggle internally and externally with paternal—I mean, *patriarchal* shit."

"Freudian slip?" The muscles in Tyler's jaw tighten, and it reminds me of the way Dad used to look when deep in thought. "Nonbinary energy," he ruminates. "I like it."

I blush. "So, why *Guardians*?"

"A ragtag bunch of misfits who make mistakes learn to come together and create a family." He stops short. Maybe I didn't give him enough credit. He's staring at the AstroTurf. "Practice shots while we wait for everyone?"

"Warning: I'm very competitive when it comes to mini golf."

"Even practicing?"

"It's a Brucke thing. Alex once gave me stitches after she flung a golf club at me when she was losing." I swivel my arm to show him the scar. His eyes widen and I laugh. "Alex doesn't know her own strength. She started taking karate lessons because she was obsessed with Wonder Woman. Our mom likes comic books, so she got Alex into them. Anyway, we quickly learned Alex can't control her temper." I laugh, but Tyler's eyes widen in horror. I take a practice swing and my ball ricochets off the stone wall and slingshots around the hole. "Fuck!" I slam my putter into the green.

Tyler's nose scrunches, the corners of his mouth twitching. He lines up his own practice shot. "So you don't like sports, but you're competitive at mini golf?" His ball sails smoothly into the hole.

"I'm an enigma." I bend down, pluck Tyler's ball from the hole, and toss it back. "I'd give you some tips and tricks for beating me on this course, but what fun would that be?" Like on the Spain hole,

149

where the green is shaped like a guitar, with a series of metal "strings" leading to the hole. If you aim for the center string and it hits, it'll catch a groove and sail straight for the hole every single time. Or the perfectly angled ring shot around the sombrero on the Mexico hole.

"Challenge accepted," he says. Then he clears his throat. "Can I ask you a question?" When I nod, he exhales. "What was our father like?"

Suddenly, it's hard to breathe. "A liar." I grind my teeth. I don't want to talk about Dad. It makes me think about all the shit he did to keep Tyler secret, all the horrible shit he did to Mom, like cheating on her and lying and blackmailing, how the last thing I said to him before he died was he *belonged* there. I don't want to tell Tyler any of this. I don't want him to think I'm a reflection of our Dad. So I flash him an exaggerated, toothy grin.

"Sorry," Tyler says. "I mean, like, what he was like every day. I only know little bits and pieces my mom felt like telling me."

"Like what?" My foot taps the green restlessly, urgently.

He leans forward, like he's telling me a secret. "She said when they were together, he was kind, generous."

"Together? *Together?*" The words spill out of my mouth before I can stop myself. "They were never really 'together' because when they were 'together,' he was married to my mom. So how kind could he have been?" I remember what Mom told me about Tyler's mom, how Dad threatened to destroy her if she contacted us.

Lamplight illuminates worry lines in Tyler's face. "Sorry, I didn't mean—I just wanted to know more about him." His stare implies he's waiting for me to jump right in and tell him a story or something.

This is *not* story time.

"Trust me, you don't," I say out of the corner of my mouth. Both of my legs are shaking now, tapping the ground like two jackhammers. "You were better off without him." Without the embezzlement scandal, the ugliness in the press, the way he tore us apart from the inside out and left us without so much as a cheap needle and thread to stitch ourselves back together. I'm fresh out of Dad-related warm and fuzzies for at least the next few lifetimes. "I envy you."

His breathing is staggered. "I, uh, I'm gonna go find Lia."

"Don't, I'm sorry." But it's too late.

He walks off.

I want Tyler to stay, but I don't know how to let him in.

ALEX BRUCKE

The bass is so fucking loud my bones shake.

I light a joint, wrap myself in one of Hunter's flannel shirts, sip on whatever puke potion his dumbass friends cooked up.

As long as my eardrums hover between bleeding and popping, I don't have to think about anything.

I can live and die with the heavy *thump thump thump* of the beat.

"What's wrong, babe?" Hunter asks, nudging me with his nose like a dog that wants to be petted. The second I touch him, he'll lose interest.

"*Nothing.*" I *could* try to talk to him, but when his "friends" are around, he acts like I'm a stupid girl with stupid girl problems so his buddies laugh. Or he gets defensive, thinks he's the source of my frustration, and when I tell him he's not, he'll say he'll "fuck up" whoever I'm having an issue with. What is it with guys saying they'll "fuck people up"? Do they think it makes them sexier or manlier? They're all a bunch of bitch babies.

His kisses me, as if it's the magic cure, and strokes my knee. "Yeah, baby. Nothing's wrong." He kisses me again, shoving his tongue deep into my mouth. When he's high, it's like he's a real-life game of Hungry Hungry Hippos.

The puke juice is kicking in now. "I need something stronger."

"Here." He hands me a shot of moonshine and I toss it back. It tastes like shoe polish took a bleach bath, but it works fast.

"Is that Ashleigh?" He nods to the corner of the room.

There she is. My former BFF in all her traitorous glory.

She offers a small wave. A little white flag?

Hunter is about to hit a bowl, but I grab it from him and pull hard.

White smoke streams steadily from my lips. I don't take my eyes off her. She's so awkward, cowering in the shadows, her body language screaming, "I'm super uncomfortable" as her arms cross over her chest and her eyes dart around the room. She looks like she wants to say something, but she always looks like she wants to say something. That's the entire problem with Ashleigh Rodriguez. She never says anything.

When I found out about Dad, she didn't text or call me for days. Later she said, "I didn't know what to say." And I told her to go fuck herself, I didn't need her because everyone else in the school abandoned me years ago and she really should've followed the crowd instead of pretending to be my friend while still being friends with Becca Arnold who hated me. You know what Becca said to me the weekend of Dad's funeral? Hunter had people over and that cunt came right up to me and said, "The world is better off without him, and so are you."

I slapped the shit out of her, and Hunter threw her out as she cried about how much of a "loser bitch" I was. Or did she say "bitch loser"? Either way.

Of course she spun it to Ashleigh like *I* attacked *her*, and Ashleigh walked away from both of us. No words, only tossed hands in the air. Done.

What do I do to make everyone leave?

I remember the last time we all really hung out as friends. It was Ashleigh's birthday and she had a hotel party for me and Becca at a lodge in Glens Falls with a ridiculous indoor waterpark. It was a cold March, and the steamy chlorinated waters of the pools and slides were a welcome change from what felt like subzero temps outside. Her mom went all out, and after a catered dinner, we had a manicurist and makeup artist come to the suite we stayed in to pamper ourselves, a Bad Bitches makeover. She gave Becca and me friendship bracelets. And these weren't like cheap macramé bracelets, but legit chains. Ashleigh's was silver and white gold, mine was rose gold, and Becca's was a tacky yellow gold. Ashleigh made some impassioned speech about how we'd be friends forever.

What a bunch of bullshit.

Not long after, Dad was arrested and suddenly Becca couldn't come over to my house. She wouldn't openly tell me she didn't want to be my friend, so she hung around, but she was only there for Ashleigh, not me.

My fingers grab at my bare wrist, searching for something that isn't there anymore.

Another hit goes straight to my head and I'm floating above the party, getting a bird's eye view of Hunter funneling a beer. I'm soaking in the immense nothingness of the whole thing. Because this party is like every other party. All these faces are exactly the same. Nothing differentiates them. They're all various shades of laughter covering up pain and entangled bodies cloaked in darkness.

What a joke.

Becca appears, looking a hot mess with her frizzy red hair fried from the sun, sitting on some jerk's lap. Why is she here? She's not welcome.

I pivot quickly to avoid Becca and smack right into Ashleigh.

"Hey, Lex. I—"

Nope. "What do you want, Ash?" I sputter quickly.

She stammers. "Y-you wanna go outside?"

"For?" I'm so lit my cheeks are numb, but I'd bet anything I'm giving real bitch face right now.

"Catch up?" She seems so trepid. What happened to the tenacity she used to have? Years ago, we used to love parties like these. We ruled them together.

I pull out my phone. "I don't see any missed calls." Pulling up her text thread, I flash her the last text she sent, which was days after I found out about Dad.

I hold it up for her to jog her memory.

She avoids eye contact while hoisting the straps of an expensive new Coach bag up on her shoulder for comfort. "I'm—"

"You saw me every single day at school. Nothing." My legs are jellied.

Her eyes are two big moons. "You haven't exactly been at school every day."

"Semantics. Oh goddess, did your mom send you here or something?"

"No," she says, a little too quickly.

Of course she did. I laugh so hard I'm worried my liquid dinner will come back up. "That's why you're here? You haven't been to one of Hunter's parties in ages, so you can't be here for the good stuff."

To our left, Hunter's Neanderthal friends grunt and cheer as Becca does a line off the table. She picks up her head, coked out of her mind. The whites of her eyes are all I can see, the slack in her droopy chin making her look like a Ghostface Halloween mask.

I barely recognize her. When she first moved to town from Ticonderoga, she was a mousy-haired nerd with thick wire-framed glasses atop a freckled face. I saw her, alone, in the comic book shop with Mom, and she was reading old Batman comics, particularly Poison Ivy. She loved the female villains, I would come to learn. I went up to her and asked what she was reading, and we became instant friends. Mom asked her where her mother was, and she said, "I don't have a mom anymore." I learned later she does, in fact, have a mother, but her mother does not, in fact, have a Becca. One day, Becca's mother dropped her at school, kissed her goodbye, and never came back. Becca's dad was a deadbeat who saw her every other weekend and was perfectly fine with that arrangement, so she came to Lake George to live with her great uncle, who lived in a cabin behind the Village with no Wi-Fi. Becca made the best of her situation, and Mom and Dad did all they could to welcome Becca into the fold.

I introduced her to Ashleigh, and the three of us bonded instantly, always together. Until the summer she turned thirteen, when she got a call from her mother, who was living in LA and wanted Becca to come spend the summer with her. When Becca came back, she wasn't quite the same. Neither of us ever learned what happened to her out there, but she came back with an expensive dye job she could never afford to keep up, contacts, a cigarette habit, and a moody disposition she intended to numb with whatever alcohol she could manage to steal from her great uncle, and then whatever she could get from Hunter. Everyone fawned over her transformation. And she felt popular, which mattered to her. When I fell from grace due to Dad's arrest and scandal, I couldn't serve her social climbing, but she kept Ashleigh around because she was a goody two-shoes, so it was a shield for Becca to hide behind. Ever since Ash dumped her ass, though, I guess she has no reason to curb herself. Coke and all.

Ashleigh makes a disgusted face. "It's not *just* my mom." She pauses. "Though she *did* say you didn't show up for any finals."

I want to set this whole place on fire.

I've already heard it from Olly and Mom. Ms. Rodriguez needs to STFU.

"I thought guidance counselors were supposed to be all confidential and shit? I'm pretty sure telling my business to everyone but me is, like, illegal."

Becca stumbles her way over. "You *would* know about illegal stuff." She shoots me a slick smirk, then grabs onto Ashleigh like she used to. As if they're still besties.

"Hello, Becca. How are you? It's so very nice to see you." Kill her with a stiff kindness, as Mom always says. All Becca does is roll her eyes, which revs me up. "You can roll your eyes all you want. Or you can be a human and say hi. Doesn't cost you anything. Except maybe the soul you sold to Satan." I grab a warm beer out of some guy's hand as he's about to take a swig and chug until it's empty.

She sucks her teeth. "Whatever, Alex." Becca rolls her nonexistent hips and latches onto Ashleigh, who still looks like she has something she wants to say.

Ashleigh's jaw is tight. She pushes Becca off her, but it barely registers to Becca, who immediately rebounds and heads back toward her coke-on-the-couch fiesta.

"That was fun. Like old times," I say through gritted teeth. "We done here, Ash?"

"I'm worried about you." Ashleigh's voice softens. "Are you okay?" She plays with her friendship bracelet, the silver and white gold woven into a tight braid against her pale wrist lulling me into a false sense of security.

"Of course she's okay, Ash," Hunter interrupts, sliding his hand between my thighs. I pivot away from her toward him, and he welcomes me into his arms. "Go home. She's good with me." He paws at me and I let him. I hate myself.

Becca laughs as Hunter points to a line of white powder on the table off to the side. I do a lot of shit, but never that. Becca, on the other hand, is salivating like it's a bowl of zuppetta di moscardini, which is basically my favorite dish ever. Blow a hole in your nose, Becca. Knock yourself out.

"Come on, baby," Hunter continues. "I got some shit that'll make you forget about your bitch mom and fag brother."

Ashleigh and I lock eyes, and I yank Hunter's hand off my body, toss it to the side. "Don't *ever* use that word. Not around me. Not *ever*. Period." If I could, I'd light this whole house on fire.

"Take it easy with the Pride Parade," Hunter says loudly, so his friends hear.

It happens so quick. I pull back and, with my entire body weight behind my fist, I punch Hunter in the face so fast he stumbles back and falls to the ground.

His friends are freaking out with their bro-y "Oh shits!"

Sweat beads my forehead as pain shoots through my fingers.

I don't regret it for a second. I puff out my chest, grab my bag and Ashleigh, in that order, and walk slowly, confidently toward the door, slamming it on my way out.

I wait until I'm far enough away from the house, the thumping bass, the burning eyes of my former friends, to break down and cry.

My entire body shudders, my sobs syncing with the sounds of the crickets, a sad, lonely symphony. I wipe my wet eyes with the back of my hand. Mascara smears. "Waterproof" my dick.

"You okay?" Ashleigh asks, her voice trembling.

"Why do you care?" I blurt out. I've wanted her to care every day over the last year but she seemed lost to me. I stumble forward and grab onto her to stop myself from splatting all over Hunter's parents' stone walkway.

"You're wasted," Captain Obvious says as she uses her upper body strength to keep me steady. "We can talk another day. When you're ready?"

Her words swirl around my head.

"Why does everyone keep treating me like I'm some stupid, fragile thing?" My voice is nasally, thick with mucus. I want to scream at her, "You ditched me at my lowest point." I want to tell her exactly how I feel, but my head is so fuzzy, I can't make sense of anything right now. I burp. Or hiccup. Who can tell?

Dad's face from the last time I saw him, all gaunt and gray and sunken, floods my mind, and if it weren't for the all the shit in my system, I'd definitely be in the midst of a full-blown panic attack. But my head feels like a balloon detached from the rest of my body and my mouth tastes of battery acid, coppery and sour.

Ashleigh grabs my shoulders and points me toward the grass, grabbing my hair so I can throw up. She brushes unruly strands of hair out of my face, and I want to shake her off before she lets go, but I don't. I hold on tightly.

She grabs a Starbucks napkin from her purse and wipes the corners of my mouth.

"I don't need you," I say.

"You don't need anyone." We always joked I could rule this entire planet myself. But I hate feeling alone.

My lips quiver as I bite the chipping paint off my nails.

She hoists me to my feet. "Where can I take you?"

OLLY BRUCKE

Khal calls me a human alarm clock because I wake before the sun, a habit formed working on *Barefoot* last year. I still fume recalling the panel of old dudes saying I was too young and green after I poured my soul into making that film.

Was that my one shot?

All I can do is sit at my tiny desk and stare at hours of footage of my family, but I still have zero direction and zero idea of the story I need it to tell.

The deadline for this year's festival is in two months.

When I told Khal I was thinking about making a documentary about what happened to our family thanks to Dad, he asked the same thing Ms. R did: "What's your story?" Here's the thing: I have no inspiration, motivation. A director without direction.

Instead, I spend a good hour watching my abandoned film essay on *Star Wars* and the Cave of Evil imagery in each trilogy for the film schools I never applied to, and wondering if I'm going to get inspired enough to make a movie to get the Saratoga Film Festival grant for young aspiring filmmakers. Probably should've finished this essay and done the "standard" thing and gone to college. But that boat has sunk.

Khal is in my bed, snoring. I glance around my room full of video equipment and signs of our relationship: Khal's clothes mixed with mine in small piles on the floor, the way he organized my favorite collectible *Star Wars* Funko Pops on my shelves, the framed ticket stub collage from all the movies we've seen together.

We practically live together.

Resisting the urge to wake him, I creep out and down the hall to Alex's room. With a light push, the door opens and a tiny head pops up out of the darkness at the foot of Alex's made bed, followed by the gargle-y not-bark signaling he wants belly rubs.

"Dracarys!" I growl. Like a good boy, he rolls over and stares at me like, "What're you waiting for?" I never could resist a call for belly rubs. "You miss Alex, don't you?" I say, and he whimpers, nuzzling his tiny furry face into my bare leg.

Dracarys is many things, but a dragon is not one of them. When we got him as a puppy, Alex was convinced he looked like one of the baby dragons in *Game of Thrones*. I never saw the resemblance between a fluffy stuffed animal–like Havanese puppy and a scaly lizard with wings, but Alex thought herself the Mother of Dragons.

We've been here two years and she still hasn't unpacked most of the boxes in her room. Posters of strong women in frames stick out of the cardboard in the corner: Lorde, Daenerys Targaryen, Ruth Bader Ginsburg, AOC. Mom didn't allow us to use thumbtacks, so everything on our walls was hung in frames of our choice. A box of her old comic books rots in the corner.

I can't blame Alex for not wanting to spend time here. Her clothes are in lumpy piles on the floor or dangling haphazardly out of the dresser. If it weren't for the bed, it would look like a storage room. She didn't want to get comfortable.

After the bank repossessed the Blue Wharf house and we moved into a spare hotel room at the Lonely Bear until we could find a place to live, Dad made us temporarily move to a shack in the woods on the other side of the lake, near the border of Vermont. "Off the grid" as he put it, it was so far removed from civilization and, in Dad's mind, the cops, that the closest place to buy food was a general store selling bacon next to hunting rifles. The thick tree cover prevented any natural light from sneaking through the small, drafty windows. The rotting wooden planks on the floor in the entrance cracked with each step, some spots worse than others, and led to a carpeted living room, the edges of which were spotted with mouse or rat droppings. The kitchen was a small sink and a few cupboards, and it led out onto a rickety porch where, in the distance, you could see the distinct sparkle of the lake through lush branches.

"It's not so bad." Dad patted my back. He'd found this place on a tip from a friend who "knew someone who knew someone who had a favor to repay from a job" or something. He always spoke in vague generalities. When Mom would ask him how we're going to pay our bills, he'd say, "I have a couple of projects in the works, a couple deals."

"We have no choice, bud," he finished.

"Easy for you to say," I muttered. Puppy Dracarys squatted on his short, chubby legs and marked his territory on a nearby bush as Dad exhaled slowly, like air leaking from a tire. "Alex is gonna die when she sees this place." I sneezed from the dust. "And Mom." Mom always said, "An orderly house begets an orderly life." This would undo her, I was certain.

"You're overreacting."

"You're *under*reacting!" Once word spread around school we lived in a shack, we'd be even more ostracized than we already were. I would have preferred to leave New York State altogether than live here.

"Oliver." He tried desperately to collect himself by puffing out his chest and taking long, deep breaths instead of lashing out like he usually did. "This is the best I can do right now. All our money is . . ." He stopped short of uttering the truth out loud.

"I can sell my stuff in storage?" I rattled off a list of my most prized possessions: original *Star Wars* action figures from grandpa, my kayak, my mountain bike, even my camera equipment. I was willing to do anything.

Dad looked down. "Oliver, everything is gone."

"What do you mean, *everything*? How?"

"The bank" was his answer. All we had left were the few boxes and suitcases in the hotel room the four of us—and Dracarys—shared. His eyes were as glassy as the lake in the early morning. He picked his head up and cleared his throat.

The realization this was only the beginning was starting to weigh me down like wet cement settling into place.

"How could you do this to us!"

"Oliver, watch your tone. I'm still your—"

"My what? My father? I thought dads were supposed to protect their kids from stuff like this." He always got so defensive. He never listened to anything I had to say. If I had an issue with him, he took it personally. He could never talk anything out. So I didn't wait for him to respond. I dashed through the corridors of the dusty, dank house and out the front door, slamming it shut behind me. Dad hated slamming doors.

I slumped down on the front stoop. My chest fluttered rapidly. I wanted to cry, the bile in the back of my throat and the sharp pain around my eyes needed release, but I couldn't. I'd cried too many times that summer. I stomped through the yard and around the rickety house, past standing oaks and fallen pines to the rocky edge of the lake, and let out a guttural scream, as loud as I could; my voice carried across the lake, vibrating through the trees and up the mountains until my cries echoed back.

Is this the stuff Tyler wants to know? Or does he want warm, fuzzy stories? Fresh out of those. *Sorry, Tyler.*

It's clear I'm not going to find inspiration in Alex's room. "Come on, Dracarys, let's go wake up Khal." I scoop him up, and he squirms his way up my chest to bury his head into the nape of my neck.

Khal looks so peaceful: the soft lines of his face, his almost Grecian nose, his dark curly hair mashed into the pillow, it all drives me crazy. I jump on the bed and hold Dracarys over his face and, in my best Mother of Dragons, shout, "DRACARYS!" In true dragon fashion, he opens his tiny mouth, yawns, and sticks out his tongue to lap at Khal's face. Khal's eyes squeeze shut, and he swats Dracarys's face away. He curses in Arabic.

"I reject your insult and offer you a very cute dragon puppy with morning breath."

"Go away!" Khal's body rolls over and he buries his face into the pillow.

"Okay," I place Dracarys on the floor and watch him scamper away.

But Khal's hand shoots up and he grabs at me. "No, don't go. Cuddle me."

I take a quick glance at my phone. "We have exactly five minutes of cuddle time before we have to get up or we'll be late for work. Ugh." *Work.* Tyler. Alex. I groan as an email from Sheila dings through.

FROM: SheilaAddington@LonelyBear.com   June 28
TO: DirectoryOlly@gmail.com
SUBJECT: Showing the ropes

Hey Ol,

As I'm sure you've heard, this summer the Lonely Bear has an intern from the Cornell School of Hotel Admin, Tyler Dell. I've created a position for him to get the most out of his experience with us. He's now the Assistant Manager of Operations. It sounds fancier than it is. Essentially, he'll be learning to do what I do in running the resort. This means I need him to know every aspect of what we offer. I want you and Khalid to take him out on the boat today and put him to work.

"Way to kill my morning wood," Khal says as I read the email aloud. "Come on, thirty seconds."

"That's hardly enough time to cum."

"Shut up and spoon me."

I big spoon him and he backs his body into mine and I melt into him. He smells like maple syrup. His body chemistry intoxicates me and I want to stay here forever and not deal with anything, but as I close my eyes, the alarm clock blares, screaming at me:

Wake up!

ALEX BRUCKE

I wake up in the spare bedroom of Sheila's spacious apartment, which is connected to the Lonely Bear, above the main office. There's so much natural light from all the windows, I'm bathed in the early morning glory of the sun. I rub the sleep out of my eyes and try my best to piece together what happened and how I got here, but all I get are bits and pieces: Hunter calling Olly the F word, Becca snorting a line, Ashleigh holding my hair back as I puked.

How'd I become this much of a wreck?

I stumble out of the guest room and toward the kitchen, following the rich, earthly smell of freshly brewed coffee.

"Morning, sunshine," Sheila says. She grabs a mug from a nearby cabinet and quickly fills it with the dark liquid. There's a bottle of aspirin already on the counter. She pushes it toward me with the coffee. "Take three and drink the whole cup."

"Do you have cream?"

"Not good for a hangover. Drink it black."

"Harsh," I mumble. The liquid burns my lips, but I slurp it anyway and hold it in my mouth until it's cool enough to swallow. "Sorry about last night," I say, for good measure. I'm not sure if there's anything I should be sorry for since I don't remember actually ending up here, but it doesn't hurt.

"Don't be sorry. I'm glad you came here. *I'm* sorry about my nephew. Hunter is a privileged young man who has never been challenged a day in his life," Sheila says, and I wince thinking what I could've told her about her own nephew. Rays of sunlight highlight the golden streaks in her Karen-esque hair. She looks like a camp counselor from the nineties who may be twenty, but could also be fifty, and you're not sure because it all depends upon her mood and the way the light hits her. This morning, she looks barely a few years older than me. I've always looked up to her as a single woman who never wanted to get married or have kids. She does what she wants. "I did call your mother this morning." This makes me groan. "She's happy you're staying here. You *are* staying here, right?"

"What are my options?" I say, half-joking.

"You can go home."

"No," I say quickly.

"Okay, then. Fresh towels are in the linen closet right outside your room. I expect you to keep your shit in your room and to keep your room clean. Your mom said she'll send a bag of your clothes with Olly today." Sheila moves quickly around the kitchen, tossing dirty dishes into the sink. "There are fresh rolls with butter from the bakery, if you want." She walks over and pulls me into a quick hug and kisses my forehead. "I have to go train a new mentee. I'll see you down there." She squeezes me longer than I expected, but it's nice. Warm. Comfortable. Like coffee.

Once downstairs, I wander into the kitchen of the Lonely Bear, which used to be the one place I could go to escape. The immaculate stainless steel, white cinder block walls, terra-cotta tile floors. Every inch of this space is familiar from spending two years working on the line, like a place I used to live. Nothing's changed. All the pots and pans, white ceramic dishes, tubs of cooking utensils, the walk-in box, the refrigerators under the line, the cellophane-wrapped herbs, spices, and butter. Everything is exactly the same.

So why does it feel like a stranger's house?

Mom pops into my head, and I imagine her behind the line tossing oregano and basil into a pot of bubbling tomato sauce. Ever since I can remember, Mom had me at the counter with her whipping up some dish from scratch. Fresh homemade pasta, lobster ravioli with sage brown butter, chicken enchiladas with a tangy tomatillo sauce, blueberry-stuffed pierogies sautéed in butter, citrus octopus salad with tentacles that pop when you chew. Mom was never married to one type of cuisine; it was whatever moved her that day. She never measured anything, either. She grabbed with her heart, measured with her nose, and perfected with her taste buds. And I watched in awe. Cooking was our thing. *Was* being the operative word.

Is it possible for the things we were once passionate about to change, shift, vanish? To die and be buried in the dirt with the people we loved?

"Thought I saw you," Ritchie says from behind me. He's holding a cup of fresh coffee, which he offers to me. I gladly take it. Give me all the coffee. "Nice to have you back."

Ritchie leans casually against one of the counters and faces me. Unlike Hunter, Hunter's dad, and Sheila, who are all model-tall and brown-haired, he's short and broad and hairy; Olly says he's a "bear," but he's more like a perfectly groomed, sassy golden retriever with a handlebar moustache. I've always loved talking to Ritchie. Unlike most of the people in this awful town, he hasn't spent his whole life here. He left home when he was seventeen after he was kicked out for being gay. He lived in New York City for a few years before moving to San Francisco where he met his drag queen husband. But they moved back here a few years ago to live a quieter life in the woods. Why he chose to willingly come back here, I'll never understand.

"It's been quiet without you, girl," he says. "Chef's missed you. He's excited to have his wingman back."

I blow on the hot liquid. "Not too sure about that." I don't want to face Chef, who I abandoned completely. I couldn't handle hearing from him, feeling like I was burden to him or I was letting him down. On top of everything else, it was too much to even think about, so I blocked his number and begged Sheila to put me on laundry duty. The only reason I'm returning to the kitchen is because, a few weeks ago, Sheila asked me if I would come back for the summer rush. I knew I wouldn't be graduating, and I heard Dad's voice in my head from the last time I saw him: "You *need* to set yourself up for success. When opportunities come, take them." This is for Dad and Sheila. Not me.

His smile is better than coffee. "I dropped to my knees in prayer when I heard you clocked my dumbass nephew." Looking to the ceiling, he clasps his hands in silent prayer.

"I'm sorry," I say.

"Don't apologize. For Hunter or anyone else." He leans forward to ensure what he says is kept between us. "It's no secret my nephew is a scumbag-in-training."

"The training wheels are off." I could never tell him the horrible thing he said about Olly. It would crush him. Add it to the mountains of shit Hunter's done and said to me I'd rather pack away into neat boxes and store away in an underground bunker far, far away. "Can I ask you a question?"

"Sure, kid." He motions for me to give him back his coffee. He takes a gulp.

"Why'd you come back to Lake George?"

He laughs. "I never expected to come back. But the older I got, the more I looked around at my wonderful life in San Francisco—and it was truly wonderful—the more I realized there was a lot I left undone here."

"Undone?" I don't get it. He got out of this hellhole. Statistically, that's a huge feat. Most people who graduate from Lake George High don't go to college or leave the area at all. It's not like there's any data for this, but so many locals end up addicted to cocaine or starting meth labs, unless they're lucky enough to have super rich parents who can afford to send them off to expensive schools. But even then, many come back as soon as they've graduated, like their souls are tethered here.

It's become impossible for me to see the lush mountains and crystal-clear lake. That's not *my* Lake George. Mine is a series of local newspaper articles, a trial, a sentencing, all the friends who abandoned me, being left alone while Dad was in prison and Mom was either comatose on the couch or working a billion jobs.

"When I graduate, I'm gone. And I sure as hell won't look in the rearview mirror."

"I said the same thing." He hops up onto the counter and motions for me to join him. "When I came out, it was a *very* different time. My family was awful. Hunter's father, my brother, was the opposite of supportive. One night, I packed up what I could carry and left. Sheila was amazing, she helped me for years emotionally and financially, until I met my husband. But it felt like I needed to protect myself from everyone else."

My mind drifts to Olly. I can't imagine a world where we don't live in the same town. If I allow myself to think of all the lonely nights we've spent apart since Dad died because I've been blacked out at Hunter's, my lungs stop contracting and I have to force myself to breathe.

"When we adopted my son, I didn't want him to grow up without his family." Ritchie's son is five with red hair and freckles and glasses, like a toddler Archie Andrews. Basically the most adorable kid I've ever seen. And I hate kids. "We had a beautiful chosen family in San Francisco, but I wanted him to know Sheila."

"What about Hunter's dad?"

"A work in progress." There's a weird light in his eyes.

"That's enough for you?"

"You learn pretty quickly who is important and who isn't. The people who want to know you—all of you—will be there. Even if it takes them a while to come around."

I grab at my wrist, looking for Ashleigh's friendship bracelet. For a moment, I forgot I tossed it into the firepit in Hunter's backyard after I told her off last summer.

"How did you deal with all the shit people say about you?" I ask.

"What other people say about you is a reflection on them. It's what you know about yourself that really matters. Too many people run from their own truths. So this is what I've learned: we all tell ourselves stories. About the world. Other people. *Ourselves*. We construct these elaborate fairy tales to help us cope and make sense of the world around us. Everyone does this. Sometimes we do it alone, sometimes with or through our people. And other people's stories often challenge our own. I'm not saying it's right or wrong, it just *is*." He pauses and takes another sip of coffee, waiting for me to respond, which is fair because I usually have something to say. But this time, I want to listen. "There are the stories we tell ourselves, and there are stories we tell other people. It's up to us to figure out how to blend both narratives."

Reminds me of my favorite Lorde song, "Supercut."

The door to the kitchen opens, and Sheila enters, waving her hands in the air as she explains the restaurant to a new guy I haven't seen before. There's something vaguely familiar about him I can't quite pinpoint. Locking eyes with me, he stops walking. My instinct is to snarl and give major "back off" energy. Instead, I offer a terse wave.

Turning back to Ritchie, I ask, "What if those stories never converge?"

He sighs, then looks me right in the eyes. "You'll never stop running."

OLLY BRUCKE

Tyler avoids eye contact with me as he follows Khal and me to the beach, and I can't blame him. We've had zero interaction since mini golf.

Khalid readies the beach, instructing Tyler on how to position the loungers exactly as Sheila likes them, angled toward the rising sun and facing the lake, in clean, straight lines. I record them, hoping the footage will be useful one day.

After power washing the docks, I turn my attention to the Lonely Bear's twenty-nine-foot Sea Ray bow rider; it's an up-to-date version of the boat we had growing up. From the moment I could walk, Dad started teaching me how to take care of our boat. It's the only thing of value he ever did for me. Besides dying.

Barefoot, I carefully climb onto the back, dip my feet into the water to wash away any sand, and start to unsnap the cover until I'm able to hop inside the belly of the boat. Once inside I wipe down the sundeck with an old towel, and I'm sweating, so I toss my shirt on one of the seats.

"Can I help?" Khal rests his arm on the dock. Tyler is nowhere in sight.

I look down at his feet. "Not with those dirty feet on *my* boat."

"I love it when you call it your boat. It's so hot." He strong-arms a dock post and uses his upper body strength to lower himself, one leg at a time, into the water to let the sand melt off his skin. His biceps pop, sculpted from hours of playing lacrosse.

I readjust the elastic on my Sheila-approved Lonely Bear swim trunks—the ones I would normally wear are much too tight and short for guests—to hide a growing boner. Khalid catches me and lifts his eyebrows before pole-vaulting himself into the boat.

The boat rocks with the added weight.

He kisses me, his soft lips coaxing me to let my guard down. His warm hand tugs on the elastic waistband of my shorts and my previous effort to conceal is basically null and void. He presses his body into mine.

"What was that for?"

He pulls back and his beautiful brown eyes hypnotize me. "I love you."

"And?" There's always more. He likes to butter me up before opening the library for a good read.

"Tyler is a nice guy. Been talking all morning."

My lips purse. "About what?"

"Lacrosse, the lake. You. He wants to get to know you," he says.

"Then he should stop asking about my dad."

"Olly, come on." He kisses my hand. "Is it really so wild he'd have questions? He didn't know your dad. You did. You're all he has. Alex too, but you know—"

"He should've thought about that before his sneak attack."

Khal raises an eyebrow. "You're being petty." He knows me too well.

"Am I?"

He rolls his eyes. "Yes, Mr. Make-A-Movie-About-My-Daddy-Issues."

"It's not about that," I say.

"Then what is it about?"

"I dunno. Intimate portraits of three siblings." Wow. I sound like a film snob.

"With footage they didn't consent to." Khal nods to my camera, which is pointed at Tyler on the beach.

"Hate you," I say, kissing the tip of his nose. "Fine, I get it. You're right."

Tyler's flip-flops smack the dock, and we both look up at him. I offer a head nod, and Tyler returns the gesture, asking, "What's her name?"

Khal nudges me.

I clear my throat. "Welcome aboard, *Buoy*," pronouncing it like a fratbro: *boh-yee!*

Tyler laughs. "Sounds like a gay porno."

"Speaking directly to me," Khal mumbles.

Tyler's eyes widen. "I wouldn't know."

"We get it, you're straight and heterosexuality is important to you," Khal says.

"Straight Pride solidary." My fist pumps the air.

"No, no," Tyler says, his cheeks bright red. "I mean, I am. Straight."

"Relax, we're teasing," Khal says.

"Boat's name is actually *Buoys Will Be Buoys*." I point to the decal on the stern. "He's a he."

"Olly likes saying, 'Let's go ride him.'"

I pat the hard steering wheel. "Can neither confirm nor deny. I'm a lady."

Tyler mutters, "This is a lot of information very early in the morning."

Khal leans in. "You're doing great, sweetie."

"Shoes off," I command, and Tyler kicks off his flip-flops and flings them into the air, catching them in his hand. "Dip your feet in the water and towel dry them." It's easier to direct him to do stuff, to act like I'm in charge, than to apologize for flipping on him the other night. I offer him my hand, which he reluctantly takes as he hops onto the back of the boat. Then I point toward the edge of the dock, by the back of the boat. "Toss the cooler in the back." Sheila always makes sure the boat is stocked so we stay hydrated because the sun is a liability.

Once fully inside the boat, Tyler says, "I'm ready to learn."

"So what are you learning, exactly?" Khal asks.

"Part of my internship credit is to basically perform every job at a hotel," Tyler explains. "I have to write up this whole fifty-page report by the end of the summer detailing how each job is staffed and how it contributes to guest satisfaction and revenue."

"My head hurts," I say. "You sure you can't make a movie? I got you covered." I remember my camera on the dock and quickly hop out to get it.

"I wish," Tyler says. "So, what do I need to know?"

I take a deep breath. "The boat excursions are really popular, so from Sheila's point of view, it's important to have people who know how to operate a boat properly, and someone who knows the lake."

Tyler starts taking notes on his phone. "Tell me about the lake."

"It's thirty-two miles long." I motion for Khal to untie the lines. "And I pretty much know all of it. The, uh, older crowd tend to like when I cruise along the shoreline. We have some pretty insane houses. The owner of the Red Sox has an enormous house on the flipside." Tyler's eyes widen, impressed, as suspected. I can't help but feel a tinge of excitement at the prospect of getting to show him my world. "I love the remoteness of Steere Island in the Mother Bunch. Cruise into Paradise Bay if you want to go off of a rope swing. Anchor in Log Bay and hike to Shelving Rock Falls." As I ramble, his face scrunches in confusion. "Oh! Or we could go to Calves Pen or Dollar Island, if you want to cliff jump. Or—"

"I wanna cliff jump!" His voice gets higher, like a kid on Christmas morning.

"Professional," I jest.

Khal checks his watch. "It's nine now. We have three hours until we have to be back for the Jacksons' lunch tour."

"The Jacksons?" Tyler cocks his head.

"This sweet old couple who come this same week every year," Khal explains. "They usually arrive around eleven a.m., check in, unpack, and Sheila packs them a small cooler with food from the restaurant and we take them out for a cruise along the shoreline."

"They tip us like a hundred bucks each." I flip the blower and bilge switches. "It's wild. Easy money."

For a full minute, nobody says anything.

Khal nudges me.

As I'm about to speak up, Tyler blurts out, "About the other night—"

"Can we start over?" I say, desperate to bypass any conversation about Dad.

Tyler smiles and holds out a fist for me to bump; it's foreign straight-bro culture, but I take the bait and it feels nice.

I start the engine as Khal unhooks the dock lines from the cleats on the bow and stern of the boat. The boat planes off, and I motion for Tyler to sit at the bow of the boat because it feels a lot like flying when there's nothing else in front of you as the boat glides across the water.

"How fast does he go?" Tyler yells, his voice cutting through the headwind.

"Chewie, let's jump to light speed!" I push down on the throttle and max out, sailing across the water. Tyler arches his back like an excited child, looking around at boats and islands and animal-shaped clouds. He throws his hands in the air like he's on a roller coaster, letting out a hearty, "Whoooooo!"

There aren't any other boats in my periphery.

The middle of the lake is relatively empty for such a beautiful summer morning, so the water is a sheet of smooth glass.

It really does feel like flying.

I slow down at Calves Pen to see if Tyler wants to jump off the cliffs. It's an opening carved into a rocky mountainside. There are three different jump-off points, one close to the water, but the others are a good forty or sixty-five feet high. A few climbers reach up for footholds along the face of the mountain like Gollum from *Lord of the Rings*, and I watch carefully as five other boats wade close to the opening. It's tricky to navigate, despite how open the water is, because of how many boats crowd around the cliffs, and more boats mean more loose bodies in the water.

Nudging him to jump in and swim to shore, he recoils hesitantly, staring at the cut in the rocks at the base of the mountain.

"It looks choppy here," Tyler says. "Can you come?"

I look to Khal. "I would, but Khal hates wading here by himself."

Tyler turns to Khal. "So you jump with me." His voice breaks. It's cute.

"Hell no!" Khal says. "Not my thing. Babe, let's go to Dollar Island. They're less than half the height and we can dock there."

"Done," Tyler says.

I reverse course and navigate us through the choppiest part of the lake, sailing past Dome Island, the only untouched island on the lake. The bow of the boat breaks and bends with the shape of the water, and Tyler grabs for support with both hands as the boat momentarily dips beneath the neck of a large wave and soaks his entire body. All three of us burst out into laughter.

"You've been christened by the lake," I yell as he continues to laugh.

"It's cold!" he screams.

We round Fourteenmile Island, and the chaos of the white-capped waters ebbs and the boat gently floats down and steadies.

"This is gorgeous," Tyler yells. "Where are we?"

"The Narrows," I say.

The mountains at this stretch of the lake taper inward and the pines are closer, so it looks lusher against calmer waters. Most of the islands here are reserved for camping. Maybe I'll take him to the ranger station at the center of a cluster of islands up ahead. They sell the best frozen candy bars and beef jerky. I loved going there as a kid. Maybe he'd like it, too.

"Why was the water so rough back there?" he asks.

Straightening the sunglasses on the bridge of my sunscreen-greased nose, I say, "Most folks—*tourists*—" My voice sours. "Think the lake ends right past Dome Island." I point behind me to the biggest island on the lake, which gets its name because it's a perfectly shaped dome. When we were kids, Alex and I spent hours drawing maps of the islands and making up our own history of how they got their names. Dome Island got its name because a sea witch who lived at the bottom of the lake fell in love with a man named Domé. He wanted to trap her magic and use it for his own gain, so she turned him into an island as a reminder of what she almost lost so she could always navigate around him to calmer water. Alex made up that part one particularly brutal night after we watched Dad get so mad at Mom he charged after her. She threw a wine glass at him and it shattered on the slate kitchen floor. She threatened to call the police, so Dad grabbed her phone and shattered it in the same spot as the wine glass, almost out of spite. I held onto Alex as she cried, and I tried to be strong for her.

"Between all the boat traffic there and the wind channel from north end through the Narrows, the waters get rough. Oceanic. But if you know how to navigate the buoys, you can escape the craziness."

"Dome Island, eh?" Tyler says. "Sounds like porn."

Khal bursts out laughing.

"I'm sensing a pattern," Tyler says.

"Everything is gay here," Khal adds. "Yes."

Ignoring both comments, I add, "It's protected land, so nobody is allowed on the island, but we snuck on last year to film scenes for *Barefoot*. It's untouched by man. Gorgeous. Magic."

Once beyond the Narrows, I shoot across to West Dollar Island, slowing down as we reach the strait between the island and Tongue

Mountain, known for its rattlesnakes, letting the boat idle through the no-wake zone. As we near the rock ledges, I let the boat drift close to the mainland and point to the spot where a few swimmers are shimmying up the rocks and climbing to the top to jump.

"See, these cliffs are much lower than Calves Pen," Khal boasts, happy with himself.

"Y'all wanna jump?" I ask.

"How deep is the water?" Tyler asks.

"Deep. You can't see bottom." I leave out the part about how rattlesnakes tend to swim around this island, but I haven't seen one here in years.

"Hell yes. Let's do it!" Tyler digs into the cooler and grabs three waters, tossing one to me, then Khal, and opening one for himself. He downs it in one gulp, squeezing the bottle to get every last drop.

I coast around the island, and Khal helps me dock in the slip closest in walking distance to the cliffs. I direct Tyler too, showing him how to tie a line to a post: twist the course rope under and over the top of the post and pull tight. Repeat a few times for good measure. "Nice job," I say. He smiles.

The three of us walk to the other side of the small island, to the edge of the twenty-foot drop.

Tyler takes his sunglasses off and rips his shirt off in one swift motion, tossing both items into a pile on a nearby picnic table.

Khal hardcore ogles Tyler's bare chest.

"Down, boy," I whisper to Khal, who straightens up quickly. "Gross." I will admit, he's ripped and it makes me feel incredibly self-conscious about my own dad body.

"Sorry." Khal shrugs with a smirk. "I have a type."

Tyler's skin erupts in goose bumps and he noticeably shivers. "You sure about this? What if I die on impact? What if I can't climb back up the rocks? What if . . ."

I laugh as he searches for a new excuse. "Don't belly flop. Or land on your back. The water slaps."

Tyler rocks back and forth on the balls of his feet, his arms folded so it looks like he's hugging himself.

I place my hand on his shoulder. "It's good to get a running start. It builds momentum." You need the momentum, the courage, the reassurance. Alex and I were maybe six or seven the first time Dad and Mom let us jump. Back then, the cliffs seemed two-hundred-feet high. I didn't want to jump, but Alex was too eager to go. She waited with me for over an hour, slowly coaxing me into believing I was ready. She didn't need any convincing. She didn't even need to look over the edge. All it took for her was the thrill of the jump. She finally convinced me by saying we could hold hands and jump together. Dad said we'd have to trust we were both ready to jump, or else we could get seriously hurt. Alex promised not to let go. So we took a running start, built up the momentum, and leaped. At some point in midair, Alex released and, shocked, I crashed through the surface, water shooting up my nose.

Ready. Tyler and I stand side-by-side at the edge of the same cliff.

Set. Our emails over the last year were momentum.

All that's left is the leap.

Tyler cranes his neck to get a better look at what lies beneath our feet.

"I can jump in and wade out there for you." I quickly add, "I did the same thing with Khalid the first time I brought him here."

His lead-weight body dropped and sailed through the water like a bullet, and he doggy-paddled his way to the surface. I had to let him latch onto me, koala-style, so he wouldn't sink.

"That'd be great," Tyler says.

I don't waste any time kicking off my flip-flops and tossing my sunglasses and shirt to the ground. "Ready?"

"Ready," Tyler says.

I bolt forward, pushing off the edge with a leap. The moment my feet leave the ground is always the most exhilarating because, even though I'm only midair for a few seconds, I can pretend I'm weightless; I can close my eyes and I'm no longer tethered to Planet Earth, but I move with the wind because I am the wind and the lake and the mountains. In those few seconds, I am invincible.

But the crash always happens.

Once I break through the surface, I wait for Tyler to follow suit.

"Come on," I shout up, wondering if he's ready to leap.

But he's already midair, nosediving right toward me.

Go.

ALEX BRUCKE

I dab my face with a cool paper towel, smudging my makeup.

My damn feet are throbbing, and my hair is a frizzy, tangled mess.

Working the dinner rush during the summer is like voluntarily walking up to a hornet's nest and rattling it. It's been so long since I'd been in the kitchen, I forgot how utterly destructive it is to the visage.

"I got a filet mignon, medium rare, béarnaise on the side, and chicken capriccioso, no onions, extra tomatoes for the pickiest table all night, table twenty!" I shout after Chef gives me the "final order of the night is out" signal.

Chef has barely acknowledged my existence all night. I mean, he's had to talk to me, but it's been short and only about the orders coming in. No small talk, no banter, no joking around about anything at all.

Silence.

I put the finishing touches on the plates, and Chef slams them on the counter.

Dinging the done bell, he wipes his brow and walks fast out of the kitchen. He's probably heading to the bar to grab an ice-cold beer or get away from me.

For the first time all night, the kitchen is quiet.

Too quiet.

This is when my mind whirls and buzzes and all I want to do is turn off all the voices and subdue the urge to cry.

"Knock knock!" Lia Francisco peeks her head through the double doors. "Hey, girl! Wanted to pop in and say hi! Haven't seen you in a while!"

I wouldn't call us *friends*, exactly, but she's been sweet whenever we cross paths, and it seems genuine. Not to mention she always looks flawless. She's wearing a skintight black leotard, with a Lonely Bear patch she must've ironed onto the breast to appease Sheila, tucked into baggy khakis with white open-toed heels.

She tosses me a cold bottle of water. "Figured you could use this." She eyes my frizzed hair and hops up on one of the only clean prep counters. "Fresh off front desk duty with Ritchie. He's a trip, girl."

"Thanks. I love him."

"Wouldn't stop talking about you," she says. "I figured since my shift was over and I knew you were here, I'd check in with you."

I hate small talk, especially when it's wrapped up in a pity visit. I bet Olly put her up to it. So, I'll match her: "How do you like working here?"

"A job is a job," she says. "You?"

"A job is a job."

She nods, not sure what to say next. "But the boys are hot, so."

My eyeballs pop out of my skull. "Where? Who? Nothing against anybody here, but what?"

Lia laughs. "Fair. Most of the guys here are—" she shakes her head. "But have you met the new guy, Tyler? Tall. Blond. Abs."

"Oh, I think so? A few mornings ago, sort of. He looked out of it."

"You don't think he's cute?"

"Meh. I mean, aesthetically and objectively, yes, but not my type," I say.

She breathes a sigh of relief.

"You like him?"

"Is it that obvious?" Lia asks.

I shrug. "You're glowing. I mean, more than usual."

She hops off the counter and walks toward me. "This is between us, I haven't even told Khal yet, but I kinda maybe sorta hooked up with him last night."

"Spill," I command, and Lia outlines exactly how it happened, adding some flourishes about "instant sparks" and "electricity" and he's the "perfect summer fling before college" and how she had the "best orgasm ever." I missed talking about anything outside of me or my family. It's like coming up for air. "I'm happy you found your summer boyfriend. Get *it*!"

"Thanks for listening, sis," Lia says. "I have to go. Mom expects me home tonight. I got in a bit of trouble last night for staying out past my curfew. But let's hang out soon?"

"I'd love that," I say.

She wraps me in a big hug, and I return the favor, holding on a bit longer than I probably should. "It's good to see you, Lex. Really—" Her hug tells me she means it.

When she's gone, I look around the empty kitchen and wonder why Chef hasn't come back yet. Is he avoiding me?

I walk out to the bar to look for him, but there's no trace of him.

But I do spot Ritchie next to the new guy, Tyler.

"Rich, have you seen Chef?"

"Hey, babygirl," Ritchie says, pulling me into a very dad-like hug. "He left a little while ago. Everything okay?"

I roll my eyes. "I think Chef hates me."

Tyler nods hello, and I return the gesture.

"He doesn't hate you," Ritchie says.

"He's avoiding me. And we worked together all night," I say. "Wouldn't even look at me. If that's not hate, *girl*."

Ritchie shakes his head. "I could say a lot right now."

"I'm all ears," I say.

"Maybe you should ask him yourself," he says.

"Sounds like conflict," I say.

He snickers. "Kids," he says, turning to Tyler. "Forgot, you're one too. Uh, do you two know each other?"

"We waved awkwardly in the kitchen a couple days ago." I stretch out my hand to him. "Alex Brucke. Nice to officially meet you. I've already heard *a lot* about you."

"Tyler Dell." Taking my hand, his grip is strong but his palms are sweaty. "Uh, you have?"

Stealthily, I dry myself on my stained linen pants. Can't go against Girl Code and blow up Lia's spot, especially in front of Ritchie. "Yeah, Sheila filled me in," I lie.

"Oh, yeah, cool." His voice has a familiar cadence I can't quite place.

"Have we met before?"

Tyler's cheeks turn a rosy shade of pink. He takes a sip of his cola. "Nope. Just here, at the hotel, I mean, briefly."

I study him until he looks away. "Right."

Ritchie glances between us. "Straight people are so weird. I gotta get the hell outta here. You kids coming to the bonfire tonight? Olly and Khalid will be there. We have sparklers and fireworks and Whitney Houston's 'Star Spangled Banner.'"

"You convinced old lady Olly to leave his rocker for a night?" I ask.

"Be nice," Ritchie says.

"I'm always nice. I'll go if you do, new guy." It beats sitting in Sheila's spare bedroom thinking about Hunter or Dad or what I said to Mom and getting high alone.

Plus, Tyler doesn't know me. I'm not Alexandra, first fuck-up of her name, daughter of Cameron the Convict of House Brucke, Breaker of Curfews, Dropout of High School, Queen of Blackouts.

I'm a stranger.

"I'm flying solo," Tyler says, referring to Lia. "Let's do it."

Goddess.

I always forget how peaceful the lake is at night. The stillness, the rich smell of burning wood from the bonfire raging behind me, the deep black sky full of endless stars.

It's hard to hate.

I wrap myself up in my favorite oversized and faded red-plaid flannel shirt and sink into the squishy sun lounger of Ritchie's boat, and take a sip of the fruity, sickly sweet mocktail his husband handed me upon arrival. It's cute. But it could use vodka.

It's weird being sober. Nice, maybe? To a degree. I would give myself a pat on the back if I wanted to move, but I'm way too comfortable for that shit, so some mental praise and self-love will have to do.

Brava, bitch.

I should want to tell Olly, but nothing I do ever seems good enough for him. He holds me to these ridiculous standards and judges me for having a good time. Sometimes I want to shake him and say, "Smoke a blunt, Ol. Get fucked up. Loosen up."

Footsteps on the creaky dock break my thoughts. I release the tension in my jaw into the night sky.

"The bonfire is nice." Tyler's holding way too many drinks in his hands. "Ritchie didn't have any orange soda, but I got root beer and water, and a Diet Dr. Pepper, if you're feeling spicy."

"No beer?" I ask, half-joking. "No merit badge for you, scout."

He offers a hesitant smirk. "Well, Ritchie's husband thought I was twenty-one and he offered me one, but I was in the mood for soda."

"Good call." I hold the root beer bottle in my hand, the condensation running down my hand. I lick my lips and clack my nails against the thick brown glass. "I don't want to drink anyway." I repeat it to myself a few times, for good measure. The moment the fizzy, earthy, vanilla-tinged liquid hits my lips, all the tension in my body releases. I don't even like root beer, but this shit is quenching my thirst better than Gatorade. "Okay, I lied, you get the merit badge. Very good call."

"I honor the creed. Always be prepared," he says.

"Oh goddess, you were totally a boy scout, weren't you?" I ask. Before he can answer, I say, "Boy Scouts is a bullshit patriarchal club perpetuating gender stereotypes and ignoring women as equal members of society."

"Fair," he says. "I'll delete my childhood memories."

I laugh. "Well, you definitely get the Lonely Bear merit badge for fastest hook-up. I'm impressed." I purse my lips.

His cheeks are so red they're basically heirloom tomatoes. I didn't know it was possible for human skin to ripen. He berries—get it?—his face in his hands.

"Relax, it's cool," I say. "Lia is incredible. You won't find anyone better."

"She seems great," he says. "I'm hoping to get to know her."

"*Get to know?*" I clutch my nonexistent pearls. "You're not from around here."

"Huh?"

"Most guys aren't interested in *getting to know* girls," I explain. "They wanna smoke and fuck."

"That's really sad," he says, and I let his sincerity sit. "Well, if it means anything, I'd like to get to know you."

Nobody's ever said something like that to me. "Sure, whatever."

He teeters on the dock. I want to invite him inside the boat, but I barely know him, and don't want to give him the wrong idea. "Cool. Tell me about you."

Without a clue how to answer, I shrug and bite the inside of my cheeks.

"Okay, fine," Tyler says. "I'll start. Three things about me. I don't know what I'm doing half the time. I really love reality shows where angry old white dudes go into failing hotels and scream at their owners. I eat that up like chocolate cake." He cheeses, flashing all his super white teeth.

"Three things?" What kind of cornball nonsense is this? "I love Lorde and I'm convinced she writes songs for me. I'm obsessed with

Game of Thrones, but I was utterly devastated when they decimated Daenerys's character in the final season and refuse to acknowledge the existence of the last three episodes. Also, you only gave me two pieces of info about you, so that's all you're getting from me."

He laughs. "Fair, fair. Um, I have a thing for Buzz Lightyear."

My eyes widen.

"Not like *that*," Tyler shouts and waves his hands around as if he can turn back time by the sheer force of movement. "I used to live in a Buzz costume from the time I was like, two to maybe three, according to my mom. He's my favorite character ever. I have—" He rotates his arm to show me a Buzz Lightyear tattoo, a black and white outline of the Star Command logo. "And I've been known to buy old video game consoles to play vintage *Toy Story* games. Love anything Buzz."

"Even that awful *Lightyear* movie?"

His cheeks redden. "I plead the fifth."

"Nerd. I'm obsessed," I say. "So you gonna hover or hop in the boat?"

He attempts to move, but I stop him.

"Shoes off. Don't be an animal."

"Sounds like Olly," he says, and I scoff.

He settles on the back platform, a few feet away, and I smell the bonfire on him: burnt cedar, smoky pine. It brings me back to nights Olly and I spent camping with our parents, who would stay up late around the campfire, drinking and talking like they liked each other. They would laugh and retell the same stories Olly and I can recite by heart. Dad would tell us scary stories about boogiemen who lurk in the woods, and Mom would ask us to put on music she could dance to with her wine. But as the fire dwindled, their silences would become awkward, soaked with tension wrung out by the reprieve of sleep. I would sneak out of the tent and stare up at the stars and feel so small and hope to wake up in a normal, happy family. I wondered how much of their marriage was for show, how much of our lives was one giant show.

"You okay?" Tyler asks.

"Ever think about how fake everything is? Like, what does it mean to get a high school diploma? It's a piece of paper. Doesn't mean you actually are ready for what comes next. We're told all our lives college is what we're *supposed* to do, but why? Everything is a list of expectations or guidelines, but there's no rulebook for losing a parent or what happens when everything goes dark. Or, like, what does it mean to fall in love? Are two people ever really in love or is it an act for like tax benefits or some shit?" I down more of the liquid than my stomach can hold. I cough and have to sit up. "What is this bottle of root beer? Why are we here right now? What is all of this for?"

"Damn." Tyler takes a swig. "You're deep."

"Ever look up at the stars and feel insignificant? Like there's something so much larger than this bullshit and our tiny little lives?"

He stares up at the endless blanket of stars suspended above us. "I don't know why we're here, but I like to think everything happens for a reason."

"Bullshit," I blurt.

He recoils, then moves closer. "Maybe there's a reason we're here, right now."

"What's that?" I ask.

"My mom and I were on our own until she met the man she ended up marrying, who adopted me. And for a while, we were happy. I never knew my biological father. I only ever saw him in my imagination. I loved Buzz Lightyear so much because I used to pretend he was my dad. It's weird."

"Not at all." Guilt for yelling nibbles at me.

Moonlight reflects hurt in his blue-speckled irises.

It's like looking in a mirror.

A busted, shattered mirror.

It's my superpower, being able to recognize the same shit I suffer from in others.

"You said your parents *were* happy?" I'm prodding but I can't help my curiosity.

"He passed away a couple years ago. Car accident."

I lower my head. You're supposed to say, "I'm sorry" in these moments, but I'm not sorry, I'm pissed for him.

"Mine too," I say. "Not car accident. Heart attack. Fuck cars and heart attacks."

"Fuck car *accidents*," he corrects. "And fuck heart attacks."

"Why does bad shit happen to good people?" I ask.

"I don't think there's an answer. But maybe the universe knows what it's doing by putting people in the same place, at the same time, who need to not feel so alone." Tyler avoids looking directly at me. He takes a swig of his root beer. "It's like hope or something. For something beyond all the nonsensical shit."

Hope. I want to grab it, stuff it in my pocket or inside this empty root beer bottle and store it in the fridge for a day when I can savor it.

"My dad went to prison," I blurt out, but he doesn't flinch. It was a split-second admission, but honestly, I'd rather this new guy who seems sweet and could actually be a friend, maybe, find out all the sordid details of my identity from me, and not from some gossipy bitch. "I don't say that out loud a lot. I don't really have a safe space to talk about all the crushing shit I experience daily."

He places his hand on my upper back super awkwardly, yet lovingly. "Thank you for sharing that with me."

"You don't judge me?"

"Why would I?" Tyler says. "Whatever your father did, that's him. Not you."

Well, fuck. That hits me like a dose of Adderall.

Opening up to Tyler like this makes me feel like I'm not alone.

He exhales hard and his lips flap. "Now that I've sufficiently stumbled into an existential crisis with someone I barely know, it's time for another root beer." He tips the empty bottle in his hand upside down and a droplet falls onto his bare leg. "Want one?"

"Yes, please."

He almost tips over trying to stand up. The boat rocks gently with the rolling waves. "I'm still not used to being on a boat."

I sigh. "I grew up on boats. They're my happy place."

"Olly said the same thing the other day."

"Twinning," I deadpan. My fingers comb through my hair, which smells like the damn kitchen at the Bear, all deep fryers and butter.

"Now *he's* a hard one to get to know."

"He's stubborn and overbearing and idealistic and a bit of a movie snob," I begin. "But he's a great sibling. If you tell him, I'll filet you."

I scroll through the Olly stories in the timeline of my mind. I motion for Tyler to sit down again. Root beer can wait.

"Picture it: junior year," I begin. "I was assigned a civics project where I had to organize and budget a pretend fundraiser, which was cool. I was obsessed with learning about Ruth Bader Ginsburg because she changed the landscape of gender politics by fighting discrimination from the inside. A true inspiration! So I took my fake fundraising project and made it real for Planned Parenthood. Olly was the first to support me. I had the idea to do a benefit dinner for women in need, and people could buy tickets and shit. I would cook. I enlisted Sheila and the whole hotel to help. Some assholes got wind of it and started sending threatening messages on social media. Then came the protests. The talent we booked to play backed out. But Olly got Ritchie and his husband, who is a drag queen in a band called Thot Process, to play. Olly and I dressed in drag and performed 'Lady Marmalade.' That's Olly."

I study Tyler's face, the way the moonlight illuminates his cheekbones. He feels familiar, and I like sitting here and talking to him, and the Olly memories he's triggering are comforting. I have the urge to word vomit, spill my guts all over the boat.

"The Bruckes are hard bitches. We don't make it easy to know us."

"*This* feels easy." He motions toward me.

"Touché."

He laughs. "I don't have a lot of friends. In general. I keep to myself most of the time. I tend to latch on when I see potential." The light from the moon no longer illuminates his softness, but rather carves straighter, tighter lines around his eyes, which appear stony. "But there's always a wall."

"You should let people know you," I say.

We sit in silence for a few minutes.

He clears his throat and hands me his phone. "If you're in the market for a friend."

"I could use one of those." I grab his phone, punch in my number, and send myself a text with an eye rolling emoji. A text from Lia pops on his screen: **We still on for later?** 🖤 "Oop—" I say, handing the phone back to him. He blushes.

Car tires screech, followed by slamming doors and a loud, "Where is she?"

My blood runs cold.

Hunter sprints down the yard and skids onto the dock.

He barrels toward Tyler. "You fucking my girl?"

I hop out of the boat.

"Whoa, dude," Tyler tries, but saying "dude" to Hunter is an invitation to fight.

Ritchie and his husband run down from the bonfire, Olly and Khalid in tow.

"Hunter, stop!" I scream.

His head whips around and when he sees me, his face softens. "There you are. Did you fuck this guy?"

"Hunter, shut up. He's a friend."

"*Friend*, huh?" Hunter puffs out his chest. "That's not what I heard."

"What're you doing here?" I ask through gritted teeth.

"I got a boy who works at the restaurant. Says you've been flirty with him all night." Hunter has reach everywhere. I should have known.

"Come on, man, don't cause a scene. We're *just* friends." Tyler's shoulder blades spread like wings as he moves to block me.

Behind Hunter, Ritchie is trying to restrain Olly, whose fists are clenched.

"The fuck are you?" Hunter yells.

I have to stop this.

"Hunter, Hunter." I'm out of breath. "Please. Not here." My hands shake." Hunter, please," I whisper, pulling him into a hug. It's the only way to get him to stop. I've learned if I devote my entire attention to him, he'll calm down.

He squeezes me tight, burying his face in the crook of my neck. His hot breath makes me shiver. "Why'd you leave me alone, baby?" His mouth makes its way to my ear, and he whispers, "Does he know who you really are? Does he know you're the daughter of a convict? I'm the only one who has been here for you. Not this guy. I never left your side, despite who you are. Because *I* love you. These people don't love you like I love you."

Right. I'm small. Nothing. Nobody. The daughter of a convicted criminal. Hunter's an aggressive poker player, and he's playing all the cards in the deck.

He won't leave unless I go with him.

He won't let this go.

He'll fight his own uncle. My brother. Khalid. Tyler. I've seen him like this too many times not to know the outcome if he goes unchecked.

I intertwine my fingers in his and bat my eyelashes and press my boobs against him, and he's so predictable because he immediately powers down.

"Let's go." I grab Hunter's hand and yank him away.

"Exactly, baby." He pushes past Olly and Khalid, knocking into both like a heavy bowling ball into wobbly pins.

When he's not looking, I quickly text Sheila to let her know I won't be sleeping at her place tonight.

He tries to kiss me, mashing his lips against mine, but I don't reciprocate. His breath is curdled milk, the stubbled skin around his mouth sandpaper.

"What's wrong?" he asks, but he doesn't mean it. He knows what he did. "You know I love you, right?" He throws his car into drive and peels out of his uncle's driveway.

I rest my head against the cool window as he drives. It's not a long drive, but it feels like hours.

At his house, he peels off his shirt and crawls on top of me. "Come on, baby. I've missed you so much. You left me alone. I told you to never do that."

My entire body shakes under his weight, and my mind goes blank as he slobber kisses my ear and cheek and neck and his hand runs up my shirt.

I shove him off me.

Shock splashes across his face, but like an angry ocean wave, he rebounds quickly, retreating, gathering his strength before rushing toward me, hovering, threatening to crash. "What's wrong, babe?" His voice isn't one of concern but filled with malice.

I *have* to think quick.

"I need a drink." I grab his hand. "You know it's always better when we're hammered." Every guy thinks he fucks like a porn star when wasted. Delusional. No girl wants a whiskey dick.

I have to get him blacked out.

So much for sobriety.

I ply him with shots, making it seem like every shot he takes, every beer he funnels, makes me hotter for him. I call him a "champion," a "man," and it drives him wild, like lighter fluid to his blazing masculinity.

He comes in for a kiss, but I give him the mouth of a bottle.

When he paws at the waist of his boxers and can't grip the elastic hard enough to pull them down, he's too far gone to try anything and I can put him to bed. The smell of Hunter's shitty cologne mixed with sweat and the stench of skunked beer from old keg cups makes my stomach sour.

It doesn't take more than thirty seconds of incoherent whining before he's zonked.

I wait until I hear him snore before moving to the couch. I swig from a half-drunk bottle of vodka.

Breathe.

In no time at all, I'll be back at the Lonely Bear. I may not love working in the kitchen anymore, but anything beats this.

My phone buzzes. It's a text from Tyler: **If you need to talk. Or want a ride back. Hope you're okay.**

I heart his message and delete the thread.

I'm fine.

I'm fine.

I'm fine.

I repeat this until words mean nothing at all.

OLLY BRUCKE

I pace back and forth as Khal and Tyler help Ritchie and Noah clean.

I check my phone again and again. Alex hasn't responded to the dozens of texts and voice messages I've left for her.

Maybe she's sleeping? Doubtful.

Maybe her phone is off? Her "read" receipts betray her.

Maybe she'll be fine? Except this is what she does right before going off the grid.

Maybe I'm overreacting and she's ignoring me like usual and Hunter is using his Sith-like powers of manipulation on her? Any way I slice it, my twin brain is telling me something isn't right.

When Khal and I got to the bonfire, and I saw Tyler sitting with Alex on Ritchie's boat, my entire system shut down. I knew it was bound to happen, but I figured I could ignore it and hope their paths never crossed. But now, keeping this secret feels a lot like dancing blindfolded across a minefield.

Except I'm not sure if the mines are buried, or if I'm the mine.

I plop down on a nearby Adirondack chair next to the still-crackling fire and bury my face in my hands.

Tyler comes up behind me, plastic garbage bag full of sticky red Solo cups in hand. "I wish I knew what to do." He puts his free hand on my shoulder and squeezes. "I wanna mess that Hunter kid up. I don't like him," he says through gritted teeth.

"Big same."

He's stony-faced as he stares at the flames in the pit.

"I saw you guys together. On Ritchie's boat," I say, and he turns to face me. "Not gonna lie, it made me deeply uncomfortable. But I'm glad you're getting to know her."

"You should've come down," he says.

I hum. "She looked like she was doing good. I didn't wanna interrupt."

"Like trigger her or something?" he asks, and I shrug. "She looks up to you. All the stuff she told me about, she—"

"What'd she say?"

He sings a line from "Lady Marmalade," and I bury my face in my hands.

"Nooooooo."

He chuckles. "Seriously though, talk to her, but do more *listening*."

I let his words sink in.

"Can I ask if—" Tyler begins. "If you're ever going to tell Alex? About me?"

I want to. "Soon. I promise. I need to feel her out more."

He bites his bottom lip, furrows his brows, and looks away.

Ritchie walks up to the pit and sits down, and Tyler lets go of my shoulder.

Ritchie eyes us, his gaze lingering on Tyler a bit too long. "I called my brother. She's safe at Hunter's."

That doesn't mean Alex is safe. But Ritchie is trying to help. "Thanks."

"Why don't we all go inside and watch a movie?" Ritchie says. "You can pick."

My head perks up. Ritchie and Noah have a ginormous TV in their living room the size of our shitty little apartment. When Khal and I come over for our ritual dinners, we always end up on the couch, watching movies. Usually documentary films about LGBTQ+ history. Noah introduced us to *Paris is Burning* and I became obsessed.

"Something fun." The first thing popping to mind is, "*Guardians of the Galaxy?*"

Tyler smiles. "Nice."

"Not my first choice," Ritchie says, "But we can make it happen." He turns to Tyler. "Grab Khal and ask Noah to get it set up. We'll be in, in a second to make some popcorn." When they're out of earshot, Ritchie leans forward. "You're playing with fire."

"Huh?"

"Your *brother*."

My head whips toward him so fast I give myself whiplash. "How'd you know?"

"Oh, honey. That boy looks more like your father than Alex does." He places a comforting hand on my knee. "It was the worst-kept secret he had affairs. It was in all the papers during the trial, the 'rumors,'" he says with air quotes. "But you know that. I figured it was only a matter of time before something like this would happen. I remember a long time ago, your mother told Sheila and me about a letter she got from some woman claiming to be the mother of a boy. It had to be a cool sixteen years ago. I wondered when he'd show up." He notices the way I'm squirming, how my chest is heaving as I struggle to breathe, how sweat trickles down the side of my face, and he moves his chair to sit in front of me to block the fire. "Whenever he's around, you look like you're in the presence of Steven Spielberg. And Tyler's body language is like a protective bear over its cub when he's with you *and* Alex. When you live as many lives as I have, you notice patterns, looks."

"Does anyone else know?" My voice shakes.

He nods. "Sheila."

"And she hired him anyway?" I haven't felt so betrayed in a long, long time. "She should have told me!"

"Listen, kid, she didn't realize until he was here," Ritchie says, his tone calm. "I recognized his name." He points to his head. "Steel trap. I pulled her aside and she really had no idea."

"You know I didn't invite him here, right? He showed up," I say. "But Mom and Alex don't know."

"All the Bruckes certainly love their secrets." Ritchie's lips purse.

I run my tongue along my dry, chapped lips. Despite the fire, there's a chill in the air and it travels through my entire body.

"They *both* deserve to know about Tyler." He squeezes my knee. "*Tyler* deserves that, too. I'm sure he's been through a different kind of hell being rejected by your dad."

Doubt creeps down my back like a spider.

"What if Alex never speaks to me again?" It sounds much worse out loud and I wince. "And I've kept Tyler at arm's length too." Inside Ritchie's house, bathed in golden light, Tyler laughs with Khal and Noah. He's already a part of my life.

This isn't *Back to the Future*. I can't go back in time, but even if I could, I don't think I would.

He sighs, picking up a nearby poker to stoke the fire, stabbing at the burned wood so it'll go out quicker. The embers flare quickly, then start to die as soon as the wood crumbles to ash. "You should be prepared for her to be so mad at you she doesn't talk to you for a long time. But if you play with that boy's heart, you'll be down *two* siblings." I wait for him to finish it with something like, "But she'll come around," though Yoda Ritchie doesn't know everything.

Doubt and fear consume me like the black smoke from the embers.

And I have to sit with that.

ALEX BRUCKE

Hunter picks me up and drops me off every day, like a concerned helicopter parent. It would be endearing if it weren't absolutely suffocating. But if it keeps him from tearing Tyler apart for no good reason, so be it.

I'm biding my time until I find a way out.

Surprisingly, Tyler isn't spooked by Hunter's bravado. He spends much of his free time in the restaurant. Granted, it's sort of part of his job. Or internship. Whatever. But every day he does *the most* to try to talk to me. He never once mentions what Hunter said to me, even though I'm certain he heard it. I wonder if Tyler pities me or, worse, thinks I'm a no-good burnout like everyone else does.

Today is a particularly slow lunch shift, so Tyler asks me to join him outside on the patio. Chef still won't talk to me, so I don't bother asking him if it's okay to eat outside. I'm getting into this new rhythm with Chef. It's easy to stop trying when I've had so much practice, but it's not as easy to stop caring. Why won't Chef talk to me? Something. *Anything.*

You know who won't leave me alone, though? Ms. Rodriguez.

She emailed me twice in the past week, asking me to come to her office at the school. Even Ashleigh texted me: **Hey Lex! Hope you're doing okay**, right around the same time, which felt like a coordinated attack. I feel like telling everyone, "It's summer. Stop worrying about me and enjoy the sun." Instead, I deleted them.

Tyler orders the hand-battered chicken fingers, and I bring them out to him with a lettuce-wrapped burger with bleu cheese and crispy onions. He's not saying anything, fiddling with his nuggets, swirling them in puddles of ranch and barbecue sauce.

"You okay?" I ask. "You seem weird."

"So remember the other night?"

I groan. "I almost thought you'd be cool and not bring anything up."

He ignores me. "I keep thinking how you said you never really had a space to talk about what you were experiencing with your dad incarcerated. When I was in high school, I used to work at a hotel my granddad owned. I grew up in a town in Pennsylvania close to a federal prison."

"Odd factoid." I suck at my teeth.

"Every week there was a meeting for families, *kids* whose parents were incarcerated, at the hotel. I was curious if there was something similar up here."

I crack my fingers. "Doubtful."

"Actually, there is." He slides his phone out of his pocket and pulls up a website. "It's called ADVOCATE. They're a support group, but also a grassroots org helping families of incarcerated people. They're meeting Sunday night."

"Tomorrow?"

He nods. "If you're interested, I'll drive."

I choose to hold in my anger, trapping it on my tongue behind clenched teeth.

Then it hits me: I'm not angry. I'm afraid. All I've wanted is to feel less alone, like there were other people who existed out there besides Olly who might be able to understand me.

My heart beats, beats, beats, faster, faster, faster.

I don't want to do this.

But I want to say yes.

"Why are you doing this?" I ask. "You don't even know me."

He shrugs. "Sometimes the universe brings people together who need to be."

"How's everything going over here?" Chef's voice booms from behind me; he must be doing his lunchtime rounds on the tables, schmoozing the guests.

I swivel quickly and it takes a second for Chef to focus on our faces—the sun overhead is beaming down strong, and it's blinding. Clearly Chef didn't register who we were before greeting us because as soon as he does, he clenches up.

"Get back to work!" He grits. "Both of you." And walks away.

"I should, um—" Tyler gathers his plate.

"No, hang here." It's time I figured out what the hell is up Chef's ass. "Chef!"

He waves me away, not bothering to turn around as he barrels toward the kitchen.

"Come on, Chef, stop acting like a big baby and talk to me!"

His heels screech against the tile.

"Listen, Alexandra, you don't get to speak to me like that." He doesn't face me.

"Alexandra?" I scoff. He used to call me "mija." I never heard him say my full, legal name. Ever. "Come on, Chef, why are you acting like this? It's a little ridiculous—"

"Ridiculous? No, ridiculous is you never returning my texts or phone calls. Not having the cojones to tell me to my face you were quitting the kitchen after all the time I put into you." He's breathing heavy, and I move around him so I can see his face. There are tears in his eyes. "You blocked me, mija. I never heard from you. And then one day you show up again but you don't come see me. You don't work the kitchen. And now you're back and you want me to act like everything is okay?"

"Chef, I—"

"You had an unimaginably tough year," he says, and holy shit I wish people would stop reminding me! "My heart goes out to you, mija. I wish I could've been there to protect you. Instead, I had to watch from afar as you torpedoed your life."

Way harsh.

"What happened to the little girl with the big restaurant dreams?"

I sigh, fighting back tears. "Doesn't exist, Chef. Cooking was all I wanted and then I wanted nothing at all. Do you understand what it's like to wake up and not want to do anything? Zero future!" Now I'm full-on waterfall crying.

Chef takes me into his arms, the way Dad used to. "It's okay, mija."

"I'm lost, and I don't want to be anymore. It hurts to be in pain."

He holds me tight. "Then free yourself, mija. You are not in prison."

"What if I never love cooking again?" I ask him.

"Then you will find a new passion," he says. "You're young. So very young. When you get to be my abuela's age, and you still haven't figured it out, then we can worry. But you will fall in love with something again. Something *worth* doing."

"How do you know?"

"Because, mija, I knew the girl you were, fearless and stupid, and I see the woman you're going to become, measured and strong. Right now, they're both trapped by this current version of you. She's fearful. She wants to keep you in between." He pulls back and kisses my forehead. "Kick her bitch ass to the curb."

That makes me laugh.

"See, you're okay."

"Thank you, Chef," I say. "For everything." For more than he'll ever know. "And I'm sorry for shutting you out."

"We're okay, mija." He makes a soft shhhhh. "*You're* okay." When I'm feeling better, he says, "Come on, let's go back to work. Maybe another couple burn marks will ignite the fire again. I know how much you love those."

"In an effort to kick the bitch to the curb, I have to do something first."

"Good girl." He's let me go and walks back into the kitchen.

I have to get back to Tyler. But Olly, Khal, and Lia are sitting with Tyler at the table now, Olly and Tyler laughing together. My breath catches. Something about the way they're both smiling sends shockwaves down my body.

I want to go over and be part of them, but something pulls me away.

Instead, I take out my phone and send Tyler a text: **i'm in.**

OLLY BRUCKE

Mom stumbles through the apartment door. Dracarys, who had been curled up at my feet, barks and bounces toward her on his short, stubby legs.

"Morning, my sweet boy," she says, scooping up the dog. "You too, Ol. Where's Khal? Did you eat? What do you want? I can whip up something real quick. You look hungry. Did you feed the dog?"

"What? Yes." I'm nursing a tall glass of orange juice.

"Yes to which question?" Mom always asks a billion questions at once.

"All of them. And Khal is home. *His*."

"That's a first." Mom immediately jumps into the kitchen, pulling out pots and pans and whatever she can find in the cabinets. "How's your sister?"

"Seems better." I take a sip.

Mom says, "And your *brother*?"

I inhale the sweet juice and choke. "Uh, what?"

Nonchalantly, she hands me a knife and points me toward the cutting board with a red bell pepper, red onion, and tomato.

I suck in a breath. "How'd you find out?"

"I'm all-knowing," she says. "All-powerful. I used the Force."

"Not how it works," I gripe as I chop.

She offers a tightlipped smile. "I dropped off some clothes for Alex at the Lonely Bear, and I saw him. I took one look and I knew who he was. When I asked Sheila, she caved." She fills a pot with some water and turns on the stove burners. *Click, click, click.* Followed by a gassy whoosh and silence. "I'm not mad Tyler is here. I'm disappointed you didn't tell me, and sad you didn't think you could."

"I didn't want to upset you or worry you."

"Oliver, *I* told you to do what you thought was best. I knew you would contact your brother. I raised you to do the right thing." Her tone is calm, measured, which makes me feel even guiltier. "What's the *real* reason?" Her wrist flicks the pan, and the veggies I chopped sauté. The sweet onion and pepper smells permeate the small kitchen.

"Alex doesn't know."

"I figured." Her hand trembles.

"I'm so used to keeping Dad's secrets it's become second nature."

She snorts. "Your father didn't believe in telling whole truths, only pieces of stories. Sometimes fact, mostly fiction. Don't be like him." She cracks two eggs into the sizzling pan and I watch it bubble. "He made his bed, and he died in it."

I wonder if anyone knew the real Cameron Brucke.

I wonder if anyone knows anyone, really.

I only know Carefully Constructed Email Version of Tyler.

I thought I knew Alex, but she's been shattered and I've been trying to piece together shards of glass, rebuild her myself.

It feels wrong to maintain the pedestal Dad erected for himself.

But while a broken Alex is worshiping at his fallen altar, I'm getting crushed beneath them.

"Aside from Tyler, I've always been one hundred percent honest with her. But this seems like it'll crush her."

"It might." Her bottom lip quivers. She turns and braces herself against the sink.

"You know she didn't mean what she said," I say. "She'll come around. One day."

She snaps out of her haze and plates the omelet, sliding it in front of me. "Please let her know her bed isn't made. Not yet."

By keeping Tyler's identity a secret, am I no better than Dad?

I think about Luke Skywalker at the Cave of Evil and how he wasn't ready to face Darth Vader in *The Empire Strikes Back*. He swung his lightsaber, chopped off Vader's head, and when the mask exploded, all he saw was himself.

Ms. Rodriguez was trying to tell me I've been running from Dad for too long, afraid to confront my biggest fear: I'm destined to become him. Dad's voice echoes in the back of my head, telling me Alex can never know the truth, and it's like a Force choke. At the climax of *Return of the Jedi*, Luke very easily could have turned to the Dark Side. He could have given in to his impulses and killed the Emperor, ruled the galaxy. It would have been easy. But he chose to put down his lightsaber.

I have to break the cycle of lies and half-truths.

My brain whirs, synapses firing, strips of film spinning in the projector of my mind, and on the screen, I see myself, Alex, and Tyler. Vignettes. Newspaper headlines and reporters and noise, noise, noise, silenced. This idea is still an unpopped kernel.

My phone buzzes. Alex: you're off monday right? can we hang at log bay? maybe a group thing with everyone?

Maybe this is a sign. Our movie might have a happy ending after all.

Maybe.

ALEX BRUCKE

I yawn and my entire body shivers as Tyler pulls up to a dilapidated brownstone in downtown Albany. The neon-orange sun setting in the distance casts a long shadow over the façade, making it look a bit more run-down than it might with proper lighting.

I'm not ready for this.

For so long, having a family member in prison felt like an anomaly, something belonging solely to our family, a concrete reason for why everyone pulled away from us, why we're all such miserable jerks. Even when we visited Dad in prison and saw dozens of families, it still didn't feel like something I could ever share with anybody else. I don't know how I'm going to relate to a room full of people my age who know exactly what it's like to have a parent go to prison.

"It'll be okay," he says. "If it sucks, we'll bail."

Easy for you to say.

I groan. *Goddess, help me.*

A sign on the dull brown brick reads:

Advocacy

Defense and

Vindication

Of

Children

And

Teens

Everywhere Affected by Parental Incarceration

He knocks but doesn't say anything.

Nobody answers. He knocks again, a little louder this time.

The door creaks open and a short, older Black woman stands on the other side, holding it in place wide enough for us to see her full figure, but not enough so she can't slam it shut at an instant.

"Can I help you?" Her voice is smooth like raw honey drizzled over buttered toast. She's smiling, but it's hesitant, held up by strings.

"Is this the meeting place for ADVOCATE? I'm Tyler. That's Alex."

She pushes the door open. "Of course you are!" Her arms stretch out and before I can refuse, she pulls me into a hug. "Welcome, welcome! Please, come in. I'm June, but everyone here calls me Mom or MJ. You're the last two we're expecting tonight, and everyone is in the living room, right down the hall. Bathroom's to the right. Make yourselves at home. You want something to drink? I have some Coke, Mountain Dew, water."

"Coke sounds amazing," I say. "Thank you."

"Same, please," Tyler adds.

As we pass by the kitchen, the hot-and-sweet smell of tangy

buffalo wing sauce hits my nostrils, and I nearly stop dead in my tracks. There's nothing like a good wing sauce. When I used to experiment with flavors, I came up with my own concoction with a mixture of fresh muddled jalapenos, cayenne, and sweet orange bell peppers, white vinegar, garlic, and lots of creamy butter, and the smell filled up our whole apartment. An easy dinner for the nights Mom worked late hours. It carries me to a warm, safe place in my mind.

Tyler's eyes bug.

A circle of ten chairs lines the living room, four of which are empty. The other six are filled with people almost huddled together. Two of them can't be more than thirteen, and they're on their phones next to each other playing some game, but it's hard to tell how old the others are, though Tyler is by far the oldest.

Everyone stops what they're doing and looks up at us.

I give an awkward half-wave, but Tyler jumps right in, reaching out for a high-five-handshake combo from the boy nearest us.

"Everyone, this is Tyler and Alex," June says. "I expect all of you to be on your best behavior with our new guests. I'll be back. Gotta check on dinner. You're staying, right? We have more than enough."

"Oh, um," I start, but Tyler finishes for me.

"We'd love to." He's beaming.

She clasps her hands excitedly and makes it a point to make eye contact with the guy Tyler is talking to.

"Alex, Tyler," June says, "This is Javier, my son."

"Call me Javy. He/him." He smiles and offers a "welcome" nod and something about him immediately puts me at ease. He has dark skin, a goatee, and a slick fade haircut the white bros in LG would kill to pull off. "Loosen up," he says. "It's weird at first, but we're all pretty great. Even Chris."

The girl next to him snickers. A skintight white tank top shows a little bit of her belly, and her jeans look painted onto her body. It's simple, but she carries herself fiercely, like she owns every thread.

"Here, do what I do." Javy instructs me. He shakes his entire body as if he's possessed, but it quickly morphs into a hypnotizing dance.

"Leave the poor girl alone, Javy." She runs her fingers through short, curly hair. She nods. Her skin is porcelain, so paper white I can see her veins. "I'm Ems."

A bigger girl with black lipstick to the right of Ems adds, "He does this with all the new inmates." She snickers and the boy sitting next to her nudges her in the stomach. "What? If we can't joke, who can?"

"Alex and Tyler," Javy starts. "The mouth over there is Lisbet, she/her, her little brother Eric—we call him Possum." He points at them one by one. "Kat, she/her, but she doesn't talk much, so don't take it personally, we all got our thing." Kat nods and offers the tiniest smile. I immediately recognize the tired lines on her face, and my heart aches. "And Maya, they/them."

Maya blushes. The way they stare at Javy, it's clear they've got it bad for him. I can't blame them at all. Javy owns the room, and it's magnetic.

June returns with two tall glasses of Coke for us. "Settle down, everyone. Let's go around the room, introduce ourselves, and tell our stories; it's been a good while since we've done that." She looks at me. "Would you like to go first?"

Bubbles catch in my throat and I cough. "Do I have to?"

Lisbet groans. Her eyerolls put mine to shame. Impressive.

June cranes her neck to shoot Lisbet a death glare. "Of course not. Most first timers prefer going last. Everyone here, *every single one* of you has asked to go last on their first time. Let's remember that, shall we?"

Lisbet clears her throat. "Sorry."

"I'll go first," he says. "Javy, eighteen. Just graduated high school." He dances in his seat. "First in my family to go to college next year, which is pretty cool, especially because my pops was undocumented when he came to the States. He married my moms," he reaches for June's hand, and she squeezes it back as he talks. "He had his green card but not a driver's license. One day, the first of December back when the orange white supremacist was president, Pops was driving Mom's car and got pulled over for a busted taillight. Between no license, not having any documentation on him, and his English not being great, they detained him. Called ICE." His voice is anger, bitter. "They didn't even let him call Moms for days."

"How is that legal?" The words slip out. "Sorry."

"Our broken immigration system. By the time everything was processed and Moms knew what was happening, the green card didn't matter. He was in the system already. We're some of the 'lucky ones.' The judge said since his 'crime' was nonviolent, he wouldn't recommend deportation. He's been locked up for five years, stuck."

June coughs. "I saw how it affected Javy, having his father cycle through the system, watching what was happening in the country at the same time to folks and children like him. So I started this group for him. I was fighting for my husband, but I also needed to fight for Javy. For *all* of you."

I long for someone to fight for me. I study the creases in June's face, around her eyes and across her forehead, and wonder about the stories behind each one. Mom has the same lines. But it would never have occurred to her to do something like this for us.

"I'll go next," Ems offers, crossing her legs regally. "My mom used to be the head of the choir at church. I used to love going with her every Sunday to sit in the front pew and watch her sing. She taught me how to sit like a lady and how to carry yourself like a queen. She also taught me to close my eyes when her boyfriend would come over and they'd shoot up heroin in the bathroom. He was a pretty well-known dealer and started coming around a lot. When the cops busted a deal going down in our kitchen, they took her down with him. He didn't hesitate to throw her under the bus. She's serving nine years." Her legs start to twitch. "But at least she's only two hours away, so I get to see her every weekend. When I can afford to take the bus, you know. It's hard. I was in the system for a little while, but June took me in. Gave me a roof."

I couldn't imagine being completely on my own, though I've certainly felt like I've been on my own most of the time since Dad surrendered himself, but there's a difference between feeling alone and actually *being* alone.

I instinctively reach for Tyler's hand but jerk away before he notices.

Lisbet moves to the edge of her seat and puts one hand on Possum the way a mother bear protects her cub. He's immersed in his Nintendo Switch as she talks about how, when they were younger, their dad was taking care of their abuela, who was suffering from an incurable cancer, and how one night, after buying marijuana so she could better deal with the pain, he was a victim of a random stop and frisk. Since he was carrying more than eight ounces, he was sent to prison for four years.

221

"But weed is legal now," I say.

"It wasn't then," she corrects.

"How is that fair?" I can't help but think about how discriminatory it is their father was sent away for buying something so accessible and now legal when Hunter is pushing hard shit to kids at school. When Olly and I first visited Dad, he told us how most of the men were in for "drug-related offenses." Almost all were men of color. Dad said many were in possession of weed. *Weed!* Meanwhile Hunter is running around Lake George with all his white powder privilege getting girls like Becca to snort lines.

And I'm a hypocrite for letting him.

My clammy fingers wrap underneath the bottom of my chair, reaching for something solid to grab hold of.

"The prison industrial complex is a business," Lisbet says. "Bodies equal money."

June nods and says, "Before we let beautiful Maya tell their story, I have to let you all know why Chris is not here tonight." June turns to me. "His father is already serving time for dealing. I told him all the time, be careful who you associate with." She looks to the rest of the group. "I got word from Chris's mom that Child Protective Services came and took him away."

Ems buries her head in her hands in frustration.

"Another victim of an unjust system," Lisbet mumbles.

Fists clench. I want to burn the entire "justice" system to the ground. "What happened?"

Javy leans in. "Once you open your eyes, you see the same shit over and over."

"Father's in the system, mother's a sweet woman, but she can't handle him. So he's been staying with a close relative, but I guess he'd been alone a lot, and running with some kids who were dealing upstate," June explains.

"What the hell, man? I told him to stop running with those damn—" Lisbet takes a deep breath and looks at me. "Rich white kids."

"Is there anything we can do?" I ask, unable to stop myself. "For him."

"You don't even know him," Lisbet says.

She's right. It's not my place. I sink further into my chair and try to disappear.

"Lisbet!" June scolds. "We don't turn away help. Right now, the best we can do is take up donations for Chris and his mom. She's going to need a good lawyer. And those are hard to find around here. I have some donations in reserve from our last charity event, but if anyone has any ideas on new ways to raise money, let me know. Brainstorm. I already have some wheels in motion. And you know how slow everything moves, especially for people like us. He'll be in the system for . . ." June sighs. "He still has half a year before he's eighteen."

A million different ideas pop into my mind at once, and I can't focus on any of them long enough to know if they're good. Maybe a fundraiser. But how?

"Maya, baby, I'm sorry. You didn't get to tell your story," Mama June urges.

Maya waves and I immediately recognize their awkwardness. Half of Maya's head is shaved, and the other half is a brilliant sapphire blue tumbling across their face and stretching down past their shoulders. Their Doc Martens are clearly vintage, and they're wearing a faded, broken-in flannel to hide their body.

"My story is a little different. My father was never really a nice person." They shift in their seat and don't make eye contact with anyone. "At first, he wasn't violent. Said a lot of shitty things that tore me and my mom down. Until I came out as trans." They pause, slowly breathing in and out. "And he graduated from saying mean stuff to beating me. And my mom. But nobody knew because to the outside world, he was a model neighbor and a cop everyone loved." Their jaw is stiff and their eyes are full and wet. "The night he found estrogen pills my mom had gotten for me, he went into a rage . . ." Their voice shakes. "But before he put a hand on me, Mom hit him in the head with a mini baseball bat she kept hidden in the couch."

I haven't taken a breath since they started talking.

"He's currently a vegetable, and mom is serving time for attempted murder. They didn't care she was defending me from him. As far as everyone knew, he was a 'great person' she beat unprovoked. I told a jury what had happened, but the lawyer his parents hired to convict my mom discredited me because I'd gotten into trouble a few times for shoplifting. I guess that made me a 'liar.'"

I move to the empty chair next to Maya and take their hand.

"We're working with the ACLU to get Maya's mom out," Javy says.

"We're hopeful," June adds.

"Everyone outside of this group told me if I kept my mouth shut and played his game and came out when I moved out of the house, my mom would still be around." Tears stream down their cheeks. "Sometimes, I wish I weren't."

A cold shiver runs down my back. Every single time I've given in to Hunter, every day I've been blacked out, one single thought has always crossed my mind: it would be so much easier if I weren't around. If I were gone. I wouldn't be a burden to Olly or Mom. I'm tired of holding on to the past, to these feelings. I want to move on, to live again.

But I don't know how.

I squeeze Maya's hand tighter. It's all I can do.

Nobody says anything. You could hear a cotton ball drop.

Javy and June move in closer to Maya.

June's voice is a warm gust of air on a cloudy day. "What your dad did is not your fault. What happened to your mother is not your fault. This was never a burden you should have had to bear. You're safe now. The world is better for having you in it. And don't you forget it."

She's talking to Maya, but it's like she's speaking directly to me, too.

"People gaslight us into thinking we're wrong for feeling what we're feeling," Javy adds. "That we don't feel what we feel. The system tells us we're crazy for seeing the very clear flaws and pushing back. Our friends pretend like we're fine or their desertion is normal, *what should we expect?*"

Wounds I've pretended had scarred over are open now, raw, and if I move or say anything I'll bleed out all over June's floor.

June turns to me and asks if I'd like to share, but I can't respond.

Voices sound far away as they call my name and I disassociate.

Suddenly the volume ratchets up and they sound like foghorns calling me to speak about all the shit I'd rather pretend isn't real.

Then.

Silence.

I look around. Breaths short and heavy.

All eyes are on me.

"Excuse me," I mumble.

I rush out of the living room, down the hall, and burst through the front door so I can finally breathe.

I collapse on the front stoop and slowly count to ten over and over again until the numbers don't matter.

My phone slips out of my pocket. I pick it up and somehow the email app opens, and I almost slam down on the lock button because my inbox is nothing but old emails from Dad. Instead, I open them. One after another. They all begin with, "Hey kiddo" and end with "Be good to each other," a rule for Olly and me to adhere to, and an "I love you." I fixate on one in particular: I'll always protect you.

The sun disappears behind nearby buildings and the shadows are cold.

Too cold.

I hate it.

The door opens behind me and I expect it to be Tyler, but it's not.

Javy hands me a plate of crispy chicken wings. How long have I been out here?

"Thanks." I don't know if I can stomach food right now. I push a wing around the paper plate with my finger.

"If you're not a fan of wings, I don't know if we can hang." Javy offers a wing-saucy smirk, but he's careful not to get too close. I appreciate his distance.

I snort. "I *am* a *connoisseur*. But I'm also feeling messed up."

"Those are the best times to eat, according to Moms," he says.

"I'm sorry I ran out," I say.

"It's a lot to take in," he says. "I can't tell you how many times other people's stories have made me feel my feelings."

"I hate feeling *anything*."

"I've been there." He hops up on the wrought-iron railing. "Don't be sorry."

"Everyone opened up and I—I can't even talk about this with my own family."

"You will when you're ready." He has such kind, beautiful eyes. The kind I could get lost in, and I can't afford to get lost. Not again.

"How do you know I'll ever be ready?"

"I don't. But my guess is you will or you wouldn't be here. It's hard to talk about this stuff with anyone, but I bet your brother is ready to talk with you, or he wouldn't have brought you here."

My face scrunches. "Olly isn't here."

"I thought his name was Tyler?" Javy says.

"Oh, yeah, no, that's Tyler. He's not my brother."

Javy looks at me skeptically. "White people all look the same." He winks.

I chuckle. "You know, it doesn't seem fair we get punished for what happens to our parents. What they do to us."

His smile vanishes. "You mean what the *system* does *to* them. To us all."

I want to bury my face in my hands because Javy's dad, and all the folks incarcerated for something so common as possession, did nothing wrong.

"It's a horrible, horrible joke. And *we're* the punch lines."

"We all got stories." He stares into my eyes. "But our truths are not defined by theirs. Once you realize that, you can let yourself out."

My stomach cramps thinking of Dad. He always told Olly and me he was the victim, it was "all a misunderstanding," and what happened didn't really happen. If I kept my head held high, stuck by him, I'd get through anything because the "witch hunt" against him was taking him. It wasn't his fault. I wanted to believe him.

"I'm afraid to say mine out loud." My voice is so low it's barely audible.

"There's no right or wrong way to process all the stuff you're feeling. But we're here as a resource. And if you ever want to talk—" Javy hands me a business card with his phone number. "I'll pick up." His incredible smile twists my insides. "Moms thought business cards would be a good idea. I think they're corny and outdated, but—"

"They're legit," I say.

"Exactly."

Olly told me when he first met Khal he got "butterflies." Gross, right? I called bullshit. *So* disgustingly cliché. But.

A nervous flutter in my gut travels up my chest and my breathing is shallow. But a good shallow, not a panic attack where everything gets dark and the world closes in.

This feels like the world is opening up, letting in a tiny sliver of light.

It's been a while since I've seen any light.

OLLY BRUCKE

"Can I get a large orange cream twist in a cone with rainbow sprin-kles. And a cup of extra sprinkles on the side. Oh, with googly eyes! Please." The worker at Martha's Dandee Creme blinks a few times in a "googly eyes, seriously?" way, so I flash her a toothy grin. I love the tiny little sugared eyes they put on the kiddie cones. Sue me.

Khal and I make our way to the picnic tables on the side of the building. I check my phone for any missed texts from Tyler; I texted him asking him to meet us at Martha's after finding out from Lia that Tyler and Alex were doing something "secret" tonight.

No response.

He has me on read.

This, of course, has rendered my entire body stiff from fear that *everything* is going to come out if they hang out. Hence the large ice cream. Figured a mountain of sugar wouldn't hurt. Part of me wishes Alex would find out about Tyler on her own and save me the trouble.

"Earth to Olly." Khal waves his hands in front of my face.

I chuckle when I notice he has chocolate ice cream smeared on his upper lip and the tip of his nose. I lean in to lick it off, but he stops me and nervously looks around.

"Not in public, babe." He dabs his face with a napkin.

I frown. Khal isn't comfortable with public displays of affection. He doesn't even let us hold hands in public places. Well, at least not in places filled to the brim with dozens of randoms. It doesn't matter how many times I tell him he shouldn't care what people think, he worries about the one person who could possibly have a problem with us. I respect his feelings, but it pains me because I want to be able to kiss him. An hour ago he was inside me and now we have to act like acquaintances. But I guess a kiss isn't just a kiss in Upstate New York.

"Sorry."

He reaches under the table and grabs my knee. "In other news, my parents are going to Lebanon next week. For a month."

"What?" Khal's parents hate to travel. "Did you *just* find out?"

"Yep." His head droops to the ground. "They didn't even ask if I wanted to go."

"They're going to see your brother?"

He nods. "You know how long it's been since I've seen him. They said, 'You're working all summer and we know you want to be with your *friend*.'" Khal's parents call me his *friend*. We spend virtually no time at Khal's house because even though he's out to them, they don't approve of his quote-unquote "lifestyle." But he loves them so much. Everything he does, how hard he works at school, his plans to get his doctorate in psychology, it's all for them. For their approval. And they can't be bothered to even tell him they're leaving the country. If he would let me, I would hug him and never let go. "They'll be gone for my—"

"Birthday," I finish for him because it's too painful for Khal to get out. He's a July baby, and I want to tell him about the surprise party I have planned for him at the Closet, the gay bar in Saratoga where Ritchie's husband does drag, next weekend, and the hot-air balloon ride I've booked for the end of the summer, a few days before he leaves for NYU, but none of that is a replacement for his parents.

"They wonder why I rarely sleep at home," Khal says. The chocolate ice cream is melting, dribbling onto his hands. He can never eat when he gets like this.

I take the cone from him and toss it in a nearby trash can. Using napkins and water from a fountain, I clean his fingers for him. He lets me, but his shoulders are tense and he keeps a lookout for nasty stares.

"I don't want to talk about them anymore," he says when I'm done.

When he's uncomfortable or angry, it's best to let him decompress because he has a tendency to blow up if pressured. Still, I can't help myself. "You sure?"

He blinks and a smile appears, like a droid powering up. He's *done*, done. "Any update from Tyler? What do you think he's doing with Alex tonight?"

"No idea, but I'm glad she's getting to know him."

He glares at me.

"I mean it!" I say quickly. "Maybe it'll sting less when she finds out."

"Whatever you need to tell yourself." Khal shakes his head. "I don't want to see all this blow up in your face. I read a lot about compartmentalization and—"

"Olly!" It takes me a second to register the voice.

Ashleigh bounds toward us. "I thought it was you. I'm on my way home, but I wanted to come say hi and see how Alex is doing." She runs her fingers through her long black hair, and I spot the matching friendship bracelet she gave Alex. I study it, still fuzzy on why Ashleigh abandoned Alex beyond the standard "our dad is a criminal" reason every other person used. While we were never close, it's like Ashleigh abandoned me too. She notices me staring at the bracelet and hides her wrist behind her back. "My girlfriend is waiting for me. I gotta go, but please tell Alex I said hi."

Girlfriend? I clock it, register it, and I'll come back to it later.

"Actually, a bunch of us are anchoring at Log Bay tomorrow, around noonish." After Alex texted me the other day to hang out, it snowballed into her wanting to bring Lia, and then I said Khal should come, and suggested Tyler, which made me freak out a little bit but I knew they've been having lunch together and I might have been humming the "Let's Get Together" song from *The Parent Trap* in my head, because it does seem a little too perfect? I asked Sheila if we could use the Bear's boat and take it to Log Bay, since I checked the calendar and there were no excursions or tours booked past ten a.m., and she gave the go-ahead. "You should come. Take your parents' boat and tie up to us. You can tell Alex yourself."

She chews on the inside of her mouth and looks behind her to a big SUV. I can't see who's behind the wheel, but I can tell Ashleigh is ready to bolt. "I miss her."

"Then tell her," I urge.

She taps her foot. "Noonish?"

"Noonish," I confirm. "Text me. And no Becca, please."

"We're not friends anymore." She heads toward the parking lot. "Thanks, Ol."

When she's gone, Khal chuckles. "First, I always knew Ash was a lesbian." He pronounces it lez-bean. "She always gave me Big Queer Boss energy."

"We must discuss this revelation!"

"Yes, but also. I see what you're doing."

I lick around the base of the cone suggestively, and he swats at me.

"Sorry." I choke on sprinkles. "But what am I doing?"

"Where do I start?" He raises a brow. "Your documentary—telling your version of what happened to your family through intimate portraits of you, Alex, and Tyler?"

Brain freeze.

Body freeze.

"You're hoping you can get everyone together and it'll be this big movie moment. Twin Lindsay Lohans piecing a photograph together or something. And maybe you're even thinking you'll get your own movie out of it."

"No, I'm not—" I toss the rest of my cone in the trash because suddenly my stomach sours. "I don't mean to. But wouldn't it be great if Alex inherently *knew* about Tyler without me having to tell her?"

He glares at me. "Life isn't a movie, Ol. Stop scripting fantasies." Tension pools at his jawline. "You like creating scenes, but real life is messy, and you're putting these people together under false pretenses. I hope you know what you're doing."

I don't bother refuting him because if I do, I would be lying to myself, too.

All I can say is, "Me too."

ALEX BRUCKE

I'm high AF. A natural high, to clarify. "It scared me to acknowledge all their stories, but it was like those electric paddles doctors use to bring a bitch back to life after she codes!" Tyler laughs, so I explain. "I watch a lot of medical dramas. But anyway! I can't wait to go back, get more involved, and help out." Use my voice and my story. If I can muster up the courage. "Thank you. Seriously. I needed this."

Javy's voice echoes in my head: *our truths are not defined by theirs* and *people gaslight us into thinking we're wrong for feeling what we're feeling.* It's a lot to take in, but I haven't felt this alive in far too long.

Tyler smiles as he pulls into the parking of the Lonely Bear. "I'm glad we—"

The headlights flood the darkness, illuminating Hunter in front of the main office.

Goddess, *no.* Fear coils around my body like a snake.

He's waving his hands wildly in the air, clearly yelling at Sheila and Ritchie, whose face is a red bomb about to explode. Sheila is staring at him blankly, her arms folded, far enough away that she can't slap him.

"Stay in the car." I don't need Hunter going after Tyler.

Hunter swivels around and squints, trying to make out the driver behind the blinding headlights. "I come here to surprise you, and you're out with this guy?"

I'm trapped in the same cycle, over and over again, and every time I get close to escaping, he yanks me back.

Before I can say anything, he charges toward me, but Ritchie steps forward and grabs his nephew by the collar of his shirt.

"It's time for you to g—" Ritchie starts, but Hunter whirls around and throws a punch to Ritchie's face.

Ritchie stumbles backward, grabs at his face. Sheila gasps in horror and rushes to her brother. Hunter looks at his fist. Unclenches and clenches again. He looks as if he might actually say sorry, but no words come.

"You little piece of shit." Blood streams down from Ritchie's nostrils.

Sheila's face is stark white, her lips stretched thin across her face. She has her arm locked around Ritchie. "Hunter, if you don't get out of here right now . . ." She doesn't finish, staring Hunter down, anger shading her face like a haunted tombstone.

"Let's go," Hunter commands. "Now!"

Sheila motions for me to come to her.

"Alex," Tyler says, having emerged from his car during the brawl. "Stay here."

Hunter's fists are shaking as he curls and unfurls his fingers over and over again. His eyes are filled with tears. But they don't fall.

They never do. It's like he swallows them up too quickly, and what's left is vacuous rage.

I don't want to go with him ever again, but I'm afraid if I don't, something way worse will happen. Hunter is on the verge of more violence, and I have to keep Tyler, Ritchie, and Sheila safe.

Looking to Tyler, I plead, "Please don't tell Olly." My entire body shakes as I get into Hunter's car.

As Hunter peels out of the Lonely Bear, I lock eyes with Tyler, whose face falls in disappointment at the same moment Hunter grabs my hand and punches down on the gas pedal, burning rubber.

Back at Hunter's, he immediately jumps into the shower, and I don't know what to do or how I feel, so I sit on his bed and pull out my phone. Javy's business card tumbles out of my pocket and falls on the floor.

I pick it up and stare at it.

I can't text Javy. But I want to. I liked the way he looked at me. Like I was a person, not a possession. Like I was someone who had something to say, not someone with glass bones, one blow away from shattering.

The water turns off. I quickly input Javy's number and rip up the card into incomprehensibly small pieces and bury them in the trash can next to Hunter's bed. I slam my phone onto the bed as Hunter walks out of the bathroom.

A loose towel drapes his waist as he stands over me.

Pangs twist in my chest.

I miss my mom. I need her. I want her to pick me up and hold me without a lecture about how disappointing I am.

He moves to grab me, but I shove him away.

He falls backward, pretending like I pushed him harder than I did. Then he smirks and his towel drops. "Oops. Look what you did." He grabs my chin and bends down to kiss me, but I don't reciprocate, keeping my lips tight.

The summer before sixth grade, when we first "dated," we were at Martha's Dandee Cream and I was eating a chocolate–peanut butter twist, which dripped onto my chin. Hunter bent down and gently wiped it from my skin with his thumb. Then he said, "You got a little more," and when I said, "Where?" he planted a soft peck on my lips. So corny, but adorable.

That Hunter is long gone.

I turn my head from him.

His grip tightens.

"Come on, kiss me. Why're you acting like this?" His fingers coil around my neck, and he jerks my head toward him, so I have to look at him.

"You're hurting me!"

He rolls his eyes. "Oh, please. You like it rough." He mashes his lips against mine and weasels his tongue in between my lips.

I jam my knee into his chest and he stumbles back, for real this time. I extend my leg so my foot is against his bare stomach, hoping it'll keep him at bay. He lunges at me, slamming my leg to the side, and I yelp in pain because of the way it twists under his force. His hand bolts for my face and I can't tell if he's going to punch me or grab me, but I don't wait to find out; I scramble up the bed toward the pillows and yank my legs to my chest.

"Help! Get the fuck away from me! Help!" I don't know if anybody can hear me. His parents soundproofed the basement, but I don't care. I can't move, but I can feel my body shake.

His face softens. "No, baby, I'm playing. Don't overreact. I thought we were doing that thing we do." He cautiously walks around the bed and sits down next to me.

My body is atrophied, frozen in place. "No, we're *not.*"

He reaches out a hand for me. "Come on, baby, you know I love you, right? I would never hurt you. You know that, right?" He stares at me and his eyes become glassy. "I'm the only person who would never, ever hurt you. You need to stick by me. Nobody gets me, Lexi, nobody." He starts to cry, his cheeks red tomatoes. "Please forgive me, you have to."

My head is fuzzy and nothing makes sense anymore and for a second, he's convinced me I overreacted.

I touch his palm and he coils his fingers around mine. He brings our hands to his chest and places them in the spot above his heart. It's thump-thump-thumping rapidly.

"See? I would never hurt you. You believe me?" He slides closer to me on the bed until he's able to wrap me up in his arms. "You really hurt my feelings," he whispers. "I know you didn't mean it, did you?" His hand grazes my inner thigh as he kisses me. "I forgive you, Alex."

I hold my breath until I'm lightheaded.

Release to feel my lungs expand, watch my chest rise and fall.

In World History, we learned about Mount Vesuvius, how it erupted and buried the entire city of Pompeii in volcanic ash, perfectly preserving the bodies of thousands of victims until the city was unearthed thousands of years later. I'm paralyzed in place, the world outside of Hunter's basement buzzing so loudly, but it's so far in the distance it sounds like a faded memory.

A volcano named Cameron Brucke exploded and blanketed the sky in a thick, dark cloud of ash, and preserved me in place. I'm trapped beneath the rubble and every time I try to escape, the ground caves in again, trapping me beneath more rubble. It rains, and a mudslide carries me away. It snows and I'm frozen in the ground, hoping to thaw.

Here lies Alexandra Brucke, watching the gradual erosion of her life. Release.

"I'm the only one here for you," he says. "If you leave me, you'll have nothing."

He rolls over. Maybe he'll finally sleep.

But I don't.

The entire night replays over and over again until the sun comes up. *If you leave me, you'll have nothing.*

After hours of silent spiraling, I brace myself as he stirs.

"Morning, babe." His voice shatters my shaky composure. He presses a fancy button on his fancy remote thing and fancy shades open, flooding the room with fancy light. "I love you so much, you know that, right?" He touches my arm so gently, so sweetly it immediately causes bile to rise into my throat and it's all I need to finally move.

I run to the bathroom and slam the door behind me.

When you're drunk, you never *really* remember throwing up. In the moment, it's the worst feeling in the world, and it seems like it never ends. But it does and you rally and forget and drink enough to puke again.

When you're stone-cold sober, it actually *is* the worst fucking feeling to wretch and dry heave so hard your entire head is a water balloon filled to capacity, about to burst. Acid coats my lips and teeth, and I want to rinse it with water, but I'm glued to the porcelain, crying.

I want my mom. I should have texted her last night to come get me.

"You're a champ, babe!" Hunter laughs on the other side of the door. He must think I'm puking.

I don't recognize the reflection in the mirror; I fucking hate this bitch. This *girl*. Her curly hair and fake-tanned skin. Lips and nose shaped like Dad's. She sought out the one person who could numb her from the pain of his death and kept numbing herself beyond recognition because she was taught to stick by the people who hurt her the most.

Run the water.

Splash my face.

Think for a second about opening my mouth and letting the water fill my lungs.

Turn the faucet off.

Breathe. Keep breathing, Alex.

When I finally emerge, I don't know what time it is, but Hunter's bros—and Becca—are here, and I'm another empty Solo cup on Hunter's floor.

Suddenly, I want Becca to see me, really see me, the girl she used to be friends with back when all we cared about was binge-watching *Chilling Adventures of Sabrina* and eating our weight in buffalo chicken pizza with extra bleu cheese while pretending to conjure hot boys.

"Yo, what're we doing, Hunt. It's like eleven, man," one of his friends says.

"I missed the breakfast shift. Sheila's gonna kill me," I manage to say.

Hunter comes up behind me and puts his arm around me.

"Don't worry, babe. I texted her from your phone and said you were sick." He makes a fake coughing sound and his stupid friends laugh. Even Becca, who I didn't think I could hate more than I already did. Turns out, I was wrong.

He invaded my privacy. First my head, then my body, now my privacy. I shouldn't be surprised his hands are wrapped around every square of my life.

"I don't want you around that kid." Hunter's pretending to whisper, but his boys are quiet and they're all listening.

"Leave him alone," I say through my teeth.

"Baby, c'mon now. I would never hurt anyone. What am I? Some kinda animal?"

Yes.

"Why would you think that?" He kisses my cheek. "You good to go?"

"Where?" I ask.

"Out on the boat for the day. My boy got the hook up, so we'll be flying." Hunter's slimy fingers try to massage my shoulders. "You're too tense, you need to relax."

I wince and pull away. "I have plans." After my breakfast shift at the restaurant, Olly was taking us out on Sheila's boat. Me, Tyler, Khal, Lia.

"Yeah, with us," Hunter says. "A day out on the water would be good for you. Like how your old man used to take you out for the day. I got you like that." He smiles, and it's almost sweet. Almost. "Let me do that for you." He walks me over to the couch and sits me down next to Becca. "Loosen her up, Bec." He walks away low-fiving his boy.

Becca is crushing a white pill and mixing it with powder in a baggy. She uses her license to divvy it up into two straight lines. She snorts one, then leans back. "You look like shit."

"So do you." My eyes roll.

"How the mighty have fallen," she says smugly.

"What're you talking about?"

"I used to be so jealous of you. With your perfect life in your perfect house with your perfect parents and perfect gay twin. It was like one of those storybooks my ma read to me before she kicked me to the curb." The whites of Becca's eyes haunt me. She's unable to focus, and she's slurring a bit, but she doesn't mince her words. "I knew I'd never have what you have, but your family made me feel nice."

"What happened to us?" I ask, against my better judgement.

"Your father, man." Her head sways side to side. "My uncle lost his job because of your dad. He became a statistic in those articles about your dad's company. *Your dad* convinced him to invest and he lost everything. He didn't want me to talk to you anymore, and it felt so much worse because all you said was your dad was innocent. He didn't do anything wrong." She sniffles and coughs, rubs her nose until it's red and inflamed. "Then my uncle told me it's all my fault because I had to go and make friends with *you*. I started selling for Hunter, then last summer you got me kicked out of his circle." She grinds her teeth. "I *really* hate you."

"Bec, I'm sorry, I didn't—"

"Shut up." She uses her gas card to set another thin line of coke on the table. "I don't need your pity, or your fake friendship. I wanna forget ever meeting your family." She bends down and sniffs line after line. "I can't. But this helps." Then, she motions for me to go next.

I'm tired of fighting the voices in my head telling me to push back, to say no, to tell Hunter and Becca to go fuck themselves, to run screaming, to get out of this cycle.

I'm a liability.

No matter what I do, the darkness always pulls me back.

And I let it.

OLLY BRUCKE

Something about Tyler is off.

He keeps fidgeting. Staring at his phone as I navigate *Buoys Will Be Buoys* across the lake toward Log Bay, my teeth grinding as I study him.

Swipes up on his screen, then slams it down in frustration or worry, I can't tell.

Contorted body facing away from me.

Restless leg.

Another quick phone check.

The silence on the ride is killing me. Granted, it's early and it's hard to talk while driving a boat, but Khal and Lia are curled up into each other at the stern, no doubt gossiping back and forth, and Tyler is in the bow, and in my head I pictured all of us—Alex included—laughing and soaking up the sun like a scene in a teen Netflix comedy.

Instead, I have a migraine and the unshakeable feeling something bad happened.

The Lonely Bear was eerily quiet this morning. Sheila was

nowhere to be seen, and I heard Ritchie called out. Alex wasn't responding to my texts until she was supposed to be here. **don't wait for me.** That's all I got. Now I'm worried something happened between Tyler and Alex last night.

He must've told her.

Khal was right. I should never have tried to direct this whole thing. Real people are not actors under my control, and now the plot has gotten lost. I thought I was doing what was best: keeping Alex safe and doing what she wanted me to do, not tell her any sort of truth about Dad because she couldn't handle it; not freaking out at Tyler for showing up, but keeping him at arm's length because I'm afraid to really get close to him—what if he abandons me the way Dad and Alex have? This entire summer has been one orchestrated movie set, and I'm trying to control everything, but I didn't account for Tyler and Alex actually becoming friends.

It's like Dad, who always did his best to keep certain important details away from people. He told me something but told Alex something different. It was his way of controlling his narrative.

Is that what I've been doing? I shudder and force myself to push the thought out of my head entirely.

Everything is fine.

I'm overreacting.

I'm not my father.

Pulling into Log Bay, I jolt Tyler to attention. "Ty, ready the anchor. Like I showed you the other day." Tyler figures out the mechanics of tossing an anchor pretty quickly.

Neither Khal nor Lia offer to help; they're "off duty."

Log Bay is one of the most popular destinations on the southern end of the lake, a spot lined with boats tied to one another, filled with the sounds of music blasting out of boat speakers and children laughing and splashing and the smell of portable barbecues grilling up boat-side burgers and nearby remnant campfires. There's a volleyball net by the marshes in the shallows, and a golden retriever hopping in the water to catch a Frisbee in its mouth.

Tyler grabs bottles of ice-cold water from the cooler and tosses one to everyone, except Lia. He uncaps hers and hands it to her because she's busy applying sunscreen.

Lia offers me her lotion, but it's SPF-15. "It's SPF-100 for me, unless I want to look—and feel—like a dried-out chili pepper." If Alex were here, she'd be baking right alongside Lia. She was blessed with Mom's Italian genes, while I got Dad's fair German skin.

"Any word from Alex?" Khal asks, and I sigh and shake my head. "Wasn't it *her* idea for all of us to go out on the boat?"

I take a deep breath and try to release my anger with it.

Triple check the anchor, to make sure it's secure.

"Relax, babe," Khal says, coming up behind me and rubbing my back.

It's clearly not working, but then my phone buzzes and my heartbeat quickens hoping it's Alex, but then crashes too quick. Ashleigh: **Omw, running a bit late.**

"Who's down for the waterfall?" I can't sit still. I have to move.

Khal shakes his head and waves my suggestion away. "I'm tanning today."

"Hell yes," Tyler yells, a bit too excitedly.

Lia squirts sunscreen on her hands and starts methodically kneading it into Tyler's muscular back.

"They're cute together," Khal whispers. "Right?"

"Sure," I say.

"Don't be like that," he says.

"Like what?"

"You're angry with Alex for not showing, but that's her, not Tyler."

I suck in a breath as the realization hits me: I *am* angry with her. Alex and I haven't had any real conversation since she stormed out on Mom, and sadness pulls at me like gravity hurtling a meteor into the atmosphere. "You know me too well."

"Olly, we going to this waterfall or what?" Tyler shouts.

Khal nudges me. "See, he wants to spend time with you."

"You okay to stay and wait for Ash?" I say.

"Go bond," he answers.

"You coming, babe?" Tyler asks Lia.

"Sounds cute," Lia begins. "Except I have zero wilderness skills, so if we get lost, we'll probably die." She's been to the waterfall at least a half dozen times with me and Khal and every time she's managed to wander off and get lost. Khal is no better, so it usually ends in me having to search them out, and between the two of them, it's a lot like herding cats.

Tyler dots her nose with lotion. "Adorable."

"I'll stay with Khal and sunbathe," Lia says. Her shoulders slump a bit, like maybe I'm impeding on their alone time. But she rebounds quickly. "You two go."

Tyler pulls Lia into his body and kisses her deeply.

There's a longing on Khal's face I immediately recognize. He'll let me kiss him on the boat if we're not immediately surrounded by other boats. Which is definitely not the case here. So I settle for a quick hand squeeze.

To get to the falls, we have to swim to shore. Tyler and I load dry towels and dry flip-flops on a raft. My camera is strapped around my neck, but I hold it high above the water. He squirms a bit when his bare feet touch the layers of slimy sticks on the bottom.

There are two paths: the wide, flat, easy way, which is a solid twenty minutes, or the narrow, perilous path with the downed trees to climb over, which takes about half the time. Unsurprisingly, Tyler chooses adventure over safety.

Tyler ties his Lonely Bear staff shirt around his head like a bandana. He moves with grace and agility around every obstacle, treating it like a magical quest to find the long-lost fountain of youth. I hit the record button as he swats through wild brush and yells, "five points" like he's in a video game. He grunts as he hops over rocks and scales up the side of the mountain to get a better view.

When he meets up with me again, he says, "Put that down and experience *this*." He motions with his hands at the thick forest in front of us.

"I'm getting great footage."

"Of me? Again? Where's my consent form?" He winks. "What's your next movie about? My dumb ass acting like Indiana Jones?"

"Indiana Jones, huh?"

He flexes the muscles in his biceps. "I could be an Indiana Jones."

"Dream big," I snicker.

He punches my arm the way a brother would. It stings, but it's nice, like we've been having this sort of back and forth for years. "Without thinking about it, your dream movie project would be?"

"*Star Wars*, but like queer and my own original story."

"You're *obsessed*, little sib."

Tyler's being his goofy self; calling me "little sib" makes my heart swell like the Grinch after he learns to love.

He bites the corners of his lips and looks to the ground, deep in thought. "Been meaning to ask. Why are you so obsessed with *Star Wars*? It never appealed to me. Bad acting. Corny dialogue. Puppet aliens."

Dad introduced me to the original *Star Wars* trilogy, insisting I start there before backtracking to the prequel trilogy. Beyond being immediately drawn to Leia Organa because what budding queer kid isn't immediately able to see themselves in a badass woman who knows her way around a diplomatic discussion and a blaster, I was fascinated with Darth Vader.

"I needed to know how one person could torture an entire galaxy and still be redeemed. It's kind of what I want to explore in my new movie. Except real life, not sci-fi. *Me*." I leave out the part about wanting him and Alex to be equal parts of it because saying it out loud might make me sound like I'm using him.

And I'm not.

Am I?

It's so quiet we can hear the sound of rushing water in the distance. We forge ahead, but Tyler's silence is killing me, and I want him to say something, react, anything at all. But he doesn't. Not until we reach the falls.

Cascading water spills out from the top of the shelving rock and crashes onto the mountain below, rocks that have been pounded and smoothed like the finest Italian marble. As we step closer to Shelving Rock Mountain waterfall, I point out the different layers of strata: the first plateau of connected boulders, which is an easy-to-climb-to spot; the foot-wide path underneath the heaviest fall that leads to a series of elevated pools; the small pools at the base, some with stagnant water filled with leeches. Alex had four or five down her legs once.

He soaks in every square inch of the majestic waterfall.

I perch on a boulder facing the falls.

Tyler follows suit and rests back on his arms. "This is incredible, damn." He bites the corners of his lips again. "I think anyone can be redeemed, by the way."

"How?"

"People make mistakes. Shouldn't they be allowed to learn from them and grow and be better people? I get being held accountable for hurting people, that's important, and obviously actions speak louder than words when it comes to making amends, but." He shrugs. "It feels like mistakes aren't allowed."

"Darth Vader literally killed, like, a gazillion people." I mimic his force choke.

He laughs. "Okay, violent serial killers aside. Obviously there are exceptions." He nudges me with his elbow. He turns away from me and toward the waterfall. "My philosophy professor said two things last semester that stuck with me: *Nothing is a coincidence*, and *Are we worth more than the sum of our mistakes?*"

That knocks the wind out of me. "I hope so."

"I spent my whole life with one dad. I knew he wasn't my biological father, but when he died and I learned the truth about your—*our* dad, I was so angry. I wrote him a letter in prison and he never wrote back. Not even federal corrections could change his mind." He tries to laugh, but it comes out like water spitting from a bilge pump. He wipes a tear away. "I hated you and Alex and our father. I wanted to know him and found out he wanted nothing to do with me."

"Screw him for not wanting you." I put my hand on his back.

"But then *you* emailed me," Tyler says. "I hated your dad, Olly. But I realized you and Alex had nothing to do with him and his actions. And I didn't want my anger to prevent me from knowing you both. As I got to know you, and talked to my therapist about it, I realized I don't hate him. I don't know him. He never got a chance to make real amends. To you, or Alex." He looks at me.

"Or you. You're part of this crazy mess." I pepper it with a "Big bro."

He looks up at me, eyes wet. "I never apologized for showing up unannounced. That was wrong. But I'm not sorry for getting to know you. Or Alex." He wraps his arm around my shoulder. "It's super awkward sometimes, but also nice."

"I haven't really let you in. I've been afraid," I mutter under my breath.

"I am too." He pulls me closer, but it feels fragile. "And I get that's why you haven't told Alex about me yet." He sighs in frustration. "I wish I weren't a secret."

"I don't wanna make any more mistakes. Sometimes it feels like it's all I do," I admit. "But I will. Soon. Promise."

"I've heard that before." His jaw clenches. "So I told you about my granddad, who owned the B&B back in PA? His dream was for me to take it over when I was old enough. That's why I'm at Cornell for hotel admin. It's a family expectation. I loved working for him growing up, but I never felt like I was born for it. Then he died and left me this letter outlining how being a hotelier was my legacy.

How do you tell a dead guy you're not sure you want *his* legacy? So I did what I thought I was supposed to do. I placated a dead guy even after my mom sold the B&B. Stupid, huh?"

"Do you like it?"

"I don't hate it," he says. "But it's not my passion. I don't know what is. I'm not like you, born to direct movies and tell stories. When my professor said that thing about nothing being coincidental, I started thinking about how weird it was you and Alex worked at a hotel, the thing I'm in school for, and part of me hoped I'd get here and things would fall into place, but they haven't." He grinds his teeth, and I know I'm part of the reason he's so frustrated. I don't blame him. I want to tell Alex more than anything.

"Have you thought about studying something else?" I ask.

"I feel like if I stop, I'd be letting him, and my mom, down. And myself. So I stay the course. Even though it makes me feel anxious and lost and like I'm suspended in midair. Like a helium balloon on a string. I dunno if I'm making any sense."

I exhale long and hard and loud until my lips sound like a balloon letting air out. "You are."

"I didn't want to hold any anger. I felt like you would never meet me, and I was waiting for nothing. I spent my whole life waiting for other people to love me or want to know me or let me do what I want to do. I want a life bigger than everything I don't have, or had, then lost. So I came here, and it was shitty not to tell you, but it was the first decision I ever made for me." His voice is small now. "I don't regret it."

"I don't either." I hope we can be more than the sum of our mistakes.

He exhales loudly and removes his arm from around my shoulder.

"I have to tell you something, Ol. I didn't wanna worry you. She told me not to say anything." Worry paints his cheekbones as he tells me about Hunter being at the hotel and punching Ritchie and how she left with him.

It takes all of me not to punch the shit out of *him*. "Are you kidding? You let her leave with him?" I hop off the boulder to face him.

"What was *I* supposed to do?" His jaw sets. "*You* let her leave with him the night of the bonfire."

"You could have told me!" I pace back and forth. "Alex is a powder keg, man, I'm trying to look out for her, but—"

"I am so tired of hearing that, Ol," Tyler says, jumping to the ground and getting directly in my face, stopping me dead. "It's your excuse for everything. I'm not taking the fall for doing *exactly* what you always do. You're *such* a hypocrite!" His words slap me across the face. "You claim to be looking out for Alex by keeping me a secret, but you're not!"

I shove him. Hard.

He stumbles backward but quickly gains his footing and barrels toward me.

I brace myself for impact. Close my eyes tight.

But nothing happens.

I wait a few seconds before I sneak a peek, and Tyler is gone.

He's storming back to the path, wrestling to pull his shirt over his head.

"Tyler, wait."

He turns around quickly. His red eyes are filled with tears. The last thing he says is, "This whole thing was a *mistake*, Olly."

Maybe I am destined to be Dad: the sum of all of our mistakes.

ALEX BRUCKE

Speakers emit an awful country-rap song.

Heart beats with the beat.

If I had the strength, I'd scream.

Sun melts into water.

Gaseous, cosmic lava rays spit from wakes.

Burst into clouds of glitter.

The sky dissolves and I float into a wave of nothingness.

I fade away, hands and feet and head disconnected from my body, like one of those dolls where feet and heads could be popped off and interchanged. I had a bin full of plastic parts. I used to wish I could pluck my own head off my body and stick it on someone else's. Maybe I'd make better decisions.

My body reassembles on the floor of my old bedroom in the Blue Wharf house. The room is exactly how I remember it, each wall a different color: white, purple, green, pink. Olly and I are playing with dolls as our parents scream. Mom finds a bra in the wash that doesn't belong to her. Dad is adamant it must belong to one of her friends.

"What kind of person walks into someone's house and takes off their bra?!" Mom screams. "Don't take me for a fool, Cameron!"

"You're overreacting." Dad is eerily calm. "Why would I cheat?"

It curdles my stomach.

Fast-forward to Mom in fuzzy pink pajamas, comatose in front of a blank television set with two empty wine bottles on the counter, a full glass in hand.

"Mom?" I set my backpack down on the floor.

She swivels her head around and her eyes are slow to follow. Her cheeks are crusted with dried tears, her hair a frazzled nest, a jumble of twigs and grass.

"Your father's gone."

"What?" I ask.

She flings the television remote across the room and emits a high-pitched squeal as it cracks and explodes. "Your bastard father left us! Again."

I can't stop my tears. "What do you mean?"

She snickers. "He packed a bag and left a note saying, 'I can't do this.'" She gets up, stumbles sideways, grabs the arm of the couch for support.

"Do what?" My heart races. There were no legal troubles yet.

She shakes her head and mumbles something incoherent.

"He must've gone out of town for a few days on a business trip, like always." That's the only scenario that made sense.

"You don't know what I deal with, Alexandra!" She clumsily places her wine on the table before gesturing wildly with her arms and knocking it over. The glass shatters on the tabletop. Silky red liquid cascades onto the carpeted floor.

Years later, after he came home time and again, she's still scrubbing out his mess.

I wake with a start, gasping for air.

Where am I?

I squint, but it's hard to see anything, so I grope the space around me for something, anything I can grab onto to.

"Thank goddess you're awake." The voice is immediate. Ashleigh's outline is fuzzy and I can barely make out her face, but her long black hair is unmistakable. She grabs under my arm and hoists me upright. "Here, sit up."

My body isn't mine.

"Neck hurt?" she asks, and I nod. "Not surprised. I basically found you crumpled on the floor under the seat. It looked like you'd been killed and stuffed there." Her face slowly comes into focus and the panic in her eyes hits me hard.

"How'd you get here?" I ask. "Where is here?" The sun is still too bright for me to see past the boat, but I can tell we're anchored somewhere shallow by the sounds of kids splashing in the water nearby.

"Log Bay," she says. "I saw Hunter's boat pull in. They all went to shore. Olly and Khal are here somewhere, but—"

"Where is Becca?" There's no way she could've swum ashore.

"Passed out in the cabin." Her eyes dart around again; there's tension in her jawline. She hands me a bottle of warm water. "Why're you here with them?"

The judgment is *real*. "Why do you care?" Even though it feels like drinking piss, I down the entire thing. "Seriously." I gasp for air after finishing the water. "What's with the sudden pivot? Nothing for a year then you're chasing after me at parties and offering to drive me home and taking care of me on boats. Why?" I wish I could tell her how Hunter makes me feel powerless, but I can't choke out the words, so I bury them somewhere in the rubble. It's easier to lash out at her.

"Because you're my friend, and I'm worried about you."

Empty keg cups and beer bottles roll around the floor as the boat rocks. There are a couple of cashed bowls. Thankfully Hunter isn't dumb enough to leave hard shit out.

"Don't be."

"You're numbing yourself, Lex." She reaches for my arm, but I yank it away. Maybe if she'd been through a tenth of what I've been through, she'd want to numb herself too. Her life is perfect. She's the prettiest girl in school. Everyone still loves *her.* "I want to help," she says. "I ran into Olly last night and he told me to come today. I figured maybe we could, like, start over. I talked to my mom and she said you can retake all your finals, and—"

Something inside snaps.

Like a twig.

"First, leave me and my family alone! You're like, obsessed. Second, I don't know where your mom gets off saying anything about me. She can be fired for that. I'm sure the school administration would *love* to know Ms. Rodriguez has been telling personal, confidential information to other students."

Ashleigh's hands shake. She folds her arms and her body concaves.

"Doesn't feel good, does it? Someone threatening your parent's *whole* life? That's what it's been like for years. And where were you?" Tears I didn't know I could cry for Ashleigh and our friendship pool in the corners of my eyes. "I needed you, and you ignored me. Fuck off, Ash. Leave me alone." I turn my back toward her. It's not like I can storm off. The most I can do is maybe duck below deck and hide in the cabin and wait for her to leave, but it's a zillion degrees outside, which means it's twice as hot down there. And Becca, who hates me, is there.

Sweat from my forehead mixes with my tears.

"I was scared." Her voice breaks. "I didn't know how to be your friend."

Goddess, that admission is horrible but honest. It takes all of my strength not to crumble to the floor, but I keep my body upright. She won't see me fall. Not again.

"I miss you. I regret turning my back on you. But between all the stuff going on with your dad, it felt like you checked out of the friendship. I needed you, too. There was a lot I was dealing with, especially junior year and I felt like I couldn't even talk to you about it because you wanted everything we did or talked about to be light and surface level. And I get it, you were dealing with your dad being away. I didn't know how to pretend for you, or for me. So I kinda stopped talking. I put up a wall." She wipes tears from her cheeks. The way she looks at me, not with pity, but with regret, tells me she means it. I want to reach out to her and hug her and feel her arms around me the way we used to hug each other like we'd never let go. But so much time has passed.

"I'm so sorry, Ash. I—I'm broken." A shard of glass that slices anyone who tries to clean me up.

"We all are, Lex." She moves closer and her arms twitch like she wants to hug me.

I let her, and it feels so warm, safe, empowering. "I missed you, Ash."

"Me too," she whispers.

I start to cry, and try to stop the tears, but they won't stop and I'm sobbing into her shoulder. She shhhhhes as she squeezes me tightly. "I got you now, bitch."

That makes me sob harder.

Eventually, it ebbs, and I feel a million pounds lighter. I take a deep breath, but my lungs feel tight, my insides corroded. I don't want to feel like this anymore. Numbing has only brought me pain. I want to feel as alive as I did at the ADVOCATE meeting.

"What was going on with you last year?" I ask, a small gesture to make up for far too much lost time.

But she doesn't look pained. Instead, she smiles and looks behind her and points to a girl I've never seen before who's sunbathing across a pale yellow towel on Ashleigh's mom's boat. "See her? That's my girlfriend."

"Girlfriend?" My eyes widen. "You're—lesbian? Bi? Pan?" My mind spins.

"Lesbian and fabulous!" Her voice shakes. "That's why I stopped hanging out with LG people. I didn't want anyone talking about me. I hang at her school a lot."

"Hey, don't be nervous," I say. "I'm so happy for you and oh my goddess what an absolute bitch I am for not giving you space to talk to me about what you were going through." I think about Olly and how I was there for him every day from the second he was ready to tell me until he came out to our parents, and how much he leaned on me, and I hate how Ashleigh felt alone.

"It's okay—" she starts.

"It's not," I interrupt her. "I own it a thousand percent. I promise, if you let me back in, to be a real friend."

She rolls her eyes, then sighs the happiest sigh I've ever heard. It's like a damn love song. "She's incredible. You'd love her." As Ashleigh fills me in about how much she loves this girl, my chest warms and I'm genuinely overwhelmed with happiness.

Maybe this friendship has a shot.

I can't put too much stock into it because around here, nothing stays for very long.

But for now, I'll take it.

Before she's done, I blurt, "I need off this boat, Ash. Please."

Together, we look out at the lake.

"Get in the water, don't look back," she whispers.

Then I remember Becca. As much as she hates me, we can't leave her with Hunter. "I think I brought a bag with me. I'm gonna check the cabin. And grab Becca, too."

It's the right thing to do.

Dipping my head below deck, I scan the cabin for my shit. It smells like a dumpster fire down here. Becca is splayed across the gray cushions lining the walls of the cabin. It's so hot inside I can't think. I push Hunter's wakeboarding gear and lifejacket onto Becca. I shove her leg out of the way to get my bag. She's out cold, heavy, so I need to put my weight behind it, and due to my residual high, it unmoors me. I'm pretty sure the flannel shirt beneath Becca's head is mine.

"Bitch, get up, let's go. I want my shirt." I yank the fabric and her head skids downward. I see vomit and fling it away.

My heart races. I'm no longer sweating from the heat. "Becca! Wake up!"

I'm shaking her body, but it jiggles lifelessly like one of those CPR dummies from health class. I get on top of her because there's nowhere else to go. I climb toward her head and brush her wet hair off her face. Vomit spills from blue lips and pools beneath her chin. Her eyes are open, cold, pupils dilated.

The cabin closes in around me as I scream for help.

OLLY BRUCKE

Dad always stressed the importance of watching the sky when out on the lake.

The weather on Lake George can change in an instant. I've seen it go from bright blue and cloudless to a sea of whitecaps, and black skies moving with precision over the mountains, bringing with it a wall of rain and thunder.

Most of the time, if you're paying attention, you can outrun the storms and make it back to the docks.

But not always.

The tea kettle whistles and I shakily pour the hot water into a lumpy art project mug Alex made for Mom for Mother's Day when we were kids.

I tiptoe past Lia and Tyler, who have been passed out on the couch all night. Even though Alex didn't want to see anyone and locked herself in her bedroom after the cops questioned her, she also didn't protest when they all said they wanted to stay. Khal is passed out in my bed, and I make sure the door is closed so he doesn't wake up.

Taking a deep breath, I knock on Alex's door.

Mom opens it from the inside.

I hold up the mug. "How is she?"

Mom shrugs. "She won't talk to me."

"Can I try?"

Mom gently pushes me out into the hallway and shuts the door behind her. "Who knows about Tyler?" There's an edge to her voice.

There was so much chaos: Tyler and I racing back to the lake to find the bay crowded with LG patrol boats, fireboats, and ambulance boats whirring red lights. Calling Mom and flying down the highway to meet her at the hospital, where the medics took Alex and Ashleigh. Watching as the cops questioned her. Getting the news Becca had died, and Hunter was at the police station. My head pounds thinking about it. I realize now I didn't even have a chance to talk about Tyler's presence with Mom, to check in with her. Hell, I haven't thought about my fight with Tyler.

"Only Khal knows."

Mom peeks her head down the hall to check for lurkers. "This is a lot for me, Oliver." She crosses her arms to hold herself. "With him in my house." She's trembling.

I'm so stupid. I should have known him being here would be a shock to Mom's system. "Do you want me to ask him to leave?"

She shakes her head. "I'll be fine. It's one thing to think he's out there somewhere, and another to know he's here. With you. But this isn't about me." She takes a deep breath and gives me a hug. "I'm relieved Alex is the one who made it off that boat. Am I a horrible person?"

I bury my face in her shoulder. "No—I keep thinking the same thing." Guilt and relief overwhelm me at the same time. Tears sting the corners of my eyes.

Mom pulls away. "If you need me, I'll be making breakfast. For *everyone.*"

In front of Alex's bedroom door, I imagine her body in a bag. In a morgue. In a freezer somewhere, toes tagged like an animal.

Grab the handle, hold my breath.

She's lying on her side on the unmade bed, buried under covers, messy brown hair, which I'm still not used to, poking out, and I immediately exhale.

"I don't wanna talk, Mom." Her voice is eerily stoic.

Sitting down next to her, I place a hand on her shoulder. "I brought tea."

The lump under the blankets rolls until she faces me. "Chamomile?"

"With orange honey."

She pushes herself up like it's been years since she's moved.

"You look rough," I say with a smirk.

She turns to look in the mirror. "Oof." She grabs chunks of hair and twirls them. Her eyes are bloodshot. "I don't even care."

"That's when you know it's bad." I want to tell her I'm happy she's alive, home.

"What happened?" She nurses the tea, holding the mug for warmth. "How did I get here?" She stares blankly at me. "One day, we were happy, living in the Blue Wharf house, playing with our dolls. Now—" Her cloudy eyes, a maelstrom of emotions, meet my gaze. "I'm scared."

I scoot closer. "What do you need?"

"I don't wanna talk. Or get a lecture. Just . . ." She reaches out for me. "This."

Squeezing her hand, I swallow everything I wanted to say. "Can do, Sis."

Sometimes all you can do is wait out the storm.

ALEX BRUCKE

i don't think i can do this

Immediately, Javy FaceTimes me. "Yes you can. Be strong. You got this." He smiles so big it fills me with hope.

"Funerals are historically not my thang."

"Did you say 'thang'?" He furrows his brow.

"I did. Fight me."

"Something tells me you'd win."

"You learn quick." I pause, suck in a breath. "I feel like everyone is waiting for me to lose it."

"And? What's it to them if you do? Channel June. Puff out your chest and act like nobody bothers you." He holds out his phone and demonstrates, encouraging me to join him, but I'm not about to do that in public. "Do what you need to do and take care of your business. You don't need to be anything for anyone."

"Thanks, Javy."

He winks. "Solidarity. I'm here if you need me."

I tuck my phone away, puff out my chest, and walk inside.

Strangers stare at me like I'm an untamed, unpredictable animal in a cage at a zoo as I meander through Becca's uncle's house during the reception. What do they think I'm going to do, pounce on them?

Probably.

I haven't cried yet. Not when I saw Becca in a body bag. Neither time the police questioned me. Not even when they cleared me and said it easily could have been me who died.

I'm a clogged drain. Every minute of every day, I think, *Why didn't I stop her from taking the drugs that morning?*

Everyone here is probably thinking the same thing.

I can't blame them. Once upon a time, I was her friend.

Olly hasn't left my side over the last week. It's been nice, if not a bit suffocating.

I wanted to come here alone. Ashleigh said she would meet me, but she's late, and I want to get this over with.

The stairs creak as I wind upward toward Becca's bedroom, missing years passing through me like ghosts. Too much time has passed since I've been here. The railing still jiggles if you hold onto it too tightly and the way the third step from the top still creaks so loudly, like it did when we snuck out at night during sleepovers. The black-and-white photo of her great-grandfather stares at me. I always thought he looked exactly like Colonel Sanders, and one day, Becca and I posed next to the picture with a bucket of KFC. Spoiler: her uncle did not find us humorous.

So many of my Becca-flavored memories have faded so completely it's more of a residual stomachache after a virus. I'm not the Alex I was the last time I was here.

The door to Becca's room is ajar and I nudge it open with my shoulder. Ashleigh is sitting on the bed holding her mother's hand.

"I'm sorry," I say, backing out. "I didn't know you were here."

"No, don't go." Ashleigh gets up and holds out her hand for me to take.

Ms. Rodriguez offers a kind smile that makes me want to wrap my arms around her and never let go. "I'll leave you girls alone." She kisses her daughter on the top of her forehead, and I look away because hot anger and discomfort prickles at the back of my neck and makes me sweat. She looks like she might try to hug me, her arms outstretched toward me, but I pretend not to notice and instead make my way to Becca's wall of pictures and stare at a selfie of her and Ashleigh at Black Mountain from a few summers ago. My entire body stiffens until she's gone.

"You okay?" Ashleigh asks, coming up behind me. She grabs hold of the picture I was staring at and plucks it off the wall. Lavender paint chips fall to the carpet. "Oops."

"Are you?"

Ashleigh snorts. "Is it weird if I said I am?" She stares at Becca's face for a while, then places a thumb over it. She's been biting her nails. Her cuticles are raw and the tops of her nails are gnawed and mangled. I grab onto her hand and squeeze. "Obviously I'm sad. But I'm also relieved."

Relieved?

The guilt I've been carrying has coagulated with the other toxic emotions I've been harboring for literally everyone in my life. I don't know if I can handle what she's saying. The day Dad reported to prison floods me, and Becca's room is washed away and I'm sitting on the edge of the docks at the Lonely Bear. Olly wanted to go to our old house, but I couldn't. I dangled my feet over the surface of the water with Olly, my head on his shoulder, silently sobbing.

"What do you think he's doing right now? You think he's okay?"

I asked. It didn't feel real, like he could stroll through the doors of our crappy apartment at any minute.

Olly shrugged. He wasn't there, not really. He was far away, maybe off on the lake somewhere, drifting in an empty cove, screaming where no one could hear him.

"We should have driven him." Watching him get onto a bus in Albany was excruciating. I couldn't move though I wanted to run to him. To know his last few hours as a free man were spent on a gross bus with strangers was horrible. We knew we wouldn't hear from him for a few days. He told us it might take a while to get phone privileges once he was processed.

"He's a big boy, Lex." Olly's shoulders tensed up. He leaned back, and for the first time since all of Dad's dumpster-fire legal shit happened, he looked like the old Olly. Happy. "It feels like I can finally breathe."

The muscles in my face tightened then, as they do now, with Ashleigh. How can anyone be relieved?

Make it make sense.

"It could've been me." I rip my hand away from hers.

Ashleigh sucks in a breath and holds it there.

"She's dead, Ash. Like. Dead. Gone. Not coming home." My lips start to tremble because all I can see is Dad's face in every one of Becca's pictures.

Air leaks from Ashleigh's lungs and out through her nostrils. "It was exhausting to be her friend."

"But you *were* her friend once."

"So were you." She looks away. "She took so much from us."

"I don't get it," I repeat over and over again as I start to pace

Becca's room. Bubbling anxiety rises to the back of my throat until I choke out the words. "She was alive that morning. *Alive.* And then." Her gray face, face-down in the cabin of Hunter's boat, flashes in my mind, but this time, as I push back the hair, it's Dad's face, not Becca's, and he's on the floor of the prison where we left him to die. "He died alone."

"He?" Ashleigh repeats.

"He died alone." My voice squeaks out the words, and I have to breathe to prevent myself from losing it, but my lungs can't find any oxygen. "Nobody cared about him. Not the system. Not the guards. Not even Mom or Olly. Now he's gone and—"

Becca's room is spinning, the natural light from the windows erasing everything else around us. Ashleigh puts her hand on my back to steady me, and it's as if her touch draws breath back into my chest cavity because almost immediately my lungs suck in air and I nearly collapse to the floor.

"Shhh." Ashleigh's hand rubs my back and she whispers, "You're okay, Lex. I got you. You're okay." I try to focus on her words, but it's all I can do to breathe.

Using Becca's squeaky bed as leverage, I prop myself up.

I have to get out of here.

My legs are Jell-O, betraying me with every step I take, threatening to take me out.

But I make it to the door.

Ashleigh calls out for me, but all I can manage is a "leave me alone" as I traverse the stairwell. The reception is loud. Bile pools at the back of my throat. I propel my body out the front door—I can't be the girl who pukes in her dead ex-friend's house.

There's a rickety bench off to the side of the house where Becca and I would go to talk shit about people at school so her uncle wouldn't hear us.

Ms. Rodriguez picks up her head. As her eyes adjust to whatever horrific state I must look like I'm in, she offers a smile and taps the bench, "There's enough room here."

I almost decline because I want to be alone. Except I don't want to be alone.

She shifts over so I can sit. Then she waits for me to say something, anything. I've known her long enough to know she never presses anyone to talk outside of her office at school. She likes to wait for you to make the first move. Which, good luck because the last thing I want to do is talk. I swallow the urge to vomit, and we sit in silence.

For a long while.

Until she breaks. "How's everything over at the Lonely Bear?" I notice out of the corner of my eye she's looking at me, but I don't turn to acknowledge her.

"Fine. I guess." It's not enough for her. She's going to keep asking questions. "Sheila's been great, you know, the last week. It's nice to keep my mind busy." I wonder if Ms. R knows anything about Hunter. His parents closed ranks around him and nobody has heard so much as a peep since the cops took him in for questioning. Even Sheila and Ritchie are locked fortresses. Mom and Olly forbade me from contacting him because he could go down for Becca's death since he was the source of the drugs she overdosed on.

I'd bet my left tit Ms. R already knows everything.

"Must be nice to be in the kitchen again." Her voice is soothing, like the rhythm of a boat engine.

I pick at my cuticles. "I don't feel like it's my place anymore. Is that bad?"

"Why would you think so?" She shifts toward me with her Guidance Counselor Face on, her eyebrows bent with concern and her eyes soft. It works.

"I always thought I'd be a chef. But—" I shake my head. "It doesn't feel right anymore. But if not cooking, what do I do with my life?"

She sighs. "I remember you teaching Ashleigh to make pierogies at Christmastime. The way you two would pinch the dough. So precise."

"Ashleigh's always looked mangled."

"Like a Muppet had a stroke. I love my daughter, but a natural chef, she is not."

I laugh. It feels . . . nice. "Do you think I should stick with it? Even if it doesn't make me happy anymore?"

"Not at all. Just because something made you happy once doesn't mean it will forever. It's silly to think you'll have everything figured out before you can drink. Legally, of course." She gives me a sideways glance.

"That's not very guidance counselor–like," I say.

She chuckles. "We push you to make decisions, yes, life is a series of choices. But the truth is you have your entire life ahead of you, and you'll probably change direction a hundred times."

I keep picking at my cuticles, and Ms. R puts her hand on mine to stop me.

You have your entire life ahead of you seems heavier a phrase now than it ever was, like those zero-gravity carnival rides spinning so fast they pin you to the wall hard, slowly crushing your lungs.

"Ashleigh told me you two have been reconnecting." She looks out toward the road, slick from last night's rain. "My daughter lost her way for a bit. Perhaps she was influenced a bit too much by the people around her." You don't have to be a mind reader to know she's talking about Becca. "But I'm so proud of her for being her authentic self, and she's come a long way. She loves you. Always has. We all make mistakes. What we do next matters most."

I clench my teeth.

What do *I* do next?

"It's hard not to feel like I've been abandoned," I say quietly.

"Nobody has abandoned you, Alex. We're all right here. Waiting. When you're ready for us. When you're ready to show up for *yourself.* You're *alive.* You get the chance to show up for yourself. And if you come to my office at school Monday morning, I might have a way to help you graduate."

For the first time since Becca died, I ugly cry.

And it feels amazing.

OLLY BRUCKE

Soft fingertips dance across my bare chest in swirling pirouettes to a soundless symphony. My eyes slowly open and I roll over to find Khalid staring at me and smiling.

I play with the soft cartilage of his earlobe. "Creeper." My voice is froggy.

Wrapping my arm around him, I glance up at the glow-in-the-dark neon stars he gave me after we moved here because he knew I missed sneaking down to the lake at night with Alex and staring at the real ones. Around here stars are harder to see surrounded by the soft glow of yellow streetlamps, car headlights, and checkered windows from nearby apartment buildings.

His lips graze mine, soft at first, until his body drifts closer to mine, our legs entangled. When he pulls away, he says, "Happy birthday to me!"

"Oops. I totally forgot." I deadpan, offering a sly smile.

"It's okay. I'll take your essence as my gift." He makes a sound like a Hoover and pretends to suck out my soul the way an evil sorceress might after brewing a potion for youth in a cauldron.

I flop down next to him on my back, rigid. "I'm withering away . . ."

He hops to his feet and bounces on the mattress. "I live again! Praise Allah!" He cackles like a witch.

I grab onto his arms and pull him on top of me.

"Do you want some of your essence back?" His big brown eyes gaze into mine as I nod. He opens his mouth and places his lips on my cheek and blows out.

I pout. "It's not working."

He kisses the tip of my nose as his hand travels down my body and reaches under the band of my boxer briefs. My eyes roll to the back of my head as he strokes me. My fingers explore his hairy chest and down to his waist. I slip off his underwear.

"It's fine if you *did* forget." His breath is hot against my cheek.

"Shut up," I say back. "Are you . . . ?"

"I woke up early this morning. Full routine. I'm ready." His breathing is staggered. He yanks my boxer briefs down to my ankles and tosses them onto the floor.

"Damn." His eagerness ignites me. I flip him onto his back, hoist his legs into the air, and grind my body against his until we're all breath and tangled limbs.

"Since it's your birthday, I *guess* I'll let you bottom."

He grabs a condom and a bottle of lube from my nightstand. "Do that thing first?"

I grin. "Alex is still home so you have to be quiet."

I move below his waist and in perfect rhythm with my movement, his back arches and I push a pillow underneath him.

His skin tastes so sweet. He tries to grab himself as I work my tongue, getting him ready for me, but I stop him.

"It's *your* birthday, but my rules."

He moans: "Happy birthday to *meeeeee*."

———————

As Alex, Khal, and I walk into the front office of the Lonely Bear to clock in, an unruly guest is parked at the desk complaining to Lia about how there weren't enough lounge chairs at the beach yesterday.

"Ma'am, I'm sorry but we do not reserve lounge chairs for guests," Ritchie says, jumping in for Lia, who is clearly flustered. "Bear policy. You're more than welcome to wake up early, walk down to the lake, and set your stuff up for later." He takes a sip of his coffee, unbothered. His affect truly is goals.

"Excuse me," Khal says. "I can bring towels to the water for you, if you'd like."

She whips around. "Aren't you sweet? At least someone here is." She doesn't bother to look at Ritchie. "Come to my cabin, you can help me with the cooler too."

Khal's eyes widen as he realizes what he's gotten himself into. He mouths "Help me" as he backs out of the office, but we all wave him off.

"We set for this weekend?" I say the second Khal is gone.

"Yes," Ritchie says. "The Closet is all set. They know you're coming, but you have to wear under-twenty-one bracelets, no exceptions." He looks to Alex.

She rolls her eyes. "I'm good. No booze for me. Trust me, I'm good."

"What's the Closet?" Lia asks.

"A fabulous gay bar Ritchie has gotten us into before," Alex says. "Is Thot Process playing?" She clasps her hands together in silent prayer.

"Thot Process?" Lia asks, again.

"Ritchie's husband's drag band," I say. "Full of thots, processing."

"Obsessed. Tyler's never been to a drag show," Lia says. "This'll be fun."

"It's a religious experience," Ritchie says. "He'll be baptized, devirginized, and reborn." He rubs his eye and winces. The shiner Hunter gave him is ripe and, by the way he twitches, obviously still tender.

"Is it okay if we bring balloons?" I ask.

"Oh my goddess, and a tiara for him to wear!" Alex chimes in.

"Yes!" Lia shouts, high-fiving her.

"All of the above," Ritchie says. "Is the short king having a good birthday so far?"

"I called him this morning, but he didn't answer," Lia says.

"Judging from the gross sounds through the wall," Alex begins. "I'd say Khal had a really orgasmic—I mean *fantastic*—morning so far."

My cheeks get hot as Ritchie snickers. "ANYWAY!" I yell. "Is Ashleigh coming?"

"Yeah, she's driving," Alex says. "She's bringing her dot dot dot *girlfriend*!"

"I knew it!" Lia jumps up and down. "I'm so happy you two are friends again!"

"Good things happen sometimes," Alex says. "I gotta get to

the kitchen and help Chef prep for the breakfast rush." She air kisses Lia.

"I gotta prep the boat for a whole day with the Fleury family." I salute Alex and pull Ritchie aside. "Do you think you can get us more of those special, um, cleansers for, uh, bottoming? We're all out."

"I got you covered, kid," Ritchie says. "You're staying safe, right?"

"Absolutely."

He nods as a new customer walks in. I thank him and start to make my way out of the office when Lia grabs me.

"What's up?"

"Look," she starts. "I don't know what's been up between you and Tyler, but—"

"Don't get involved." It's cold, but it's not Lia's fight. Though Tyler has been physically around for Alex, he and I haven't made much progress past our fight at Shelving Rock.

Her eyes widen, and she takes a step backward. "Seriously? He's my whateverfriend. I care about him. He's been a wreck ever since you two went off to the waterfall together."

"A wreck?"

She nods. "Moody as hell. Said you got into a fight but won't tell me what about."

Shit. She's too close. "I'll talk to him. I don't want drama on Khal's birthday."

She gives me a quick hug. "Thanks, Ol." She turns to leave but hesitates. "Tyler's a good person. Treat him like one."

I sigh because I already know.

Boat cleaning supplies in hand, I'm trekking down the hill toward the docks when I notice Tyler with a clipboard examining the siding of one of the cottage rooms.

"What're you doing?" I ask.

He turns quickly, and when he sees it's me, he returns to his clipboard. "Property assessment. Part of my internship."

"Cool, cool."

"What do you want, Olly?" He still doesn't look at me.

I gnaw at my thumbnail. I have two choices. I could tell him the truth—I miss him and hate how we fought even though I think he should have told me about Alex. Or I could do the bro-thing and sweep it under the rug. "To thank you for helping with Alex."

"How is she?" He turns around.

"Good. *Better*," I correct. "She and our mom haven't even picked fights with each other while she's been home. Baby steps. She's been texting some new guy. She smiles when she thinks no one is looking, which is weird for her. She won't tell me much, except his name is Javy."

He hmms and looks away, avoiding me. "How's the new movie coming?"

"Stalled. Haven't been inspired." The thought of the looming deadline for festival submission fries my nerves.

He shifts leg to leg, waiting for me to say something else.

"Look, I don't want things to be awkward between us. And I really want you to come to Khal's party. In case you weren't sure."

Tyler's brows furrow. "Did Lia say something?"

"No, why would she?" I hate how good I've gotten at lying. "Does she know?"

"Not at all. She knows something is weird between the three of us, but I don't think she suspects." His jaw muscles tense. "I hate being a secret. You're doing what you think's best for Alex, but I—I feel like I'm gonna end up collateral damage."

His words settle as he starts back toward the main cottage.

I have to make things right and do what I should have fourteen months ago.

ALEX BRUCKE

Ashleigh's obnoxious gas-guzzling SUV rips into the Lonely Bear parking lot. Her girlfriend is in the front seat, and the back is filled to the brim with rainbow balloons with HAPPY 18th BIRTH-DAY next to the astrological sign for Cancer in glitter.

I wipe my sweaty palms on my jeans before yanking on the heavy door handle and catapulting myself in.

"Thank goddess you're here. My hair is frizzy and gross in this heat." I check my reflection in the rearview mirror. "At least I don't have to look cute at a gay bar."

"Lies. Who're you kidding?" Without hesitation, Ashleigh hands me her makeup bag like we're back into our old Bad Bitches routines. "You want *all* the gays to love you."

I crunch my hair and stare at my reflection in the rearview mirror.

"You look hot," Ashleigh's girlfriend says. Her face is angular, but her cheeks are plump and rosy. She has long, luscious black hair and her green eyes pierce right through me. *She's* the hot one. "I'm Dusk."

"Dusk? As in . . ." I motion toward the sky.

"I was born at dusk, in those quiet moments between night and day. My parents said they could see the fiery sun in my eyes, but the twilight moon in my aura. Dusk."

That's some out-there shit.

"My parents were hippies on a commune in the Catskills until I was five." Her voice floats above my head.

"I have no words."

"Alex is short-circuiting," Ashleigh says. There's an energy swirling around Ashleigh I haven't seen in a long, long time. She's relaxed like a pair of broken-in red-bottomed heels.

"It's okay, let it out. I've heard worse," Dusk says.

Normally, I'd burst out laughing because, honestly, Dusk? But looking at this badass with the cheekbones? "I'm kinda in love with you."

Ashleigh reaches behind and grabs my hand.

"*I* can't believe I'm finally meeting the famous Alex," Dusk says.

"Everything Ash told you is a lie." There's something about a mascara wand, a bold lipstick, and a rearview mirror that makes me feel alive again.

Dusk looks at Ash and gives her a crooked half smile. "So you didn't organize a charity event to raise money for Planned Parenthood?"

I shift uncomfortably. "Ahh, the good, selective stuff."

"And you didn't spend basically an entire month at Leigh's house after her grandma died and cook her entire family dinner, like, basically every night?"

"You told her?"

"I did a deep aura cleanse where we unearthed and examined

her core memories, and that was one. Actually, a few revolved around you," Dusk says, matter-of-factly. "It took a long time for us to work through the shame she felt when she wasn't there for you." Dusk reaches out for my hand, and I'm drawn to it. This bitch is casting some sort of spell, and I'm okay with it. She does the same to Ashleigh and somehow weaves our hands together, our fingers the thread, our bones and blood the fabric. "Feel the healing energy?" Her hands hover above ours.

I'm so relaxed I can't even be snarky.

"Love you, bitch," Ashleigh says.

I smile. "You too, bitch."

"This is lovely," Dusk hums.

"Before everyone else comes," I say quietly, not really wanting to break the moment. "I met a guy."

Ashleigh glances at me in the rearview mirror. "Tell me everything. Immediately."

"His name is Javy. He lives in Albany. I sort of invited him to come out tonight."

"Boyfriend material?" Dusk asks.

I shrug. "I dunno. I'm not looking for that after—" My voice trails off, lost in thought about Hunter. Though we're beyond over, we never technically broke up. I blocked his number and have zero intention of talking to him ever again, but he's always there. A demon in the dark corners of my mind. He probably will always be. I shudder but shake it off as best I can. "Anyway, I started going to this group for kids of incarcerated parents. His mom runs it, and he's been a great resource. He gets me, you know?"

"What about your sibling?" Dusk asks, and the car gets awkwardly silent because right on cue, Olly knocks on the window, his handheld camera around his neck because of course. Tyler stands behind him, squinting from the setting neon-orange sun.

Ashleigh catches my eyeroll in the rearview mirror.

"There's a weird energy here," Dusk says, looking at Olly and Tyler.

"I have no idea what those two have going on, but it's weird," I say.

Olly opens the door, and he and Tyler file in.

Ashleigh introduces them to Dusk, then says, "So what's the plan?"

"Lia is with Khal now," Olly says. "She made him help her with some reception task to stall. Ritchie should be here any second, and as soon as she hears the horn, she'll bring Khal out and we'll do the whole 'Surprise!' thing." Olly acts it out like we're idiots.

As Tyler settles in next to me, an electric Volkswagen Microbus pulls up next to Ashleigh's truck.

Noah, Ritchie's husband, is in full drag in the driver's seat, cigarette hanging out of her mouth. Ritchie waves excitedly from the passenger seat. "Y'all ready for tonight? I can't wait to embarrass the piss outta Khal, that sweet thing!" Noah's drag voice is a southern twang that bites at the end of every sentence. Her aesthetic is Dolly Parton on acid: tall blond wig teased out, features drawn out in glitter paint, and a breastplate built for a porn star.

"Let's do this!" Olly yells.

"I'm so excited," I whisper to Tyler. "I love Khal!"

"Same." Tyler looks shook, though. "That's *Noah*?"

"Not *Noah*, *Petty White*," I state. "Get it right."

Petty White pops her tongue in affirmation. Then she blares on the horn, which plays an analog "9 to 5."

"We should all hang out of the windows," Dusk says, and who am I to argue.

Lia, who is killing the game with short shorts and a skintight yellow sequin jumpsuit with a dramatic back cut-out, emerges from the office first.

Still no Khal.

She holds up a finger.

We dangle our torsos out of all the windows, ready to scream for Khal.

Still nothing. Really?

Petty White shimmies out of the driver seat and primps her enormous wig. She does a runway walk halfway around the car and then, upon realizing a few of the hotel guests have gathered, stops and says, "I don't perform for free. Come to the Closet for a real show. Spoiler: I have a penis!"

Lia lurches back into the office and yanks Khal's arm, and he tumbles out.

"Surprise, bitch!" and "Happy birthday!" are followed by Petty White's amazing "9 to 5" car horn and incoherent callouts and snaps and claps from each of us.

Khal's face gets fire-engine red, and he's laughing so hard he doubles over in pain.

Olly hops out and rushes to Khal, scooping him up into a hug and Khal lets him, which is kind of a big deal for Khal, given the amount of randoms who have gathered on the grass around our cars.

It's enough to warm my cold, dead heart.

Petty White claps her hands. "Adorable. But get your asses in the car."

The Closet is barely visible from the street, but we follow the sounds of Beyoncé's *RENAISSANCE*, traversing down a poorly lit alley, to find the entrance. It's a circular door inside a small, enclosed concrete courtyard whose brick walls are covered in remnants of weathered posters and unrecognizable decals.

The bouncer doesn't look twice at us as we tail Petty White and Ritchie. They don't even bother giving us under-twenty-one bracelets, like Ritchie thought they would. But Ritchie makes it a point to tell us not to drink before they disappear backstage.

The space is pretty big, and we immediately get to work tying the balloons to the small area in a far corner Betty said was designated for us. It's dimly lit, and most of the walls are painted black with chips in the paint everywhere. Red light bulbs light the hallways to the bathroom, and strings of Edison bulbs are strategically hung around the perimeter of the bar and nearby stage. High-top tables line the walls, but the center of the room is clear, probably for dancing. The floors are sticky and every step I take toward the bar is accompanied by a squishy wet sound like duct tape being yanked off the roll. And these are new heels, too.

There are two guys behind the bar, one All-American with a chiseled jawline, perfect salon-styled brown hair, and the body of an Olympic swimmer, and the other a weathered trucker-looking dude with giant arms, tattoos, and a handlebar moustache. They don't waste time asking Olly, Khal, and Tyler if they want drinks.

Ignoring Ritchie's orders, they all say yes. So do Dusk and Lia.

I guess I'll be the responsible one?

There's a first for everything.

Olly hands me a glass of ice-cold Coke. The bubbles tickle my throat, and while it doesn't go straight to my head the way vodka might, it gives me a bit more energy.

I'll take it.

Khal comes up behind me and wraps his arms around me. "I'm so happy you're here!" I smell liquor on his breath already.

"Anything for you!" I kiss his cheek.

"What about me?" Olly says.

"Meh," I say with a shrug and a smirk.

"That tracks," Olly says.

Lia hands Olly a drink and he stops himself from taking it. His eyes dart between me and the glass. "Sorry, Alex, I didn't—" Lia starts.

"Ol, you can drink," I interrupt, directing my ire at Olly. "I *promise* I'll be okay. For once, don't hover. Have fun. Leave me alone." I move away from him, toward Ashleigh.

"You okay?" she asks.

"Olly's been walking on eggshells since Becca. I want everyone to be cool."

Ashleigh looks toward our circle. Olly has his camera out, capturing Dusk as she dances like a flower child, arms billowing and completely out of sync to an Ariana Grande song.

The bar is filling up, wall-to-wall bodies. Men in short shorts and sequin tank tops and leather harnesses across their bare chests crowd the bar. Women of all shapes and sizes, arm-in-arm, huddle in groups far smaller than the men. Nonbinary folks in all their layers of fabulousness sprinkled in between.

Ashleigh clinks her Sprite glass against mine. It's nice to not be the only sober one. She takes my hand and drags me toward the group.

Lia pulls us in and we're dancing, grinding, feeling ourselves.

She grabs my face with her hands and kisses me on the lips. Her eyes are droopy, lazy.

"How the hell are you drunk already?" I ask.

"I dunno," she slurs. "Tyler got me drinks."

"Where is Tyler?" I ask.

Her head whips around. "He's with Oliver. *Again*."

"Has it been better?"

Lia tries to focus on me. "He's so preoccupied lately. Boy has demons."

"Don't we all," I say.

"True." Lia's eyes well up.

"Bitch, don't cry," I say.

A tear falls down her cheek. "I'm not crying, I'm drunk."

"Real talk. You like, like him, huh?"

"I care about him." She takes a long-ass sip of her vodka cranberry. "I dunno what's gonna happen after the summer." Her tone is softer, sadder. "He's in Bumblefuck, New York. I'm going to the city. I'd like to stay friends. Plus the dick is good."

I burst out laughing.

"What? It is." Another sip and all that's left in her glass is pink ice and a tattered lime. "But as close as we are, and as much time as we spend together, it's like he won't get close to me. Around Olly, he's like an excited puppy, but then he gets so sad. Then I see him with *you* and it's like *all* the heaviness there is, like, gone."

"Oh, girl, no. Hard pass. *Nope*. Not my type."

"Excuse me!" she sucks her teeth, then bursts into laughs.

"Honestly, I'm curious about Olly and Tyler," I say. "Should we spy?"

Her eyes widen. "Yes!"

Ashleigh and Dusk are grinding up against either side of Khal, whose eyes are in that sweet spot between buzzed and sloshed. We sneak away unnoticed.

We snake around bodies easily due to the dim lighting and how crowded it is until we're right behind Olly and Tyler. Lia and I stand shoulder to shoulder, our backs to Olly, and strain to hear what they're talking about.

"Give me a little more time," Olly begs.

"Why?" Tyler shouts. "You've had all summer."

"Why are you bringing this up now?" Olly asks. "We're both drunk, it's Khal's birthday, I said I would—"

"I'm tired of being on *your* timetable!" Tyler shoves Olly hard in the chest, and he topples into us, causing me to spill the rest of my Coke on the floor. "Go make your fucking movie, which you care more about than actually fixing your family!"

"Tyler!" Olly shouts, but Tyler's already beelining through the crowd. Lia wobbles to regain her footing and immediately goes after him.

Olly turns and starts apologizing, then realizes it's me. "What did you hear?"

"Really, Olly?" I shout, noticing the camera dangling around his neck. It's not on, but still, I get Tyler's frustration. What I don't get is what Tyler meant with the part about Olly fixing his family.

Lia grabs Tyler. "Babe, you okay? Talk to me!"

"I wanna be alone," Tyler says through gritted teeth. His chest heaves rapidly, and he looks like me when I'm about to have a panic attack.

Lia reaches for him again, but her drunk arms are like rubber and they flop back down to her side as he slips out of reach.

Some guy yells, "Who let the straights in?" He's the MVP of the night.

Lia's face changes from hurt to pissed in nanoseconds, and she storms straight past me. Tyler takes off down a tight hallway.

I could go after Lia, but I have to find out what Tyler meant.

The hallway he disappeared down is dark and I have no idea where I'm going, so I use the walls to guide me. My fingers come across a door jamb, and since it's the first sign of an exit, I push through and stumble headfirst into the backstage dressing room where three drag queens are painting their faces.

"Oh goddess, I'm so sorry," I say, backing out quickly.

"Somebody order another straight bachelorette party?" says a slender brown queen with an eighties-era Whitney Houston wig and blue sequin gown dangling around her waist. I catch her mid-hoist and she scuttles over to me as she finishes pulling up the gown and turns her back to me. She points to the zipper. "Make yourself useful."

This is definitely *not* how I pictured tonight going, but this is kind of awesome.

"Ooh, she got muscles," the queen says, pronouncing the C like a K. "I'm Ivanna. Ivanna C. Receipts. And you are?" Her contouring is flawless.

"Alex?" Tyler's voice is far away, and I turn to see him rounding a tight corner at the back of the room with Petty White.

"Does this straight boy belong to you?" Ivanna asks. "We kidnapped him for a little midnight snack."

I can't help but laugh as I nod.

"What's wrong with him?" Ivanna asks.

"Same thing as her, I presume," a much-older queen says with ire, in the lowest, deepest voice I've ever heard out of anyone, let alone someone in six-inch heels and long, pink nails. She explains how her look is modeled after Dorothy from the *Golden Girls*, but glam. "Look at that face. Hiding behind laughs. You can't fool a bunch of queens who paint for a living."

Sobering. I straighten up.

"Pay no attention to Sir Phyllis. But she's not wrong," Petty White says.

"Well then, what's wrong with you?" Ivanna asks me.

"Asking a straight white girl what's wrong is like asking a pampered dog why it's whining. You ain't gonna get anywhere and she's gonna expect belly rubs," Sir Phyllis says between beating her face with a giant pad.

Ivanna rolls her eyes. "Sir Phyllis's heart dried up a long time ago, around the same time as her syphilis." She points to Tyler, then me. "Both of you. Sit. Now."

The room is cramped, and I'm careful not to step on ruffled gowns or fallen wigs. The air smells like talcum and copper pennies and fruity body spray. Tables are littered with tiny bottles of sweet-tart-flavored energy drinks and used eyeliner kits. Walls are papered with posters of naked men with oiled muscles and flyers for old drag shows with bubbly, outdated fonts. There are mirror stations for multiple queens. One in the very back uses the overhead light to contour her face with dark makeup, doing a good job of pretending like she doesn't see us.

"That's Lisa Dick," Ivanna whispers, noticing the direction of my stares. "Drag mother. Best leave her alone while she paints."

Petty White ushers Tyler forward. "He won't talk to me, but I found him in the hallway hyperventilating." She sidles up next to Ivanna and they both cross their arms.

"Spill," Ivanna demands.

Tyler and I look at each other. He has the same look Olly gets when he's holding something back. All creases and furrowed brows and dilated pupils. The familiarity sends a chill down my spine.

Ivanna purses her lips. "It always helps me to talk when I'm getting my makeup done, which doesn't happen very often." She pulls up a stool. "Neither does this gift I'm about to bestow."

"Huh?"

Ivanna rolls her eyes. "Who did your mug? You're a mess." She ruffles through a Mary Poppins bag of dusty makeup searching for something to match my tone. "Cool it with the tanning beds. And fix this shitty dye job." She wipes my face with a makeup remover wipe. "You gonna talk or what?"

"My twin is being an ass," I say, and Tyler nods.

"A tale as old as time," Petty White says.

"What I don't get is why," I say. "Tyler? Care to jump in here?"

"Nope." Tyler's lips are so tight they're bone white.

"What is with you two, seriously?" I snap. "What kind of secret shit are you involved in? Olly literally never hangs out with anybody but Khal, yet he seems to make exceptions for you."

"You two siblings?" Ivanna asks.

Petty White coughs.

I shake my head no.

"Mm-hmm. Could've fooled me." She blows on a brush. "Close your eyes."

"Well, what do you have to say, handsome?" Ivanna asks.

291

"It's complicated," Tyler says, defiance in his voice.

"Uncomplicate it."

"I—" Tyler whispers. "Can't."

The sound of feet pounds the linoleum floor.

"Don't leave!" I shout, eyes still closed. "Please. I'm so sick of everyone around me leaving or lying. Someone has to stay!"

Ivanna's hand hovers inches from my eyes with a lash brush. "Heavy stuff."

I open my eyes and Tyler is in the same place. He didn't move, but Petty White is gone. I blush. "You weren't leaving?"

He smirks. "Nope."

But I'm not smiling. "Look, you've been a great friend, and I've barely known you a couple weeks."

"You don't really know me."

"You took me to ADVOCATE and honestly that's more than anybody has done for me in a long-ass time. I don't know who I am or who I want to be, but around you, that's okay. For what it's worth."

Ivanna brushes my T-zone and moves away from the mirror so I can see myself. It's natural, save for the purple lip. I don't recognize the girl staring back at me. Yet. But I'm willing to get to know her.

"You're allowed to be messy and in control at the same time," Ivanna says. "You get to be right *and* wrong at the same time. You look snatched, by the way."

Sir Phyllis clears her throat. "Let the kids have a moment, willya, Ivanna?"

Ivanna winks at me, then punches Tyler in the shoulder playfully.

"I don't have everything figured out," Tyler continues.

"So what's your story?" I ask.

His lips go tight again.

"Oh, he's frustrating," Ivanna says.

"Welcome to my life," I say. "Beauty, alcohol, and debilitatingly annoying guys."

Ivanna snaps. "Yes, bitch!"

Sir Phyllis, who has been leaning in watching intently like we're some sort of reality show, says, "So what's your story, sassypants?"

"Oh, you know," I say. "Dad does crime. Dad gets arrested. Friends ditch me. Dad goes to prison. Mom disappears. Dad dies in prison. Twin hovers but maybe hates me too. Boyfriend turns out to be an American Psycho. Your standard fairy tale, really."

Ivanna takes a step back. "The son always suffers the sins of the father. In this case, the daughter, too. You know how many people I grew up with in Baltimore who had incarcerated parents? I learned there are two types of people: the people who let the system take from them until there's nothing left but to follow in the footsteps of their parents, or the people who take their pain and do something positive with it, like trying to change the system." She crosses her arms and leans back against a vanity, the sequins clanking against the fiberglass. "I've been listening to you for a while now, and I have one question: Have you talked to your twin about why he's acting the way he is? Seems like there are four victims here. You, your dad, this handsome boy here judging by the tears in his eyes, and this twin you're pissed at."

Guilt cramps my sides. I never considered how Olly must feel. I didn't want to.

Tyler's staring at my reflection in the mirror, but he looks far away.

I study his face.

The lines on his forehead.

The crinkles next to his eyes when he smiles.

His nose. *My* nose.

My breathing is belabored as I connect the dots.

Olly in the car the day Dad died: *I wanted to talk to you about something.*

Olly outside our apartment the day Tyler showed up at the Lonely Bear: *There's something I need to tell you. About Dad.*

Tyler's words to Olly: *I'm sick and tired of everything being on your timetable . . . which you care more about than actually fixing your family.*

The way Tyler reminds me of Dad when he says certain words or smiles a certain way. It all makes sense now. He's been trying to get close to me because—

I stop breathing.

Everything comes into sharp focus.

Ivanna taps my cheeks. "Sweetie, you okay? You look pale."

Sir Phyllis hands me a glass of water, and they all command me to drink.

I bring the cup to my lips and lap at it.

Ritchie bursts through the doors from the dark hallway, panic in his eyes. Petty White is behind him, fiddling with her fingers. "Alex, are you okay?"

Tyler's eyes betray him.

OLLY BRUCKE

Shot after shot, song after song, Ashleigh, Dusk, Khal, and I grind in the middle of the bar until we're all so close I can feel all of them breathing heavily. Ritchie is next to us getting his life to Kim Petras's "Throat Goat" booming through the speakers.

I grab Khal's shirt and pull him toward me until his tongue dances with mine.

This is all I need. Screw Tyler.

"You're the throat goat," he warbles in my ear.

Petty White pushes her way through the crowd toward Ritchie. She whispers something in his ear and he looks toward me, wide-eyed, before disappearing with her.

Khal wobbles, and he looks like he's about to fall over.

"You having a good birthday?" I shout, not sure what to make of Ritchie's reaction.

Khal kisses me again and reaches for the top button of my jeans.

"Whoa, down boy." I may be drunk, but not trashy. "You need some air."

The second we get outside, some dude by the door stares at me, squinting.

"Hey, Tyler, remember me?" He's short like Khal and looks like that hot actor Angel Bismark Curiel. I've never seen him before.

"Tyler's my brother," I say absentmindedly. "He's in there somewhere."

"My bad. You must be Olly. I'm Javy." His grip is tight.

"Oh, Javy." It takes me a second to register the name. "Alex's Javy?"

He laughs and nods. "It's really nice to meet you. Alex has told me a lot about you." She has? He turns to Khal and quickly says, "You must be Khalid then! Happy birthday, brother!" He pulls Khal into a bro-hug.

Did I call Tyler my brother?

My mouth is dry. "I, uh, yeah, same." My head pounds. Is it possible to have a hangover so soon? "How do you know Tyler?"

"ADVOCATE. You gotta come. It's really great."

"What is ADVOCATE?" I don't register anything he's saying.

As Javy explains the organization his mother founded and how he met Alex and Tyler, it dawns on me that Tyler knows Javy, but he didn't say anything when I brought it up at Shelving Rock.

Why hasn't Tyler invited me to this group?

Why does everyone in this fucking family keep secrets?

Tyler dashes outside. He's out of breath, his face drained of all color. "She knows."

My body goes into panic mode like the whole building—no, *world*—is on fire and all I have is a half-drunk glass of watered rum and ginger ale.

"How?" is all I can manage, but it doesn't matter because she knows and I've likely ruined everything with my sister, my soul mate, the one person I tried so hard not to hurt.

I'm a hollowed-out jack-o'-lantern, guts splayed all over the floor, nothing inside but rotting flesh.

"I tried to find her, but I lost her inside," Tyler says. "I'm so sorry, Ol."

Then I see her.

And I know.

It's over.

ALEX BRUCKE

My body is on fire.

"I'm sorry, Lex. I didn't want you to find out like this." Olly tries to take a step toward me, but I back away. It takes every ounce of strength not to punch him out.

"So it's true?" My temples throb. I never wanted to know any of this, but now anger and confusion swirl around me like a category-five hurricane.

Olly's guilty, traitorous, lying-ass face is the eye of the storm.

I feel *his* heartbeat in my chest, racing.

I hope he has a heart attack.

"Lex, please! Dad didn't want me to tell you, he—"

His words are meaningless.

"How long did you know?" I interrupt. There's a steady stream of tears I don't bother to wipe away. He hesitates, fumbles, so I shout, "Be honest!"

"Since last May. When I got Tyler's letter."

Letter? There's so much I don't know. But the worst part is he brought Tyler into my life and I *unloaded* on him. Seeing Tyler and

Olly together now makes me physically ill. Betrayed isn't the right word. It's a violation of my heart and mind.

"Fuck you, Olly. You're no better than the father you hate. Leave me alone. Pretend *I* died. You're good at pretending." I turn around to bulldoze my way back inside. "I called Mom and she's picking me up because honestly, I can't stand to be around any of you." I didn't actually call Mom. She's at work and wouldn't pick up her phone. "You know what, Olly? You think Dad is the villain in your story, but it's you. Keep telling yourself you're the fucking hero and I'm a damsel in distress. We're done."

I grab onto Javy and yank him away.

"Are you okay?" he asks, and I shake my head.

My legs have to keep going or I'm afraid I might collapse.

I don't know where I'm going, but once I'm back inside, the bodies stacked on top of each other, shoulder to shoulder, pelvis to pelvis, sweat dripping to some Dua Lipa song, my head swells. It's too much.

I will not break down.

I will not break down.

Javy stops moving. Tentatively, he places his hands on my shoulders like I'm a frightened animal. "What do you need?"

I spot Ashleigh and Dusk under a pink glowing light.

I can't bring down their high. I have to get out of here. "You have a car?"

OLLY BRUCKE

We're done.

I can't breathe.

I hold onto Khal for support, but he's so drunk his body is Jell-O.

Tyler is sitting on the curb, head buried in his hands.

Alex screaming at me loops inside my head like an old black-and-white film, but her cries go silent as the camera zooms into a close-up of her face, the shadows around her eyes, the betrayal etched in her makeup.

This is all my fault. If I had told the truth from the start, everything between the three of us would have been different. If Dad had been the father we needed—to all three of us—none of this would have happened.

Alex hasn't been sober long. She can slip. Probably will.

I can't hold back a loud, "Fuck!"

"It's okay," Khal coos, but it doesn't help.

"It's not." My breathing increases. "I have to find her . . ." The oxygen flowing rapidly to my brain makes me dizzy, but I can't stop the heaving of my chest and the short manic breaths. The concrete feels like quicksand.

Tyler is beside me, telling me to breathe. He has the face of my dead father.

All the hurt I've been holding inside since Dad died erupts.

"Get away from me," I shout. "You've done enough."

"Olly, stop," Khal pleads, suddenly sober.

"If you had stayed away, none of this would have happened." I'm in his face now. "We were doing fine before you showed up. We were *fine*. *I* was fine." My fists are clenched and I hate the vile garbage spewing from my mouth, but I can't stop it.

Tyler holds up both middle fingers. "Have a nice life, Oliver." He starts walking toward the street, Lia chasing after him. "I'll Uber back and be gone by morning."

"See. I knew you'd leave. Bruckes always do."

My body is on fire.

A raging tempest of anger and regret.

Air leaks violently from my lungs as one thought screams at me:

I am my father.

ALEX BRUCKE

Javy lowers the music. "Where are we going?" he asks, one hand at the top of the wheel. I don't know how long we've been driving. Javy swerves and brakes to a halt in a metered spot along a dark, deserted street dotted with streetlamps.

"What the hell?" I snip.

"You don't have to tell me what happened back there." His eyes are soft and full of concern. His voice calm and steady. "But you *do* need to tell me where I'm going."

"I don't care." I suck in a breath. "That was bitchy. Sorry. It's my natural affect."

He laughs and it's such a charming, confident chuckle I immediately ease up.

"I feel like I need to scream," I admit.

"So do it," Javy urges. "Let it go. Full chest."

Don't have to tell me twice.

I scream so loudly my entire body convulses and my lungs rip to shreds.

Javy has to cover his ears. "Damn. Could've used a warning or something."

I hold my breath.

But he bursts out laughing again, and I exhale.

"You're an ass."

"I know, I know," he says. "Feel better?"

"I don't feel like I'm about to disintegrate, so. Winning."

"A good place to start." He clears his throat. "You live in Lake George, right?" I nod. "I can take you someplace you feel safe."

Only one place comes to mind.

The silence in the car as we drive up the Northway is welcome.

Javy winds around dark streets bordering the lake until we arrive at the Blue Wharf house.

"Park there." I point to a side street where we can cut through the brush and into the yard to get to the dock.

"This where you live?" he asks.

"Once upon a time," I whisper.

"So. Are we—" Javy hesitates. "Trespassing right now, 'cause—"

"Not really." I peer through the thick pines to my old house. All the lights are off, save for a nightlight in the child's room. My old one. "I used to live here and we know the new owners well. They let us use the dock."

"If you're sure." His tone is unstintingly cautious.

I don't get why he's being weird. "Yeah, follow me."

We quietly make our way to the dock and walk to the end, where Olly and I used to sit and dangle our feet over the edge.

His body is stiff, tense, and he keeps looking around like he's checking to make sure the coast is clear. Once he sits, he lets out a deep breath.

"What's wrong?" I ask.

There's an edge to him that wasn't there before. "Only white people can get away with sneaking onto someone else's property in the middle of the night in a bougie neighborhood and think it's no big deal."

My body goes cold. "I didn't think—"

"Why would you?" He swivels to face me. "No disrespect *at all*, I like you, but I'm not about to get the cops called on me. When was the last time *you* worried about that?"

My privilege affords me so much, which I know in theory, but this is the first time I've had to confront it. I squirm. "Never," I whisper.

"Good you recognize it," he says. "But it's not enough. You have to use it to bring about equity. Sit with that."

I stare out over the black lake, the stars and moon reflecting on its surface like specks of silver in a cave. "I'm sorry."

"Don't apologize. You're coming out of a hard time. You're opening your eyes."

"Trying."

"That's all we can do." He clears his throat. "So, why here? Why not go home?"

"Nosy." I nudge him gently in the ribs.

"You owe me after this"—his hands wave in circles—"grand white privilege flex."

"Fair. I don't want to be around any of my family."

"Olly," he tests himself, and I nod. "Yeah, he looked all sorts of stressed. I was worried the vein in his neck would pop."

"Fuck him."

"Oof, so bitter," Javy says.

"How would you feel if you found out you had a half brother—Tyler, by the way, which I didn't know until, like, two seconds before I saw you tonight—and the twin you thought would never lie to you has been keeping said half brother a secret for over a year? You'd be bitter too." My toes kick up water until I'm basically stomping the waves.

"Damn." He pauses, and the way he's crinkling his forehead says he's carefully constructing his next thought. "Can I ask you something?"

I shrug.

"What changes now? Besides you being mad, which is warranted."

"I can't trust my own brother. Either of them." A chill travels through my body. "That was weird to say."

"Weird how? Like it doesn't sit right?"

"No. The opposite. It—" My foot twitches restlessly on the floor and the vibration ripples out around me, creating a steady rhythm in my bones. "Makes sense, somehow. I need vodka." I laugh nervously.

"Fresh out," Javy says. "So that's your thing?"

"My thing?"

"Kids of incarcerated parents always have a thing, a way to cope," Javy explains. "It's the burden we bear."

"I liked vodka, or whatever puke juice I got my hands on. Weed, which isn't bad or illegal. Sometimes something harder. That scared me."

"Good. It should. It takes something from us. We've already

had so much taken, you know? What do you gain from a drink besides a nasty hangover and a lot of shit you wish you could take back?"

One sip would be easy. Freeing. Once I get past that first swig where it feels like fire, the burn fades and in its wake is a warm comfort in my belly that spreads to the rest of my body, like hot nutmeg-y butternut squash soup on a cold fall day. With a poisonous twist. The next sip is easier still.

If I were alone right now, I might have downed my demons in something.

But I silently thank Javy for not leaving me alone, for being a safe space.

Glancing back toward the Blue Wharf house, I remember how I used to get scared from a creak in the foundation or water gushing through pipes and would rush into Olly's room and fling myself into the bottom bunk bed. It was our forever-fortress, blankets hung like tapestried walls created our own world filled with pillows and stuffed plush toys. Knowing Olly was asleep on the top bunk me made me feel safe.

I wish I could feel that now, but Olly isn't my safe space anymore.

"I don't need to drink," I say resolutely. "I choose not to."

He smiles, but it flickers. "The worst part of having a parent in the system is we somehow get stuck in a prison of our minds."

"Trapped in the past," I say, not sure if it's an addition to his thought or a question.

"Past, present, future," he says.

"How do you break free? I'm so tired of holding on to how bitter and angry and sad I've been. It's exhausting."

"I'll let you know when it happens for me." He gazes up at the stars. "The way I see it, unlike our folks who are involuntarily locked up and forgotten, we're not. We can do something about it."

"Fight back?"

"Exactly. Not everyone can. Awareness is key. Of self, circumstance. Privilege. And how much you can withstand."

I can wallow in this prison, or I can bust down the walls. I remember what Ritchie said, about how people tell themselves the stories they want to believe to get through the day. Is letting go of the hurt and pain and choosing myself another form of storytelling? I don't want to tell myself a bedtime story so I can sleep at night. I want to be proud of who I am. What I've done. I don't want to be angry anymore.

Hunter infiltrates my thoughts. He manipulated me, destroyed me, and then apologized and said he loved me so he could fuck me. He always blamed me for everything and I never realized it before, but it's the same thing Dad used to do to Mom. Tell her she was "crazy" when he'd leave for days on end and return like it was nothing. Or when she found that bra she eventually bought Dad's excuse to keep the peace. I wonder what he told her about Tyler. Now I feel guilty for every horrible thing I've ever said to her. The strength she must've had to endure.

Olly said Dad knew about Tyler, and he wanted Olly and Mom to keep it secret. If true, I have to confront it and separate the man who loved me from the one who hid his son away, emotionally abused Mom, and defrauded a bank, causing dozens of people, including Becca's uncle, to lose everything. This is the first time I've admitted his guilt, and it makes me lightheaded, unable to breathe for fear of breaking down completely.

"You okay?" Javy offers me a sleeve to wipe the tears from my cheeks.

"Trying to figure a way out of my head." My voice is mucusy and thick.

"You got the key." He jangles his car keys.

"One last favor. Can you drop me off down the road?"

As Javy pulls into the Lonely Bear, and I think about Chef and our conversation the other day, I blurt out, "I wanna get more involved with ADVOCATE." Tearing down the walls built by a corrupt justice system is something *worth* doing. Seeing Javy more would be an added bonus. "What's next?"

He raises his brows but doesn't miss a beat. "We need to think about what we can do to raise money for Chris, the kid we were talking about at the last meeting in child protective services. No lawyer. His mom is struggling to make ends meet. If you have any ideas, bring them. We've had luck in the past with local businesses sponsoring our events, but the wells are running dry. Come to the next meeting, and the fundraising and street team meetings too."

"I'll help do it all." I want to take his hand, but I'm not ready. "Thank you."

"For what?" Javy asks.

Everything. "For bringing me home. And listening."

"Sometimes all we need is to know someone's listening."

The Lonely Bear is still.

Except the humming crickets.

There's a bite to the breeze, so I unlock Sheila's apartment and run to the room I used to sleep in and grab the first hoodie I spot.

Of course it's one of Olly's with his favorite *Star Wars* character Ahsoka Tano screen-pressed to the front. He's such a nerd.

For a second, I forget I hate him.

Dark skies fade to lighter blues as the sun spills over lush green mountains. This is my favorite time of the morning, though I'm rarely up this early to feel it. It's like the entire world is waking up at the exact same time: the trees stretch out their limbs, searching for warmth from the sun's rays, and the birds sing to each other, calling out from their nests to let us know they've been waiting to take flight again, and the breaks on the beach are soft like yawns. Dad loved mornings like these, where he could wear a long-sleeved shirt and baseball cap and take the boat out on the glassy lake.

My legs carry me directly to cabin 120.

Tyler's room.

I plop down on the plastic basket chair right outside his door and my leg begins to bounce restlessly. *Don't be a little bitch, knock!* My leg bounces higher, faster.

When I start to chew on my chipping nails, I spasm forward and knock.

No answer.

I knock again, this time a little louder.

Nothing.

Okay, now I'm impatient. I resist my natural impulses to pound the door and yell, "Wake up, bitch!" But I *do* knock a little louder and call out his name.

Nada.

Cupping my hands against the glass, I peer into the window, smashing my cheek against it to get a better look, but he's not inside.

Maybe he's hiding in the bathroom because he doesn't want to see me. I wouldn't blame him.

I take advantage of the early morning quiet when all the guests' kids are still sleeping and head down to the lake. The sun reflects off the glassy water and although I'm freezing, it makes me want to take a dip. I fling my shoes into the sand and wade into the water, which is warmer than the air, until I'm ankle-deep. I close my eyes, feel the smooth sand between my toes, and sink down ever so slightly until I'm part of the lake.

A moment of perfection in a sea of shit.

Something splashes in the water near the rocks. It's probably a beaver, but it's followed by a hollow thwack like a body slapping the surface of the water. Figures there'd be someone here to destroy the zen I'm trying to summon.

My eyes open enough to see a fully clothed Tyler floating in the water like a crocodile stealthily stalking his prey. Or, in his case, trying to escape a larger predator.

"Tyler?"

He stops moving. Then stands up, his basketball jersey and loose fit jeans dripping, and turns around. "Oh. Hey. What's up?" he says, not at all suspicious and jumpy.

"Trying to be zen."

"How's that working out?"

"Meditation is garbage. What're you doing?"

"Going for a swim." He looks down at himself, sheepishly. "I fell in."

I nod and a laugh escapes me.

He waddles over to me the way a baby with a full diaper might. "I've been sitting on the rocks for I don't know how long, thinking."

"Anything good?"

"I'm heading back to Pennsylvania," he blurts.

There's a pull inside, like a child stretching a ball of almost dried-out Play-Doh; knead too hard and it crumbles completely.

"I don't think you can swim all the way back to PA," I say, swallowing sadness.

He chortles, fake as hell. "Didn't think you'd want to see me. I thought I could be stealth and get away. My feet had other plans." He animates his hands to illustrate his epic downfall.

"So you went full-on crocodile to hide from me?"

"Pretty much." There's that goofy smile again. I never noticed before, but it's eerily similar to the one Dad had when he'd read Olly and me bedtime stories and did the voices of the characters in the books.

"If it makes you feel better," I say. "I sat in front of your cabin for a good ten minutes this morning like an idiot, and you never would've known if I didn't tell you. So, even?"

He wrings out his soaking-wet shirt, hesitation pulling at the skin around his eyes.

"I figured you were at Lia's."

He looks at the ground.

"What happened?"

"We had a fight in the Uber on our way back here." He looks like he's trying to figure out what to say. "She didn't get why we lied to you. She said she couldn't trust me." He swings an invisible baseball bat and drops his arms in defeat.

"For what it's worth, same." I purse my lips.

He shifts awkwardly in his wet clothes.

"Olly usually keeps a change of clothes in Sheila's boat," I say, hoping he won't say he has clothes in his cabin and split, which would be way more logical.

I want him to stay.

He's squinting from the early morning orange sun, but also rolling his eyes. "Olly might kill me if I wear his clothes. I've already done a good job of ruining his life."

I make a jerk-off motion with my hand. "Please. Olly is so dramatic he can power all of Times Square on his hysterics alone."

"Runs in the family." He sticks out his tongue. His head sways a little bit, something he does when he's contemplating what to do next. "Race ya to Sheila's boat?" He dives into the water, splashing me, and shoots toward the dock.

I rip the hoodie up over my head, toss it onto my shoes, and dive in after him.

The cool water frees something inside of me. My feet and arms propel me forward, and I cut through the water effortlessly. I'm weightless. Nothing is holding me back anymore. Breaking through the surface and gulping up air feels like drinking cold water after being in the sun all day, but as soon as my lungs fill, I'm back below the surface again, passing Tyler's slow Pennsylvania ass, and coming up on the back of Sheila's boat. I use my upper body strength to leverage myself up to the swim platform so I can let down the ladder for Tyler. Something tells me he needs it.

He bobs up and water sputters out of his mouth. He does the wet-hair toss golden retriever boys do to shake the excess water off their heads. Do they not realize they look like dogs? Especially Tyler, paddling rapidly to stay afloat.

"What took you so long?"

"Ha ha," he tries to say, but water flows into his mouth and he spits.

I point toward the ladder, and he takes to it quickly, panting as he climbs.

"You're fast." He drops next to me. "Clothes weighed me down."

"Sure, sure." I debate whether or not to joke around with him or get straight to the point. Time isn't on my side, so might as well get to it. "So you're really leaving?"

He stretches back behind him and rests on the covered seat. "It's time."

"Is it? We barely started."

"Maybe it would have been different if you knew about me from the jump."

He looks out toward the water, his eyes following a seagull dipping with the wind.

I wonder what home is like for him. If he has a favorite ice cream shop, or if he and his friends from high school have a secret place they go to get high. Will he feel relieved to go back? Lake George is all I've ever known, for better or worse. Mostly worse. It's messy and complicated and mostly awful, but it's a part of me, or maybe I've become a part of it. I want to know Tyler that way. Which probably never could have happened from the start.

"It wouldn't have been different, because I didn't want to know," I admit, the words getting lodged in my throat. "I told Olly not to tell me. I knew whatever secret he was holding onto would ruin my image of our dad. I couldn't deal." My feet splash the water. The world feels both larger and smaller than it once did.

He takes a deep breath and pulls out a soggy photograph.

I immediately recognize myself with Olly, and what is an unmistakably young Tyler. "I *wanted* to know you. And Olly wanted me to know you too, for what it's worth."

The little girl in the photograph slyly staring back at me is a virtual stranger, a reminder of everything I've lost. I wish I could reach out and hug her and tell her to guard her heart. A tear runs down my cheek and mixes with the lake water.

One question gnaws at me like gnats on sweaty skin. "So my dad, our dad, didn't want to have anything to do with you? I don't get it." It's like swallowing broken glass realizing Dad wasn't perfect.

He shrugs. "I've stopped wondering. I'm sadder I didn't get to grow up with you and Olly. He denied me *that*."

"I thought parents were supposed to be *good*." I'm starting to understand why Olly wanted to protect me. "How can they turn into the people who hurt you the most?"

"I wish I knew." Tyler smiles softly, but it flickers then fades like an old neon sign. "I'm sorry I hurt you, too." Then he unravels. Tells me everything. About his letter, the emails with Olly, and how he felt like Olly was starting to become a sibling. "Is it possible to love someone who doesn't want you?"

I'm not sure if he's talking about Dad or Olly.

"Olly doesn't let people in. Must be a twin thing." I chuckle, but he doesn't. "He wouldn't have gone through everything he did if he didn't want you in his life."

"I don't know if I believe that."

"I'm sorry," I say. "For everything our dad put you through." I let Tyler's version of Dad sink in, like kicked-up sand settling to the bottom of the lake. *Good* people don't hide their secret children away and lie to their families until the day they die. If he could do that, what else was Dad lying about?

"He may have been my father, but he wasn't my dad," Tyler says. I remember what he told me about his stepdad.

I rest my head on his shoulder. He awkwardly tries to side-hug me.

It's not perfect. Not in sync like Olly and I used to be. But it doesn't have to be. It's distinctly Alex and Tyler.

We sit in silence for a long while as the rest of the world wakes up. Small fishing boats emerge from other docks, plane off around the bend, and come back.

Then, for a second, the breeze stops blowing and the waves don't crash and no engines roar, and it feels like the lake is holding its breath. For us.

I don't want to move from this spot. If I do, everything will change.

Part of me feels like if I lose him, I'll lose another piece of myself.

The sun is higher in the sky than it should be.

Hopping off the boat, I say, "I get why you're leaving. But I wish you wouldn't."

I speed-walk so he doesn't see me cry.

Later that day, when I check my phone after the lunch shift, there's a long text from Tyler:

Alex,
When I mailed the letter to you and Olly last year, I hoped to find a family. I should never have lied to you, but Olly did what he

thought was best. A lesson I learned from playing basketball is bones may break, but they mend stronger if you treat them properly. I think that applies to family too.

Thanks for the goodbye at the lake. It was like a full-circle moment for me, since the first time we met was at the beach. I think I came here looking for something more real than an old photograph. It's easy to make something real, but hard to make something last. Relationships that last take time. Maybe it wasn't in the cards for the three of us to get it together. I get to decide what's real, like a night spent on the back of a boat having an existential conversation. For a little while, it felt like I could be part of something with you and Olly, and it would have been nice for all three of us to figure it out together.

For what it's worth, I'm happy I got to know you. You're stronger than you think you are. But you don't need me to tell you that.

Love,
Tyler Dell

THE END OF SUMMER

OLLY BRUCKE

I start recording. "Who am I?"

My face is framed in shadows against a dark backdrop. I've turned my bedroom into a small studio, two cameras rigged on either side to capture every emotion.

But I can't find the emotional core.

I've been throwing myself into making this movie, ever since Tyler moved back to Pennsylvania and Alex stopped talking to me. *Again.* I should be used to this by now, but nope. Consumes me like the flu.

"Everything comes down to my father." I sound so robotic, rehearsed.

This morning, before he left to go home, Khal said to me, "The reason this documentary isn't working is because you're trying to prove something to your dad. Tell *your* story, Ol."

Ms. R was right: I *am* Luke Skywalker walking into the Cave of Evil, headstrong and believing I'm ready to face Darth Vader. Like Luke, who was so focused on becoming a Jedi he couldn't see the biggest blocks in that path were his own shortcomings and fears, I haven't been able to see past the tip of my camera lens.

Vader tried to coerce Luke to the Dark Side. But Luke's destiny was the *choice* he made to be good. To believe his father still had good in him instead of choosing power. But it's not like Luke is some ultimate good either. He's a perfect gray of contradiction guided by the knowledge of choice.

I had a choice. I chose to keep Dad's secrets and treat Tyler like he was expendable.

I resume. "I carry the burden of my father's action. And I keep coming back to this one question: Am *I* worthy of redemption?"

I stare into the lens until it's no longer a lens, but a mirror.

A tear falls, and I look away.

That's enough of that for one day. I settle in front of my computer and open up all the footage I've compiled. I sift through fresh reels, clips of old home videos, and news stories about Dad on my laptop, piecing together a supercut of my life.

Home video footage of me and Alex playing in piles of colorful leaves in the yard with Dad.

News footage of Dad getting arrested.

Alex and I dancing to aughties pop music on Dad's boat as he laughs in the background.

A female newscaster's voice over zoomed-in shots of Dad's face, highlighted red and blue from police cars.

Alex in the kitchen, covered in caked-on flour, pinching dough with Mom while Dad steals freshly baked cookies.

Aerial footage of the Blue Wharf house from a helicopter after his company shuttered.

Me, at six, sitting on Dad's lap as he teaches me how to drive his boat.

Protests from angry ex-workers outside of Dad's office building.

Dad giving Alex and me a push in a sled down a steep, snowy mountain overlooking Lake George, saying, "Hold on tight, you're in for a ride!"

Tyler on the boat, laughing with Khal.

An establishing shot of Tyler and Alex on Ritchie's boat during the bonfire, moonlight illuminating their silhouettes.

Shirtless Tyler Indiana Jones*ing up the mountain to the waterfall.*

Tyler in Ashleigh's car on the way to the Closet, laughing with Alex.

Something Dad said to me the last time I saw him infiltrates my thoughts: *"Don't open doors you can't close, kid."*

My mind flips through scenes from my favorite movies and lands on *Star Wars, Episode VIII: The Last Jedi* where Rey is in the Mirror Cave, much like Luke in *Empire Strikes Back*, looking for answers about who she is, and, after searching, she comes face-to-face with her greatest fear: only she can define herself and choose her path forward.

I think about the last thing I said to Tyler: *I knew you'd leave. Bruckes always do.* A tear streams down my cheek. Dad left us repeatedly, unapologetically, and when he died, he left me with no path forward. No way to figure out who I am in his wake.

After that visit at the prison, I ignored his calls and had all emails forwarded to a locked folder marked VADER I haven't looked at since.

Curiosity gets the best of me now.

There is one unread email, from the day he died, no subject line, and the only preview is,

Hey Pal.

My hands shake, unable to bring myself to open it.

This is why I make movies. It's the greatest escape I have. The only escape. Alex, Tyler, and I have had to conquer a galaxy of our father's real-life secrets, a lake as deep as an ocean. How could we ever have real relationships with each other when he designed it so we couldn't? Everything was determined by him, to protect himself, while sacrificing us.

Dad sought to control *our* narratives. He always told me everything before he told anything to Alex. He drilled in me the need to protect Alex, make sure she wore "appropriate" clothes to prison. He brought me with him first to visit the shack he made us move into. It was like he wanted me to be him, to take over his role when he went away, to be a "man," be tough, "take care of things," and I internalized his heteronormative crap. He made me responsible for her, instead of sitting alongside her and being there for her. Alex deserves a real sibling, and I have to try to make things right. To equalize us. To not try to control her narrative the way Dad wanted. All of this has been holding us back and kept Alex in this box of helpless little girl, damsel in distress.

But she is not helpless; she's the badass hero of her own story, even if she doesn't know it yet.

And I am not my father. My fault is imagining myself as the main character in everyone else's story, and trying to play architect, like Khal said. I've been so in my head about trying to create another docu-style film, this time about my family, that I haven't considered making something entirely fictional to process and tell my story.

I need to create my own Cave of Evil, to find my way out.

Fingers to keypad, I write.

I don't have an exact plot yet, but I'm thinking it's a mostly silent film, relying on raw white noise and natural sounds.

Three characters, two boys, one girl, lost in a cave trying to find their way out. Each ends up confronting a mirrored reflection, a trial, and what they see and how they confront their fears will determine whether they leave the cave. I type out the treatment until my fingers bleed and my ass aches from sitting.

———————————

Heart racing, I type THE END on my script, scroll back to the first page, and stare:

SUBMISSION: Saratoga Film Festival

THE GREAT ESCAPE
Written and Directed by
Olly Brucke

After a full week of all-nighters, I have a script.

A path forward.

A story.

My story, not my father's.

I'll never get an apology from him, so it's time to leave the prison in my mind, once and for all. When someone is alive, there are infinite opportunities to fix what broke. But once they're gone, so is their potential to make things right. I've been mourning him, us, for *years*, but what I'm really mourning is the time we all lost.

ALEX BRUCKE

Late afternoon August sun blares down on me as I linger on June and Javy's front stoop after the latest ADVOCATE meeting.

"Great ideas tonight, Alex," June says. "We're well on our way to being able to help Chris and his family." At the start of tonight's meeting, she told us fundraising had hit a wall. It's been hard to find a lawyer willing to take on Chris's case pro bono, especially because he'll be eighteen next year, so there's no real "urgency," and his mom is struggling to pay bills. But people are still willing to donate time. I had been talking with Sheila and she agreed to let us throw a fundraiser on the Lonely Bear's grounds next weekend. Sheila's inviting all the privileged rich folks who "live" on the lake seasonally, donating food from the restaurant, and pledged a free weekend at the resort in the fall for a raffle. We've secured giveaways from local boutiques and shops in the Village and Bolton Landing. Javy and the other ADVOCATE members were on board, and we spent the rest of the evening working out the logistics.

"You did good, you hear me?" June grabs my shoulders and squeezes. She smells like the giant pot of linguini with sweet fire-roasted tomatoes, pungent garlic, and clams, giving it a hint of fresh ocean water, she made the group for dinner. It nourishes me all over again. "Call me if you need anything. And love the new blonde hair on you. Very natural, beautiful." Her grip is strong as she wraps her arms around me and hugs me tightly. I lean into it. Hard. When she's done, she taps my cheek in a "good kid" kind of way and eyes Javy before slipping back inside.

I tousle my hair, and it spills effortlessly over my shoulders. Going blonde again was a small act, but it feels more *me*.

"I'm impressed." Javy sits on the top step near the front door. He tips his chin toward me like he's the lead in one of those old black-and-white movies Olly used to watch. "The way you organized everyone in there and got the ball rolling on the fundraiser. Gives the new kids hope. Next up, you actually have to share *your* story."

Don't get me wrong. It's a nice sentiment. But goddess, I hate that since I've been coming to these meetings—nearly two months now—there have been two new members. Sometimes it's hard to think anything can get better when there are constant flesh-and-blood reminders that the criminal justice system is corrupt, unjust, irreparable. Yet inevitable. Javy says it fuels him to study law and community activism to make change. His optimism is like the flint of a lighter. A few clicks, a spark from him, and I'm aflame.

"Hey," he says, noticing my faraway glances. "You're doing good things here." When I nod, he asks, "Can I hug you?" His asks of consent are *everything*. I nod, and he scoops me in his arms.

"Thanks to you and June," I say once he lets go. "You know she checks in with me once a day?" I could go on and on about June and how her warm, energetic phone calls every morning not only get me ready for the day but keep me focused. When Tyler split, I told her what happened and she offered to be my unofficial sobriety sponsor. She gives me strength not to give in to the urge to drink or smoke, and she always asks if I'm staying on top of summer school so I don't let Ms. R down, and maybe can graduate.

"She's got many 'kids.'" He makes air quotes with his fingers. "Hard to keep up."

"I'm her favorite, though." I wag my tongue at him.

"Runs in the family, I guess." He jingles his car keys. "You ready?" He hops up in front of me and holds both hands out toward me. I don't move, so he reaches for one of my hands, and I let it go limp like a dead fish. It flops to my side, and I let my whole body slump toward the ground. I try hard not to laugh, but a snicker slips out. "Oh, she's playing games." He rubs his chin, thinking of his next move. "I guess you give me no choice." His head ducks and he moves like a bull about to ram me, but instead he grabs my legs and upper body and hoists me over his shoulders.

He's laughing too hard, which I've learned physically weakens him, so he puts me down pretty quickly.

"Take me someplace?" I ask. "Anywhere but home."

"You hungry?" he asks.

The hot orange skies are the perfect backdrop for Butter Together, a 1950s-style diner with a neon yellow sign in the shape of melting butter on top of a waffle.

"This is for the soul." I follow him to the open counter on one side of the building.

The menu is simple, written in swirly white chalk: waffles.

"What's the best here?" I ask.

He sucks in a breath. "Everything."

"Order for me. Decisions are not my thing."

"Could've fooled me. All that talk during the meeting. Everything you organized with your boss. Sounds pretty decisive."

"When I know I'm right, sure." I think about Olly and bite my lip.

"Always a puzzle." Javy shakes his head, turning to the girl behind the counter, who can't be more than fifteen. "What's up, Jaz?" They fist bump. He turns to me. "Family friend."

"Haven't seen you in a minute," she says.

"Been busy." He rocks on his heels. "Give us two Cocoa Butter Specials and two cups of water."

A few minutes later, Jaz hands over two plates, each with a hot, crispy waffle topped with a perfect mound of melty chocolate ice cream.

We perch on top of a picnic table overlooking a small creek.

I'm hypnotized by the waffle's beauty. "Wreck me."

He laughs. "It's impressive. But it tastes better."

He's not wrong. It's brown and crisp on the outside, but warm and soft inside, and it's coated with a layer of butter. The ice cream is luscious and velvety, super dark, but not bitter, the right amount of sweetness to complement the salty notes of the waffle. Its recipe is simple, its execution perfect. The ultimate in comfort food made with love. Reminds me of why I loved to cook in the first place, and why I'm so passionate about ADVOCATE now: it's exciting, fulfilling, comforting.

I don't stop until it's gone, then I try to steal Javy's.

"Good, huh?" Javy hands over his scraps, which I polish off easily.

"*Ridiculous!*" I wipe away chocolate from my lips. "Thanks for bringing me here."

"I wanted to ever since the night you took me to your old house and we sat on the docks," he says. "My pops used to bring me every Sunday. It was our thing. I knew no matter what happened that week at school, we would get our waffles. It was our time, you know? We talked about life and he cared about what I was going through at school and whatnot. Ever since he went away, it hurts to come back."

"Is this your first time back?"

He nods, then turns to look at me. "I drive by it all the time. Friends pick up food for me sometimes. Can never bring myself to get out of the car."

"Why now?" I ball the napkin in my hand, fiddling with it.

"June says we have to live." He clears his throat. "Can I ask you something?"

"Of course." I grind my teeth nervously.

"I figured you would at some point, but you *never* talk about your siblings. Why?"

Ignorance is bliss, Javy.

"Look, I'm not saying you need to talk about that part of you because that's your thing to deal with in your own way when you want, but I want you to know if you need to talk, I'm all ears." He smiles. "Or we could eat more waffles."

A ladybug lands on my knee and crawls across my skin.

"Sorry, I shouldn't have said anything," he says.

"You're right. I've avoided Olly and Tyler since Tyler left." The ladybug lifts its little red shell and its translucent wings flutter for a second before it continues the crawl up my thigh. "I can't help it, I'm mad. Too mad. I can't get past it."

"Have you talked to Olly?" Javy leans back, using his arms as kickstands for his upper body, propping him up against the table.

"About Tyler?" I shake my head. "He's tried, but I'm not ready to hear him out."

"Why not?" Javy asks.

Good question. "Everyone in my family protects themselves. I have to look out for myself now."

"What about Tyler?"

I don't know. As much as I was pissed that Tyler lied to me, I get why he did what he did. But I lost the chance to get to know him. My gaze fixes on the ladybug.

Noting my silence, he takes another approach. "Have you tried to contact him?"

I shake my head.

"Why not?"

I shrug.

He exhales so long and so loud it's obvious he wants to say something.

"What?" I ask. "Say it."

He sucks his teeth. "Well, first, you have every right to be fuming mad at everyone for what happened. But. Your anger *miiiight* be misplaced. From what you told me, your dad is the one who lied *and* made Olly lie. He was the one who didn't want to be involved in Tyler's life. I don't know what it's like to have a brother I didn't know about, but if I did, and I was in Olly's shoes, I probably would have done the same thing. Second, you're avoiding talking to Olly and reaching out to Tyler because if you did, you'd *really* have to deal with all the anger you have toward your dad."

My mouth is dry. "Maybe."

"It's okay to be angry but realize where that comes from. I didn't realize I had my own anger to deal with in regard to my pops, too. The what ifs. Avoiding doesn't help. Give him a chance." Javy moves as close as he can without touching me and it's the most intimate, vulnerable feeling I've ever experienced. "It's got to be exhausting, running all the time. Confront that shit. Eat a waffle. Sometimes, it's the best we can do."

OLLY BRUCKE

Past the Narrows, across from the Mother Bunch Islands, just beyond the oasis of Steere Island, is a little known but deep cavern nestled into a mountainside where waves lick the rocks.

It's perfect.

After "hiring" (aka paying them in free boat rides and Martha's ice cream) three young kids and a father to act in the roles, maxing out Mom's credit card for rental film equipment, and hustling for a solid week of filming all day, every day—thanks to Sheila giving me time off—it's finished. Sure, I have to edit in special effects, smooth out the transitions, and add in some haunting music to increase tension and suspense and create the perfect mood.

But I love it.

The Great Escape, a cautionary tale of three siblings lost and separated in a cave, each encountering their own trial, and having to confront their fears without their father.

It's the perfect follow-up to *Barefoot*. I can taste the win and smell the grant money, seeds for an eventual move to Los Angeles.

Academy Award worthy, no question.

Golden Globes are a shoo-in.

Cannes doesn't stand a chance!

At least first place at Saratoga material.

And the ending! It's a risk, and I have no idea if I pulled it off, but it's objectively good. I *think*. If anything, it's given me clarity on what I need to do with Alex and Tyler.

Still, I'm terrified as I hit play on the file in the editing bay on my laptop.

FADE IN:

EXT. OPENING OF A CAVE—ESTABLISHING—DUSK

At the edge of the lake, waves crash on ancient rock, splashing up and toward the cave's dark entrance. Hot orange sun illuminates the glittering stone, each crack and crevice becoming more visible as we zoom in closer, pushing in until the opening of the cave swallows the shot and turns 180 degrees so the outline of the entrance of the cave frames the lens from the inside, bright sunlight quickly dimming until it's pitch black.

CUT TO:

EXT. ISOLATED BEACH—AERIAL VIEW—

ESTABLISHING—DAWN

A metal rowboat rocks back and forth gently with the waves, brushing up against a sandy, natural shore. Inside, a father sets sail with three children, two boys, one older, one younger, and a girl, each eager to be on the water and go exploring with gifts bestowed upon them by their father. The youngest boy has a shovel and a pail. The girl carries a rosy-pink pair of goggles. Both sit in the bow in the boat, while the older boy, who was given nothing, sits behind his father, out of sight.

CUT TO:

EXT. THE CAVE—DAYTIME

The bow of the metal boat taps into a rock. The father motions for the boy and girl to settle down as he grabs the dock line and hops onto a rocky landing. Once the children are safe on land, the father gets back in the boat and unties it.

FATHER

I'll be right back. *Don't* go inside the cave.

I'm breathing heavily as a tear falls down my cheek. I wish he'd never left us.

ALEX BRUCKE

Windows down, Ashleigh and I scream-sing Lorde's "Supercut" while mimicking the bonkers Kristen Wiig and Maya Rudolph choreography from our favorite classic comedy, *Bridesmaids*, as Ashleigh coasts through backroads. Déjà vu of all the times we'd dance and Mom would shout for us to stop. In the backseat Lia glares at us as she records us in our natural habitat.

A text from Javy breaks my intense focus. **Can't wait to see you tonight!**

I show the girls, and they immediately start making fun of me.

Javy sends another text. **You bringing Olly?**

I send back a grimacing emoji because I still haven't spoken to him, then slide my phone into my back pocket.

"I am ready for this ADVOCATE meeting!" Lia shouts. Both have been coming to the last two ADVOCATE meetings with me to help plan the fundraiser for Chris.

"What's on the agenda tonight?" Ashleigh asks.

"Finalizing details. I went over logistics with Sheila and Chef today, timing and food and setup. We're doing a final count of all the vendors who agreed to participate and all the giveaways. Oh, and I got Noah to convince Thot Process to play and some other drag queens he knows to do some stand-up and lip-synching."

"I love Petty White," Ashleigh says brightly. "Dusk will be so excited."

"If only we got to see her that night," Lia says under her breath. We've hung out nearly every day since, but neither one of us brings Tyler up. I wonder if she talks to him.

Sweat droplets pool at my hairline. I pull down the mirror. "I look like fresh hell after being in the kitchen all day."

"Javy would like you even if you showed up wearing a potato sack," Lia says.

"It's beyond obvious. When're you guys gonna make it official?" Ashleigh asks.

Javy is possibility, a gulp of fresh air after swimming underwater too long. But it's too soon. We haven't kissed. I don't even know if he likes me. All I know is he feels like a center of gravity. "After Hunter, I need to be with myself for a while."

Ashleigh chokes at the sound of Hunter's name.

News broke that the district attorney is not pursuing a case against Hunter for supplying Becca's drugs, and the judge gave him a hundred days of community service and court-ordered rehab for possession. Slap on the wrist for everything he's had a hand in. When I found out last night, I lost my shit. Broke my lamp in a rage. Wanted to drink, but instead threw myself into listing out everything I could do for Chris and this fundraiser to make sure no stone went unturned. I couldn't call Javy because of how ashamed I felt even telling him.

"I can't believe Hunter got off," Ashleigh says.

"Nothing happens to the Hunters of the world," Lia says, exhaustion in her voice. "The ultimate in straight white male privilege."

My insides twist at the guilt and anger I feel for enabling him, for letting him manipulate me, for ever caring about him and thinking he could change. For being there when Becca overdosed and doing nothing to stop her. I'll spend a lifetime repairing the damage to myself and others.

"You have to drop off homework with my mom before we head down to Albany, right?" Ashleigh asks, adjusting her rearview mirror.

I nod and Lia asks, "How's all that going?"

I groan. "Intense. Only two weeks left, thank goddess. A whole year's worth of shit in six weeks is a lot. If I pass everything, I'll be invincible."

"Someone once told me, 'Bones may break, but they mend stronger,'" Lia adds.

A wave of sadness washes over me. Tyler wrote that to me in his goodbye text. I lean my head against the glass and feel Lia's hand on my arm.

"You talking to Olly yet?" Lia asks.

"No," Ashleigh answers for me.

"Why not?" Lia asks. "Oh, I forgot, stubbornness runs strong in your family."

"Ouch, bitch," I sneer.

"Did I lie?" Lia asks.

I roll my eyes.

"What are you waiting for?" Ashleigh asks as she turns down her street.

"Well, he's been so busy making his latest film, I didn't wanna distract. He's on deadline," I say.

"Sounds like an excuse," Lia says, and Ashleigh hums a loud "Mm-hmm!"

Mom's car is in Ashleigh's driveway. "What's my mom doing here?"

"No idea," Ashleigh says.

"Mess. I'm waiting in the car," Lia says, waving us away.

Ashleigh pushes open the front door. "Mom? You home?"

"In here, Ash," Ms. R calls out from the kitchen.

Mom and Ms. R are sitting around the island sipping coffee and sharing a package of Mom's favorite Italian cookies, the kind she loves to dip into her coffee so the flavor drenches the biscuit, effectively turning it into mush. Ms. R doesn't waste time getting each of us a mug, and I go right for a biscuit.

"What's going on?" I ask, mouth full of soft cookie.

"We're having coffee," Mom says as if no time has passed. "Telling Amelia how special my surprise birthday breakfast was yesterday. My talented chef daughter *actually* did something nice for her mother."

I force a smile. Guilt pools in my gut because the truth is, I forgot her birthday, so I improvised. I'm trying, but most days, it feels impossible.

"I was telling your mom how amazing you're doing in summer school. I got a report today from all your teachers, and they're blown away."

"Alex always was the smart one," Mom says.

Uneasiness stirs in my chest; I'm not used to compliments, and I don't know if I deserve it, but I shove the feeling down.

"That's why I'm here." I dig through my backpack and hand her a packet of work. "I forgot it this morning."

Ms. R takes it and flips through it quickly. "Quite a lot."

"Yeah, well, I fucked up most of this last year, so."

Mom chokes on her coffee. "Alex. Watch your mouth."

"On that note, we need to head out," I say. "Thanks, Ms. R."

Ashleigh hugs her mom, and it makes me feel slightly rotten I don't hug mine, but we're not there yet.

I'm about to step outside when Mom grabs my shoulder. "Can we talk?" she asks.

"I'm gonna wait with Lia," Ashleigh says. "Bye, Mrs. Brucke!"

I sling my backpack over my shoulder. "What's up, Mom?"

"How's it going with your group, ADVOCATE?"

"Fine."

"That's nice you're bringing Ashleigh and Lia," she says.

"Yep."

"What about Olly?"

"Nope."

Her eyes narrow and she puts her hands on her hips. "I'm sure he'd like to go."

I bet he would. "Whatever."

"Can I get a little more than a one-word answer?" Mom is hovering between concerned and battle-ready.

I can easily push her off that tightrope, but I'm too tired to fight, so I'll leave.

She takes a deep breath and says, "Wait, please. I'm trying."

I stop and wait. It feels like I'm dangling on the edge of a cliff.

"What I'm trying to say is, I'm sorry."

To say I'm stunned by her admission would be the understatement of the century. Olly's the one who gets the apologies from Mom. I get lectured.

"I don't think I've been the best mom I can be," she admits.

Mom is killing it with the revelations today.

"Olly is helping me see I wasn't there for you kids in the way you needed. I did what I thought was best. I thought working my ass off and providing for you both was enough because it was all I could manage. I realize now, seeing the rift between you and Olly, I didn't do enough to protect you. To be there for you and listen. And hold you." Mom has been trapped in her own prison, one of self-preservation. And while it's no excuse for leaving Olly and me to fend for ourselves, an apology is all I've ever wanted.

She takes a step forward.

I fight my instinct to back away.

"It's not enough, but I hope one day you'll forgive me. Because I love you—and Olly—more than anything. It kills me that I failed you. I failed you." She repeats it until it sinks in, truly sinks in. She tries to hug me and I hesitate. She's a bit shorter than I am, but she still hugs as fiercely as she did when I was small and would fall and skin my knee, like I'm the only person in the world who matters to her, and only she can make the pain go away. I bury my face into her shoulder. She strokes the back of my head and says, "I'm here now. Everything will be okay. I'm sorry." It's like a skinned knee—there's a residual sting, but I can walk, even if I'm a bit more cautious with where I step now.

I don't say anything because words can't repair damage the way time can.

But it's a good start.

As I walk out of Ashleigh's house, I send Olly a text and exhale.

OLLY BRUCKE

On the first night of the Hot-Air Balloon Festival, I lead a blindfolded Khal through the launch field toward the balloon with bird silhouettes against stripes the colors of a vibrant Lake George sunset: hot pink, blood red, warm orange, golden yellow. Tonight, all the balloons are lifting off from the fields next to Battlefield Park in the Village. Hundreds of people are propped up on lawn chairs and stretched out on blankets to watch as the balloons sail above the lake. I stop walking and carefully position Khal so that he can see everything. Untying the blindfold, I study the muscles in his face, the way his cheeks redden and ball in excitement. His body is a lit rocket, ready to zoom into the atmosphere. He kisses me and thanks me, kisses and thanks, kisses and thanks, until we're both giddy with laughter. I point to our balloon, and he takes off, pulling me forward by the hand.

Khal is practically skipping, his steps lighter than I've seen in a long time. In four days, he'll be gone, off to college without me. But tonight, he's still here, with me, snapping photos of the balloons lined up in a row like they're round rolling clouds or exotic, colorful mountain ranges.

A floating staircase sits halfway up the basket at the base of our balloon, and I wait for Khal to go first. Our pilot, a short spitfire with choppy lavender hair and a tattoo creeping up her neck, offers her hand to Khal from the inside and he uses her strength to balance himself as he hops in. She introduces herself as Ace.

Once I'm inside, Ace goes over safety instructions, mostly to stay away from the burner and to not make sudden movements once we're midair, and Khal presses up against me, his heart beating so hard I absorb his nerves; as much as Khal loves the idea of hot-air balloons, he also has a slight fear of heights.

I lean into him, my hand on his back. "I got you."

"We've got perfect weather." Ace peers out over the lake with her hands shading her eyes. "Yesterday was windy as all get-out. Looks like the wind is coming from the south."

"Northern winds are never good," I say.

Dad always warned us about storms blowing in from the north. We've been stuck in a few storms out in the middle of the lake, and Dad always predicted them based on the change in wind direction.

"Exactly." She stares at us, furrowing her brows and shifting her weight from leg to leg. I almost step away from Khal because it's the look of someone figuring out we're together, and you never know how people will react. I shudder at how horrifying it would be to be trapped a bazillion feet in the air with someone queerphobic. "How long y'all cuties been together?"

Khal breathes a sigh of relief.

"Almost two years," I say.

"You're so young!" she says.

"But when you know, you know," Khal says. "You know?"

"I do." She places a hand over her heart. "You're safe." She flicks her wrist to show us a visible tattoo of two interlocking "female" symbols. "I'm getting the signal we can go. It's gonna be a little loud, but once we're high enough, you'll forget and won't hear a thing."

Slowly, the balloon lifts off the ground, and we glide effortlessly above the heads of onlookers. Higher and higher, we float above the dark sapphire waters. Peering out over the rim of the basket at the vast expanse of trees and mountains and boats zipping across waves, I am finally flying.

Khal moves in closer to me and we drift together against the backdrop of a golden sun. "This is incredible, right, babe?" He turns to look at me. His hand grazes the peach fuzz of my newly shaved head—when I wrapped production on my film, I decided it was time for a fresh buzzcut, to prune out the bad dye job and allow my ashy blonde roots to grow.

Up this high, magic exists. I can see so far in every direction, and the land stretches endlessly before us. From here, Lake George isn't the town I grew up in; it's a collection of houses and people and memories. Beyond that? Possibility. *Khal.*

Khal *is* magic.

I sneak a glance at Ace, but she's busying herself so we can be "alone" as we glide over the lake.

I nuzzle my nose against his.

"With you, I feel like I'm flying." He's all breath and breeze. He spreads his arms along the rim of the basket and hesitantly lifts them into the air. Khal is the type of guy who grips tightly to safety bars on roller coasters; he loves the thrill but needs the safety more.

"You are." I move behind him and run my hands along his arms and lift them higher. He hmms.

Once he's confident enough to leave his hands in the air by

himself, I wrap my arms around his chest and hold him tight. I rest my chin on his shoulder.

Khal cranes his neck to kiss my cheek. He closes his eyes and whispers, "I'm the king of the world." It's not a *Titanic*-level shout, yet it carries so much more power.

He deserves to feel like this every day. When he opens his eyes and looks up into mine, he says, "You look far away. Where are you? The movie? Tyler? Alex? Me leaving?"

"For once, none of the above." I take a deep breath. "Thinking about how I wouldn't have gotten through the last few years, especially the last month, without you. You gave me space when I needed it to finish my movie, you never judged me for anything I did with Tyler or Alex. If I could give you the entire world, shrink it down to the size of a marble and inflate it like a balloon, I would."

He looks out over the lake. "I'll take *this*."

All of this. The endless mountains like green blankets over sleeping giants, the possibility of magic, of leaving this town for something bigger and better. As cliché as it is, the edge of the horizon isn't as far as we'll go. He's shown me anything is possible.

He swivels until he faces me.

"You're missing the view," I say.

But he kisses me, pulls me into him, devours me. He buries his face in my chest and hugs me. "I wish we could stay up here forever."

"Every day with you is like flying," I say.

He makes a vomit sound. "Gross." Still, it makes him smile, the balls of his cheeks rosy and round.

"Do we have to go to Pennsylvania tomorrow?" I whine.

He shushes. "Be here now."

My phone vibrates.

"Careful," Ace says as I pull it out. "If it goes over the edge, it's gone."

"Speaking of going over the edge, Alex texted." I flash the screen to Khal. hey! would you mind helping me saturday and film the fundraiser? i'd really appreciate it. maybe we can talk after?

"See! Good things happen in hot-air balloons." Khal beams.

I hold him tighter. "Ana bahebak," I whisper.

"I love you too," he says back, his voice strong and clear.

Whatever happens next, my future with Khal exists way up here, where there are no limitations.

———

The next morning, Khal is pulling a Megan Rapinoe soccer jersey over his naked body when he asks, "What're you gonna say when you see him?"

The alarm clock behind him flashes five a.m.

The Great Escape is open on my laptop, the final edit saved and uploaded to the submission form along with the script and the rest of the materials on the Saratoga Film Festival's website. The deadline is today, but I can't bring myself to hit "submit." Even though it's a work of fiction, it's about Tyler and Alex and me, and it feels like tearing open my chest and spilling out my insides for the world to see. And that's terrifying.

I upload the short film to send to TyeDye1505@gmail.com and save it in my drafts.

I hold my breath for the entire five-hour trip to Swarthmore, Pennsylvania, where Tyler lives. It's a secluded neighborhood full of stately colonial homes. We park in front of a modest house with a white picket fence, a rusted soccer net in the yard, and a basketball hoop over the garage. I imagine a younger Tyler running around the yard, volleying the ball back and forth with his dad, and practicing his layups in the driveway. Maybe he'd take his bike into town and stop at the Archie Comics–themed ice cream parlor we drove past on the way here. I wonder if, had Dad brought us together, we would have done all those things together.

It feels too late in the day.

How do we make up for lost time? How do we find places that belong to us?

"This was a mistake," I say. "Tyler is better off without me."

Khal groans, but I can't blame him. It must be exhausting to deal with me. "Babe, I love you. I don't care if we drove all the way down here to turn around and go home, if that's what you want. But damn, Olly—" He puts his hand on my chest. "What's going to make you whole again?"

"Making everything right. But what if he thinks I'm no good, like our father—"

"Your dad has nothing to do with what happened between you and Tyler. What happens now is on you."

"That's what I'm afraid of."

Inhale through my nose, exhale through my mouth.

"Go backward you can't, forward only," he mimics Yoda.

I turn off the ignition and get out, but when we get to the front door, I hesitate.

"Move," Khal mumbles, lunging forward and knocking for me. He kisses my ear and shuffles behind me.

Tyler's voice calls out from other side of the door. "Got it, Mom!"

It swings open.

As does Tyler's mouth. He yells, "Mom, it's Sean. I forgot we were hanging out," and shuts the door behind him. This is pretty much in every movie I've ever seen where a character randomly shows up at the person's house they're estranged from. In one breath, he says, "*What'reyouguysdoinghere?*"

"Can we talk?"

Tyler folds his arms. "Talk."

"Here?"

He looks behind him. "Right. Let's go somewhere else."

Jughead's Shoppe is wall-to-wall Archie paraphernalia: shelves of mint condition Archie Comics, murals painted on walls and windows, toys—you name it, Jughead's has it. Mom would love this. Alex too. I order a Veronica on a cone, black cherry soft serve with a white chocolate swirl and edible red glitter dust. Khal takes his ice cream and sets off to explore town so we can be alone.

We sit by the window. Passersby wander aimlessly, mostly in packs, down the busy street. Tyler sips on a chocolate milkshake, waiting for me to say something. I want to lead with, "I'm sorry," but those two words don't seem to be enough.

Tyler's eyes are weighed down by dark circles. I realize I don't know him at all. That's not his fault. It's a fact, one I'd like the opportunity to change.

"When I first found out about you, I was angry at you." I pause, thinking about the short film I made. "Because if you existed, and our dad didn't want you, it meant I could never forgive him. I wasn't ready. I always thought once he got out of prison, we'd get to have a real relationship, one I wanted my whole life. Finding out about you complicated that, and then he died, and I let my fears control me."

Tyler flicks the lid on his cup with his index finger.

I gnaw on my bottom lip. "I felt guilty I didn't know you all those years, and jealous you grew up without our father. Like somehow you got the better end of the Brucke deal. I hated how you showed up and I lost control, yet I felt weirdly complete when you were around."

His eyes meet mine. "That's messed up." He cracks a smile. I'll take it.

"Right?" My voice is shaking, but I have to get this next part out. "I've been doing nothing but thinking since you left." Tears cloud my vision and I try to blink them away. "I made you feel like you didn't belong with us. But you do. You're our brother."

He wipes his wet eyes and takes a sip of his shake, but it's empty, so he sucks the excess from the bottom like a vacuum. "Can we get outta here?"

I follow him out of Jughead's down the main drag, but we don't talk. He takes out his phone and checks his messages.

"Lia? Are you guys . . . ?" I can't help myself.

"Damn. Nosy." He slides his phone back into his pocket. "We've been talking."

It's comforting to know the summer wasn't a complete loss for him.

We round the corner and an elementary school comes into view in the distance. The parking lot is deserted, and beyond is a thicket of dense woods.

"You planning on killing me?" I ask. "I've seen this movie before."

He snickers. We reach the playground, a large, intricate sculpture of metal and plastic woven together into an obstacle course. He settles onto one swing and I sit next to him, facing the opposite direction. I walk backward, winding up the rubber ground to spring forward.

"After we met at the boardwalk as kids, I asked my mom every day for a year when we would see you and Alex again. And every day, she would say, 'soon.' Until one day, she stopped answering."

I wish I could tell him I did the same thing. But I don't remember.

"I was six when she said he wanted to meet me."

My feet grind to a halt.

Tyler continues. "We were living at my granddad's B&B, so she decided we were gonna meet here, after school, and we'd go for ice cream at Jughead's and maybe play catch." His head droops toward his lap. Dark shadows color his face. "I waited and waited and waited. Everyone got picked up. The school was pretty much empty, except maybe the custodians. Mom told me she'd bring me to get ice cream and we could go see a movie. But I wanted to wait. So I sat right here. My mom was where you are. It was pretty much pitch black before I finally gave up. That was the first time I remember feeling like I was nothing, unwanted." Tyler tries to smile away the hurt, but he's fragile, held together by scotch tape.

There's a basketball court on the other side of the playground, and a dirty old ball in the grass nearby. I hop off the swing. It's not a glove and a baseball, but it's the closest thing to a game of "catch" here.

"Play with me." I jog toward the court.

He hops to his feet. "You don't."

I suck at all the sportsballs. I'm so uncoordinated, I'm basically those inflatable tube people you see at car washes; my limbs will attempt to go after the ball, but there's a 99.99 percent chance it'll either go over my head, under my legs, or my natural fight or flight instincts will kick in and I'll dive in the opposite direction.

"Teach me."

He trails me and when he gets to the sidelines, I use my whole chest and heave the ball at him; it almost reaches him, and he easily catches it with his strong hands. We play one-on-one, and apparently it's important to dribble(?) the ball. I nearly trip over my legs multiple times. I set up a shot, and he slams the ball away. He apologizes, but shrugs and darts after the ball.

I attempt to block his bank shot, then propel off my heels and fly through the air but it turns into a stop-drop-and-roll maneuver.

He bowls over in laughter before offering me the ball, but it fumbles out of my hand. Together, our laughs grow until I can't breathe.

Catching his breath, he dribbles close enough to the net to make a good layup, and I use whatever strength I have left to run at full speed, hop on his back, and latch onto him. He tries to shake me, but he's laughing too hard and cursing and the ball slips through his fingers. I hop off and dive for it, but apparently basketball isn't football. Like I have any idea what the hell the differences are anyway. By the time he's made twenty shots, and I've made a pitiful five, he calls the game. I'm not ready for it to be over.

I wipe sweat from my brow.

He drops the ball to the ground, all the one-on-one games we could have had bouncing off the court.

"What time do you have to get back?" he asks.

"No rush," I say, a little too quickly. "As long as I'm there tomorrow for Alex's ADVOCATE event. She asked me to film it. She still won't talk to me otherwise, but it's a start." I check my phone to see if Khal messaged me, but he hasn't. Knowing him, he found a coffee shop and is sipping on more espresso than any human should consume.

"I'm happy for her," he says.

"You know about the event?" It wouldn't surprise me if Alex has been secretly talking to him. In fact, I'd be relieved.

"Lia's been filling me in." He nods toward the road so I sprint to catch up. "I'm sorry you and Alex aren't talking."

"Alex and I were fractured long before you showed up. I'm the one who chose to lie to her."

"I think about her a lot, but water and bridges and stuff."

I wonder if he's thought about me at all. We cross back over to Main Street.

"I think about a lot of shit," I say.

"Like what?"

"There's so much left unresolved. I made a mess. Is sorry even enough?"

"I messed up too." Tension tightens his jaw, like a boat line on a dock post.

"I don't want to be let off the hook," I say.

On the opposite side of the street is a small boy no more than two next to his dad. In his hand is the loose ribbon of a red balloon.

Tyler grits his teeth. "Why did you come here?"

The child fidgets with the knotted string.

"To apologize." I could use a movie metaphor and wrap it in a parable. Or I can give Tyler what I never got from Dad. "I'm sorry. For everything. I wish I could take it back, but I can't. I have to live with that."

The child across the street yanks down hard on the balloon and it taps him in the face, which catches him off guard and he laughs and lets go of the string. The dad doesn't notice the balloon fly out of reach until the kid screams.

Tyler turns away as the father scoops up his son.

"It's probably not enough, but I miss you," I say.

He dries his wet eyes and looks to the sky. "How's your movie?"

My eyes widen in hope. "You really wanna know?"

"I let you film me, like, every day for a month. Curious if my footage made it in. Maybe I can quit school and go into acting. Be the next Timothée Chalamet or whatever."

My eyes widen. "Lofty goals, bro." The word "bro" catches in my throat.

He chuckles and shoves me off the sidewalk. I gain my footing and run back to slam into his side until we're both laughing.

"Well, I scrapped the documentary idea. This is more of a parable, I guess. It's hard to describe, but I wanted to tell a story that was a test of what I've learned."

He hums curiously. "What's it called?"

"*The Great Escape.*"

"And did you? Escape?"

I let the question hover in the air above us like the red balloon, just out of reach.

"As I edited the movie, I realized I might never truly escape my fears. But I can recognize them and not let them shadow my life. I can't protect anyone, all I can do is be the best version of Olly and do right by everyone I hurt. You can hate me if you want, Ty. But I am truly, genuinely sorry, and if you give me a chance, I'll show you." I take out my phone, pull up the email draft to him that says: Ty, this is my short film, hot off the presses, an exclusive preview! I'm working on finding my way out of the cave. Maybe one day, you can forgive me. Sorry, big bro. Tap send.

Hopefully he'll get it after I leave.

He puts a hand on my shoulder. "I think you broke the cycle."

I exhale.

Tyler points to a figure in the window of a nearby coffee shop surrounded by tiny ceramic espresso cups. "Is that Khal?"

I laugh. "Great. He's gonna have to pee every five minutes on the drive home."

Khal sees us and waves excitedly. He gives me a "Do you need more time alone?" look and I shake my head, so he bounds out of the shop speed-talking. "This place has incredible espresso I can't even handle how good it is I had ten shots I lost count I was waiting for you guys for so long and they looked at me like I had five heads when I asked if they had any lemon rind apparently they don't do that here which is crazy but they were probably shocked to see a brown kid here what are you guys up to did you bond?" He puts his arm around my shoulder, and another around Tyler's.

"Easy, buddy," Tyler says.

"We played basketball."

Khal's eyebrows fly off his face. "You? Basketball?" he puts all of his weight on us and swings like a child. "Hell has frozen over."

"He wasn't *horrible*," Tyler says. "I see potential."

Khal, small and slippery as he is, ducks out from underneath both of us. Tyler and I collide awkwardly, neither one of us knowing if we should bridge the gap.

His body is stiff at first, then his muscles relax and he squeezes my arm.

It's hesitant, but that's okay.

The three of us walk back through his neighborhood until we reach the empty driveway. "My mom's car isn't here, so looks like I got the house to myself. Wanna watch a movie?" Tyler asks. "If you guys have time?"

I look to Khal, the gleam in his eye and smirk on his lips giving me permission.

"What did you have in mind?"

Tyler shrugs. "I got this email a few minutes ago. Coming attractions, I guess." He pulls out his phone.

I look up at the sky, the clouds drifting peacefully. It's not as clear or as breezy here as it is back home. But clouds are clouds.

"You came this far," Khal says.

And so I swallow my fears, my chest thumping wildly, and follow Tyler into his house, down to his basement, which is chilly and unfinished, with an old, comfy brown couch and an out-of-place Smart TV with a PS4 hooked up, controllers on the floor. He hooks up his laptop to the TV and presses play.

But I don't watch the screen.

I watch Tyler, especially during the scenes with the eldest brother, based on him:

INT. ELDEST BROTHER, DEEP INSIDE CAVE—NIGHT

The walls of the cave close in around him and he begs silently for help as he hears his younger brother and sister cry out.

353

FATHER (VOICE-OVER)

All you have to do is use what you
brought, and you can leave.

ELDEST BROTHER

But I brought nothing. I had nothing.

He closes his eyes and thinks. Images of waves
beating against the shores of his mind are
transparent and layered over his face until his
eyes widen with realization and the waves
disappear. His face sharp and determined.

ELDEST BROTHER

It's—all an illusion.

He may have gotten no tangible object from their
father, but he has his siblings, and there is no
way out without them.

The walls fall away, and the eldest brother is
left in the center of the cave, still unsure of
where to turn until light fills both ends of the
tunnel. He hears the sound of his youngest
brother's voice and takes off running.

Tyler glances over to me, and I wonder what's going on inside
his head. I want to scream out to him: "Run after me! Don't leave
me behind!" But I don't.

At the end of the fifteen-minute short film, after all three siblings faced their own trials lost in the cave, I look away.

As much as I love it, and am convinced it's totally brilliant, it hurts too much to take it in this way, as a viewer. Not when the wounds I have are still so raw.

EXT. OPENING OF THE CAVE—DAYTIME

After encountering their trials inside the cave, the brothers find their way out, where their sister waits by the metal rowboat.

As the sides clang against the rocky cliffs, they take one last look at the cave as all three row away.

CUT TO:

INT. DEEP INSIDE CAVE—NIGHT

Camera winds through the dark tunnels, snaking down pathways until a body comes into view.

The youngest boy, flat on the floor of the cave, bloodshot eyes, screaming without sound. His skin is discolored, like it's part of the cave. In the reflection of his irises, a metal rowboat.

Tyler doesn't say anything as the credits roll. He reaches over, squeezes my shoulder, and nods. And that's all I need.

I instinctively stand up.

Khal follows suit, and Tyler leads the way upstairs. He sends us off with a couple bottles of water, and I'm not sure he's going to say anything.

Does he need to?

Is there anything left *to* say?

The past can't be changed. If we're lucky, we can learn how to be in the present moment and make conscious decisions to take one step forward, however small. There's no way to know if where we're going will be worth it, but I have to trust that it will. The point is to take the step at all, right?

It takes all of me not to ask Tyler if we'll ever see each other again.

When Tyler hugs me goodbye, he whispers, "See you round, little sib."

ALEX BRUCKE

Who says justice can't be served alongside drag? Because Petty White is the MVP of the ADVOCATE fundraiser.

A gaggle of drag queens draw the biggest crowd the Lonely Bear has ever seen, and Petty White leads the charge, sending queens around the resort to get donations. The looks from guests are a potent cocktail of genuine shock and awe. Hilarious.

I've been busting my ass trying to keep up with food and making sure everything runs smoothly. The Lonely Bear is basically Coachella, if Coachella weren't run by assholes and actually did good for the world.

Javy rushes over to me. "June's about to take the stage." He grabs my hand and I ignore the silent rush as we race to the side of the stage.

The late afternoon August sun beats down on her, but June doesn't break a sweat.

"Did y'all know there are 2.3 million people, across all genders, all ages, all races who are incarcerated across state and federal prisons, juvenile correctional facilities, local jails, military prisons, and the concentration camps they're calling immigration detention centers?"

A hush falls over the entire resort.

"Over forty percent of those incarcerated are Black, but Black Americans only make up thirteen percent of the entire US population." Her pause allows for the statistic to sink in, and people start to visibly squirm and murmur.

"She's good," Javy says. "That's the sound of realization."

June holds up her pointer finger. "One in five incarcerated people are locked up for drug-related offenses. The majority of men, especially Black men, in the prison system are nonviolent drug offenders, and men account for around ninety percent of incarcerated parents, but there have been spikes in the incarceration of women, which increases the number of incarcerated parents. In state and federal prisons, there are more African American parents than parents of any other race. How does this impact our children?" She looks to Javy first, then to me, and one by one to all of the other ADVOCATE members. Each of us nod in solidarity.

Olly is front and center, capturing everything on film.

Mom, Sheila, and Ritchie are in the audience next to Khal and Lia, and behind them sit Ashleigh, Dusk, and Ms. Rodriguez. My heart swells. A few months ago, I convinced myself I was alone. I built walls out of cement and mortar and barbed wire, locked myself inside, and threw away the key.

"I can't believe so many people showed up," Javy says.

I slip my hand inside his. "It's incredible."

The only one missing is Tyler.

June continues, "I want to bring up someone without whose

help we would not be here today. She is someone I've come to know quite recently, but I've seen her incredible strength grow every day. Please welcome Alex Brucke!"

Javy's eyes widen. Olly nearly drops his camera. The cheers and applause from the audience is so loud it carries me to the podium.

I steady myself and breathe out.

June whispers, "Like we practiced."

I catch Chef's gaze in the crowd, and he nods and mouths, "Go, mija."

"Children of incarcerated parents need your help," I begin. "We are suffering in silence. We experience rejection from our peers and exhibit behavioral problems and we have been failed at every turn: our criminal justice system has failed us, our school systems have failed us, and our communities have failed us. Everyone fails to listen to our pain, our stories. That's not acceptable. My father was arrested three years ago, and he died trapped in the system." My voice shakes but I do my best to tell my story, about a father I loved who, yes, made mistakes, but was taken away from me. I speak about how I wanted to numb myself, make myself cold, disappear into snow angels and drown in the idealized version of Dad because it was all I had. There were no mental health or financial resources for me and Olly, for Mom, nothing to help what remained of our family to heal.

Mom and Olly are bawling. Thank goddess for tripods because there's no way he'd be able to hold the camera steady.

Javy wipes his face and smiles so proudly it gives me the strength to finish.

"I was lost for a long time, but I'm slowly finding a new me. But I should never have had to endure the consequences of my father's actions. The system, all of us, we need to do better for children of incarcerated parents." Maya walks up and hands me a note. "My good friend Maya informed me we raised more than enough money to get Chris a good lawyer and help his mom!" The crowd erupts. "But this isn't only about Chris. This is about the next Chris, and all the ones after. I need to believe our stories are important." I look to Maya, Javy, June. All the ADVOCATE members. Olly. "We're here."

I take a deep breath and close my eyes.

"Please listen to June," I command the crowd, but the words get lodged in my throat as I spot Hunter, his nostrils flared. "As a white person, I recognize my privilege here. I am aware of the opportunities I was granted because of my skin color. My dad told me stories about the Black men and men of color with whom he was imprisoned and the unfair treatment they received: grossly unjust sentencings and rampant arrests due to racial profiling. Unfair drug laws still plague these folks even though marijuana laws have changed in many states across the country. Even with mixed legal statuses, it's not decriminalized in about forty percent of states. This has to change." I take a deep breath. "It's taken me awhile to realize it, but I hope to one day be part of the change. *Be part of the change.*" I hand the mic back to June and a rush of emotions floods me as she hugs me tightly, then releases me. I run behind the stage and Javy scoops me up into a hug. My entire body trembles, but I feel alive.

"You did *that!*" he shouts.

"What the hell is this?" Hunter's voice breaks through my happiness. I look up and see him barging through the crowd toward us. The pounding of adrenaline in my chest I felt onstage quickly turns to fear.

"Is there a problem here?" Javy deepens his voice and puffs out his chest.

"The fuck are you?" Hunter looks at me, rage turning his face a blood red like those old coffee mugs that change color depending on the temperature of the liquid inside. "This your new boyfriend?"

I step in between them. "Hunter, please. Go away."

"What the hell, Alex? I don't hear from you for almost two months and then I hear you and my aunt are throwing a party for convicts?"

"What did you say?" Javy paces. His breathing is hard and heavy.

"Javy, walk away. I got this. He's not worth it." I'm trying my best not to soak up Javy's anger, but it mixes with my own, imbuing me with enough energy to take on Hunter.

Javy slams his hands in his pockets and storms back to the other side of the stage. I catch a glimpse of Mom, who is hanging on to every one of June's words, and realize there's an empty space between her and Khalid, who is now holding Olly's camera. Olly is nowhere in sight. Fuck, I hope he didn't see Hunter.

I turn back to Hunter. I'm done with this shit. I'm not giving him a chance to get to me. Not anymore. "You need to leave. And if you don't, I'll call the cops."

"You wouldn't dare, weak bitch. You don't have the balls." He grabs my arm hard, and the trauma I've been suppressing for years erupts and my knee whips up at full speed and smashes into his groin. He crumples to the concrete and writhes.

Sheila runs down the driveway toward us.

"No, *you* don't have the balls." I kneel down next to him and whisper in his ear. "You're nothing. You have no power over me."

Sheila is quick to grab Hunter by the arms.

"Why don't you tell your aunt what you did to me?" My voice shakes, but I don't stop. As I tell her how he lunged at me, how he spent months gaslighting me, her pupils become pinpricks and the color drains from her face.

Sheila's knuckles are white. "Get off my property, Hunter. Before I call the police and tell them you're driving with a suspended license. And you punched your uncle in the face. Did you forget we covered for you when the police questioned us about your character?"

"Aunt Sheila," Hunter pleads, his eyes filling with tears.

"Go." She points to his car, then shoves him away from us. "Now."

When Hunter's car whizzes out of the parking lot, Sheila's chest heaves and she lets out a cry so stifled it sounds painful.

"I'm sor—"

"*I'm* sorry, Alex," she interrupts, tears streaming down her cheeks. "Never apologize or make excuses for the monsters. Hear me? Never."

I should feel better, but I don't. Hunter, Sheila, Javy, this event, it's all swirling around me in a complicated tornado and I have to get away before it sweeps me up and I lose all the ground I've gained.

I wriggle out from Sheila's grip. "Tell everyone I'll be back." Before she can say anything, I follow it up with, "I'm okay. Promise. I need to be alone for a bit," because she's worried. I've earned her—and everyone else's—worry. "If Javy is looking for me, tell him I'm *safe*."

Disappearing into the woods, everything fades into white noise. I pop my AirPods in and play Lorde's "Perfect Places." The trees along the lake provide cover from the sun, and my legs carry me across private property and through untouched woods until I reach a familiar mountain stream carving its way through dead leaves and rock to the lake. Olly and I used to hike here, pretending the high rocks were fortresses where we could hide from zombie invaders.

Up ahead is the back of our old Blue Wharf house.

As I trudge across the lush green lawn, I remember how we used to chase Dracarys around the high trees and if we dropped and rolled into the grass, he would fly through the air and leap on top of us. One summer, Olly and I spent all week making our own version of the Iron Throne for him out of sticks we tied together with twine we found in the shed. We even put the metal Targaryen house symbol on the top. It only lasted until the next lightning storm, when a thick yellow bolt streaked through the trees and set it ablaze. The fire trucks had to come because the flames almost spread to the house. Dad was not happy.

I chuckle to myself.

The planks on the dock creak.

Olly's at the end, staring out at the lake. He glances behind his shoulder and smiles. All the anger I've held inside melts and my steps get a little quicker. When I reach him I use his shoulder for support as I maneuver myself down and dangle my feet over the edge.

"I left after you spoke," he says. "Khal's filming the rest. You were *beyond*."

"Thanks." My voice is small. "You should come with me sometime. To ADVOCATE." I want to lean my head on his shoulders, but it feels like too much has happened, or not happened.

"I'd like that," he says. "Did you see the For Sale sign?" He turns and points to the lawn behind us.

"No! Really?" It's too weird to think of the house we grew up in belonging to yet another new family. It's already had a completely new life since we had to leave. "Think the new people will let us hang out on the dock?"

He chuckles. "We need to let go of this place, Lex."

Tears threaten the corners of my eyes. I bite my lower lip. "I'm tired of being angry."

"Me too."

I grab his hand and fold my fingers into his. I used to think I wanted an apology from him for hovering over me, lying to me, scaring Tyler away, but I don't.

I wanted him to be here *with* me.

"I finished my next movie."

"Another masterpiece."

"You know it." He pauses. "I sent it to Tyler."

"Tyler?"

"Khal and I drove down to see him yesterday. I tried to make things right. I don't know if it did any good, but it felt nice to see him."

"I wouldn't be where I am right now without Tyler."

He takes a few seconds before saying, "You would have. Maybe it would have taken you longer, but you're strong."

"Everyone tells me that, but *I'm* trying to figure that out for myself." My toes touch the surface of the water, and I kick up a little splash.

"You'll get there." He tells me how he played basketball with Tyler and sadness creeps into my bones.

"When I think about how much he's missed in our lives, and how much we've missed in his, I almost can't breathe I get so sad. Can we ever make up for that?"

"Probably not," he says.

"You think we'll ever see him again?" I ask.

"I hope so." His voice is soaked in hope like tie-dye.

I want to ask why Dad kept Tyler from us, but I'm not sure the answer matters; it won't change the outcome.

"Ol, is it okay to be mad at Dad?"

He sighs. "If you'd asked me a month ago, I would've said it was about time. I realized I've been so damn pissed because I'll never hear him say he's sorry for *everything*. I have to make peace with it. I'm also angry because, despite everything, I still love him and I don't know how."

I was so convinced he hated Dad.

His voice is small. "Is it okay to still love him?"

"It has to be."

He pulls out his phone, launches his email app, and pulls up a long-ass message. He pulls it to his chest. "It's the last email I got from Dad. I haven't been able to read it." He cradles the phone in his hand.

"I'll do it." I reach for the phone, take a deep breath, and read it aloud:

Hey Pal,

I wanted to give you time, but I haven't been feeling so great. Still can't get a pass to see the doctor for a while. That's the prison system for you: doesn't give a shit about you until you're no longer taking up a bed. I'm trying to eat healthy, but commissary money is out.

I have the brochure with *Barefoot* from the Saratoga Film Festival hanging on my wall. I convinced the guard to let us watch it next weekend instead of Judge Judy reruns. Ha ha. I'm proud of you. I wanted to tell you this in person, but, well, you know. I'm not perfect. It's difficult confronting your failures. There is so much I want to say to you, but I can't find the right words. I always thought I had nerves of steel, but leaving you and your sister tore me apart. All I have left are my thoughts, and those scare me. What could I have done differently? A hundred things, none of which I can forgive myself for. I'm no superhero, just a man who made a lifetime of mistakes. You and Alex are the two things I've done right. Be good to each other.

Love always,
Dad

Olly licks away his tears. It's not the apology he wanted, but I don't think Dad was capable of admitting he was wrong, and this is the closest he could ever get.

The first of the hot-air balloons from the last night of the festival emerges from behind the trees and floats over the lake.

Salty tears drip off the tip of my nose. "We haven't been good to each other."

A red balloon drifts over Diamond Island, followed by a brilliant emerald-green one decorated with ribbons.

"But the hard part is over," he whispers.

I move closer to him. "How do you know?"

"I don't. But we can figure the rest out together." His promise settles as his body trembles. I wish I could take away his uncertainty and pain. All his time spent "protecting" me was what he needed for *himself*, for someone to protect him.

"I'm so sorry, Lex. For everything."

I grab onto him and hold him tight. "Me too, Ol." Suddenly, I'm five years old again making snow angels for fun. It's been too long since I let that little girl run free.

I close my eyes.

Set her free.

Car tires roll across gravel. A door slams shut. The family who lives here now must be home. Even though they're cool with us on their dock, it still feels weird. Like we're trespassing in the past.

Olly's right. We can't come back here anymore.

There are no perfect places left for us.

But one last sunset won't hurt us.

***

After a while of silence, the dock creaks.

Olly and I don't turn around because we fully expect the owners of our old house to destroy the moment and we both want to savor it for as long as we can.

Then we hear Tyler's voice. "Mind if I sit?"

I look over and Olly has tears in his eyes.

"You don't have to ask," I say, for both of us.

He crouches down next to Olly and dangles his legs over the edge.

"How'd you know where we were?" Olly asks.

"Khal and Javy," Tyler says. "I went to the Bear. Caught your speech, Alex. Never been prouder. I tried to find you after. They both knew where you guys were, oddly enough." Tension pulls at Tyler's jaw. "I didn't know I was gonna come until I got in the car. But you know me, I love a good plot twist." He looks around, waiting for us to say something.

"What made you come back?" I ask.

"I wanted to come back to support you." Tyler avoids my gaze, instead staring out at the lake. "And Olly was pretty convincing, especially after I watched his movie, again."

My eyes go wide because I used to be the one to see Olly's work first. But maybe it's okay that things have changed. It doesn't have to be bad. Not anymore. "What did you think? Oscar-worthy?"

Tyler nods. "Lots to unpack."

"When do *I* get to see it?" I ask.

"At the film festival," Tyler says. "Because it's gonna win, and we're all gonna be there to cheer you on." He holds out a hand for Olly, and whispers, "You're not trapped anymore, little sib. You made it out. We all did."

Dozens of hot-air balloons float above us, reflecting in the surface of the water, a magical dreamscape bursting with color. The sun's bright-orange bulb kisses mountaintops. Rolling waves shine like ripples of gold foil.

"So, what'd I miss?" Tyler asks cheekily.

Olly sighs. "That's a loaded question." He wraps one arm around our brother and the other around me.

I exhale. "Where do I begin?"

THE BEGINNING

ACKNOWLEDGMENTS

For all those who make up stories to get through the bad days: I see you, and hope you receive this story in kind. This book was a real, raw labor of necessity; first aid for wounds that haven't quite healed. It's one story, told through one lens, and certainly not *the* only story of children with incarcerated parents; this work of fiction is *not* meant to encompass the entire broken criminal justice system, nor should it—that would be an impossible task. With that in mind, this book is especially for people who have incarcerated parents, like me, whose voices and stories largely go unheard, who have had to unfairly suffer the same sentences as their parents. It's an impossible thing to navigate, and this book is my way of trying to make sense of things that don't.

No Perfect Places is by no means a perfect book. It was deliberately written to be imperfect, full of messy characters who make mistake after mistake, who deal with hard yet very real situations. My enduring appreciation and endless thanks to Olly + Alex's biggest champions: My superstar agent, Jess Regel, who never,

ever stopped believing in and pushing for this book, even when I wasn't sure it could or would ever be publishable: I'm forever grateful to have you in my corner as my advocate, cheerleader, idea confidante, and backboard. Allison Moore, who fought for and believed in the Bruckes' messy story, *you* gave them life! Camille Kellogg, editor extraordinaire, who swooped in and energized me so I could tackle the massive undertaking that was this book; thank you for always showing me a way forward! The entire team at Bloomsbury, especially Lex Higbee and Briana Williams who deal with my incessant emails: I couldn't ask for a better squad! Most importantly for Erica Barmash, because our unheard stories matter.

The award for *Most Gorgeous Book Cover Ever* goes to David Curtis! You captured the beauty and stillness of the setting, and the mood/entire essence of the book perfectly!

It takes a village to foster a creative, like me, and the people I've collected since my author journey began sustain me. Nicolas DiDomizio: I wouldn't be here without you, my wonderful friend, our friendship is invaluable and means the world to me. To Jason June, Jess Verdi, Abdi Nazemian, Daniel Aleman, Becky Albertalli, Claribel A. Ortega, Julian Winters, David Levithan, Tracy Deonn, Matthew Hubbard, Naz Katub, Amy Ewing, and so many more beautiful souls: Y'all have filled up my cup, offered shoulders and guidance, and helped me believe in myself and my stories. And to all the readers who have sent emails and DMs about how my books make you feel seen: y'all make *me* feel seen. Because of you, it's all worth it.

To my family and extended tribe: I love you all in more ways than I can count, and in more words than all the stories combined.

Thank you all for raising me, in all ways, every day. For Steve, who never stopped believing in me, you've been my rock. Thank you, *Khal*. Ana bahebak. Some things never end, even when they do; but here, *we live*.

And finally, to Lake George for allowing me to dream and find peace in chaos.

CREDITS

ART AND DESIGN
David Curtis
Donna Mark
Jeannette Levy

CONTRACTS
Christelle Chamouton

COPYEDITORS AND PROOFREADERS
Jill Amack
Elizabeth Degenhard

EDITORS
Allison Moore
Camille Kellogg

MANAGING EDITORIAL
Laura Phillips
Oona Patrick

MARKETING AND PUBLICITY
Erica Barmash
Faye Bi
Alexa Higbee
Briana Williams
Beth Eller
Kathleen Morandini
Alona Fryman

PRODUCTION
Nicholas Church

SALES
Valentina Rice
Jaclyn Sassa
Valerie Esposito

AUDIO
Jo Forshaw
Tom Skipp
Geo Willis

HELM LITERARY
Jess Regel